# THE RIGHTEOUS

Dave Wragg really got into writing stories just as he finished his English GCSE, then took about twenty years to get back to it. In the meantime, he studied software engineering, worked in global shipping and technical consultancy, and once spent a year in the Foreign Office 'hiding in the basement'.

Dave lives in Hertfordshire with his wife, two small daughters, and two smaller cats. He has a dog now, too.

# THE RIGHTEOUS

## DAVID WRAGG

HARPER
Voyager

Harper*Voyager*
An imprint of HarperCollins*Publishers* Ltd
1 London Bridge Street
London SE1 9GF

www.harpercollins.co.uk

HarperCollins*Publishers*
1st Floor, Watermarque Building, Ringsend Road
Dublin 4, Ireland

First published by HarperCollins*Publishers* Ltd 2021
This paperback original edition 2021
1

A catalogue record for this book is
available from the British Library

ISBN: 978-0-00-833144-3

Set in Sabon by Palimpsest Book Production Ltd,
Falkirk, Stirlingshire

Printed and bound in the UK by CPI Group (UK) Ltd,
Croydon CR0 4YY

MIX
Paper from
responsible sources
FSC C007454

This book is produced from independently certified FSC™ paper
to ensure responsible forest management.

For more information visit: www.harpercollins.co.uk/green

*For my parents,*
*Who thought they'd raised me better*

# PREVIOUSLY . . .

Aye, right, where were we? So our boys Rennic (aka boss) and Chel (aka wee bear, cub, dipstick) have got themselves locked in the dungeons below the old royal citadel, along with a whole bunch of hapless folk who thought they were on the verge of liberating the kingdom from your good old-fashioned tyrannical regime. I'd say execution at the hands of the murderous red confessors is imminent, on account of the steady procession of corpses that's been rolling out of said citadel in the time since, often in stages.

How did it come to this, dear Lemon, I hear you ask? Ah, well, it all started back in Denirnas Port, where the Black Hawks (the greatest mercenary company the world has yet to recognize) – the boss Rennic, the big lad Foss, the tart Loveless, the tireless Whisper, the tiresome Spider and the wise and scintillating Lemon – were engaged in the blameless act of unregulated commerce. Then out of the clear blue morning, in come the whopping black ships of the Norts from over the sea, blockade the bay and blast the fuck out of the port's various edifices strategic with their heathen witchfire.

It's fair to say some chaos and bedlam ensued. Being attentive and charitable souls, we snatched a prince from the melee: Tarfel, the runt prince, the spare heir. Chel, his sworn man, came too – not my fault, the boss insisted. Plan was we'd shop said wee prince over to the Rau Rel, the great partisan underground, who were gathering their strength to overthrow the hated church.

Course, like any good plan it's fucked sideways from the off. Seems the wee bear has made it his sworn mission to drop a bollock at every opportunity, and boss has to relocate one of his arms to knock off his aggro. We're forced cross-country, chased by a steaming stack of confessors, Mawnish mercenaries, cannibals, and toothy wolves. Fucken wolves, man. At least we saw the last of that prick Brother Hurkel – Loveless took a hand off him and we left him to die on a mountain. No chance he made it back from that, no chance at all.

Anyway, all's grand in the end. We get princeling to the Rau Rel, they arrange a meetup with his big bro, the dim Crown Prince Mendel, and we're all set for taking the citadel. Off we dutifully march, with nary a pause to renegotiate our fee, and set up guard in the courtyard while the others bust in. Now I don't know exactly what happened next, but friend Spider came steaming out in short order and bellowed a morsel as he passed, to wit: the 'regime' we'd come all that way to perform said overthrowing upon is our bosom pal the fucken crown prince. Except he's not the dim one, Mendel the thickie. He's the dead one, Corvel the bastard – who offed his own twin to lay a trap for the churchy

# PART I

# ONE

The crack on the ceiling was patterned with frost, frozen tendrils spidering the length of the cell. Chel stared up at it in the dull light, watching his breath plume in the frigid air.

The wind blew through the narrow cell window and he hunched into the thin blanket wrapped around him. The noise it made was eerie through the dungeon, moaning down the hallway. Snow lay piled beneath the narrow windows, small drifts resting undisturbed on the broken flagstones beyond the cell's bars. The vast bulk of the gaoler blocked what thin light and warmth spread from the brazier by the stairs, her infrequent shuffles, farts, and mutterings the only reminder that another soul dwelt alongside them.

Chel sat up on the pallet and opened his mouth to speak. His cellmate was already staring at him from the opposite pallet, glaring from beneath thunderous dark brows, bearded jaw set hard.

Chel closed his mouth. Today would not be a talking day.

The clatter and jingle of armoured footsteps from the stairwell roused the dungeon's denizens and the gaoler knocked over her stool in her haste to stand. She slapped at the cell bars with the brazier's poker, her wordless command to stand and look presentable, and a moment later the procession reached the foot of the stairs. Armoured confessors tramped around the corner and out of sight, away from the cells, spears tightly angled against the low ceilings. Chel couldn't see who marched at their centre. The gaoler sagged back to her righted stool as they disappeared, the clang of a distant iron door reverberating down the cold stone hall from the block's far end.

Chel's heart fluttered. He felt an electric surge of hope and fear every time the confessors appeared. Their visits were less frequent, the prince coming weekly now that most of the cells had been emptied, sometimes stopping at their cell, sometimes going only to the iron door. Every time, Chel tried to scrutinize his escort without staring, looking for signs that his sister survived, that she hid still within their ranks. That she could still free them, before their cell, too, was emptied.

He slid back from the bars, back to the pallet, lost in melancholy, as the red procession swept back past the cell in a tumult. Gold flashed amid the red, then Prince Corvel Merimonsun was there, standing to address the occupants of the last two cells. Chel risked a look at the escort, but the forms were hooded and dim, their rust-coloured robes murky in the gloom.

'Here we are again.' The crown prince, now king-in-waiting, sounded cordial, even cheerful. 'This really is your last chance. I've waited as long as I can.'

Silence came in answer from both cells. Chel began to

edge forward, but a confessor's hood twitched in his direction and he shrank back.

'I'm offering you a way to survive. I'm a man of my word. Tell me all you have, confirm what I already know, and you live out your days. All of you, saved from confession.'

He paused, waiting for an answer that would not come. He began to move away, footsteps echoing off the stone walls, hesitated, and turned back.

'I could have tortured you, you know? I could have had you ripped into pieces, but I wanted to keep this civil. I wanted to set an example. Well, you've done me no favours there, have you? Now Brother Hurkel will tell me he was right all along.'

The prince took a long breath. The gaoler shuffled in the lull.

'Enough is enough. My mercy is not inexhaustible. Prepare the court. These two can go today. In fact, they can go now.'

Something stirred within the cell. A moaning cry, a wordless expulsion of woe and denial. A pair of confessors peeled off from the escort, running back up the stairs with their gear jangling. The gaoler was sitting up straight now, keys in her blistered hand. Chel felt numb, even the cold in his fingers was distant.

'Oh, you have something to say, do you?'

The crying continued, becoming a repeating syllable, *no, no, no, no, no*. Shifting, becoming hoarse, pleading screams. 'Take them! Take the others! They're to blame! It wasn't me!'

Dalim, the erstwhile glaive-wielding mercenary, had spoken little since Brother Hurkel had crushed him against the wall of the Primarch's tower, and what he'd said had been indistinct. This was the most vocal he'd been since the cells had welcomed them.

Corvel addressed the cell's other occupant. 'You see, Palo? You could have saved them all, every soul in this place. What kind of monster are you?'

Without another word, Corvel swept back past Chel's cell, a flowing wave of golden hair and robes. The clank of the cell door opening was followed by the grunting and cursing of the confessors as they extracted the kicking and wailing Dalim. His screams echoed down the stairwell as they carried him up, weakened but struggling, out of the light and out of sight.

'It's their fault! Their fault! They did this!'

Ayla Palo, last survivor of the Rau Rel leadership, emerged from the cell and followed at her own slow pace, a confessor on either side. Chel hadn't seen her since they'd been confined, countless weeks before. She looked thin, colourless, diminished, but her expression was resolute.

She paused as she passed their cell, the confessors stopping alongside. Chel started to find his cellmate at his elbow, his gaze locked on Palo's.

'He's right, you know.'

Her first words in weeks. Chel tried to puzzle out who she meant.

Beside him, Rennic nodded.

'He is.'

'Should have listened to me.'

'I should.'

She nodded, eyes blank, then turned to follow Dalim up the stairs.

'Palo?'

Rennic called after her, and she paused. His fingers were wrapped around the freezing bars, but he wasn't letting go.

'Yes?'

'Be seeing you.'

*  *  *

The gaoler was roasting something over the brazier and greasy fat drops were sizzling on the glowing coals. The smell reached Chel's nostrils, making his mouth water, despite his growing unease at the cries and creaks from the courtyard beyond the narrow window. The sounds of a gathering crowd.

Chel leaned against the freezing bars. His mind drifted, thoughts blurry, indistinct, whirling like a leaf in a gale.

'Hey.'

Rennic called from across the cell, past where Chel was slumped. The founder and chief executive of the Black Hawk Company was upside-down, feet against the back wall, pushing himself slowly up and down on his hands. Chel's shoulder ached to look at him.

'Hey!'

The gaoler glared over one meaty shoulder. 'What?'

'When are we eating?'

The gaoler stirred, pushing herself to her feet. The keys jangled at her belt as she lumbered forward, the poker back in her hand. She came to rest before the bars, a fraction beyond arm's reach. A sickly grin spread across her bulbous features, revealing an excellent set of teeth.

'No food for you today, fuckers. No food ever again.' She chuckled, her robes shuddering in waves.

Rennic took one foot off the wall, then the other. He

maintained the handstand for a breath, then lowered his head to the floor, raised it again, and rolled down into a crouch. Flushed and panting, he fixed a fearsome glare on the gaoler.

'No last meal? We die hungry? Prince Dick-head decree that, did he? Or is this your initiative, you pearl-grinned fuck-fountain?'

The poker slammed against the bars. 'You die hungry,' the gaoler growled, and turned to waddle back toward the brazier.

Torchlight flickered in the stairwell. Someone was coming.

The gaoler brandished the poker again, grunting them back from the bars, then straightened her stool and stood tall beside the brazier. Footsteps echoed from the stairwell, less numerous than usual, less weighty. A moment later, a bright torch flared into the dungeon, held aloft by a skinny but well-tailored arm. The gaoler dropped to one knee.

'Your highness!'

Prince Tarfel Merimonsun stumbled into the dungeon, keeping the torch overhead, blinking in its dancing light. A hooded confessor followed at his heel. Tarfel cleared his throat, eyes scanning the now-empty cells, the unease growing on his face. He looked healthy, at least, whole and well-fed, although his sunless pallor had returned.

'I . . . I need to speak to the prisoners. Alone.'

The gaoler frowned. She was still on her knees, the poker still in her hand.

'Alone, highness? I can't leave them unattended. You understand, these are dangerous, vile men. Damned criminals and traitors.'

12

Tarfel nodded, distracted. Despite the cold, he appeared to be sweating. 'Yes, yes, indeed. Indeed. That's why I brought protection,' he added, with a wave toward the accompanying confessor. 'Open the cell, please?'

The gaoler's frown deepened, and she raised her gaze a fraction, narrow eyes moving from the prince to his escort and back. 'I cannot, your highness.'

Tarfel turned back to the confessor with a helpless look, a shrug forming. The confessor's hood gave a firm nod, one hand reaching for the thin mace dangling from the rope belt. The gaoler caught the movement, shifting her focus from the hapless prince to the confessor, her furry brow now lowered in bullish suspicion. Chel edged closer to the bars. The light was weak, his view blocked, but the confessor looked small to his eye. His pulse quickened.

The gaoler had risen to a half-crouch. 'Is there something else I can help you with, highness? Perhaps you'd like me to call for someone?' The dungeon bell was two paces away, the far side of the brazier.

Tarfel swallowed. His torch arm was beginning to tremble. 'Give me the keys. Please.'

'I don't think that would be appropriate, highness.'

'I'm a prince!' His voice rose in panic. 'You have to do what I say!'

'Perhaps I should check with the duty prelate. I'll call for him.'

The gaoler stood, already lurching toward the bell. The confessor pushed past the prince, mace in hand, blocking the gaoler's path, dwarfed by her.

'Are you lost, brother?' the gaoler sneered. 'Stand aside.'

Tarfel had his free hand out in desperate placation. 'Now there's really no need for—'

The gaoler swung, the poker whistling in an arc and smashing shards from the stone beside the stumbling confessor's head. The mace swung back, pinging from the poker as it came back around. It flew from the confessor's grip and skittered across the icy flagstones.

With a gleeful chuckle, the gaoler advanced on the confessor, who scuttled and dodged back and around the bleating prince. The gaoler followed, the bell forgotten, swiping with the poker like a butcher swatting flies. The confessor scrambled around, kicking snow, before standing before Chel's cell, back pressed to the bars.

The gaoler lunged, the confessor ducked, and something shunted Chel aside. A ringing clang filled the hallway, a muffled grunting in its echoes. Chel looked back to see the gaoler's beefy arm dragged through the bars, held fast at a punishing angle in Rennic's unyielding grip. His other arm was through the bars in the other direction, wrapped around the wide-eyed gaoler's neck, jamming her back against the rusty iron. The poker dropped with a clatter.

Rennic's eyes shone white in the gloom. 'Get. The. Keys.'

The confessor pushed out from beneath the gaoler's shadow and stood, a touch unsteady. A quick hand snapped the keys from the gaoler's belt, another beckoned Tarfel and his torch over to find the right key. A moment later, the door clanked open and swung wide. The gaoler looked around with wild eyes, her every attempt to speak or cry choked by Rennic's grip.

Rennic peered over her at the confessor. 'Lemon, is that you in there? How the fuck did you get in?'

The confessor pulled back her hood. Straight black hair, pulled tight, tumbled out from within. Defiant grey eyes glowed in the torchlight.

14

Chel's heart burst. 'Sab!'

'Hello, Brother Bear. I told you I'd be back for you, didn't I?'

Rennic looked from one to the other. 'Fuck me, this is your sister?'

'Rennic, this is Sab—'

'Don't care. We need to get the fuck out of here. I assume you have a plan for what's next, Chel's sister?'

Sab nodded. 'There's a way out, while everyone's distracted by the confession.'

'Then let's go.'

Sab looked around the dungeon, the barred cells stretching off either side of the hallway.

'What about the others?'

Chel shook his head. 'There are no others.'

'Oh. I'm . . . I'm sorry. I came as soon as I could . . .'

'You're here now.'

The gaoler struggled in Rennic's grip, and he clamped down with a growl.

'Either of you got a knife?'

Tarfel wiped at his face, smudging his cold sweat with torch soot. 'Can we just lock her away? The cell's open.'

The gaoler struggled again, fighting against his grip, her muffled cries rising in pitch.

Rennic's voice was grave-flat.

'No.'

The muscles of his arm bulged like the gaoler's eyes as he began to crush the life from her. Chel turned away, reaching out an instinctive arm to steer Sab with him, but she stood firm, expression fixed. He tugged at her shoulder.

'Let's go.'

'I can take it.'

15

'I'm sure you can, but we need to go, remember?'

She relaxed and turned with him, and he nodded to Tarfel to lead the way out.

'Good to see you, highness.'

Tarfel sniffed, a small smile tweaking his mouth. His trembling had almost subsided. 'How about a thank you?'

'How about we get out of here first?'

Chel had his foot on the bottom step when he heard the sound, this time clear enough to make him pause. It was coming from the opposite end of the dungeon hallway, the darkened end, the end with the iron door. It sounded like a cry.

Rennic bumped into his back. 'Get moving, fuck-stick.'

'I think there's someone in there.'

'You can pity them later.'

Chel stepped back from the winding stairwell. He walked quickly to the iron door, Rennic's exasperation at his back palpable, the weak light from the fading brazier picking out only the scores and divots from the shadows. A small, barred grille was cut from the door's mass. From it, a pair of wide, frightened eyes peered, glimmering tearful.

'Please?'

Chel stared into deep wells of the eyes, locked in pleading entreaty. The face was small, dark, dirty, young.

'Who are you?'

'Please?'

Chel yelled for the keys. 'Fuck it, you're coming with us.'

Rennic's hand was rough on his shoulder, spinning him. Behind them, Sab's approaching footsteps jingled.

'—the fuck are you doing, boy? You think we have eternity to bolt?'

16

Chel reached past him, snatching the keys from Sab's outstretched hand and rummaging in the half-light.

'I'm getting this boy out.'

'Please,' came again from the grille.

'This is not one of ours! There's none of us left!'

'He's trapped here just the same. We can't leave him – my father would have called it a sin to leave an unfortunate in peril.'

'*We're* pretty unfortunate by any measure, and our peril is not in dispute!'

Chel fumbled with cold, rusty iron, trying one of the keys to no avail. 'You can either stand there and shout at me while I ignore you and do the right thing anyway, or you can fucking help. We'd all get out sooner.'

Rennic's nostrils flared, and his mouth shaped to speak, but he held his tongue. Finally, he snatched the ring from Chel's hand, flicking it around before seizing one from the mass.

'Here you go, merciful sister. Keyhole's a different shape from the cells.' He sighed. 'Sooner or later, your fucking sanctimony will be our deaths.'

The lock sprang, and the great dark door swung open with a clang and an alchemical waft.

A shrivelled creature looked up at them, rag-clad and hunched.

'Fuck me,' Rennic said, head tilted. 'A Nort.'

# TWO

The stark, snow-reflected light from the tall windows along the upper hallway stung Chel's eyes, and by now his weakened legs were aching, begging for rest. Only the little Nort fared worse; his shuffling steps were timid and unsteady, and a rough sack of belongings gathered from shelving beside the iron cell was slung over his shoulder, clinking with each halting pace. Rennic was doing better – Chel wasn't sure if he'd never abandoned hope of rescue, or if he was too bloody-minded to change his routine, but the big man had kept himself as fit and strong as possible during their stay in the cells. Chel's early attempts to match him had led only to sharp pain from his ruined shoulder, and he'd felt too cold and hungry to try again since.

'Come on, Bear, keep moving!' Sab's arm wrapped around him.

He nodded back at the Nort. 'Think our friend needs help more than I do.'

'"Our friend" flinches whenever I get near him, so you're all I've got.'

They struggled on in awkward synchronicity.

'Where are we heading?'

'The gatehouse. I've stashed some cloaks and things there, we should be able to slip out of the side door, mingle with the crowd at chucking-out time, get down the hill with the masses.'

'At the end of the confession?'

She paused.

'Yes.'

'Where are all the guards?'

'Prince Tarfel told them it was fine to go and watch the confession. Only that beast in the cells looked twice at us.'

Chel nodded, wincing at the burning sensation in his legs. He'd not walked so many steps in a row for weeks, nor climbed anything more than his creaking pallet.

'How did you get Tarfel to help? How did you even come to speak to him? How . . .' He fell silent. There were too many questions, too many things he felt eluded him.

She sensed his mood, the tide of enquiries dammed by his silence. 'Don't fret, Bear. You know I can be persuasive. We can go into detail later, once we're clear. If you want, that is . . .'

He nodded, waved her words away.

'How long do we have?'

A scream rent the air, something awful and animal and in utter agony. It lasted far longer than Chel thought possible, its pitch and intensity shaking his bones, making his guts tremble.

Sab's eyes were wide, her breath sharp.

'Not long.'

Rennic was already at the window, peering into the courtyard below, but keeping as low as he could. Chel thumped down next to him as the next scream ripped across the citadel. It subsided into sobs, screeching, mewling, pleading.

'Any chance they're just skinning a goat down there?'

Rennic shook his head. His expression was grave-cold, his years wearing as heavy on his face as Chel had ever seen.

'Dalim,' he said.

Chel nodded, because he could think of nothing else to do. Then he said, 'Palo will give them nothing. She'll make fools of them all.'

Rennic took a long breath, steadying himself to stand. 'I doubt it.'

\* \* \*

At the door to the frozen battlement, their burning climb behind them, Tarfel stopped to wait. 'The gatehouse is at the far end. Just stay out of sight until the confession ends, then go for the side door. I need to get back upstairs, before they notice I'm gone,' he said. 'We both do.' He was looking at Sab.

Chel looked back in horror. 'Get back? What are you talking about?'

The prince shrugged, apologetic. 'I'm technically under house arrest, confined to chambers, you see. If your sister hadn't got me out, I'd still be stuck there.'

'But people saw you, you sent them to watch the confession!'

'Indeed, indeed. My status is all a bit hush-hush, a bit need-to-know. Corvel's not keen to explain why he's imprisoned his own brother, you understand.'

'And you're going back?!'

'Plausible deniability, Vedren. Best big bro never finds out I've been on a jaunt.'

'And you?' Chel turned to his sister. 'Why would you stay here?'

'Nobody knows about me,' she said, jaw set in an expression he remembered from years before. 'I can do more good here, working on the inside.'

'Corvel knows a thrice-damned sight more than anyone ever believed,' he said, skin prickling with inner heat. 'He knows I have a sister, and he'll sure as day-old shit know that we're gone and his gaoler is dead. He'll know we had help. He'll look.'

Another scream tore through the morning air, this one layered thick with madness.

'And everyone confesses in the end.'

Rennic elbowed his way into their huddle. 'It's guarded,' he snarled. 'The fucking gatehouse has three men I can see and who knows how many more within. What the fuck are we supposed to do about them? Cough our way past? Why do you have no weapons?'

Sab stood her ground. 'If you'd let me *get* to it, I'd tell you I planned for this.' She gripped his arm and led him back to the battlement doorway. She pointed at a stack of bundles, piled against the base of the wall. 'There, see it? It's stacked with tinder and dried wood, plenty of green piled on top for some nasty smoke. I even rolled up a barrel of brandy from the cellars. Set that lot off, nobody is going to be looking at the gatehouse.'

Rennic gave a nod of the head. 'Impressive. How do we set it off?'

Sab went a little pale, and Rennic's expression darkened.

21

'I . . . er . . .'

'Jingling dick-bells, are you serious?'

'I had a lot to do, all right, and not much time to do it in! And in *absolute secrecy*!'

'Shepherd's tits, there's no way to light it.'

Sab was flushed but defiant. 'Hey, there are plenty of ways to light it. I could go down there, and—'

Before Chel could throw himself into the argument, Tarfel spoke up. 'I know where they put your stuff. Your weapons and armour.'

Rennic turned to him, very slowly.

'Yes, princeling?'

'It's in the armoury, above the stables. There are bows there, and crossbows. You could light the pile with a flaming arrow, right?'

Rennic stared at him for a long time, eyes burning, then he shrugged. 'Not very subtle, but fuck it, yeah.'

Outside in the courtyard the chanting of the crowd reached a crescendo, and the final, agonising scream ended with abrupt certainty.

'Show me.'

\*\*\*

Rennic stalked along the empty hallways like a great prowling cat, sliding from one pool of shadow to the next, his fists clenching and unclenching as he went. Tarfel trotted in his wake, pointing the way in mute distress, while Chel brought up the rear, casting pinched looks back down the passageway to where his sister and the Nort huddled on the battlement. Tension radiated from the man in front. Until he held a weapon, Rennic would not relax.

Not every occupant of the keep was at the confession, and their progress was skittering and irregular as they ducked in and out of doorways to avoid the occasional squeamish clerk. Overhead, the early bell had begun to toll once more. The second confession was imminent.

The smell announced that the stables were close. They peered through a narrow window into a low, separate courtyard, strewn with straw and dung piles. A stone-walled building occupied the far wall, plumes of steam billowing from the horses tied in the stalls within.

'Up there, above the stables. The room with the narrow windows.' Tarfel gestured redundantly upward, and Rennic rewarded him with a withering look.

A sound pricked Chel's ears: footsteps.

'Someone's com—' he began, but Rennic was already bundling them out of the hallway and into a side room. The big man followed, staying pressed against the cold stone of the door-frame, breathing into his arm to hide his breath-fog.

Chel counted the footsteps, four sets. No, five, moving fast but heavy. Armed men, most of them. Approaching from the main keep, either heading for the stables or the walls. Rennic met his eye. They were both unarmed. He knew Rennic was perfectly capable of incapacitating an adversary with little more than his thumbs, even a couple if he had the drop, but five was pushing it.

Rennic was scanning the gloomy room, an office from the look of it, as most of them seemed to be on this floor: rolled scrolls, writing desks, quills, and ink. He plucked a quill from its holder, tested the point against his finger, then sighed in disgust, snapped it and discarded the remains.

'. . . *cannot* be allowed to escape the citadel, you

understand? There's no way he drugged that guard himself, and if he's loose, he's had help.' A voice, pompous, northern. Familiar. Chel's gaze snapped back to meet Rennic's. He recognized it too. 'You two, check the walls, make sure he's not sneaking out that way. We'll look in the stables, count the horses. That ghastly little shit may have his brother's indulgence, but he does *not* have mine.'

The footsteps split, two sets heading up the hallway toward them, the rest continuing toward the stables. Chel slid deeper inside the room, ushering the prince into the shadows. The two men flashed past down the hallway, swords at their hips and shields on their arms. Their colours confirmed his suspicions – the freshly minted Grand Duke of Denirnas, Esen Basar, was hunting the prince.

Tarfel poked his head up, jaw flapping. 'Esen Basar!'

'Esen fucking Basar,' Chel growled, feeling the throb of his shoulder. The cowardly count who'd killed his own father and tried to murder Tarfel in the process.

'Prick-weasel escaped me once at the winter palace.' Rennic was already moving, padding out into the hallway. 'Not going to let that become a habit.'

'Two of his men are going to the wall, Rennic. They'll find my sister!'

'No shit.' He changed direction. 'I'll deal with it. Stay here, keep princeling quiet.'

Rennic's hand moved to the knives at his belt.

He had no knives. He had no belt.

Chel held his gaze. 'What are you going to do?'

The big man paused only a moment.

'Improvise.'

\* \* \*

Rennic came barrelling back into the office only a short time later, before Chel had started to really panic. One side of his face was sprayed dark and a guard's sword hung loose and bloodied in each hand; he left dark footprints in his wake. He looked out of breath.

Chel was on his feet immediately. 'What happened? Are you hurt?'

Rennic pushed one of the weapons into Chel's grip. Its hilt was sticky. 'Fine. Where are Count Pig-Dog and his minions? Have they left the stables?'

Chel shook his head. 'We haven't heard—'

'Fucking hells. Fine. Princeling! Take us to the armoury.'

The thick door to the armoury was unguarded. Tarfel fished around for a set of keys, gabbling the whole time.

'Borrowed these from the seneschal's office, didn't even have to use subterfuge, turns out nobody wants to refuse a prince, well, aside from that monster in the dungeon. I suppose, that could have been—'

'Shut up.' Rennic cuffed the back of his head.

'Righto.'

The armoury was less impressive inside than Chel had hoped: a rack of spears that had seen better days, some rusted mail and low-grade swords. Wherever the confessors were keeping their blessed blades and fancy new breast-plates, it wasn't here. Chel poked at a pile of unstrung bows, their wood cracked and snarled. Through the narrow windows, voices drifted up from the stables below. Pressed to the wall at the window-side, Rennic's scowl deepened. 'Basar is down there, he's searching the stables.' He looked up at the others. 'Find me something that can shoot.'

Chel went back to the cracked bows, hoping to find one he could salvage. Tarfel began to sift in the room's other corner, looking under canvas coverings and rummaging in crates. A moment later, he cried in triumph. 'Crossbows!'

'Levers and quarrels?'

'Er . . .'

'Keep looking, dung-muncher!'

Rennic marched to a long, low chest that sat beneath the windows. He ripped it open then crowed with delight, reaching in a gleeful hand to make sure. Chel looked up from his search. 'What, what is it? Quarrels?'

Rennic withdrew an armful of interwoven panels of leather and steel, a little frayed but still robust. His lamellar armour. He shook it out, then slung it straight around his shoulders.

'Little man, come and give me a hand with this.'

Tarfel piped up. 'I've found crossbow bolts, I think. And some kind of rod.'

'Good, good, now . . . Oh . . .'

Chel peered over Rennic's shoulder into the chest. Under the grotty collection of mail and broken blades piled within lay something long and slender, one end thick and tightly wrapped. Rennic reached in and levered up one end, sliding it out with great care. The shaft was carved, inlaid and ornate. And under the wrapping would be a long, sharp blade, inscribed with swirling patterns.

'Dalim's glaive,' Chel murmured, his gaze fixed on the gleam of the day's grey light on the shaft's carvings.

'He won't be needing it.' Rennic hoisted it over his shoulder.

'Anything else in there? My good knife?'

'Come on, let's get back to the battlements while those dick-heads are rifling the stables. Keep a tight hold of that sword, eh?'

Armour hanging open, wrapped glaive over his shoulder, Rennic strode back toward the door, waving for Tarfel to bring the crossbow, quarrels, and lever. The prince stumbled along behind them, bent double over his load, and Chel went back to assist him. Rennic sighed, turned and marched out through the doorway and straight into Esen Basar, Grand Duke of Denirnas.

Both stood in shocked silence for a moment, agape. Then recognition bloomed in the young duke's eyes, an instinctive hand going straight to the puckered scar across his otherwise perfect cheek. Rennic had given him that, Chel remembered with satisfaction.

'You!'

Rennic unfroze, swinging the glaive off his shoulder and tearing at the blade's wrapping. The duke's eyes moved from Rennic's face to the weapon and back, his nostrils flared, then he turned and ran, jostling past the two guards filling the hall. '*Kill him!*' he screeched as he fled, soft boots slapping against the flagstones. Chel tried to step in to help, the sticky sword heavy in his hand, but Rennic blocked the door. The wrapping wasn't coming free. The two guards closed, shields up, swords drawn.

'Fuck,' Rennic snarled. 'Fuck, fuck fu—'

Chel lunged forward and swiped at the last of the bindings around the glaive, narrowly missing Rennic's fingers. The blade abruptly freed, the big man feinted a back-step then pivoted, slashing the razor-sharp blade in a tight arc below the shield-line. Both guards, caught mid-advance, buckled and squealed. One managed to keep his shield up, the other took the blade's driving point in his neck. As he fell, Rennic was already shifting, spinning the haft around to crunch the pommel into the surviving guard's helmet, then slashing the blade again to his undefended legs. He collapsed, and Rennic moved fast to cut both throats.

'Can we—'

'*Shh!*'

Rennic cocked his head, and Chel did likewise, trying to quiet the pounding of his pulse in his ears. He could still make out the soft slap of the duke's boots, now half-muffled by straw.

'He's back downstairs. Crossbow!'

Rennic pushed the glaive toward Chel and snatched the crossbow from the prince's hands, along with the lever and a handful of bolts, and raced to one of the arrow-slit windows. Chel was an instant behind him, glaive and sword cradled uselessly in his hands, eye pressed to the next window along. There was the duke, sidling across the stable-yard, his step hesitant, his gaze over his shoulder at the lower door. Presumably waiting to see if it was safe to come back, or if he was being pursued.

Rennic dropped to one knee, working the lever into the crossbow's notch and drawing the creaking string, then slotted in a bolt. He sighted along its length, through the arrow-slit, at the oblivious duke. Chel looked down at the weapon. The quarrel was warped, the string fraying.

'It looks pretty old, are you sure you can—'

'Princeling,' Rennic growled over him, 'find another crossbow and load it.'

He pulled the trigger.

The bolt twanged from the bow, swishing through the air and smacking off the packed, frozen dirt several feet from the duke. The duke squealed and took to his heels, making for the wide gate that led to the main courtyard.

'Fuck! Rancid fucking crossbows! Give me another!'

He slung the crossbow aside, and Tarfel scurried over to press another into his waiting hand. Chel could only watch, his arms already full of weapons. Rennic checked the quarrel, raised and fired. The bolt skittered away, pinging over the duke's shoulder and into the ground, setting him squealing anew.

'Another!'

Tarfel passed him another weapon and he sighted along it. The duke had reached the wide gate and was trying to open it. It was shut fast, and the noise of the confession beyond appeared to be drowning out his hammering wails. Rennic lined up the bolt and pulled the trigger.

The string snapped.

'Fuck! Another!'

The duke had spotted the wicket gate.

'Another!'

The duke ran to the wicket gate, first trying to push, then pull.

'Another! What the fuck!'

Rennic swung around. Tarfel had the last crossbow, feebly trying to lever the string back. He looked up in misery. 'I think it's stuck, I can't—'

In the stable-yard, the wicket gate swung open, and the duke darted inside. He was gone.

Rennic's gaze swung back to the prince, and his knuckles went white.

'You useless fucking shit-heap!'

He threw himself at the prince, fists swinging. He landed only a couple of blows before Chel was on his back.

'Stop!'

Rennic stood, levering Chel clear of the ground, spinning and wrenching. He threw him clear, but Chel leapt straight back, a fresh scrape along one arm and a nasty throb in his shoulder.

'Stop! Stop. Hitting. Him.'

Rennic swayed on his feet as the rage seemed to drain from him. He seemed at once very tired. Tired and old. Chel pressed his advantage.

'He risked his life for us. He didn't have to do that. He didn't have to do a thrice-damned thing.'

Tarfel cowered behind him, whimpering. Chel kept himself between the big man and the prince. He could feel a hot trickle of blood leaking from his nose.

'We need to leave. And he's coming too.'

Rennic nodded, the fury gone from his eyes as suddenly as it had come.

'Then let's go.'

# THREE

Chel led them back at speed, ignoring the thumping pain in his head and shoulder. Rennic seemed in a daze, Tarfel likewise. They stepped over a pair of steaming corpses in the hallway as they approached the battlement. Nobody spoke.

The bell had stopped. Shouting filled the court of confession, the crowds below roiling and chanting, jostling for a better look. Confessors and clergy mixed with commoners, a great seething mass of humanity joined for the spectacle, some in ghoulish glee, some morbid fascination. And somewhere out in the courtyard, a panicked duke, screaming for guards, screaming about a missing prince and assassins in their midst.

On the central platform, beneath the gibbet, whatever remained of Dalim had been cleared away, now freed from sin – and any other earthly consideration – in the sight of the Shepherd and her merciful servants. Palo stood flanked by a pair of brawny confessors, small and hazy in the snow-glare. Over her stood Brother Hurkel, the great tin monster on metal legs, his red little head capped with the white wolf pelt. On the far side of the platform stood the royal gallery. Chel could almost make out the golden blur of Prince Corvel, front and centre.

Rennic crouched on the battlement and rubbed his eyes, peering at the gatehouse at the wall's end. He was sprayed in drying blood and looked drained. 'It's as before, no change. We still have a chance.'

Chel nodded. 'Let's light a bolt and get things moving, shall we?'

Sab hovered over them, her relief at their return tempered by their battered state. She seemed particularly disturbed by Rennic's gory appearance, and wouldn't meet his eye. 'This way.'

On the platform, Hurkel raised his arms, his missing hand replaced by a two-pronged fork. He began bellowing of Palo's crimes, real and imagined, to the baying of the crowd. Chel watched his theatrics, his absent hand, and thought for a moment of Loveless, feeling a sharp pang of something he couldn't name. His glance fell on Palo, now half-strapped to the confessor's table. Even at this distance he could see she was impassive, detached.

Rennic had taken the crossbow from Tarfel's arms without a word, slotting the bolt and tweaking the string. His gaze matched Chel's, watching Hurkel raise the glowing brand from the platform's brazier, seeing it steam in the frigid air. Chel realized he was shaking.

'Can we save her?'

Rennic's head shake was a mere twitch.

'We'd only die alongside.'

'Can we do anything?'

'We can get the fuck out of here. She'd want that at

least.' He clicked his fingers at Sab, startling her. 'Fire, girl. Where's the fire?'

'What? I thought you meant you . . .' Sab swallowed, and looked to her brother. 'I can run and get a torch—'

'Nine hells, girl, what were you doing while we were fetching the fucking weapon?'

'Keeping out of sight! Not murdering anyone! Which is—'

The little Nort appeared between them, dragging the clinking sack. He looked up from one to the other, then to the crossbow in Rennic's hands.

'Please?'

Rennic raised an eyebrow but allowed the Nort to take the bow. He placed it flat, then fished in his sack for a few small clay pots and jars. He tapped out a handful of crystals from one, added a powder from another, rubbed his hands together – Chel noticed his palms were pale and smooth with scarring – then applied the mixed powder to the shaft of the bolt. He wiped his hands and held out the crossbow to Rennic.

'Please?'

Rennic took back the weapon, frowning, and knelt to fire at the stacked fuel against the far wall. The Nort tapped his shoulder, one finger raised, then reached over with a tiny bottle in his hand. Trembling, he tilted the bottle, until a drop of something clear and acrid fell from its lip onto the powdered bolt.

The bolt began to steam, then smoke, and then it burst into flame.

'Fuck!' Rennic cried, almost dropping the weapon. Chel and Sabina fell back, recoiling from the alchemical stench. The Nort pointed at the far wall, hands urgent, and despite visible misgivings, Rennic lined up the shot through the caustic smoke.

He fired. The flaming bolt whipped through the air, leaving a plume of curling fumes, almost disintegrating. It smacked into the base of the stack, splintering into flaming shards, and almost immediately the stack began to smoke.

Rennic clenched a fist. 'Fucking have that!'

If anyone had noticed the bolt's passage, they made less noise than the clamour of confession. Chel exchanged glances with the others, then looked back to the simmering stack. Already white smoke was curling from within, the dry wood alight, licking at the green above.

'Let's give it a moment before people notice the smoke, then—'

The stack exploded. A ring of flame tore out from the base of the wall, a pulse of roaring energy ripping through the eddies of black and white smoke, tearing and stretching the atmosphere around it. A deafening crack split the air as pieces of splintered, flaming wood rained down on the shocked and screaming crowd in the courtyard.

Rennic whipped around, eyes locked on the Nort, the crossbow shaking in his hands.

'What the giddy fuck was that?'

The Nort looked equally shocked, his mouth open, hands up in warding. Chel blinked away smoke-induced tears, feeling the air burning in his lungs. The crowd in the court-yard were panicked, fleeing, streaming for the city gate in a heaving mass, even as the last echoes of the explosion died away. In the gatehouse, the guards within were milling, unsure if they should be investigating or fleeing themselves.

'We need to leave!'

Rennic nodded, immediately back on task. He stood,

waving the others forward along the wall. Tarfel and Sab led, the Nort on their heels, his clinking sack slung over one shoulder, leaving him hunched and lopsided. Rennic went to toss the crossbow, then paused, his gaze returning to the platform at the courtyard's centre. Chel followed it.

Hurkel stood on the platform, turning slowly, his big red face a picture of enraged confusion. Below him lay Palo, on the confessor's elevated table. She was still, her free hand clamped around the dagger she'd plucked from his belt in the commotion, now standing proud from her chest. Blood pooled beneath the table, joining that of the countless hordes who'd preceded her, the table's wood long since stained dark. She looked serene.

Rennic swallowed and nodded. His voice was a cracked growl.

'Be seeing you, Palo.'

They ran for the gatehouse.

\* \* \*

They didn't stop running until they reached the outer walls, melded with the fleeing crowd from the citadel. People's instincts varied – some ran for their homes, others for the river, some out into the countryside beyond – and it was only when they split from the free way into the back alleys that the human tide around them ebbed.

Chel jogged beside his sister, kidding himself that he was keeping her safe, his legs burning along with his lungs. He'd long since let the bloody sword drop, had kicked it away into an alley. He'd told himself that he needed to conserve what little strength he had, but beneath this rationale lurked an abiding desire to be rid of the thing that had little to do with any forthcoming need for self-defence. Sab kept easy pace at his side, ducking through the warren of adjoining buildings as they made for the Shanties gate.

'What happened back there?' she said, breath catching. 'What did the Nort do? What else is in that sack?'

'The Nort?' Chel gasped, flicking a glance over his shoulder. The Nort was keeping up, his mysterious sack still shouldered and a look of determination on his young face, shuffling along beside Tarfel. Rennic brought up the rear, shepherding them along with a glower from beneath the hood of his pilfered cloak. 'From his reaction, I'd say he was as surprised as us. Are you sure it was brandy in that barrel?'

She shook her head. 'It came from the lower cellars. It's *usually* where they keep the brandy . . . Shepherd's tits, there were dozens of barrels down there . . . It cracked the wall, Bear. Did you see? It cracked the citadel wall!'

The Widowgate hove into view, a dark and stubby thing festering in the brutal New Wall. Rennic stepped ahead of them. 'Who has silver? Anything valuable?'

Chel gave him an even look.

Tarfel slapped at his cloak. 'I think I have a token somewhere, it's a trifle really—'

Rennic waved him away. He slung the re-wrapped glaive at Chel, then stalked off toward the gate guards. The others huddled in the faint shadow of a workshop.

Chel found himself standing beside the little Nort. He looked down at the heavy sack, then found the Nort gazing up at him, a glare of challenge. 'So, er,' he coughed, 'they let you keep all that alchemical stuff close to your cell? That was . . . er . . .'

The Nort said nothing, holding his gaze with unblinking eyes.

Rennic stepped out from the shadow of the gate and waved them forward. They hurried through, hoods down, while the guards studiously looked the other way.

'What did you offer them?' Chel asked as Rennic took back the glaive.

'Promises,' he said. 'And we'll be long gone before they realize they were dust.'

'Ain't that the way,' Chel said. He was very tired. And hungry. Very hungry. 'Does anyone have any food?'

\* \* \*

The Shanties still reeked of smoke and soot, parts charred black and broken from Spider's fire. Their ill-starred entry to the city seemed so long ago now. They crept through the winding labyrinth of nominally temporary structures, snow and charcoal crunching underfoot. Water dripped from somewhere, always seeming to be both ahead and behind. They saw no one.

'What are you going to do about the prince? He can't go back, can he?'

Sab was beside him again, her hand on his arm, helping him around a blackened spar as his stride faltered.

'No. Not after that.'

'And nor can I.'

'No.' Chel realized that he was feeling relief, a great wash of sensation, an unwinding knot of tension. His fingers tingled from it. He was free, and his sister was safe. 'No, you can't go back there.'

She grunted, and they walked on in silence for a time.

'How did you get into this mess, Bear? Last time I saw you, you were in the favour of two princes, destined for great things. Why do I next encounter you as a condemned traitor to the crown? Did you get *very* drunk?'

'We . . . I think we made things worse.' He swallowed. 'But what about you?' He felt anger rising in his voice, now they were free, now the immediate danger had passed; a hot, raw frustration born of ignorance and insecurity. 'You were a fucking Rau Rel spy? Did you consider for a moment the risk—'

She put a hand on his arm, drew him to a stop, and his words died. She met his faltering gaze with steady, moist eyes. 'Bear, we're all growing up fast.' One hand ran down his cheek, lingering at the scar on his lip, the broken bulge of his jaw. 'I'm glad I can still recognize you. How are you, really? Are you all right? I'm so sorry I couldn't . . . Things took so long to arrange . . .'

He put his hand on hers, then wrapped his arms around her, and wept for the first time in all of it, in all the weeks of captivity, misery, and doubt. He cried on his sister's shoulder until he was a heaving, empty husk, and felt her sobbing against him in return. He realized he was talking, mumbling, forming the words 'thank you' over and over into her cloak.

'We're not out yet.' Rennic shook his shoulder, drawing him gently away. Chel looked up in tearful defiance, but he saw his emotion mirrored on the big man's face, his own eyes glazed with unshed tears. His voice was little more than a whisper. 'We need to keep moving, little man.'

Chel sniffed, nodded, and on they pressed, the weight of the Shanties pressing down around them. He remembered the children he'd seen playing therein, their rhymes and songs.

*We were supposed to be lucky.*

\* \* \*

Sab led them up into the hills, away from the slabs of the walls and the malignant gaze of the citadel's tower. She'd recovered some of her poise, and chattered as they climbed, of what she'd seen within the citadel, of her covert operations for the Rau Rel. Chel paused for breath at the edge of the woods, looking back over the city beneath its pall of winter smoke, now thickened by the alchemical plume from their distant intervention. Below them, the main road wound around to the ruined old bridge, clad in ugly stacks of wooden scaffolding, then away toward the gates. Small structures lined the road, thin poles, dotted at the top with . . .

'Best not look too close,' Rennic muttered from beside him. One of his knees seemed to be giving him trouble. 'You won't want to risk recognizing anyone.'

Of course: they were heads. Dozens upon countless dozens, girdling the road like fence-posts.

Sabina was following his gaze, and Chel heard her breath catch. 'The bastard,' she hissed. 'The unconscionable . . . Why didn't you stop him?'

Chel turned, his mouth already framing an earnest defence, but her words were addressed to Tarfel. The prince stood slumped, panting and pink-cheeked from the climb, eyebrows raised and eyes wide.

'Me? What could I do?'

'You're his brother! Who else can stand up to him?'

39

Rennic pushed himself back upright. 'Let's hope our fates don't rest on this little piss-cloth,' he muttered. 'Let's get where we're going, get to someone who can actually make a difference.'

With a pointed look at the prince, Sab led them into the woods. Before long, they reached a clearing, where she came to a hesitant stop. It looked deserted, and the sun had long since disappeared behind the hills; if it had been cold before, the coming night promised something altogether worse.

Rennic strode ahead, into the clearing, fierce eyes scanning the trees in the dying light.

'This is the place?'

'It should be.' Sab crinkled her nose. 'I've never actually been out here . . .'

'But?'

'But I left a message in the usual drop. They should know we're coming.'

'Depends if there was anyone left to listen. As our friends along the road can attest, King Corvel has been busy.'

Something rustled in the gloom beyond the clearing, and Rennic froze, hands gripping the glaive. Chel felt his pulse quicken but nothing more. His muscles were spent, his very bones exhausted, and he'd long since given up on the idea of food. He wanted to lie down on the ground and let the world wash over him. Beside him, Tarfel whimpered.

A hoot came from somewhere around them, a formless owl, too loud, too imprecise. Rennic unfroze, a broad grin spreading across his face in the twilight. He visibly relaxed, letting the end of the glaive rest on the ground, then put one hand to his mouth and hooted in return.

A figure detached from the darkness of the trees, striding

across the clearing with a sun-bright smile. Even in the low light, Chel could recognize Whisper's lithe gait anywhere, the springing confidence in every step. She raced to Rennic, embracing him with silent affection, while he let the glaive fall.

The bushes beside him rustled and crackled, then an orange-haloed figure emerged blinking into the clearing. 'All right, wankers?' said Lemon. 'How's tricks?'

# FOUR

Talking surrounded them, a happy gabbling of steaming breath in the nascent moonlight. Rennic and Whisper engaged in one-sided conversation, the mute scout straining to slow her cheerful gestures to maintain their clarity in the low light. Lemon expressed joyous disgust for their collective state, accused Chel of both improper diet and hygiene, bobbed a quick bow to Tarfel then demanded introductions to the others. She was delighted to meet Sabina, doubly so when she learnt of Sab's crucial role in their escape. Sab herself was particularly tickled to find that the mercenaries also called her brother 'Bear', or derivations thereof.

Chel was not tickled, and turned quickly to the Nort.

'And I'm afraid I don't know this young man's name, but we busted him out of the cells when we bolted. Good thing we did – he knocked up a tasty bit of alchemy on the walls, might well have been responsible for that great bang back there.'

Lemon looked from one to the other, puzzled. 'Young man?'

Chel blinked. 'What?'

'Your alchemist pal is a lady, wee bear.'

'Come again?'

As one, they turned to the Nort. He—She bristled from the attention, shrinking away behind the heavy sack. Lemon put up her hands. 'I may not know all things beneath the moon and stars, but I'm quite sure this is a Miss.'

Chel noted the Nort's look of irritation at this. He peered closer.

'Can you understand us?'

The look of irritation intensified.

'Of course. I am not a farmyard animal.' Her voice was sharp, of lower pitch than he'd expected. Far from the stripling boy he'd imagined, she could easily have been the same age as him. Her accent was utterly foreign, the consonants oddly shifted, the vowels sing-song, but the disdain beneath could be heard from a mountaintop.

Lemon's eyebrow had rocketed. 'Do you think maybe you could have mentioned being able to understand us a little earlier, perhaps?'

The Nort's baleful glare settled on Lemon.

'You are very rude. You are a stupid, rude person.'

'Aye, right, cheers. Quite the grateful sort you are.'

The Nort only sniffed. 'What have you done for me?'

Rennic interrupted, the glaive now little more than a walking-staff in his hand. 'What's the commotion?'

Lemon jerked her head at the Nort. 'Your wee northern alchemist is a girl, can understand every word we say and has not a shred of gratitude in her.'

Rennic nodded slowly, rocking slightly on his heels. The Nort glared back at him, defiant. Chel tried to stop himself gawking at her too openly, but there was a fire in her eyes

43

that he didn't remember seeing before. Had he seen it in the cells, he might have thought twice of releasing her.

'What's your name?' Rennic said.

'*Akoshtiranarayan*,' came the response, followed by a string of titles in a tongue Chel had no chance of following.

Rennic remained impassive.

'Hello, Akoshtiranarayan,' he said, and Chel saw the Nort stiffen at the competent pronunciation of her name. 'I'm guessing you have a shorter name you use, eh? To save time, and all.'

'By some, I am called—'

'What do your friends call you?'

She paused, and Rennic tilted his head.

'You do have friends, right?'

'Of course, I have friends, imbecile! You are very stupid people, and I have no duty to answer to any of you!'

'Uh-huh. Well, Akoshtiranarayan, you are a thousand or more miles from home, a wanted fugitive from the clutches of both crown and church, lost in hostile countryside without provisions or allies. If I were you, I'd be bending over backward to make some more friends, even with imbeciles.'

The Nort glared at him, her jaw working, before she sniffed again.

'I have been called Kosh, in the past.'

Rennic nodded, a smile pulling at his mouth. 'Honoured to meet you, Kosh. I'm Rennic. This is Whisper, that's Lemon, these are Chels One and Two, and this is Tarfel, younger brother of our nemesis and prince of the realm.'

Kosh's jaw dropped. She stared at the prince, who coughed and shifted in embarrassment.

Rennic's smile widened. 'It's a long story, little alchemist.

We'll fill you in as we go, and you can tell us what you were doing in the citadel's dungeon, and just what your part was in that whopping bang back in the courtyard.'

'I will tell you nothing.'

The Nort was trembling, staring at Rennic with huge black eyes, and Chel found himself shaking in sympathy. Not just in sympathy – he was freezing. His jaw had begun to judder, clattering his teeth against each other.

'That's enough,' he said. 'We need warmth, shelter, and food. Especially food. If we're not camping here, let's get where we're going.'

Rennic grunted. 'As you say, little man. Long journeys. Let's get moving, by now the boys in red will have worked out we're sprung and be on the hunt. If this alchemist is a curled hair as important to Corvel as she seems, they'll be taking her loss with great offence.'

'I was to be executed after you! I gave them nothing!'

'Either way, we need to get gone and sharpish.'

'About that—' Lemon began, but Rennic kept talking.

'We should head south and west, back toward the Sepulchre. The remains of the Rau Rel may still be in residence, and let's not forget that that prick Torht owed us a shit-pile of silver. Someone's going to pay. Lemon, how far off are the others? Are they meeting us here or do we need to signal?'

'*About that*, boss—'

'Which of you was watching the drop? Are you sure you were the only ones? How did you even know about the drop? We weren't part of Torht's little set-up . . .'

Around them, the woods rustled with more than just the passing breeze. Figures loomed from the darkness, separating from trees but never becoming distinct. Rennic whipped around, the glaive held in open challenge, but Lemon jumped in front of him.

'Calm, calm, boss, we're under control.'

'Who the fuck is this?'

Whisper was at his shoulder now, a steady hand on his arm.

'Like I was *trying* to say, boss, wasn't us watching the drop. We're here with them, not the other way around.'

'And who the fuck are they?'

'The Rau Rel, boss. What's left of them.'

A gritty figure with an eyepatch loomed close enough to make out, a nocked longbow loose in her hands.

'Spear of the South,' she said. 'You're just in time for the conclave.'

'Do I know you?'

She'd already turned away. 'We'll camp on the ridge. We'll be there in good time yet.'

Rennic watched her recede into the darkness, then exchanged a look with Chel.

'Now what shit-housery is this?'

They dragged their feet forward once more.

* * *

'Five hells, where are we?' Chel murmured as they watched the setting sun light the structure on the hilltop. It stood apart from the snowy forests that surrounded it, a three-storey pillar of wood and stone. The last rays of the weak winter sun cast it in a red the colour of blood and embers. It looked too fragile to be a fortress, too stark and windowless for a dwelling. And it was miles from *anywhere*.

Rennic shrugged. 'I suppose we'll find out.'

'I am *very tired* of surprises.'

They trudged on. At last, a full day's exhausting march from their camp on the ridge, their journey seemed to have reached its end.

The one-eyed woman – Eka, she'd said – led them on a winding path up the hillside, and a lone torch was lit at the tower's base by the time they reached the summit. It was much bigger than it had seemed from distance, its base and foundation pale Taneru stone, some of the old engraving still visible despite the weathering. A single door stood open beside the torch, although evidence of encampments around the tower lingered at the torchlight's edges. Shapes flitted in the wooded gloom around them, the same armed figures that had escorted them since the clearing outside Roniaman. Eka's people, rarely seen, hard to count.

'Four,' Rennic said, as if reading Chel's mind.

'Huh?'

'There are only four of them, plus her. Just seems more because they move around us so much.' He chuckled. 'Whisp and I could take these fuckers out in a heartbeat. Like a one-eyed archer can be any cop. No depth perception.'

'Let's hope it doesn't come to that. Sab seems rather friendly with them.'

A giant shape filled the doorway as they approached, arms held wide.

'All right, Fossy!' Lemon called from behind.

The big man grinned, bundled braids swaying as he shook his head. 'I didn't dare think it true, my friends. I didn't dare. Welcome, welcome.'

He embraced Rennic, then wrapped Chel in a mighty hug that ground his bones against each other. His greeting came out as a gasp. Once the introductions were complete, Foss gestured to the structure behind.

'Welcome, my friends, to the conclave.'

'The conclave of what?'

'The conclave of the Rau Rel. Loveless is inside, saving us a table. Our other friend is here.' He nodded toward a nearby tree.

'Other friend? Who—?' Chel turned and came to a sudden halt. There, slumped against the trunk with her ruined arm now bound tight against her body, lay Brecki the Strangler. She looked cleaner than Chel had seen her, scrubbed of war-paint and decoration, but the pallor of her already milky skin was cadaverous, even in the warm torch-light from the building's base.

'She's . . . here. Unchained.' Chel swallowed. An odd mix of feelings welled within him at seeing the reaver, seething resentment at the woman for her killings, a hot flush of shame at the thought of his own negligence in her acts, and a sliver of something altogether lighter, something that might have been . . . relief? 'Untied.'

'She is, friend.'

'Isn't that . . . risky?'

Foss released a heavy breath and ran a hand over his braids. 'Shepherd guard my words, but she seems no threat to any. She long since ceased to bite anyone, eats little, moves less.'

Lemon came up beside them. 'Aye, right. Guess she rather lost her motivation along with the use of the arm.'

'But why is she here?'

'Our partisan colleagues maintained talk of a citizens' trial for her, once matters in the capital were settled,' Foss said. 'Such talk has faded in light of recent developments.'

'She's no longer a prisoner?'

'Not of the Rau Rel. Do you believe we should restrain her, friend?'

Chel rolled his bad shoulder in its socket. It wasn't so long ago he himself had been chained, one arm damaged, and locked in a cell. 'I . . . uh . . .'

'Are we going in, or what? It's cold out – who is that?' Sabina had approached, along with the Nort, who was gazing at the slumped reaver with detached curiosity.

'That,' said Lemon, 'is Brecki, a visitor from our southern shores, who was foolish enough to tangle with your brother and his pals at Talis.'

'You broke her arm?' The disapproval in Sab's voice was unmistakable.

Chel felt the back of his neck growing hot. 'She started it! She's a bloodthirsty reaver!'

Sab's eyebrows lowered as she looked back at the pale, lethargic woman, one thumb resting against her teeth. 'What in God's name was a reaver doing that far north?'

'Not just her,' Lemon said brightly. 'Whole fucken war-band, came steaming up to attack the King's Hunt right when wee bear here was trying to arrange a princes' parley. They'd have slaughtered everyone if our boys hadn't stepped in.'

Sab's thumbnail tapped her front tooth. 'Is that so?'

'Aye, boss-man and your wee bear took this one prisoner.'

'I thought you lot just killed everyone who crossed you?' Her tone was sharp, accusatory. 'That one,' she said, indicating Rennic who was a few paces away, 'killed three people in the hour after I met him.'

'Hey!' Rennic, bristling, held up one hand. 'It was five. You missed the two in the armoury.'

'You must be very proud of the life you've lived,' she shot back, which seemed to give Rennic pause.

Eka, their one-eyed guide, cleared her throat. 'The conclave is beginning. You should go below. We can keep watch over your friend.'

Chel and the others turned for the door. 'You're not joining us?'

She shook her head. 'We are patriots, not politicians. We will watch from the gallery.'

Rennic scooped him along with a wide arm as he passed. 'Come on, little man. Wouldn't want them deciding anything without us.' He had Tarfel marching before him, encircled by his other arm. The prince turned as he saw Chel, eyes wide and watery.

'Listen, Vedren, I really don't think this is any place for me,' he began as Rennic pushed him on. 'I think perhaps I should be moving off elsewhere, and I was wondering if—'

'Keep moving, princeling, you're holding everyone up.'

'My brother will be looking for me, Vedren, he has plans – such plans! We should—'

'You're not staying out there. Now button your flap and keep your head down,' Rennic growled as they followed Foss into the dark of the tower. 'If there's anyone who can marshal against that bastard in the citadel, they're within these walls.'

\* \* \*

Stairs led both up and down, to galleries above and a stone-cut pit below. Sab and the Nort had stayed with Eka at Foss's suggestion – just political wrangling to come, very dull for outsiders, he assured them. Whisper went with them. Foss chattered as he led Chel, Tarfel, Rennic, and Lemon down the wooden stairs, which creaked beneath his feet. 'This place was once a grain-store, during Taneru days, or so I'm told. There was a settlement at the bottom of the hill. It was a temple after that, old gods . . .' He shuddered and made the sign of the crook. 'I think it was a mill after that, but now it's our watchtower. Everyone's here.'

Rennic's mouth twitched. 'Everyone?' He nudged Chel. 'This is how we get back on the horse, little man, here's how we turn the battle-tide. First, they're going to pay us, then we're going to join hands across the kingdom and deliver a steel-capped kicking to Golden King Shit-Grin, our boots front and centre. He's out in the open now, him and his red-cloth fuckers.'

Chel offered a weak grin. 'It'll be nice to hear what our rebellion is up to, I suppose.'

Bright fires burned at the base of the pit, a central blaze and braziers spaced evenly between the long tables that circled it. Figures milled around them, some sitting, some talking in small groups. Despite the cold beyond the walls, the atmosphere in the pit was sweaty and fevered. A palpable anxiety filled the crackling air.

Loveless met them at the foot of the steps. In spite of her attempts to remain aloof, she radiated visible joy at their arrival. The Black Hawk Company were reunited.

'You're just in time,' she said. Her hair was flame red now, trimmed back, shorn almost flat at the sides. 'They're about to start. You'll make for a nice surprise.'

Rennic's frown deepened. 'Who's running the show? We need words about our contract. Although everyone who signed it is dead.'

She ignored him. 'Come on, I've got us seats at the back.'

Loveless had commandeered a small table behind the outer circle, one of a handful dotted around the pit's perimeter. A clay jug of spiced wine and a collection of cups stood waiting. When Chel hesitated, Loveless clapped him on the shoulder and sat down. 'Come on, my hussies, take a seat and have a drink before this bunch of old women bore the arses off us.' She gestured with one of the wine cups toward the pit's centre, where some of the greyest heads were gathered.

Chel did as he was told. 'Who are they all?'

Loveless poured wine, pointing without looking. 'That scruffy bunch are what remains of the western leadership, brotherhood of something, small-time but vocal. That fellow behind them you may recognize, he's speaking for the lady of Wavecrest, and those dour types are some of the last Merciful Sisters.' She paused. 'Did you hear about that? The Sepulchre?'

Chel shook his head. Despite the warmth from the braziers, he could feel his skin prickling.

'We weren't exactly drowning in gossip in the cells,' Rennic growled.

Foss was looking deep into the darkness of his wine cup. 'Evil days, friends,' he said without looking up, his sonorous voice reflected from the cup.

Loveless nodded at Tarfel, who was keeping a low profile behind the table, hood pulled low. Self-concealment seemed almost habit for him now. 'Rest assured, princeling's big brother has racked up a few more stains on his soul since last we chatted.'

Chel's head was spinning, the heat of the chamber and

the first gulps of wine sending his thoughts swirling. Corvel's various crimes dimmed in his resumed proximity to Loveless, her hair glowing in the light, and he felt a dull ache return, a memory of his captive dreams. Thoughts of captivity made him think of the Nort, the young woman with a bag of alchemy and the ability to make fire on command. It was hard to shake the feeling there was a lot she wasn't telling them—

'*Aaaanyway*, the rest of them are much of a muchness: they're the peasants' collective from somewhere southern, that bunch snarling at them is the collective from down the valley. Not much in the way of Free Company representation, I have to say, bar those tedious haircuts from the Indigo Company, nor anyone I can see from the hill tribes of the Territories or the eastern marches. But we've a handful who claim to represent various free cities – or at least their earthier trades – a couple of banking house stooges and a few proxies for the Names who weren't already purged and are still inclined toward fomentation . . .'

Chel looked at her blankly.

Lemon rolled her eyes. 'Fighting back, wee bear.'

'And "earthier trades"?'

Loveless grinned, sharp and pearly in the torchlight. 'Purveyors of the necessities of quotidian alteration.'

'Eh?'

Lemon waved an expansive hand. 'What my impenetrable colleague is failing to express is that the rich and varied wealth of humanity within these walls is a fair representation of what remains of the resistance.' She paused, chuckled. 'Impenetrable, ha!'

Chel ignored it, directing his attention to Loveless. 'How can you know all that?'

Her smile twinkled. 'Didn't have much to do while I was waiting for you lot, did I? I'm a good listener.'

Before Lemon could get another word in, someone banged on the central table and a hush descended in the pit. Chel saw faces in the gantries above, pressing over the old railings like the audience of a mummers' play. Sabina was among them, and she gave him a big wave. She looked to be deep in jolly conversation with Eka the one-eyed hunter. They'd had plenty to talk about on the march to the tower, it seemed, and were not done yet. Chel found himself unnerved to see his little sister so . . . so . . . *independent*.

'Sisters and brothers,' said a gruff voice from somewhere near the main fire. A woman stood, middle-aged, soft-eyed. 'We are joined for the conclave of the free peoples.'

Various noises of agreement echoed around the pit.

'For those who don't know me, I'm Gurgen of Koronur. Thank you for coming. It's no secret that things are bleak. Since Raeden Torht launched his doomed infiltration of the citadel, we have seen systematic purges of our allies, and countless innocents, at all levels. All of us here have lost friends and family.'

Murmurs rose around the pit, loudest from the Merciful Sisters.

'So, I say again: thank you for coming. I know you do not come lightly. And unity of purpose, of belief, is now more crucial than ever. Torht failed not because his planning was poor or his preparation lacking, but because he under-estimated our enemy. We shall not do so again.'

More agreement, some growling, echoed around them.

'We must agree this evening, sisters and brothers, we must reach common understanding. Tonight, we are gath-ered to select a new watcher, a new strategist, a new spymaster. A new leader. I know that we all have our preferred candidates, but again I stress what matters most is the survival and regrowth of our movement, that we can bring others to our cause, unite the lands, and throw off once and for all the yoke of subjugation!'

This got cheers, although they seemed guarded. Chel wondered if everyone was thinking of their preferred candidates. He glanced at Tarfel to see how he was taking the talk of subjugation, but the prince remained hidden beneath his hood.

'First, a moment's silence for our fallen comrades.'

The pit fell silent, its congregation bowing heads and making the sign of the crook.

'Fuck 'em!'

The voice came from above, somewhere on the upper gantry, and shattered the silence like a hammer.

'They were twats, they fucked up, and they died.' The voice was descending, coming down the stairs into the firelight. 'We shouldn't be celebrating them, we should be spitting on their fucking names.'

A gobbet of something green arced from the stairs into a nearby brazier, hissing in the coals.

'They could have taken care of that fuck-stick prince, carved through those royal bastards and their lapdog clergy, emptied that fucking citadel in rivers of blood. They failed. And we all suffered as a result. If they'd done what they should've, there would have been no purge. Nobody would have died. Nobody who didn't fucking deserve it!'

The figure neared the bottom of the stairs, others following behind. Armed men and women. Murmurs of agreement sounded again, the growl returning.

'I should know. I saw it. I was there. And I won't make the same mistake.'

Spider stepped into the light.

Rennic was halfway to his feet when Chel's arm hauled him back. The big man rounded on him, eyes boiling with rage. 'What the f—'

'The prince!' Chel snarled, his voice a hoarse whisper against the hubbub. 'Who knows what Spider will do if he sees him?'

Rennic matched his whisper. Chel had never been more conscious of the vivid blood vessels at the fringes of the man's eyeballs. 'That *fucker* left us to *die*.'

'I remember! Just keep a lid on yourself until he's said his piece and buggered off, then you can take it up with him at your leisure. For both of us.'

Behind Spider, his followers had moved into the light, slack-faced and pale, from leaf or poppy Chel couldn't tell. They carried axes.

'What the fuck is going on?' Loveless hissed across the table. 'He told us you got separated inside the citadel, that he couldn't fight his way back to you!'

'And that,' Rennic murmured, eyes still fixed on Spider, 'would be bollocks.'

Spider was moving away from the stairs, striding toward the centre. He steered Gurgen aside, taking the floor.

'Brothers and sisters,' Spider said in mocking imitation, 'the old girl is right, we need unity. Torht played power games and lost, and took the rest of those sorry fuckers with him. I can make you a promise: the Spider will never seek the throne, nor political favour.'

Rennic was snarling. 'Because the Spider seeks only bloodshed,' he growled. Chel jerked a curt hand to shush him.

Spider circled around again. His followers, half a dozen by Chel's count, were spreading around the base of the pit, axes heavy in their hands.

'Let me make this clear to you all. We can sit here and drink wine and spout platitudes about *unity* and *common understanding*, but there is no common fucking understanding. Not between this jostling bunch I see before me. So listen carefully, because there is yet one thing we can agree on: death to the royals. Death to the church.'

The muttering fell away, and Spider repeated himself.

'Death to the royals. Death to the church.'

He said it again, and this time others picked up the refrain. He chanted with the bulk of the crowd, while those who kept their silence looked around nervously.

*Death to the royals! Death to the church!*

Spider continued the chant, moving between the tables, reaching out a hand. One of his people handed him the haft of an axe. Chel looked back at Tarfel. The young prince was pressed back against the wall, shaking beneath his cloak. Chel grabbed Rennic's arm. 'We need to get out of here. They'll kill him!'

Rennic shook him off. 'Not before I kill that fucking rat.'

Loveless was on her feet before them. 'Fuck's sake, don't draw any more attention. We can probably sneak him out if we go now.'

'Brothers and sisters! There will be no election, no selection! I will be direct, because these times call for directness, and the Spider is nothing but direct. I will make you this vow: pledge to me, and I will bleed the church, and murder every crown-wearing bastard in this land. The Spider vows it! Death to the royals!'

*Death to the church!*

Spider's minders were shuffling closer, their slack gazes falling on any failing to chant.

Chel reached back and grabbed the prince's cloak. 'We're leaving, highness. Keep your head down.'

They began to shuffle around the pit's edge, ducking away from the lights of the braziers, heading for the stairs. Chel kept the prince's hand in his, gripping against the fearful grease of his palm. His gaze rested on the bottom of the wooden staircase, counting the steps in his head. Thirty paces would do it. They were past one of Spider's men already. Twenty-nine. They were past another. Twenty-eight.

Spider was walking back to the pit's centre, almost crowing with triumph. 'No more failures, no more pitiful gambits. The Spider will deliver action!'

'The Spider's a fucking coward!'

The pit fell abruptly silent as Rennic's cry echoed from its stone walls. Chel froze, his hand gripped around the prince's. *Fu. King. Hells.*

Spider's head tilted, a quick, reptilian motion. 'Is that you, Beaky? Funny seeing you here, what with you being dead. Still, least said, soonest mended.'

Rennic's teeth were bared, but it was nothing like a smile.

'And how are you, Spider? Looking pretty perky for someone who jumped off a tower-top. They do say insects can survive long falls.'

'The Spider is not an insect, maggot-dick,' Spider replied with a glittering grin of pointed teeth. This, too, was devoid of mirth. 'Which of the gobshites did you drag down here with you? Could it be . . . ?'

He turned instantly on Chel, pinning him where he

hunched against the wall with his pointed gaze. 'Leaving already, rat-bear?' Then his eyes glimmered wide, and a grin of malicious delight split his face. He jumped onto the nearest table and bellowed for quiet.

'Brothers and sisters! The Shepherd has shown us her favour tonight! We have uncovered a spy in our midst, a traitor to land and people! That cloaked coward with the sand-crab is none other than Tarfel Merimonsun, the runt prince!'

Chel jerked on the prince's hand, but he was immobile, his eyes locked on Spider. Before them, a man rose from his chair; a mercenary with an ornate hairstyle, a muscular pile almost a head taller than Chel. He regarded Chel and the prince with a deep frown. His armour creaked and rippled as he stood.

'Whoever brings me his head shall be my first sworn!' Spider bellowed.

Chel gritted his teeth.

'Fuck.'

The mercenary lunged.

Something flowed in front of him, a blur of cloth and flame-red hair. The mercenary grunted as the pommel of Loveless' short blade rammed into his groin, and as he doubled forward her upward-facing palm smashed into the soft tissue of his nose. His backward stagger became a tumble as she kicked his trailing ankle from under him, and he crashed to the stone floor, lowing like a bleeding heifer.

The pit fell quiet.

'Next man crosses me,' Loveless said, voice carrying clear across the pit as she raised the blade, 'loses his bollocks. That's *my* fucking vow.' She gestured behind her back, urging Chel and the prince to move again. Chel grabbed Tarfel's arm with both hands and yanked.

Spider bounced on his table.

'She's full of shit! Traitors! Kill them all! Any who hesitates dies as well! Death to the royals! Death to tyrants!'

The pit erupted. The other mercenaries leapt over their fallen comrade, drawing long knives from their belts. Spider's axe-toting men were closing, as were the nameless brotherhood. Already the peasants' collectives were wrestling with each other, fists and spittle flying.

Loveless circled around, keeping her elevated blade between Chel and the prince and the oncoming mercenaries. She matched them feint for feint, and Chel dragged the prince around the pit and away. He looked up at the gantry above, making out both Whisper and Eka, arrows nocked, looking down on the tumult below. His sister was up there too, along with the Nort. He waved up, shouting over at the chaos.

'Get them out of here! We'll be right behind you!'

Whisper nodded and ducked out of sight as Chel and Tarfel raced for the stairs. Someone had knocked over a brazier, perhaps two. Already black smoke billowed from where the coals had caught on a long table, flames flickering on the pit's far side.

The western brotherhood caught them at the foot of the steps, a quartet of burly men with rough clothing and wild beards, their weapons improvised and brutal. They were already bloodied and ragged.

'Give us the prince! Death to traitors!'

Something roared to Chel's left, and a table arced through the air and smashed down into the men of the brotherhood, scattering them like straw in the wind. Foss strode into view from the smoking chaos, a vengeful old god. He grabbed the nearest brother by his smock, lifting him clean from the ground and hurling him over onto his companions. The next he grabbed by the skull, flinging him firmly, head-first, against the wall of the pit.

'You all right, my friends?'

Chel nodded. Tarfel murmured something indistinct.

Loveless ducked out of the turmoil, one arm over her face from the growing smoke, which had already choked the upper gantries. She had a small scratch on one cheek but seemed otherwise whole.

'Keep moving, nitwits!'

Lemon appeared from the other side of the stairs, looking sooty.

'Problem, folks! The boss is back there, can't get him to fucken bail!'

Loveless growled and went to duck back, but Chel found himself stepping in front. 'Get his highness out. I'll get Rennic.'

She frowned but made no argument. A heartbeat later, they were pounding up the stairs and out of sight.

Chel turned back to the pit. The scene had shifted now, as more of the furniture and furnishings caught in the roaring flames. The world glowed bright and angry, dozens of plumes of frantic smoke surging upwards into the suffo-cated structure above, lambent with the fire's rage. Bodies littered the floor of the pit, some dead or injured, others overcome from heat, smoke or exhaustion. The pit's pale stone glowed in reflected fury. It was a vision of hell.

Sleeve pressed over his face, he crept around the pit's edge, trying to keep low and out of sight should anyone still be standing. Somewhere beyond, the peasants' collectives still battled, their shouts and insults now punctuated by coughs and wheezing. He thought he saw Rennic through the flames, heard him roar over the fire's crackle and hiss.

'Spider! Spider you prick, time to repay the ferryman!'

Rennic was there. He was nearby. Chel tried to call out but his voice was cracked, smoke filling his lungs. He bent to cough, then hurled himself aside as a great dark figure loomed out of the flames, sweeping a bladed spear before it.

'Rennic! It's me!'

The big man swung around, then cocked his head. His hair hung in sweaty clumps before his eyes, the panels of his armour gleamed glossy with firelight and blood. He looked both elated and very, very angry.

'Little man, what the fuck are you doing down there?'

Chel pushed himself upright, staying hunched against the pressing fumes. 'Looking for you! We need to get out of here, this whole place is going up!'

Rennic began to shake his head, but Chel stabbed a finger back toward the stairs.

'Forget that fucker, if the stairs go, we're all dying down here. We get out, you can always finish him later.' Chel paused to hack out a ragged cough. 'You'll do no good by dying.'

The big man snarled, the glaive twitching in his hands, but nodded.

'Lead the way.'

The stairway was already thick with smoke. The fire had reached the upper gantry, and was eating its way along toward the top stair. Rennic still paused at the foot, swinging around to scream one final insult at Spider, but Chel dragged him onward. The stairs smouldered beneath their feet, steam rising as they cracked and blistered in the heat, the lowest steps already blackening.

They made it to the top before the stairway burst into flames behind them, a rushing whoosh that sent the smoking air into ripples. Chel kept his streaming eyes fixed on the oval of dark night ahead, of fresh starlit sky, impossibly black in the midst of the blazing light on all sides.

Rennic stopped again. He returned to the smoking railing and leant over into the conflagration below.

'Spider!' he called, his voice carrying over the roaring mass. 'Hey, Spider, you ghastly fuck!'

Impossibly, a figure was down there, still standing in the midst of the inferno. Spider stood in a pocket of baking stone, knives in his hands, corpses at his feet, dark eyes darting around the gantries, looking for escape.

'Fuck you, Beaky! I'll see you in hells!'

'Not if I see you first.'

Chel screamed for Rennic to follow, and at last he turned from the blaze and they fled into the cool embrace of night.

\*\*\*

A hoot from the tree-line drew Rennic and Chel out of the open, into the cool darkness of the woods. Behind them, the tower consumed itself, the fire's mad light bathing the hilltop and those around it. Those of the resistance who had made it out stood scattered, shocked and sooty.

'For once,' Chel snapped at Rennic as branches closed over them and the night wind sapped the heat from their skin, 'can you let go of your pride just long enough to do what's necessary?'

Flames lit one side of the big man's face. 'Look who's

talking.' Behind them, a flaming roof timber crashed down into the structure. Chel flinched away, but Rennic did not. 'If our pal Corvel didn't know where they were before, he will now.'

Chel looked back, worry tightening his chest in tandem with the smoke.

Whisper lurked in the trees, ever watchful, bow drawn. Blinking in the shifting, tree-split light, Chel picked out the others further back, making out Sab, his chest easing a little. He ran to her first, checking her for damage as she did likewise. The small Nort, Kosh, watched them with quiet, angry eyes, while Tarfel sat beneath a tree, huddled beneath his cloak and shaking. Eka was there too, along with two of her people. She was kneeling by the prone form of another, a young man, still and bloodied. Her lone eye wept.

'She saved me,' Sabina said softly, her eyes on the weeping archer. 'Then Whisper saved her.'

'You made it, then? We were beginning to worry.' Lemon was soot-streaked but cheerful. Whisper signalled something beside her, something Chel recognized as a question. An angry one.

Rennic wiped his hand across his forehead, leaving a smear of bloodied charcoal. His hair and beard were singed, small, truncated hairs curling away at odd angles here and there.

'Had to make sure Spider wasn't coming after us.'

'And did you?' Lemon asked.

Behind them, the rest of the tower's roof collapsed, dropping in on itself in a gout of rolling fire.

'He's not coming back,' Chel said, eyes shielded against the glare.

'That right? Saw him die, saw the body, did you?'

'Well, no, but—'

'Then you can't be certain. You don't see a body, you can't be certain. Ever. Remember that, wee bear.'

Whisper motioned again, softer this time, just at Rennic. He grunted.

'I'm all right. Not the man he was. Will someone just give me some thrice-damned food and a bed?' In the cold night air, his rage had faded, evaporating on the breeze. The need to organize returned. He turned to address the group. 'We can't stay here. Whisp says that most who made it out have scattered, but this hill's a fucking beacon and there are a lot of interested parties on the hunt for us. Hanging around here is going to get us involved in some uncomfortable conversations. We go into the forest tonight.'

Nobody disagreed. Lemon cleared her throat. 'What about her?' she said, with a nod to Brecki. The reaver was still sitting against her tree, watching the tower burn itself to ash with slack eyes.

Chel felt his sister's gaze on him, felt the weight of responsibility return to his shoulders like a stone collar. 'We can't . . . we can't leave her. This place could be crawling with confessors by morning.'

Lemon's eyebrow was a perfect sooty arch. 'You want to invite her along, wee bear? She may not eat much, but she's a nasty fucken sort deep-down. I seem to remember her trying to kill you at least twice. Your choice if you want her as a travel-pal.'

Chel worked to avoid acknowledging Sabina's stare. 'I'll . . . talk to her. Wait. We're a little short on language overlap, remember? Not even you could get through to her.'

Kosh raised her head. 'The white ghost can understand what you're saying.'

'You what?' Lemon spluttered.

'She smirked when you mentioned how terrible she is.'

'Aye, you're joking!'

Kosh frowned at this. 'No. No, I am not. Only a very stupid person would find amusement in such a bland statement.'

Chel rubbed at his eyes. They still stung from smoke. 'Everyone's so full of surprises.' He approached the reaver, who rolled her head just a fraction, her eyes pale and distant. 'Brecki. We're leaving here. You should, too.' He scratched at his neck, which still felt too hot after the fire. 'You can come with us. If you like.'

She gave no indication of hearing him, let alone understanding. Shaking his head, Chel returned to the group. He'd done the right thing, at least. He'd done the right thing.

The hunter Eka had remained on her knees, head bowed with one hand on the dead young man's chest. Rennic stood over her.

'You coming with us? No harm either way, but if so, we're leaving now, and we can't take him with us.'

She nodded, folded the young man's arms across his chest, then placed a small coin over each eye. She wiped her eye as she stood.

'Let's go.'

As the group moved away, Chel walked beside Sab, who seemed uncharacteristically withdrawn. 'Who was it,' he said, 'the dead guy back there? Do you know?'

She gave him the briefest look, her own eyes tearful.

'Her little brother.' She wiped an eye. 'What in hells happened back there?'

Chel shook his head. 'I think we made things worse.'

Sab looked over her shoulder. 'Your friend the reaver is following us.'

He looked back. Brecki was slouching along behind, pale and lean, eyes fixed on nothing. Chel tried to force a care-free smile, but inside he felt only regret, and dread.

They walked on in silence. From somewhere behind them came Lemon's voice, muttering away to Foss as they trudged.

'I'm just saying, maybe no weapons in meetings from now on, and more than one emergency exit, eh?'

# FIVE

They camped in the lee of another hillside beneath a wine-dark sky. Despite Rennic's command to go without a fire, Lemon insisted on a small one and he lacked the energy to overrule. They ate sparingly, huddled around the delicate flame.

'So, what now?' Tarfel asked quietly. Chel looked around the makeshift camp. Everyone looked exhausted. It had been scant days since they escaped the citadel, but they'd already made new enemies to add to the old and were once again on the run. Chel couldn't remember the last time tension hadn't knotted his shoulders.

The prince was still cloaked, the hood pulled over his face, as if he had become mortally afraid to show any of himself to the world. He'd been sitting off to one side, too far from the fire, and he was trembling now, either from cold or existential terror. No one seemed able to answer him.

At last, Rennic puffed out his cheeks. 'We have a few options, although we need to put distance between us and that clusterfuck earlier. Avoiding Roniaman would be wise, most major populations centres, to be honest. Your brother is going to be looking for you, as are some of our vanished friends from today.'

'Are the Rau Rel finished?'

'In this incarnation, yeah, perhaps.'

'Then where?' Tarfel's tone was surprisingly insistent. 'Where are we going to go?'

Rennic spread his hands.

'I'm not . . . well, I hadn't exactly . . . thought about it. Precisely.'

'Well, I have, all right? It's *all* I can think about!' The prince waved an angry hand. 'I've had people trying to kill me now for . . . months! Even my own brother had a go, for all I know – he seemed perfectly blasé about the concept at least. Do you know what that's like? To have people, people you know, people you've never met, actually trying to kill you? Trying to hurt you, end your life? Out of nowhere? Knives to your throat, axes, swords, spears!'

Rennic nodded slowly, a mirthless smile on his face.

'I've some idea, yes.'

'Well, I didn't! And I shouldn't have to! I'm not part of this, I want nothing to do with it!'

Loveless waved an equivocal hand.

'It's a bit of a by-product of your birth station, I'm afraid, princeling.'

'Exactly!' he cried, pointing back at her. 'But didn't you tell me once that I'm . . . I'm only prince by *consensus*? That if the world stops thinking I'm a prince, then I'm no longer a prince?'

She shrugged. 'Something like that, yeah.'

'Well, there you go. I'm not going to be a prince anymore.'

Rennic's thick eyebrows were up.

'And how are you going to manage that? You're too well-known to too many in these lands, and a unilateral declaration ain't going to cut it on this one.'

'Which brings me back to my original point. I want to go somewhere that nobody knows me. Where nobody knows who I am, where I'm from, and most of all nobody *is trying to fucking kill me*! Better a lifetime as a nonentity than a short and terrified royal existence.'

A low moan carried across the camp, a sound like someone in pain, long and rising. As those around the fire turned to look, the moan became a breathy expulsion of contempt. 'Ooooooh, whine, whine, whine.' Brecki sat at the firelight's edge, her back to the hillside, her lone arm knuckling one eye in imitation sobs. '"I don't want to be prince, my life is too hard,"' she mimicked in a sing-song imitation of Tarfel's voice. 'Pitiful coward.'

Tarfel drew back, his jaw hanging loose. 'I *beg* your pardon?'

'No pardons for worms.'

Tarfel only stammered. The others around the campfire only watched. Loveless was grinning.

'Now look here, I'm only—'

Brecki waved her hand in derision. 'Is fitting, be prince no more. Unworthy.'

Tarfel's cheeks were flushed pink. 'How dare you—'

'You are of our blood, of Horvaun. Blood of chieftains, hunters, warriors. Blood of kings. Blood of conquerors. Horvaun do not stop. Your brother is true to blood, worthy foe.' She spat toward the fire, leaving a long string of drool swinging from her chin. 'You are blood traitor. Unworthy. Gutless. Coward.'

70

Silence descended as Tarfel stared, incredulous.

'She talks, then,' said Loveless, one corner of her mouth pulled in a wry smile.

'Aye, and she seems remarkably abreast of matters political,' Lemon added with a look of deep distrust in the reaver's direction.

'Now, just hang on a moment,' Tarfel barked, one hand raised, finger wagging. 'What is your point here, you southern monster? That I should turn around and march straight back to Roniaman and . . . what, challenge my brother to single combat? Duel him in the Court of Confession?' He swept the arm across himself. 'I mean, have you *seen* me? I have no allies, no army, nothing to my name!'

Brecki only smiled, sarcastic and sour. 'You are prince, you say. Princes command. Princes rule. Princes conquer. Princes not run like whipped dog.'

Tarfel blinked and shook his head. 'So that's a yes to suicidal single combat, is it? And I thought you such a sophisticated people.'

'Hand of my queen holds no axe, but her foes hewn just same.'

Tarfel squinted. 'Eh?'

Lemon pointedly turned her back to the reaver. 'Ignore her, princeling, she's a babbling loon. She's got no idea what she's talking about.'

Beside Chel, Sabina shuffled. 'Didn't you say that she and her war-band attacked Corvel and his guards at the hunt? Back when everyone still thought he was Mendel.'

Lemon looked at her through narrowed eyes. 'Aye, and your bro and the boss saw them off. Why?'

'Well,' Sab continued, 'forgive me if I'm speaking out of turn here, but wouldn't it be accurate to say they'd have killed off our great villain once and for all . . . if you lot hadn't intervened and messed . . . things . . . up?'

Chel swallowed. Words seemed suddenly hard to come by. He couldn't bear to think through the implications of his sister's suggestion.

Lemon half-scoffed, half-shook her head, one dismissive hand waggling. 'Wha—? Nah, that can't . . . That's bollocks, right, boss?'

Rennic was staring hard at Brecki, whose grin remained, impish and mischievous and rich with malice. 'Palo said we should have let him die,' he murmured.

'You, you . . .' Tarfel was still central, waving his finger at Brecki. 'You were going to kill my brother, at Raven-Hill. Why?'

The smile broadened. 'My queen commanded. My queen conquers. My queen rules.'

'And your queen wanted my brother dead?'

'My queen commanded.'

He blinked, rubbed at his face with a pale hand, leaving soot streaks. 'Does she still want him dead?'

The reaver shrugged, one-armed. 'How I discover?'

'Mm, yes.' Tarfel's hand had moved to his chin. 'How indeed.'

Chel pushed himself to his feet at last, feeling late to contribute. 'Highness, what are you thinking?'

'This bears consideration, Vedren,' the prince said, his gaze distant.

'What does?'

'All of it. All of it.' He wrapped the cloak around himself and retreated to the shadows, far from the firelight. Brecki slumped back against the hillside, no longer animated, and a hush fell.

Sab looked around, upper teeth on her lower lip. 'Did I say something wrong?' she whispered to Chel. He shook his head, but couldn't manage more than that. The quiet was suddenly oppressive.

'My friends. We're due a circle.' Foss addressed the group as a whole, but his gaze was on Eka, who sat with the remains of her people off to one side, keeping well away from the arguing.

Sab nudged her brother.

'What's a circle?'

Chel murmured something noncommittal and waited to find out.

'We have fallen friends to mourn,' Foss went on, 'and we may not get a better chance. Eka, would you like to join, to speak for your kin?'

Eka nodded, and she and her band moved closer. The raw emotion had left her, but she seemed thinner, worn, as though holding herself erect took everything she had. The group sat around the fire in, of all things, a loose circle.

Her voice, when she spoke, was squeezed dry but still strong, clear.

'There was a man, Amaz.'

*There was a man, Amaz*, the group echoed.

'He was a son, a brother, a hunter.' She paused and wiped at her eye. 'Once, he saw a goat, a woolly, scraggly hill thing, on the slope above. He said, "I'm going to catch that goat." He was barely four. He chased that goat, it trotted away, he chased it more, it kept trotting, until they were both out of sight. Our mother raged, ha, how she roared. He was lost to us as hours passed, the sun went down, our mother was going around the farm-steads to raise a search party. Then he came trotting back, over the hill, with the fucking goat at his heel. He said they'd been playing. Playing! He'd been feeding it rice, of course.

'He and that goat were inseparable for years afterwards. It even followed him on hunts.'

She stopped again, choked by a sob.

'His name was Amaz, and he was friend to goats.'

Those around the fire repeated the words. Foss made the sign of the crook and murmured a prayer.

'While we speak their names, they ride with us still.'

*While we speak their names, they ride with us still.*

'There was a woman, Palo.' Rennic paused for the echo. 'She was a leader, a warrior, a believer. She gave her life for others' mistakes, so they might live long enough to learn better.' He sat back, jaw clenched.

'Her name was Ayla Palo, and she deserved better.'

The stories continued around the fire in similar vein. Chel was surprised and a little humble to hear of Palo's exploits, her campaigns, her tireless devotion to her beliefs. The thought of her sacrifice, her final weeks imprisoned and her death upon the confessors' table, made him almost sick with guilt and grief. At least she had robbed Hurkel of his triumph.

Foss intoned the refrain again, then looked around.

'Will anyone speak for the Watcher?'

'No,' Rennic growled. 'Spider was right about one thing, that fool brought death on us all.'

'And will anyone speak for Spider?'

'*Fuck Spider.*'

'Very well. Who will speak for Dalim?'

Loveless sat forward. She'd been quiet until then, lost in her own reflections.

'There was a man, Dalim,' she said as others turned in surprise. 'He was a fool, a narcissist, and a sex-pest.'

Whisper had a fierce eyebrow raised and Foss looked shocked, but Loveless waved them off.

'What? Nobody ever says anything bad in these things. Anything all-true. Well, this is truth: he was the greatest fighter I ever knew. For all his posturing, he had the stones to back it. He was beautiful, he was poised, and he could move like no other.' She sniffed back what could have been a tear.

'His name was Dalim, and he was physical perfection. His personality, less so.'

They repeated the first part, at least.

When the circles were done, Foss had said the last of the incantations and the group had begun to settle, talking among themselves, Tarfel returned. He approached Chel directly, who still sat with Sabina, but when he spoke it was to the assembled group.

'I've, er, I've been thinking,' he said, voice scratchy. Loveless started to make a comment, but Foss cut her off with a glare. 'About what the reaver said.'

Chel pushed himself to his feet again. It was harder and harder each time. 'Yes, highness?'

'She was . . . she was right.'

Chel struggled to keep himself upright. 'Highness?'

'She was right about Corvel. He is truly of their . . . our blood. He intends to conquer, Vedren. Controlling the church, the Names, the provinces, that is just the beginning.'

'Do you—'

'Please, Vedren, let me finish. She was right that rulers command, both loyalty and forces, and a prince who shirks his birthright is unworthy of the title.' He looked at the ground, shook his head. 'And she was right that perhaps I am not so much without allies as I imagined – or at least those who share an agenda.'

Chel paused, waiting to see if the prince had finished. He had.

'What do you intend, highness?'

'I have spoken with Brecki.' He half-turned, indicating the reaver, who once again seemed more corpse than contender. 'She has agreed to act as my guide.'

Chel's mouth fell open, his words garbling themselves. 'You surely highness can't—'

'I wish to travel south in her care, and hear out this queen of hers. Perhaps we will have fertile grounds for discussion, and perhaps not. But I cannot simply turn my back on my duties, on my father's kingdom.'

Lemon snorted. 'Aye, and perhaps she'll skin you from boredom after the first half-mile. Or they'll do it for you on arrival. Honestly, princeling, this must be the daftest—'

'It strikes me,' the Nort Kosh's voice carried over Lemon's, solid with self-confidence, 'that the meeting you attended earlier this evening was in search of gathering forces to oppose your enemies. You appear to have identified similar forces, albeit elsewhere. What basis is there for complaint?'

'Basis? I'll give you fucken . . . For a start, that bunch of Horvaun bastards are murderous savages—'

'You're all murderous savages from my perspective, so it seems a false distinction.'

'You come here and say that!'

'A distinctly non-murderous and un-savage response.'

Ignoring the escalating bickering, Chel concentrated on the prince. 'Highness, are you sure about this? Putting yourself in her care, and for such a distance, to an unknown reception? The risk is . . .'

Tarfel offered a rueful smile, and for a moment his youth shone through the creases of worry that marked his face. 'I know, Vedren, I know. But this is . . . this is the right thing to do. I feel a sense of . . . *purpose*, like nothing I've ever felt before. I believe I have you to thank for that. However . . .' he cleared his throat, rubbed his hands together in the chill. When he spoke again, his voice was quiet and his pale eyes wide and wet. 'I cannot face the journey alone. The mercenaries will follow coin, and I still have some silver and baubles with which to tempt them, but . . . but I need you at my side, Vedren.'

'You want me to come with you,' Chel murmured, a feeling like a stone dropping through his torso, 'to meet the reaver queen.'

'I know it's not what you signed up for – remember that, eh? – but I cannot face such an undertaking without my first sworn by my side. Of course, if you wish, I could release you from your oath here and now, begin walking back to my brother. If I maintain a brisk pace, I might reach the citadel before he notices I left—'

'No, no, highness, just . . . let me, uh . . . Can we discuss it in the morning? I'm too tired to stand any longer.'

'Of course, Vedren, of course. Good night.'

Chel did not sleep well.

\* \* \*

They were still arguing when he awoke, unrested, the sun crawling into the wintry sky. He kept his eyes closed, the ground cold and bruising, and waited for things to settle.

'We could just lie low, go to ground for a while.' Loveless sounded tense, tired. 'We don't have to up sticks and march down to the frozen wastes on a wild whim.'

'We hang around here, all that's guaranteed is we're caught up in the next purge, or worse.' Rennic sounded animated, too energetic. Chel wondered how much he'd slept. 'Remember what the princeling said? His brother has no intention of stopping at the provinces. He walked among us, remember, he's combing the countryside for us and his sick little brother, and we're horribly short of friendly faces in these parts.'

'Aye,' came Lemon's voice, 'and I'm saying that if we're bounding that far south, we might as well head for Clyden.'

'*Clyden?*' Rennic couldn't keep the astonishment from his voice.

'It's a safe harbour, nobody would know you lot. And I've got a bit of influence back there.'

'But . . . *Clyden?*'

'Aye, now, what's wrong with Clyden?' Lemon's tone was defensive, the warning growl of a hound. Chel cracked open his eyes.

Loveless was stretched out by the fire, while Foss cooked breakfast over it in studious silence. 'I always fancied visiting Clyden,' she said. 'They have booze there, right?'

'Oh, aye,' Lemon scoffed. 'Gallons. Seas of it. More than even you could drink.'

'How's the music and dancing?'

'Frequent and frenzied.'

Loveless arched an eyebrow. 'And where are they on baths?'

'Once a year, whether you need it or not. Regular bathing is the basis of civilization, after all.'

'Hmm. Are all the men the same colour as you?'

'Now what the fuck does that mean?'

Rennic chopped down with a hand. 'Clyden isn't an option. The straits will be frozen by now.'

'They don't freeze!' Lemon protested.

'Lemon, be silent. Our choices are this: stick with princeling on his lunatic expedition to parley with the Horvaun, or stay here.' He took a long breath, his eyes tight shut. 'And I can't believe I'm saying this, but given what we know of Corvel's intentions, I'm for heading south. Princeling still has some silver, maybe there will be more at our journey's end. I hear sometimes the Horvaun use outsiders for their dirty work.'

'Aye, but we could just take the silver off him now, boss, save the boot-leather.'

'We're mercenaries, Lemon. We need a client.'

'This is a bad idea, Gar,' Loveless sighed.

'Then it's fruit of a tall and bounteous family tree.' Rennic turned back to the fire. 'Who's coming?'

'I will not.' Kosh was on her feet, her face stern. 'You will release me immediately.'

'Release you? We're not fucking holding you!'

'Then you must escort me back to my country or my people.'

Rennic's expression remained level. 'And why would we do that? You can offer payment? Great rewards?'

'I am—'

'Because between here and the northern coast lie several armies, fortresses, and murderous bands of red confessors, all of whom would dream of seeing us meet our end in the most gruesome and painful ways imaginable, and I don't much fancy my chances of skirting the lot of them for free. How do you fancy yours?'

The Nort said nothing.

'Well, north is that way. So, you can fuck off on your own, or you can come with us. If you're coming, you make yourself useful. Understand? Some of that terrific alchemy of yours when the moment dictates, think you can manage that?' He turned his back on her. 'Rest of you coming?'

'Not an alchemist,' Chel heard the Nort mutter. 'I am an *engineer*.'

'You're awake, little man.' Rennic was staring right at him. 'I take it you'll be accompanying your precious prince on his southward jaunt?'

Chel shuffled to his knees, wincing at his aches, and rubbed at his eyes. 'I need to talk to my sister.'

Rennic nodded toward the trees. 'Over there.'

Sab was sitting beneath a frozen tree, lacing up her boots. She gave him a tight smile as he wandered over. She looked marginally better rested than him, which wasn't saying much.

'Morning,' he mumbled. Somehow his little sister was making him feel two feet tall.

'Good morning, Brother Bear,' she replied, springing to her feet. 'Have you decided what you're going to do?'

'That's what I wanted to—'

'And if you go south, would you be expecting me to come too?'

He paused, his breath coming in plumes in the chilly air. 'I hadn't really thought about it,' he said.

'Oh, that's just fucking priceless, Bear! Am I an *inconvenience* to you?'

'No, not at all, Sab, nothing like that!'

'Then what is it like?'

'I . . .'

'Far too dangerous for silly young girls, right? Trekking to the arse-end of nowhere, in the hands of a monstrous reaver? What would you do when you got there? If you got there?'

He let out a long puff of air, watching it billow amber and vanish into the morning.

'I—'

'—don't know, of course. Who does.' She cuffed him on the arm. 'I don't like you with these people, Bear. Killers and thieves, itinerants, *bad influences*. I don't think Mum would approve, do you?'

He cracked a grin. 'I don't suppose she would.'

She wrapped her arms around him and squeezed. 'I'm the only one who should be a bad influence on you.' When she stepped back her eyes were glistening. 'I'm going home, Bear. I've had it with sneaking around in disguise, hiding in shadows and passing messages. It's time to spread the word, get organized. I'm going back to whip up some resistance and defend our family, just in case those weasel-fuckers decide to come knocking in our neck of the woods.'

Something lurched hot in his gut at the thought of riders at the manse, Corvel's pennant stiff in the wintry breeze, Brother Hurkel stomping toward the door. Sab saw it in his eyes and put a cold hand on his cheek.

'Don't fret, Brother Bear, they won't catch us with our breeches round our ankles. I'm going to raise some forces, open some eyes. You can trust me. I survived long enough in the citadel on my own, didn't I?'

He nodded, feeling his cheeks burning against the cold with shame and gratitude. 'You did. You surely did. But—'

81

'Eka is going that way, with her people. After what happened to her brother, well, she's had it with centralized rebellion. She's going home too, which is Svipina – basically next door! I'll let her escort me, and we'll be keeping close if the time comes, keeping things local. So now you can decide for yourself: do you want to come home, with me – back to your family – and put all this royal nonsense behind you? Or are you sticking with your prince on the road to madness?'

Chel could feel the beat of his heart in his chest, the thump of his pulse at his throat. 'I'm his first sworn, Sab. Duty commands I . . .' He tailed off under the force of her gaze.

'You've nothing left to prove, Bear. You can choose for yourself.'

'I need to discharge my oath, to do what's right. Father would—'

'Bear! Father would be proud of you already, for all you've done. You don't have to throw your life away—'

'No, Sab. We failed, remember? We made things worse. I made things worse. I have to fix it.'

'Not everything is your fault, big brother, despite what I may have told you in the past, and not everything can be fixed. What do you want to do, Vedren? Bugger duty and oaths and all that for once. What is it that *you* want?'

He scratched at the back of his head, jaw working, trying to corral the words. What did he want? When had that last mattered? He'd been bound by obligation since before his father died, and every day since had merely brought more Tasks That Must Be Accomplished. The notion of a life without demands seemed as appealing as it was absurd.

Also, if he really thought about it, he'd be very keen to have the chance to get close to—

She was looking at him sidelong. 'If you want to go, you want to go, Bear. Just make sure you're being honest with yourself about why. Without the oath, would you be coming home to us? When this is over, when you've saved the world, will you be coming home then?'

The thought of returning home soured his guts – to slink back, face his family's disapproval, his step-father's contempt, his mother's shame . . .

His mouth opened and closed. 'I . . . I need to do what's right . . .'

'Hush, Bear of mine, don't tie yourself in knots.' She hugged him again, then cuffed him again. 'I'm still so, so angry with you, getting all mixed up in this. Why couldn't you have just stuck with hobnobbing with princes and dukes? How have you become a fugitive freedom fighter?'

He shrugged, feeling his weak shoulder click in its socket. It was worse in cold weather.

'I swore—'

'And I swear all the time, but you don't see me packing up for the armpit of the world. Oh, one more thing,' she said, delving into her pack. 'I want you to take this. It wouldn't do for the first sworn to a prince to be gallivanting around the countryside unarmed, would it?'

She produced the confessor's mace she'd sported in the cells, its heavy metal head cracked and lost; it was now little more than a steel-tipped wooden baton. Somehow it felt right in his hand.

'Thank you, Sab. It's perfect.'

She offered him a bright, beaming smile. 'I'm proud of

you, Bear. I'll tell Mother and our sisters that you're doing well. That you'd have made Father proud too.'

He hugged her then, and wept silent tears in the cold beneath the broken tree.

\* \* \*

'She's eating again. Voluntarily.' Lemon nudged Chel and gave a pointed look toward where Brecki sat, wolfing down her share of Foss's breakfast makings one-handed. 'I swear to the ancestors, wee bear, she means to stitch us up.'

'She's rediscovered her appetite,' he said doubtfully.

'Rediscovered her purpose, more like, which is *fucking us over.*'

'However you slice it, it's one pendulous cock of a trek from here to the coast.' Loveless was drawing on the snowy earth, dragging the burnt end of a branch in a semblance of a map. 'We're looking at weeks on foot, maybe a month. We'll need supplies and equipment for the duration, plus what follows. And the weather will only get worse, especially that far south.'

Eka watched from the group's edge, firelight glittering in her lone eye. 'I know somewhere you can get mules and packs for the trip, but you'll need coin. A lot of it.'

Rennic waved a hand. 'Appreciate the offer but we're a little, uh, *between contracts* as things stand.'

Lemon coughed. 'Aye, well, as it happens, we maybe have a little coin,' she said. 'A modest pile.'

Rennic's gaze slid to her, thick brows lowered.

'We do?'

Lemon looked uncomfortable. 'Could be I, uh, came into possession of some discarded silver.'

'When?'

'At the tower.'

'At the fucking tow— When?'

She put up her hands. 'When I was bezzing about trying to pluck your good self from the roaring flames, keeping my head down.' She swallowed. 'You know, from the smoke. A girl can hardly be blamed if folk departed were spilling their purses at her feet!'

No one spoke for a moment. Rennic's jaw flexed in calculation.

'Robbing the dead is a new one for you, Lem,' Loveless said, voice playful. 'What happened to pennies for the ferryman?'

'Aye, right,' Lemon scoffed, 'like you wouldn't have sullied yourself in my clod-hoppers. Rather slog all the way south in the buff, would you?'

Loveless's smile crinkled the scar at her temple. 'Well now, I didn't say that. Exactly how much did you bag?'

# SIX

They left in the snow, a stinging wind slapping gentle flakes against their skin. Eka was as good as her word, guiding them to a trading post on the edge of hill-lands where Rennic exchanged a quantity of blood-silver for as many mules and supplies as the proprietor could offer, including a couple of oversized shields that went Foss's way. She asked no questions, made no recommendations and attempted no up-sell. Rennic approved.

They parted with Sab, Eka and her people a day later, sending them off with two laden mules between them. Chel exchanged a tearful farewell with his sister, promised to return before she knew it, spoke words of thanks and implied threat to Eka who nodded them away. He tried to watch them go, to follow them with his eyes until they were over the crest and lost from view, but Brecki growled at them to follow and was away over the hillside.

She set a brutal pace from the start, too brutal even for herself. Weeks of little food and moving less than a veal-calf had left her frail, and she flagged rapidly. He was close to her when first she stumbled, one-armed, and instinctively he reached out to steady her.

She slapped his hand away with a snarl, righting herself on the slippery path. He saw the crisp gems of sweat glinting from her forehead, the flutter of the pulse in the pale cords of her neck. Her twitching eyes dared him to mock her, to make something of her weakness, her ruined arm.

'Sorry,' he mumbled, gaze fixed on the frigid earth. 'I thought you could use a . . . ah.'

She pushed on without a word, but this time a little slower, to Chel's relief. He wasn't in much better shape himself after his time in the cells, and the frequent stops and early camps that followed reassured him that however swift their southward journey, it wouldn't leave him wrecked in the snow.

He kept close to Tarfel, who was at pains to keep up with Brecki in a presumed demonstration of leadership. He cut an awkward, bulky figure in his new-bought furs, pale face peeping from within, lost in the surrounding fuzz. Chel walked at his side and kept an eye on Brecki, whom he was certainly no closer to trusting. Who knew where she might lead them, or what she might do along the way? The woman was an instinctive and merciless killer.

But then, so were most of the others in their party.

'You're quiet, Fossy,' Lemon said as she and the other Black Hawks trudged along behind Chel and the prince. 'You pondering life's great mysteries, or is it bum-gas again? Just between us, that last bit of breakfast isn't sitting too pretty in my down-belows either, and if someone sparks a flint at the wrong moment, I'm apt to go up like—'

'I am reflecting, Lem,' came Foss's tired reply.

'Like a puddle?'

'I am reflecting that while God may have a plan for us, He has a certain humour about its implementation.'

'Come again?'

'Our young friend saved this woman, this reaver, and now she leads us downmap, toward the great unknown. Toward a savage land and savage people, or toward our own salvation?'

'Aye, right, Fossy, this is a bit doom-flavoured even for me. Maybe their god is on board with yours, eh? Maybe it'll all be sunshine and rainbows.'

Foss's sigh carried the weight of centuries. 'They have their own bloody pantheon, unlike anything ever described by the church.'

'Who's to say they can't be friendly?'

'They cut the limbs from their sacrifices and hoist them on sharpened poles, while still they live.'

'. . . Oh. Bit short on manners, then.'

Chel dropped back a pace. 'Is there any way we can trust her?' he asked in a low voice, with a nod to Brecki at the head of the group.

Lemon made a face. 'Can't see how.'

'But we're getting her home, right?'

'Do they even have homes? I thought Horvaun simply sprung forth from holes in the ground and set about chewing through livestock.'

'Lemon!' Foss admonished. 'That's a terrible thing to say about an entire people.'

'Aw, come on, Fossy, have you ever met one who wasn't a cast-iron bastard?'

Foss pursed his lips. 'I've only ever met that one.'

'Well, there you go.'

'Wasn't Tarfel's mum from there?' Chel said in a hopeful

voice. 'And his grandfather? You heard her,' – another nod at Brecki – 'saying "you're of our blood".'

'Aye, just goes to show, doesn't it?'

'What?'

'You can take the most wild and savage bloodline, and it can grow up to be . . . that.'

'Will the three of you cease your prattle?' Kosh's peevish tones carried over the clear air. 'This accursed wasteland you call a country is bitter enough without the constant chirping of small-brained mammals. Spirits curse this cold!'

'Oh, cork it, Norty,' Lemon called back with a chuckle. 'Like the big man said, it's all downhill from here.'

Chel resumed his place beside the prince, his thoughts dark and churning.

\*\*\*

'Highness,' Chel said, 'what kind of reception do you expect to receive when we reach . . . when we arrive? What do you think will happen?' Aside from imagining Brecki's potential atrocities en route, it was now hard for him to think of anything beyond their journey's end. Tarfel had seemed so determined in this course that Chel had assumed on some level that the prince's inherent cowardice would preclude any decisions flagged with suicidal risk. His confidence in this conclusion was waning.

The prince sniffed. His nose had gone very pink. 'Well, Vedren, there are some treaties that cover this kind of thing – Kelsuus set a precedent, you know – even with the Horvaun. Believe it or not, relations haven't always been all axe-heads and blood.'

'Do you think this queen of Brecki's will be pleased to see us?'

'What interests me more, Vedren, is why she would have sent a war-band to kill my brother in the first place. Could they have known what he was planning? Could anyone?'

Chel blinked tiny snowflakes from his eyelashes. 'Perhaps they just like to kill royalty in neighbouring lands every so often, for sport – like how nobles hunt game.'

Tarfel offered a wry smile through the collar of fur. 'The point is, Vedren, that my brother . . .' He paused, swallowed, took a sharp breath of wintry air, '. . . is now my enemy. And if this queen thought killing him worthwhile, then we may well have fertile grounds for discussion.'

'Highness?' Chel tried to keep his reaction neutral, but the word still came out with the inflection of *you what?*

Brecki had tired again, and come to a halt in the long shadow of a copse on a small rise. The rest of the party were strung out behind them, making steady progress up the snow-dusted slope in their wake. Ahead of them rolled ever more hills, crusted white and glinting amber in the low afternoon sun. The world had a total stillness to it, frozen in time as the two young men looked out over the empty landscape, their breath coming in steady plumes.

'I never knew my mother, Vedren,' Tarfel said. 'She died, as you know, birthing me, which I don't think endeared me to anyone.' He looked away for a moment, something pained crossing his face, then continued. 'But beyond that, I barely know . . . knew my father. Not well enough to tell that he'd been dead for five years, for a start. Hells, it would almost be funny if it were someone else, wouldn't it?'

Chel offered a rueful smile. 'My father died when I was

young, highness, but there was at least no doubt that it
had happened.'

'I'm sorry to hear that, Vedren. Was it combat?'

'Plague.'

'Foul luck. My sympathies.' The prince sighed. 'I knew
my parents more by reputation than as people, let alone
family, and I've found that the more time I've spent outside
the cloisters and palaces, the more I've come to question
what I heard.'

'Such as, highness?'

'I think it's pretty obvious by now that my father was
Vassad's pawn for much of his adult life, and that much
of what I was told about his great victories and leadership
and so on was likely exaggerated to the point of outright
mendacity. Who was going to tell me the truth, after all?
I believed what I was told, never questioned it, and, had it
not been for your intervention, I'd have gone to my grave
believing that my father was a fabulous conqueror who
championed justice and the true church, and brought great
strength and stability to our kingdom. But it's all bollocks,
isn't it?'

'It is, highness.'

'It's been non-stop conflict for two decades. Battles and
strife, famine and plague – your poor father among the
victims, direct and indirect. And it was all power games, to
Vassad, the Names, the powers beyond our borders. All that
suffering, just so they might get one over on each other.'

'You've been thinking about this, highness.'

'I have, Vedren, I have. I've been thinking that I stand
here, the scales fallen from my eyes, finally understanding
the hypocrisy, the *vile waste* . . . And in Roniaman, my
brother dreams of empire.'

'Empire?'

'It's . . . it's worse than I mentioned before. When I said he had plans.' Tarfel pushed back the hood of his furs, ran a hand through his lank mass of hair. 'He hasn't seen what I've seen, he's swallowed it all, whether he realizes it or not. He thinks Father was a great man, poisoned and murdered by Vassad, and with Father avenged he can carry on his legacy. Corvel once told me as a joke that Father had some ancient scrolls falsified, lineage changed, just so he could claim to be descended from the first emperors. It was all a ridiculous stunt, or at least we thought so.

'And now I think back, I wonder how stupid, how petty a man my father was. So easily tricked, so easily used, before he was even drugged into a stupor. He probably believed it himself. That he was emperor in waiting. And now Corvel . . . Now my brother sees his duty as the rebuilding of that empire. He's going to wage wars the like we've not seen in our lifetimes, and all over a foolish lie. He will not stop unless he is made to stop.'

'What are you saying, highness?'

'I'm saying, Vedren, that I'm not going south to hide. I'm going to face up to my birthright, to my brother. I'm going to make him stop. It has to be me – that much I realized when I saw the remnants of the Rau Rel tear themselves to shreds at the slightest provocation. I cannot expect disparate groups with too much to lose to unify spontaneously against my brother and avert a catastrophe in these lands. Nobody else can do this, can unite the forces required to stop Corvel for good. And as your sister said, if I can't stand up to him, who will?'

'You're going to ask the reavers to . . . help? For alliance? To be your army?'

'Corvel has more enemies than he realizes. Why not start with the most dangerous?'

Chel could only nod and try to keep his eyebrows level. Part of his brain was beginning to sound something like an alarm bell, a sonorous and implacable suggestion that he'd made a terrible mistake in accompanying the prince, and that his death was not only inevitable but indescribably gruesome and speeding toward him at an ever-increasing rate. *They cut people's limbs off and stick poles through them while they're still alive. That's what they're going to do to you, to all of you.*

'Are you all right, Vedren? You look a little peaky.'

'I'm, uh. I'm fine, highness.'

*I was supposed to be lucky.*

\* \* \*

Tarfel was in a good mood for the rest of the day, and Chel found his own mood lifting alongside. The prince had a certain puppyish glow when he was happy, and it happened rarely enough to be infectious. For a moment, Chel even saw some of the golden bounce of Mendel the Fair in his exuberance. Perhaps they weren't so far removed after all.

'Vedren,' the prince said, 'I think our chat earlier was the longest conversation I've had with anyone in months. Years, probably.' He was quiet for a moment, then said, 'We're friends, aren't we, Vedren?'

Chel didn't permit a moment of hesitation. 'We are, highness.'

'Then I think you can probably call me Tarfel, Vedren.'

Chel concentrated on his footing in the gathering

twilight. 'As you wish, Tarfel.' Then after a moment, 'How about Tarf?'

'Yes, why not?'

'Tarfy?'

'Um . . .'

'Tarfy-Barfy?'

'Well—'

'Tarfy-Warfy-Rum-Bum?'

'Yes, all right, Vedren, you don't have to take the piss. I'm still a prince, remember?'

'Right you are, Tarf.'

Both were still grinning when they stopped to camp.

\* \* \*

The sedate pace wasn't to last. Although Brecki maintained her distance when they camped, ignoring the varied tales around the evening fires – most of which seemed to revolve around Rennic's catastrophic escapades with a string of mercenary companies – and treating the rest of the group with a blank-eyed indifference that was somehow more hostile than any direct interaction, she ate heartily and each day seemed that much more restored, ranging ever further ahead and away. Eventually only Whisper could keep pace with her.

Chel watched the reaver carefully, uneasy when she was nearby, more so when she was out of sight. He kept close to the prince out of habit, but his curiosity about the woman grew as they travelled. Occasionally he'd see her struggling to tear off a strip of meat, or snarling at a trailing bootlace. He realized the pang he felt was guilt. He'd captured her. He'd injured her. Her presence, and all its concomitant issues, was his fault.

Every so often, this sense of obligation would overwhelm him and he'd try to offer her help. Although she stopped short of physically striking him, the hot contempt in her glare was usually enough to send him scurrying, muttering apologies.

Whatever Chel's misgivings, Brecki knew the land. Despite the clotting snow and icy brooks, she kept them moving along hidden creeks and goat-paths, well out of sight of settlements much bigger than the occasional hut. They moved carefully, forever mindful of pursuit, hiding their tracks where they could. The farther south they went, the more the temperature dropped, and the thin snatches of sunlight through cloud became ever rarer until the sky was a single leaden sheet, seeping swirling flakes over a blasted and barren world.

Foss stopped on a snowy hillside, dropping to one knee and scraping at the ground's white covering. He churned black frozen earth beneath, thin black stubs crunching between his fingers. He stood, wiping charcoal streaks from his hand.

Rennic approached. 'Is it?'

He nodded. 'Crops burnt.'

'Who do you think?'

Foss spread his heavy hands. 'Take your pick. Rival claimant, local lordling, our friends in the church, Corvel himself. Or maybe even her lot, on their way north.' He jerked a thumb at Brecki, who affected indifference.

Foss sighed and resumed his trudge. 'Evil days.'

'Evil days.'

\* \* \*

The weather's deterioration was matched by declining visibility, and before long they had travelled several days without seeing the sun. Whisper alone could match Brecki's now tireless, uneven canter; the rest of them took turns to ride the mules, more so as the supplies dwindled. Tarfel and Kosh were never off theirs, the non-riding prince bobbing unsteadily on the lead-rope. Their sluggish pace and persistent griping had ensured it could be no other way.

Another sunless morning brought them to a hazy snow-covered plain, crunching over lumpy fresh snow as they descended a sharp slope at its edge. Odd shapes loomed from the snow, bulges and pillars of white fluff, standing alone or in groups. The plain itself was expansive, almost perfectly flat, stretching away into the mist around them. Brecki seemed pleased at seeing it, loping without hesitation onto the plateau and into the mist.

'Where in ancestor's fuck are we?' Chel heard Lemon grousing behind him, her voice clear in the freezing stillness. 'This fucken fog is a curse.' They trudged out onto the plain, almost snow-blind from reflected glare, the mules following with minimal protest. Hard ground thumped beneath its snowy coat.

'Where the fuck's this come from? There's no fucken flat land south of the Kharin, unless a fucken mountain has prolapsed.'

The wind was picking up, a more insistent whirling, howling at the plain's distant edges. Looking back, Chel could barely see the lumpy slope that they'd descended. Ahead, Brecki had vanished, lost from sight in the drifting grey banks.

'Only thing that's big and flat in this part of the south is Lake Saldirtse, and that's, you know, water . . .'

Chel wondered if he'd felt the slightest slip of his boot, a glossy surface beneath a thin crust of snow. The howling of the wind was louder, making it difficult to hear Lemon's grumbles.

'Of course, even if it was frozen, this couldn't be Lake Saldirtse, on account of there being a great fucken town on its banks, you know, houses and buildings and that . . .' She paused, looking back at the now invisible slope behind them, at its odd lumps and pillars beneath the snow.

The howling on the wind was loud now, insistent. Discrete. Whisper put up an urgent hand.

'Aw fucken *hells*!' Lemon was turning in small circles, clenching and unclenching her fists. 'Those Horvaun bastards couldn't have burned the whole place, could they? Razed the whole fucken town?'

Whisper had an arrow nocked, her sharp gestures bringing the group and mules together, weapons fumbled from storage.

'Where's the reaver? She's fucken stitched us!'

Chel swung around, feeling hot breath in his throat and the thump of blood in his ears. Where had Brecki got to? A new sound echoed over the frozen waste, a fierce scraping like blades on a whetstone. Something was coming.

He seized on her tracks, tried to race after her, to bring her back to them, but his foot slipped after a handful of paces and he floundered and fell, thumping against the freezing ground with enough force to drive the air from his lungs and crack his head.

*Oh, yes, that's ice all right.*

At last he could place the howls that came loud over the wind. He'd heard them before, at Raven-Hill. Reavers were upon them. Brecki had sold them down the river after all. Bitter disappointment curdled in his gut. He'd genuinely thought she was softening toward him.

Shaking snow from his head, he rolled up onto his knees, then immediately dropped back to the ice as a shape flashed through the mist, moving too fast, too smoothly, travelling around him in an arc, all the time making a noise like grinding steel. It howled as it swung around him, the howl picked up by others, more shapes gliding in and out of his vision. The shouts behind him redoubled, joined by the braying of the terrified mules, the whistle of arrows fired at nothing. Somewhere Lemon was beating something against her shield, screaming incoherently.

'They're on fucken skates? Fucken skatey-skates?'

He scrabbled to his feet. He'd travelled further than he realized. White surrounded him, shaded blue and grey. Murky ice beneath, snow-dusted, nothing but white haze above it in all directions. Sounds of combat, clangs and cries, came from one direction, one that looked the same as any other. He ran for it, feet slipping on loose powder.

One of the mules was down, its blood staining the snow bright around it. The others were huddled together, Tarfel and Kosh at their centre, the five points of a star, wide-eyed and steaming. Circling them were the howling, skating reavers, pale-skinned in pale furs, dodging in and out of the mist, flinging half-axes and knives, whooshing in close to slash at the beleaguered defenders.

Chel bolted for the mule-circle, feet slipping against the carved ice. He skittered on approach, unable to stop, and slid past an astounded Lemon with arms waving, crashing against the side of a mule and back onto the ice.

'Wee bear! Nice of you to join us!' Her shield was prickled

with thrown steel, and she had a thick wad of blood on one temple. 'Did you find that Brecki bastard?'

'Not as such,' he confessed. 'What do we do?'

She hefted a hand-axe, then ducked behind her shield as something metallic flashed out of the mist and slammed into its creaking woodwork.

'We're fucken stuck! Can't get near the pricks! We've winged a couple but I'm low on rods and Whisp is running out of sticks. Can't tell you how many more of those fuckers are out there.'

He ducked down, scrambling beneath the panicked mule, past the equally panicked Tarfel and Kosh, and popped his head out the other side.

'How are we doing over here?'

Rennic glanced down at him, maintaining a neutral expression. 'You're alive, then. Thought you'd run off.'

'I am. What's the plan?'

Two reavers screeched past, out of glaive-reach, then swung around, splitting and arcing back in a pincer manoeuvre. Rennic lunged with the glaive and retreated, snarling, as they sailed gleefully past. They really seemed to be enjoying themselves.

'You tell me, little man.'

'We can't stay here. We've got to get off the ice.' Chel was already looking around, searching for a landmark that would betray the distant shore.

'No shit. Which way would that be?'

Lemon's shout from the other side of the terrified animals curtailed his search. 'Aw hells, they're coming again! A wet ton of the fuckers!'

Chel ducked beneath the mules again. Two sets of frantic eyes met his.

'We're going to run,' he said. 'Get ready.'

'Which way are we going?' Tarfel was shaking all over, whether from fear or cold was immaterial.

'Not sure yet. Stay behind the mules, or between them at least.' He paused, eyes on Kosh's lumpen sack, cradled in her stringy arms. 'You know, now would be an excellent time for some revelatory alchemy.'

She glared at him, defiant with terror. 'I am not an alchemist—'

'Yes, yes, but if you've got any more spontaneous infernos in there, then this would be an excellent moment.' The howls and whoops were coming again, loud over the skate-scrape.

She gestured with a trembling hand. 'It's too cold for that reaction, but . . .' The fear left her eyes for a moment, their gaze distant. She whirled, delving into the saddlebags of the mule behind her. She fished out one of the wine-skins, labelled by Loveless a travelling necessity. Unstoppered, its contents hissed against the ice, splashing scarlet.

'The fuck's going on there?' Loveless had seen the splash. Her tone suggested restitution for her lost wine would feature urgently once their current situation was resolved. Kosh ignored her, now adding powders and liquids from small containers fished from her sack. The smell was appalling, and the mules began to honk with displeasure beyond their current alarm. The Nort jammed the stopper back on the skin, then held it out with a tremulous hand.

'Throw that.'

He lunged for it, and she pulled it back from his hand.

'Gently! And far, far away.'

He took the sagging skin with care. Already its surface was beginning to discolour, the skin bloating in his grip.

'Fast! Get rid of it!'

He squeezed through the mule wall, to where Lemon and Foss faced half a dozen cavorting reavers, swirling patterns on their bone-skates as they swept forward in ones and twos to swipe at them. Her shield was a splintered wreck, his was hacked and scored.

Chel lobbed the skin. It arced away from him, hissing faintly, trailing an acrid stench in its wake. Already his fingers felt stained and itchy where he'd held it. The skin flopped up through the air, then began its descent, now bulging almost spherical. The two reavers who were next in line to charge paused to watch the strange, round object travel slowly through the air, its landing spot well in front of where they lurked.

The skin hit the ice and burst. It more than burst. It erupted. It split apart with a great crack, blasting tatters of animal hide into the air. A great fountain of thick white cloud spurted outwards, while hissing liquid sprayed in all directions, coating the ice. One of the reavers was caught in the spray and collapsed screaming, clawing at the affected skin. The others were overcome with coughing as the smoke rolled over them, hands to faces, eyes streaming, failing.

Then the ice split. Whatever had sprayed from the skin had eaten through the crust, weakened by the explosion, and a great chunk reared before them, cracks widening either side of it. A moment later, a channel of black water yawned between the mules and the reavers, peppered with icy chunks, some still hissing.

'What the *fuck* was that?'

The question came from all sides. Chel looked to Kosh, who began to stammer the names of reagents.

'Move! Move, move, move!' Rennic was yanking at a

mule's rope, gesturing the others to do likewise. He began to drag the protesting mule away from the smoking ruins, where the reavers hacked and rolled.

'Which way is the shore?'

'It's a lake! It's all shore eventually!'

They ran, feet slipping against slick ice, mules resisting, leaving the one dead animal and a dozen stricken reavers behind them. Chel looked over his shoulder in time to see Dalim's beautiful glaive slip from the fractured ice and into the dark waters of the hungering lake.

Then the ice split beneath him, and he plunged.

\* \* \*

The shock was immediate. He disappeared beneath the water, his world nothing but bubbles and grey filtered light and pressure in his ears and *incredible cold*, then rose to the surface with a great rush and a watery explosion, coughing and spluttering and terrified. He trod frigid lake-water, fighting the drag of his sodden clothes, sucking him back below. His breath came in desperate little shocks of fog, bursting over the lapping black of his own waves. The cracked ice had split around him, breaking away into diminishing chunks, and his numbed and flailing hands grasped only drifting shards.

'Help! Help me!'

From somewhere he thought he heard Rennic bellowing 'little man!', but his movements were becoming urgent and spasmodic as his body started to shake. His eyes were blurry with water and panic, and he blinked furiously. The monochrome smears in his vision resolved themselves into figures, lurking at the ice's edge.

The skating reavers had dragged themselves from the caustic fog, weak on their feet, coughing and grunting. The closest had kicked off his skates, a long axe gripped in one hand, the other pressed to his streaming eyes. The moment his vision cleared, he would see Chel floundering by his feet. The great cold that had gripped Chel began to crush him.

A new figure strode into his view, moving confidently over the ice past the hunched and grunting reavers. Brecki came to a stop by the floe's jagged edge, and regarded Chel's desperate plight with a tilt of her head, her flaxen braids swaying.

'Brecki,' he gasped. 'Please! I'm . . . sorry . . .'

Her lip curled, and she shook her head with slow contempt. Beside her, the skate-less reaver had blinked himself to sight, and was staring at Brecki in surprise. From her his gaze slipped to Chel, battling to stay afloat in the freezing waves, bloodless fingertips questing for solid ice. A broad grin lit the reaver's pale face.

'Please, Brecki! Please!'

The reaver raised his axe to swing, and Brecki cuffed him around the head. Still weak on his feet, the man staggered and dropped to the ice, the axe skittering from his grasp. Brecki fixed Chel with a look of utter disgust, then extended her hand toward him.

'You apologize too much, crying boy. Look weak enough already.'

# SEVEN

The harbour boiled. Chel watched from the prow of the sword-shaped ship as they steered toward the icy wooden dock, freezing black water churning beneath them. Trickles of water, streams and brooks, cut dark, steaming lines down the snow-draped peak that loomed over the inlet, and the black seawater hissed and foamed where they met. The whole place stank of bad eggs and iron. On the horizon, the evening cloud hung thick and dark over the silhouettes of broken peaks, sporadic gouts of molten rock and earth-smoke clawing upwards from within, shot through with flashes of orange light. Beyond, odd wafting waves of emerald and indigo veiled the narrow band of stars that squeezed between earth and sky.

'Truly,' Foss said, 'we are at the end of the world. The heavens are burning, and all the hells are here.'

'C'mon, Fossy, don't be so dramatic. It's the ash-light, you can see it sometimes from Clyden.'

'And the great bursts of flame from beneath? The smell?'

He looked around, at the clusters of large and muscular reavers at the back of the boat. 'The company?'

Kosh was re-organizing the contents of her alchemy sack, cross-legged before the mast. 'That is volcanic activity. It is natural.'

Foss looked unconvinced. 'Evil days,' he muttered. 'Evil days.'

'Well,' said Loveless, joining them at the prow, 'I'm guessing that's the closest thing we'll get to an apology from a Horvaun war-band.'

'Ah, that was no war-band,' Lemon gave a dismissive wave of her hand, 'that was barely a scouting party.'

'Either way, Lem, it's fair to say they weren't expecting to meet friendlies. Our new bosom chum Brecki appears to have smoothed things over.'

'She has promised us as great weapons for her queen,' Kosh muttered. 'Including a . . . *wizard*.' She spat the last word.

Lemon was outraged. 'You can understand them? How can you fucken understand them?'

Her gaze flicked to Lemon and away. 'Honestly, I am appalled that you cannot.'

Chel crouched before Kosh. 'Can you talk back to them? Translate for us?'

The Nort looked appalled. 'Is it not enough that I sully my tongue with your mud-speech? Leave me be. Leave me to my . . . *wizard tricks*.'

Loveless put a hand on Chel's shoulder. 'You all dried out, cub? You're still shivering.'

'You're just twitching with excitement, eh, wee bear? Besides, splash of cold water's good for the muscles, you'll be in better shape than the rest of us come morning.'

Chel offered a tight smile and excused himself, with reluctance. He dreaded to think what shape they might all be in come the morning. Brecki's return and his sudden rescue from the frigid lake had been such a welcome shock that what had followed had passed in a blur; baffled, angry conversations between Brecki and their would-be murderers, a forced march, Chel still wet and shaking and half-carried by muscular reavers, from the lakeside down to the jagged coast, bundled into waiting Horvaun vessels and carted across the black water to wherever this demonic harbour lay. He'd at least had a chance to change his clothes once they were aboard and under sail, but it seemed impossible he would ever feel warmth again in his frozen bones.

Tarfel remained huddled beneath his cloak, curled beyond the mast. He'd been silent since the giant reavers had marched them down to the boats, keeping the lowest of profiles. He looked up at Chel's approach, tried to muster a smile.

'Ah, Vedren, how do things look?'

'We're coming into harbour. The landscape looks like it's on fire.'

'Jolly good, jolly good. Are we prisoners, do you think? It's hard to know exactly.'

'I wasn't aware that Horvaun reavers took prisoners, highness, so your guess at this stage is as good as mine.'

He nodded, smile cracked. 'Then let us try some old-fashioned diplomacy, and turn the screws against my brother yet.'

'C'mon, you dour sods,' Lemon called across the boat, 'we ain't dead yet, that's something to celebrate, eh?'

'It's all right for you, you're back among your people,' Rennic retorted.

'Ah, piss off!'

'Evil days,' muttered Foss, as the boat bumped against the pier.

\*\*\*

The fortress on the hill smelled even worse than the harbour, but it was wonderfully warm. Hacked and quarried into the hillside and walled in its rough grey-black stone, it offered both sweeping views over the darkening bay and respite from the blasted winter beyond. Brecki and two of the giant reavers from the boat led them out of the bitter night and through thick double doors, beneath an archway carved with a snarling parade of voracious faces. The hallway within was bright with torchlight, reflecting from racks of weaponry lining the walls, axes and pikes, shields and serrated daggers, some notched, stained, well-used, others ancient in style or appearance.

'It's half-armoury, half-museum,' Lemon muttered.

'What's a museum?'

'Aw, ancestors, Fossy, are you messing with me?'

Their escorts seemed unconcerned by their proximity to all the hardware, and they remained unchained and had not been disarmed. If anything, that made it worse: as far as the hard-faced, pale-skinned lumps marching either side of them were concerned, the group were no threat at all, armed or otherwise.

They were led into a vaulted great hall, a combination throne room and dining chamber. Tables were laid out in a spreading pattern from a dais at the far end, where a grand old throne, carved from dark wood and topped with what Chel guessed was a bear skull, looked down on the staff scurrying around, laying out preparations for what looked like a coming feast. Guards stood at regular intervals, hefty types in boiled leather with axes in their hands and at their backs.

A woman stood before the dais, taller than Brecki but not towering like the reavers who'd brought them in. She was hard-featured, inescapably pale, but frost-sharp with it, and wore a dark blue stone on a clasp at her neck. Her hair was unbraided, pulled back from her head in a loose pile, interwoven with coloured ties. On seeing Brecki, her eyebrows gave the slightest flex, and she turned half away.

'You stay,' Brecki growled, gesturing fiercely with her hand as if they were dogs of questionable obedience, then walked off toward the woman. She seemed to shrink as she approached, her stride losing its swagger, her shoulders hunching.

'We're all agreed this is Brecki's queen, right?' Loveless muttered, to general murmurs of assent. Rennic was craning forward to catch their conversation, but whatever passed between reaver and queen remained impenetrable. Chel had expected their language to be all grunts and hawking, but to his ear their speech was almost sing-song, a roll of even vowels and trills.

'What do you think, Vedren?' Tarfel pressed close to Chel, his gaze darting between the reaver guards who flanked them. The nearer one was a tall woman, beast-shouldered, with thick braids of jet-coloured hair bound beneath a helmet fashioned from an ox skull. Her furs were clean, thick, embroidered beneath. Chel caught the crystal blue of her cold eyes as she swept them over the group, and he flinched back.

'I have great faith in your diplomatic capabilities, Tarf,' he replied in a near-whisper.

'What do you reckon they're jacking on about?' Lemon said, one arm leaning on Foss, who looked peeved. 'Hardly strikes as a tearful reunion, eh?'

The attention of the group shifted very perceptibly toward Kosh, who was hunched at their centre, arms wrapped around her alchemical sack. 'Ugh,' she said, 'must I do everything for you? How is it I am surrounded by such incapable infants?'

'Strikes me you're the smallest, crunchiest person in this hall, Nort,' Rennic growled, 'and we infants are the only thing keeping you alive.'

She scoffed. 'Who was it who engineered our escape on the lake, who produced—'

'Hush,' Loveless said, 'they're finishing.'

Brecki was dismissed, sloping off toward the hall's far doors without a backward look. The woman at the dais looked over to the group, smiled, and beckoned. Something about the smile's brilliance made Chel nervous.

\*\*\*

The woman with the blue stone maintained her smile until they were all standing before the dais. Up close, there was more than a hint of a sneer about it. 'Welcome,' she said in their own language, 'I should perhaps introduce myself. Or reintroduce myself, as appropriate.' Her accent was obvious but controlled, her speech fluent, colloquial.

'What do you mean, reintroduce?' Rennic had shouldered his way to the front, trying to reassert a measure of dominance. Normally one of the biggest humans in any gathering, he seemed unnerved by so many large, brawny figures around them. 'Not sure any of us has ever travelled down to this beautiful part of the world before.'

She smile-sneered again, but it was without contempt, which Chel took as a good sign. 'You have not, but I have been north in the past, no doubt much to your surprise.' She leaned back, resting one hand on a chair that sat on the dais, small and relatively simple, before and to one side of the throne. Another matching chair sat on the throne's far side, and Chel wondered at their significance. 'I spent some time, a few years ago, studying at the Academy in Denirnas, among other things. I once met a young man, the little brother of two of my classmates, who had travelled there to visit with a great retinue.'

Her smile widened as her eyes sought Tarfel among them. 'That *is* you, isn't it, Prince Tarfel? You're taller now, I'll say that for you.'

Tarfel stepped forward from behind Rennic, holding his head high with barely a sniffle. 'I'm afraid I don't remember you, ah . . .'

She ignored the dangling pause. 'I am glad, after all, that Brecki spoke true, and you are not dead as we had heard. This will make life very interesting. We have much to discuss.' She was smiling even wider. 'The rest of you, you are . . .' She wrinkled her nose in thought, an oddly juvenile expression. '. . . Mercenaries? Sell-swords?'

'Aye, we prefer "freelance contractors".'

She nodded, unperturbed. 'And which of you is the wizard?' Again, her smile was genuine, if unnerving.

'Hold on a thrice-damned moment!' Rennic was still trying to assert himself. 'Who *are* you?'

'You may call me Ruumi.'

'And you're the queen of this place, right?'

'Ah,' she said, grin undimmed. '*Very nearly.*'

\* \* \*

The hallway they followed curled down into the hill, vaguely infernal, lined on either side with monstrous images, statues and bronze casts. Ruumi nodded to each one, a salute of sorts, remarking over her shoulder as she walked.

'You're familiar with our pantheon, your highness? You must have suffered Doctor Mesomedes' overview at the Academy.'

Tarfel mumbled, noncommittal. Chel worried that the prince's great resolve from their journey seemed to have withered now they were in a Horvaun stronghold.

'You will recognize the main players, of course,' Ruumi said, pointing as she walked. 'The Devourer, the Reaper, the Beast, everyone knows.'

'The Reaper who winnows weakness, the Beast who hews strength, the Devourer who consumes the dying world,' the prince echoed, seemingly surprising himself.

'Very good, your highness. But do you recognize that one? No? The Gatekeeper, who stands before the door? Do you remember any others?'

'The . . . Judge?'

'The Arbiter, yes, who sits in judgement. An easy one. Any others?'

'The . . . Frothing Ear-Biter?'

'Ha, no, very good, your highness. You could also have had the Tiller who sows the seed, the Sentinel who watches over, the Harbinger who heralds what comes, the Navigator who sails the starry sky. Then there are all the minor gods,

111

of course,' she continued. 'But their names vary depending on who you ask, and the time of year. I doubt even Doctor Mesomedes could name half of them.'

'They worship the Navigator in the Thousand Isles,' Chel said. 'Is it the same one?'

Ruumi's gaze travelled through him and out the other side. 'Does their Navigator sail the oceans of night in a vessel of bone, her oars fashioned from the claws of the last dragon?'

'I, uh, don't think so.'

'Perhaps not the same one.'

'Aside from the Tiller, they sound like a morbid bloody lot,' Loveless muttered from behind.

Ruumi smiled. 'The Tiller harrows with a thousand-sided plough of the swords of his conquered foes, sowing their teeth in the furrows, that they may rise as an army of slaves at the coming of the endless winter.'

'Ah. My mistake.'

The doors were thick and dark, the rooms windowless and lit by fat, reeking candles that burned with a strange, sloppy flame, their smoke vented through black gaps carved into the ceilings. Behind the candle-smell, the old eggs and brimstone odour remained, obscured but undimmed.

'You may make yourselves comfortable here,' Ruumi said, airy as a seneschal. 'The women will be in here, the men there.'

Chel frowned, peering round to see if the other chamber was better furnished. 'Why the separation?'

'I imagine you are tired after your trip. Perhaps you would care to leave your belongings here and bathe? Then we can talk.'

Rennic had burst his dam. 'God's bollocks, woman, who

the fuck *are* you? Are we prisoners? Can we not get a straight fucking answer out of you without a riddle and an enigmatic smile?'

Ruumi raised her eyebrows, but her smile remained. In the hallway beyond, the guards creaked as their hands moved to rest on their weapons.

'I apologize if I seem enigmatic, Master . . . ?'

'Rennic.'

'Master Rennic. I am only out of practice with your language, I assure you. Answers will come shortly, but rest assured, you are not prisoners. You are my honoured guests, my honoured, royal guests.'

'So, we can leave?'

'We have yet so much to discuss. Brecki told me that Prince Tarfel had a proposition for me; I will hear it, and he will hear mine in turn, then we will reach accord. This is diplomacy, yes?'

'And you are, what? "Nearly-queen"?'

'My mother was queen, if that helps?'

'Not really.'

'Where's Brecki?' Chel said. He'd half-expected to find the woman waiting for them, one-armed and gurning.

'As we speak?' Ruumi's brow crinkled. 'Preparing for her exile, I imagine.'

'What? You're exiling her? After she, she—'

'Rest assured, Andriz, she is grateful for exile. To return after such failure, our laws would demand her execution. Her redemption is cause for celebration, should your inclination yearn for mercy.'

'Huh?' Chel scratched at his brow. 'Are you saying she led us all the way here expecting to be executed for her troubles?'

Lemon whistled. 'Goes to show you can never really know a person, eh? Especially a leg-chewing head-splitter like that one,' she added quietly.

'She is a warrior,' Ruumi said, blithe and cheerful. 'Better to be sent to the gods by her own people than die a coward in the Sink. Or perhaps she was confident of her outcomes. You may yet have a chance to ask her, should you return north and survive a while.'

Lemon started. 'Hoy now, what's that supposed to—'

Ruumi gestured to the cushions and furs beyond. 'Please, rest for now. Bathe, I beg you, for others' benefit if not your own. Pikul will direct you.' One of the meaty guards nodded, incongruous as a bull. 'I must go, I have much to prepare. I will return soon, and we can discuss our proposals then.' She swept from the room, a pale, languid flourish, lost in the hallway's darkness in a moment.

'Well, she's a pain in the arse,' Loveless muttered. 'Is it just me, or does this sort of thing seem to happen to us with alarming frequency?'

Rennic sat down heavily on one of the fat cushions that littered the chambers' common area. Chel glanced at the guards, immobile as statues, their gazes fixed. 'What do we do?'

Whisper was unwinding various straps from her limbs, laying her equipment down on top of a carved wooden trunk. She gestured, one-handed, then resumed her task.

Rennic sighed and nodded. 'As the lady says, a bath wouldn't kill us.'

# EIGHT

'Aye, right, hot springs, very clever.'

Noxious alchemical steam billowed from the bathhouse, venting through a skylight into the freezing night above. Pikul, the giant guard escorting them, gestured to the women, then to the door on the left, then the men and the other door. Steam churned in the low amber light beyond.

'Why the separation?' Chel asked again, although he was both disappointed and relieved.

Lemon shrugged. 'Best not quibble, I'd say. They're not a bunch renowned for flexibility of custom.'

\*\*\*

The antechamber was hot, the sulphuric stench initially overpowering, but the effect waned as they acclimatized. They dumped clothes on wooden benches, crunching over the still-cold ground to the rocky pool beneath the slatted roof overhead. However ashamed Chel felt at his nakedness between peeling off the last of his travelling garb, scuttling through the rippling steam and sliding into the hot, hissing pool, he had nothing on the prince. Tarfel, a blushing white stripe in the rolling clouds, shuffled crabwise around the edge, hands clamped over his nether regions, then splashed into a distant, far corner of the pool.

The water was unreal, supremely warm, and Chel felt buoyant, relaxed, soothed. His shoulder pulsed, slowly, almost happily. From somewhere over the wooden divide, he heard giggles and the petulant tones of the Nort alchemist. It seemed she was having some conceptual difficulties with the shared bath.

Somewhere to Chel's left, Rennic stretched out his tattooed arms and groaned with aching happiness. To his right, Foss did likewise. One of them farted, but it was impossible to tell which. Both collapsed in laughter, streetkids at a parade.

'What do you make of her then, friends? Our illustrious host.'

Rennic blew soaking strands of hair from his face. 'Nearly-queen Ruumi? She's playing the grinning guide, but let's not forget where we are. She's something around here, and this lot tend to respect one thing above all.'

'What are you saying?' Chel said. He was beginning to feel lightheaded from the water's warmth.

'I'm saying, little man, that you don't get to be nearly-queen of a reaver tribe as established as this one without being a vicious piece of work. She said she has a proposal for us. We need to be seriously careful—'

'How are we getting on, gentlemen?'

Ruumi was standing over them, one boot on the pool's edge, hands on hips, vapours curling around her like affectionate pets.

116

Rennic sent up a chaotic spray as he thrashed to face her. 'The f—? I thought women weren't allowed in here!'

Again, the flat grin, a half-sneer devoid of malice. Perhaps it was a cultural thing. 'You misunderstand. The separation of the sexes is only to prevent the clouding of minds when concentration is required elsewhere. We are a passionate people, and the last thing our womenfolk need when they should be considering matters of tribal import is the peacocking of brutes. It impairs our progress. Much great thinking, planning, *scheming*, is done within the bathhouse.'

'Uh-*huh*. Yet here you are.'

'Here I am. You need not worry, I am fully sated for now.'

Blank looks shone up from the pool.

'Sexually,' she clarified with an encouraging nod. The blank looks became somewhat frozen. Undeterred, she continued. 'Prince Tarfel, I promised you we would talk, and now we may.'

Tarfel edged forward through the drifting steam, an amorphous white streak from the neck down below the waterline. 'I thought . . . when you said we should bathe, then we would talk . . . you meant, ah, *after* bathing.'

The smile flashed again. 'Now seems as fitting as any, does it not? Brecki informed me of the gist of your intentions, I would like to hear the words from you. She was never the most accomplished linguist.'

Chel found himself wondering about Brecki's fate, her motivations for bringing them back here after all, and had to snap himself back to the present. The hot water was definitely getting to him.

Tarfel seemed to be steeling himself, his weak chin jutting as he looked up at the elegant figure at the bath-side. 'You wanted my brother dead before.' He swallowed, larynx bobbing in and out of the water. 'I want him dead now. What will it take for you to try again?'

The bathhouse had gone quiet, but for the gentle bubble and splosh of lapping water. Murmured conversation, unintelligible, drifted over the divider.

Ruumi's smile had hardened, not with anger or dismay, but with satisfaction, small lines appearing beneath her eyes. 'It is true, then. Tarfel Merimonsun is to raise his pennant against his brother, and plunge his kingdom into civil war.'

Tarfel was shaking his head, hands out of the water spraying droplets. 'It's not like that, it's . . . it's . . . He's planning things—'

'I believe it was you and your entourage,' Ruumi said with a gesture toward Rennic and Foss, but not Chel, who flushed with injured pride, 'who despoiled the attempt in question. Perhaps you should have kept out of the way then, no?'

'We didn't know that he was . . . We couldn't have known . . .' Tarfel's brows lowered, water trickling down his pale face. Chel watched through narrowed eyes, the steam tickling his nose. Ruumi had sent Brecki and her warband to kill Tarfel's brother when few in the kingdom would have considered him anything more than a jolly simpleton. Had they known what everyone else hadn't?

Ruumi had one hand on her chin, her gaze lost somewhere in the drifting haze of the rafters. 'It will be different now: he is not living as before. He sits at the heart of a great and growing force. To reach him directly with a warband will be near impossible.'

Tarfel stood defiant in the water, his shoulders breaking

the surface. 'I realize this. I have no intention of making such an attempt.'

'What is your plan?'

Chel leaned forward. What indeed?

'My brother pretends to empire. He will consolidate his forces over winter, then come the thaw he will march his armies to each corner of the kingdom that resists central rule. There are plenty of Names, minor lords, and free cities who chafe at the thought of consolidation, but without a signal to rally they will simply capitulate, one by one.'

'You mean to unite them? Replace one crown with another?'

'He can only sweep the board if he can concentrate his forces. Give him too many enemies, no matter how small . . . If the scales tip, he will be pulled in too many directions.'

'You wish for me to be one of these small enemies?'

'I do, yes – the signal to rally. And I wish to know your price.'

Ruumi stood, her hand still at her chin. The smile was still there, as if applied and forgotten like war-paint. 'You may have less time than you realize. Already your brother has begun disbanding and absorbing the mercenary companies of the north, drawing them into his great church army. He may not wait until the thaw.'

Rennic stirred at this, half-rising from the water. 'He's doing what?'

Tarfel, too, seemed taken aback. 'That's . . . How is he going to hold the disputed territories without the free companies?'

'I know only what my spies report, Tarfel Merimonsun. Perhaps another for your list of small enemies.'

'Perhaps . . .' Tarfel was quiet for a moment. 'Do I have your interest, Queen Ruumi?'

'Only nearly, you remember. We will come to that. You have my interest.'

'What do you offer?'

She put her hands on her hips, standing tall, looming over them in her fine-cut robes. 'At an agreed time, I will land a significant force in the south-west of your kingdom, and I will seed chaos. We will set the coast aflame. Your brother will be forced to send aid, and we will fall upon it, as long as we are able. Should matters turn against us . . .' She made a face. '. . . we shall depart in earnest.'

Tarfel swallowed again. 'You'll . . . pillage?'

Ruumi's smile flashed back, beaming and brilliant. 'We like to play to our strengths.'

Chel cleared his throat, trying to manage speech. The hot water had made him light-headed. 'Surely . . . This seems, uh, disproportionately . . . bad. What about . . . isn't there another way you can help?'

She gazed straight at him, through him. 'None I am willing to countenance.'

'I will ponder it,' Tarfel said, his head dropped a span as if weighed. 'This is your price?'

This time the mirth was gone from her smile. 'It is half. As to the other . . . You expressed curiosity as to my station here. Thanks to your interventions and the failure of Brecki's war-band, my situation is less sure than it should have been. You will remedy this.'

Rennic leaned forward. 'Would this involve your conversion from nearly-queen to actual queen?'

'My half-brother has made himself an issue. As outsiders, you are . . . uniquely placed to resolve matters.'

Tarfel looked affronted, nostrils flared. 'You want us to kill your brother?'

'*Half*-brother. You must admit, it seems only fair, given your own request. He need not die, but he must be removed from contention. I will leave it to your sell-swords to determine how.'

'Surely . . . there must be something else?'

Ruumi's eyebrow arched, and she folded her arms.

'Give me your wizard.'

Despite the warmth, Chel shuddered at the thought of Kosh and her alchemy in the hands of the Horvaun.

'Something else,' protested Tarfel.

'Pledge your troth to me, unite our causes and ride at the head of my war-bands as we exterminate first my brother, then yours, then overwhelm the continent with the fruit of our union.'

Tarfel's mouth hung open.

'You may decide which option you prefer,' she said, the mirth creeping back into her smile.

'I . . .' Tarfel said. 'I need to ponder this a little longer.'

Ruumi's smile broadened. 'I do not believe that you do.'

'You all seem to be forgetting something,' Rennic said, lying back against the pool's edge with his hands folded behind his head, adopting the Posture of Unhurried Negotiation. 'To wit, we are a commercial enterprise, and there are formalities involved in the engagement of our services. We'll need explicit terms, and a contract drawn up. Then there's the matter of expenses—'

Ruumi coughed, one hand over that smile. 'Again, I apologize for my rustiness with your language. The work is already accepted in principle, by your captain. I was merely informing you as a courtesy, in case you wish to scheme while you are still bathing, once the prince agrees.'

'My cap— What fucking captain?'

'The lady with the unusual hair. I can see why you defer to her. I will leave you to make your plans. See you in the hall at your leisure, honoured guests.'

'Loveless . . . I'll . . . Nine hells!'

She vanished into the drifting fumes. The four men sat in the steaming pool in silence for a moment, brows deep, lips chewed in uneasy thought.

'What . . .' Chel said, running a hand through his hair. 'What did we just agree to?'

One of them farted again.

\*\*\*

When they returned to the hall, they found braziers burning between the long tables and fires in the great hearths at the walls. The hall teemed with activity. Tall southerners were standing in thick, boisterous knots, downcast servants weaving between them, ferrying dishes and drink; other figures, their furs and jewellery fine and well-made, were taking seats of significance around the chamber. The half-brother, a blond beast of a man, stood beside one of the modest chairs before the throne, a long table laid before him, surrounded by meat-armed and slab-chested southerners. All men, Chel noted.

The table before the other chair, the one on which Ruumi had leant before their tour, was occupied by an entirely female cast: their four companions, Ruumi herself, and her captain, the towering woman who'd brought them from the boat, finally named as Oksa. They rose as Pikul escorted the scrubbed and glowing men to the table, then withdrew to one side to maintain a presence of brooding menace. Ruumi signalled Tarfel to sit at the head of the table, a place of presumed significance.

'They make you leave your tools behind?' Lemon said as Ruumi bade them sit, before Rennic could begin a diatribe at Loveless. Loveless herself gave an arch grin, clearly aware of the big man's mood.

Chel nodded. Not that they had much equipment left between them.

'See?' Lemon said to Foss. 'They get it. Run a tighter ship than that shambles in the tower.'

'Our people,' said Oksa, each word delivered with great precision, 'need no weapon to kill.'

'Aye, right, but it's a time-saver, eh?'

The big woman frowned at that, and returned to her platter. Chel wasn't sure if she'd understood a word Lemon had said.

Ruumi gestured for a hovering servant to start pouring what Chel hoped would be wine into their horns. 'What is this? What's the occasion?' he said, directed primarily at Ruumi who was looking down on them from her chair on the dais, chewing at a haunch of something.

'Feast,' said Oksa, and no more.

Ruumi smiled again. 'As my captain says, we have something of a gathering this evening. I am glad you could be with us for it – it is to Brecki's credit that you are. We have many honoured guests, besides yourselves, many of our local . . . Names, yes? The equivalent.'

Chel looked around the smoky hall. It hummed with a pleasant chatter and munch. Given the seating arrangements, he began to pick out several figures who were being treated with deference by those around them.

Lemon nudged him. 'You've got your tribal chiefs, elders, even some of the local anointed.'

'Anointed?'

'Like a priesthood, but, you know, bloodier.'

Foss rumbled beside him. 'Warlords. Blood-lords. Godless and damned.'

'Aye, I dunno, Fossy, seems they've more than a few gods to go around.'

Ruumi raised her horn from its perch on the arm of her chair. 'A toast, my guests, to mutual benefits.'

'Tell me again how rusty your language is,' Rennic muttered, downed whatever was in his horn, then waved to the servant for a refill. A number of other horns were emptied as the servant approached.

'Can we not?' Tarfel's voice was small, the end of the table seeming a long way away in the hall's raucous hubbub. 'Given everything earlier, can we please, for once, not drink everything we can see?'

Loveless was staring at him, hard, as if he were something risen from the ocean and now walking up the beach. 'Come again?'

'Every time this happens, every time we sit down somewhere with people who seem friendly, it goes wrong. Terribly wrong. And I'm usually the one who gets hurt!'

Ruumi was watching the prince, ever-present smile held steady, muted, curious to hear more. She made no effort to reassure him over her perceived friendliness – or lack thereof.

'In all the time I've travelled with you,' Tarfel said, 'willing or otherwise, I can't think of one occasion where a feast hasn't ended badly on some level. I'm just asking if we could maybe keep clear heads this evening, given what we've been asked to do, and the kind of people we're surrounded by.' He blushed, and added, 'Meaning no disrespect, of course.'

'Of course,' Ruumi echoed with her smile.

'That,' Rennic said, voice already a touch flat with booze, 'is life, princeling. Just about everything, feast or otherwise, *ends badly on some level*.'

'Then why take the risk?'

'Where would be the fun in a life without risk? Rest assured, every life ends badly, sooner or later. Might as well get some use out of it while you can.' He waved to the servant again.

Ruumi sat forward, one elbow on her knee. 'This is where our philosophies differ, sell-sword.'

'Rennic.'

'Master Rennic. When our lives on this vessel end, when we are reaped, we are judged on a life well-lived. Those who are judged worthy will be carried across the stars in the Navigator's ship of bone, those who disappoint will be ground and resown by the Tiller to be reborn at the dawn of the endless winter, and those who have failed their people, as Brecki so nearly did, are severed and devoured.'

'So?'

'So for us, a life well-lived is a devout imperative.' She sat back, still smiling.

'And what constitutes a life well-lived?' Loveless said, genuinely curious.

'What you would expect. Great deeds. Victory, vitality, conquest, in steel and flesh.' She waved a hand, as if curving over something invisible. 'Pain endured, pleasure gained and given.'

Loveless seemed satisfied, her smile mirroring Ruumi's.

'But nothing of ethics, or moral imperative?' Foss said. 'Kindness to fellow man in all things?'

Ruumi's smile faded, her response only a quizzical glance. 'But how would that please the gods?'

'And what about your ancestors?' Lemon interjected. 'Staying true to those who went before.'

Ruumi's expression remained quizzical. 'Those already sent to the gods had their time and received their judgement. The imperative, as your friend puts it, is in living the best life for the self. Our duty to the gods is to glory in an existence lived well, no matter what, or who, came before.'

'Aye, but what about—'

'Only the pieces on the board are still in the game, Clydish wench.'

'Where does the boat go?' Chel said over Lemon's squawk. 'The bone-boat, does it ever dock?'

'Indeed: in paradise. A land of eternal conquest, eternal hunt, and eternal feast.'

'Sounds like a recipe for eternal gut-rot,' Lemon muttered. 'I mean, I sleep terribly after a big meal these days, all that pissing and farting, just imagine an eternity of that.'

Rennic's head was tilted, his eyes on Ruumi. 'And to get to this paradise, must you die with your weapon in your hand?'

'Not a problem for you, Gar,' Loveless chuckled, 'that's how you wake up most mornings.'

Even Ruumi laughed at that. Foss watched her, frown deep, distrustful. 'You laugh at your own gods? You mock them, allow others to do likewise?'

'Of course!'

'You don't worry about angering them? They seem an ill-humoured bunch.'

'Angering them? They are gods! What have they to fear from the mockery of mortals? What kind of gods would they be if they were cowed by the teasing squeals of piglets in their slaughterhouse? Ha! Can you imagine? Who would worship a god who craved the protection of men!'

Oksa was laughing, deep and mirthful. Foss's frown was unmoved.

Ruumi sat forward again, warming to the conversation. 'Tell me, I have often wondered. Your people, you have the Shepherd, yes?'

'We do.'

'And you have a god, a sole god, but one?'

'We do.'

'And are they the same?'

'Yes,' said Foss at the same time as Loveless said, 'No.' They looked at each other, irked.

'I see,' Ruumi said, stroking her chin. 'And this Shepherd, she was a real person, walked the earth?'

'No,' said Foss, firmly, while Loveless said, 'Yes,' with equal certainty.

'Master Rennic, do you have a view?'

Rennic put up his hands. 'Don't look at me, nearly-queen, my gods are silver and grape.'

'I believe we have more in common than you may have expected.'

He raised his horn. 'Maybe we do.'

They exchanged a smile, and Chel didn't like the look of it.

\* \* \*

Oksa was talking, a rapid stream of the lilting Horvaun tongue quite at odds with her ponderous speech to the northerners. Ruumi listened intently, the smile growing at the corners of her mouth, then exploded with laughter at the joke's conclusion. Oksa sat back, chuckling to herself, delighted.

'I apologize,' Ruumi said, wiping a tear from one eye with the hand that held her drinking horn. 'It's a marvellous joke, but it just won't translate well. Rest assured, it was not at your expense.'

'Until you said that, the thought hadn't occurred,' Lemon said, eyes narrow. She returned her attention to hacking at the meat on the platter in front of her, something rich and well-fatted. It wobbled and sprang beneath her knife.

'I am sorry, too, for the quality of the feast,' Ruumi said. 'Now that winter is upon us and the straits are frozen, we are forced to open the stores.'

Lemon looked up, aware of the glares in her direction. 'But the straits don't freeze!'

'Perhaps not all the way across, but enough to make them impassable for our vessels. There will be no eastern travel until the thaw. Hence, no fresh meat, I'm afraid.'

Loveless raised an eyebrow. '*Hence?* Just how long did you spend in the north? Your linguistic command appears prodigious.'

Ruumi placed a hand on her chest in modesty, false or otherwise. 'I admit, much of your language is returning to me with renewed exposure. Borre, my half-brother, and I both spent several years at the Academy, our terms overlapping. It was only toward the end of my time there that I encountered Prince Tarfel's brothers, and of course the young prince himself. I saw only a little of them, and of course it was soon after that one was dead and the other was acting an imbecile.'

Chel's gaze was back on the nearly-queen in an instant. 'What do you mean?'

'Mendel, the younger twin.'

'The one who imprisoned us, executed our friends, purged the countryside of rebellion?'

'No, no, you misunderstand. Mendel was dead. Corvel remained, behaving in a . . . strange manner, as if he were Mendel. And somehow . . .' She waved a hand beside her head. 'Damaged, his thinking.'

'How did you know it was Corvel?'

'The scar. Mendel had a scar, a failed hunt, something. Corvel, as Mendel, emerged from his trials with a fresh wound in the same area, but the old scar was gone from beneath.'

Tarfel was gazing at her, eyebrows pinched, a look of great scrutiny. 'So you did know. How? How would you notice and nobody else?'

Ruumi's smile returned, if anything a little prim. 'How would you think, your highness?'

Tarfel's mouth hung open.

'It was only a brief time,' she continued, 'but that was no great shame.'

'You . . . with my brother? *My brothers?*'

Demure, now. 'Not at the same time, your highness.'

Loveless was cackling, her head lolling with mirth. 'I think I like this one. Oh, really I do.'

Chel's memory stirred. What had Corvel said? *I cut my own face, you know that? I did this to myself. It was that or wait for a knife in the back*. He might have been called 'the Wise', but someone had clocked his act.

'Then you knew,' Rennic said, speech barely slurred. 'You knew Mendel . . . Corvel . . . whichever fucker. You knew he was acting up? Did you know he was running the church, and not the other way round?'

She sloshed the wine around in her horn. 'I considered it a strong possibility. Why else do you think I sent Brecki's war-band to kill him? Better safe than sorry, you might say.'

'Fuck me. Brecki knew it. The whole time. While we had Corvel in our camp, while we made our plans. Fuck *me*! She could have said something!'

Chel repeated Ruumi's words, mirthless. 'She was never the most accomplished linguist.'

Ruumi nodded, smile persistent. 'She was not.' From across the dais came a great roar of stone-shaking laughter, and the slapping of a thick palm against the table. Borre was amused. Ruumi's smile flickered, ever so briefly. 'Tell me, sell-swords, is your scheming complete? The sooner you have acted on my situation, the sooner I can commit to your prince's cause.'

'I never actually—' Tarfel began.

'We're on top of it,' Loveless said over him.

'We'll *discuss* it,' Rennic growled with a pointed look in her direction. Loveless flashed a brilliant smile, a perfect imitation of Ruumi's, and Chel felt a sudden pang. 'But . . . yeah, we're on top of it,' Rennic finished.

'It pleases me to hear it,' Ruumi said, 'for Borre will likely depart on a hunt in the next day or so, and could be gone for some time. I would hate you to miss your opportunity.'

'Like I said,' Rennic replied, holding up his horn for a refill. 'We're on top of it.'

'Then, my friends, let us drink, and eat, and talk of great things, as friends do.'

'Any chance we could go easy on the drinking part?' Tarfel spoke with the dejected tones of one who knows his pleas will fall on deaf ears, but feels he must make them nonetheless.

'Fuck off, princey!'

'Right you are.'

Chel looked back at the other half-throne. Borre was drinking now, his broad back to them, a massive stack of meat flanked by equally imposing hulks. Even getting close to the half-brother was going to be a challenge, let alone causing him some kind of injury. Surely there had to be a better way than this?

He kicked Rennic. 'Are you sure about this?' A nod toward Borre. 'He's . . . enormous. Have you given much thought to—'

Rennic's glance was barely even cursory. Wine stained his beard. 'Don't worry your pretty head, little man. We're on top of it.'

His words did nothing to reassure. Chel looked back at Borre, and realized the surreptitious gaze of several among Borre's table was fixed on their own. As drinking horns were refilled and drained around him, Chel saw their hard features ease, their own jugs beginning to circulate in earnest. Was this some level of competition? Were they being measured? Or was something more dangerous at play?

He turned to Rennic to raise the prospect, but the big man had eyes only for Ruumi, and likewise she for him. Not for the first time, Chel felt like an outsider, a voyeur, peering in through the window of a party to which he hadn't been invited.

'Fuck it,' he muttered, and reached for the wine.

131

# NINE

He heard it first in his dream, a starlit stroll along snow-capped mountains that had unravelled into an abattoir, the air thick with the agonized squeals of frenzied pigs. Rennic stood at the centre of the carnage, blood-soaked and aproned, sharpening a great cleaver with sweeps of a stone.

'We're on top of it, little man,' he said. 'The gods are laughing. Come and join the party.'

'Where is she?' he cried, panic mounting. 'Where is she?'

Awake. Awake but the sound continued, a scream, a roaring, excruciating scream of shock, pain and outrage.

*Where is she?*

He was out of bed, scrabbling for the mace, fingers closing on cool wood beside his pallet. The chambers were dark, the sole light a distant torch in the outside hallway. His eyes floundered in the gloom, but already he could see movement, the great lump of Foss rising from his pallet, the scrawny stick-figure of Tarfel, huddled beneath furs, wishing the world away. 'I told them, I told them, I told them,' came from somewhere beneath.

Rennic's pallet was empty.

'Shepherd's mercy, friends, what's that noise?'

'Come on!'

'I told them, I told them—'

He'd gone three steps before the magnitude of his drunkenness hit him, a great wobbly smack across his legs that sent him skittering sideways instead of toward the doorway. Whatever hour it was, he'd not yet slept his way into the coming hangover. He shook himself, pressing the cold metal of the mace-tip to his temple, then made for the doorway with renewed intent.

The hallway beyond was deserted, unguarded, dark but for the single torch at its far end. The screaming continued, barely a pause for breath, a wordless howl. It was coming from the doorway at the hallway's end. Footsteps thumped from behind, and he turned to see Oksa pounding toward them in the gloom, Ruumi a pace behind. The captain was fully dressed, still in her armour and furs, while the nearly-queen wore a long robe, belted carelessly around her waist.

Loveless came striding from the darkened doorway, moving quickly but with a certain satisfaction. 'Sorry, boys, did we wake you?' she said, noting the gathering crowd. Lemon and Whisper emerged behind her, looking a little more furtive.

'What in hells is that noise?' The screaming was like a blade scraped across Chel's eyeballs.

Loveless ignored him, approaching Ruumi directly. The nearly-queen and Oksa filled the hallway, leaving very little room for the otherwise significant figure of Rennic to slip past them. He was dressed but still lacing his shirt with one hand as he peered around Oksa. 'It's done,' Loveless said, pointedly ignoring Rennic's appearance.

'How done?' Ruumi replied, as conversational as if she were asking after the health of a distant aunt.

'Your path to the throne stands blissfully unimpeded.' She winced as another bout of screaming began, echoing from the hallway's rough stone and making Chel's teeth throb. 'Some of his night-time companions may be a little . . . scarred, but we thought precision was the order of the day.'

Chel could no longer contain himself. 'You killed him? Borre?' He rubbed at his thudding head. 'After all that wine?'

Lemon shuffled past. 'Aye, well, all a gambit, see? Classic ruse. We drink, they drink, they drink, we drink, everyone's all pissed and mellow, couple of friendly wee stabs in the dark and job's a good 'un.'

'But you're hammered! Your eyes won't focus!'

'Years of practice, wee bear,' she said with a merry wave of her hand, then walked into the doorway and bounced off. ''Scuse me. Probably shouldn't be hanging around, eh, folks? Discretion would call for a sharp exit.'

Chel's head was sore and his vision was swimming. Still trembling, he looked back at Rennic. 'Was this your plan? You said you were on top of it!'

'On top of something, no doubt,' Lemon chuckled drunkenly as she staggered into the quarters. 'Someone give me a hand with the Nort, eh? She's right cranky when she's tired.'

Ruumi leaned into Oksa, whispering urgent words. The big Horvaun turned and vanished back into the fortress behind them. Already clatter and shouts echoed from elsewhere. The screaming was finally dying away, which in some ways was worse.

She ignored it, turning to Loveless, her face impassive,

unreadable. 'As the Clyde says, you must depart. You will, of course, be hunted for your crimes against my family . . .' Her smile returned, fleeting but fierce. '. . . But not well.'

'As agreed.'

Ruumi gestured. 'Pikul will attend to your fee, and show you out.' The aforementioned guard was already waiting at the hallway's end, stone-faced, impossibly silent, bundles of furs piled over one shoulder.

Loveless held her gaze. 'And the bonus for prompt completion?'

Ruumi put one hand to her throat. 'Of course. As agreed.'

Rennic looked like a man torn, pulled between two drifting boats. 'Is this . . . Will you . . .'

'Time to go, Master Rennic,' the nearly-queen said, and a ghost of her smile rolled across her face as she ushered him toward the waiting Pikul.

Chel steadied himself against the wall with one hand. The screaming had faded, but the air seemed thick with blood and the echoes of horror, and he couldn't wait to get out.

'I'll get Tarfel.'

\* \* \*

Pikul led them from a stubby side gate, hidden in the bowels of the fortress, and into the stinging cold of the night. The sky was black with cloud, starless, the drifting curtains of hazy light of their arrival lost beneath silver-veined sheets of jet. As they descended toward the harbour, Chel saw lights sparkle in the dark block of the fortress, increasing in number. He expected bells to start ringing at any moment, and hurried his progress down the winding icy path, his breath shards of golden fog in the light from Pikul's torch.

A vessel awaited them at a lightless black-wood jetty, long, low and rigged. The helm started at their approach, standing straight and hawking a gobbet of chewed leaf over the side. It seemed they'd been expected: the helm and a lone crewman were already making ready, and the vessel looked packed with crates and barrels, as if for a long voyage. Wrapped in their new furs, they boarded under Pikul's grunted direction, casting glances of varying suspicion at the smoothness of their exit.

As the crew went to cast off, Ruumi descended onto the jetty, one hand raised in farewell. She was dressed in furs, her bearing regal. At last, she looked triumphant.

'Farewell, my friends. I regret that our time together was so short. Prince Tarfel!'

The ropes were cast, the gang withdrawn. The vessel began to drift away from the jetty, loose chunks of floating ice bumping its hull. Tarfel roused himself from his half-slumber and pushed to the rail. 'What?'

Her smile widened. 'At the first moon of northern spring, I shall set your south-west aflame. Be ready!'

His expression frozen, he nodded, one hand raised in presumed gratitude. 'I never actually agreed to—'

The very-nearly-queen moved on to Rennic. 'Safe travels, Master Rennic. I enjoyed our meeting.'

'Uh, likewise.'

Already Ruumi was shrinking, a dwindling figure beneath the dancing light of Pikul's torch, the sole light on the darkened harbour.

'Farewell, mercenaries of the north,' she called. 'Find your small enemies.'

Then she was gone, a swirl of dark fur and waning torchlight. Loveless stayed at the rail, staring back at the

diminishing harbour. At her neck, a blue stone shone in the
drifting slivers of moonlight.

Lemon flopped down next to Chel, beside Foss at the
stern. She sighed, her breath a long silver plume in the biting
night air.

'At least we're getting away from that place. Stank like
Fossy's farts, it did.'

'Hey!'

'Not your fault, big fella, it's probably just the food down
here.'

'Hey!'

'Now,' she said, humour a little restored, 'does anyone
know where we're going?'

Tarfel was at the rail beside them. 'We're committed
now,' he said in a small voice. His gaze slipped down to
Chel. 'Are we committed? This vessel could take us
anywhere.' He swallowed, his larynx bobbing pale in the
moonlight. 'We could . . . We don't have to . . .'

Chel held his gaze. 'My father said the righteous need
fear nothing but the loss of their resolve.'

'Is that the same father who died of plague?' came
Lemon's voice from beside him.

Tarfel offered a weak smile. 'Being righteous sounds
good. How do we know if we're righteous?'

Chel became aware of Rennic hovering in his peripheral
vision, but he kept his eyes on the prince. 'We do our duty.
We do what's right.'

Tarfel's quavering stilled, a touch of mirth returning to
his pale face. 'Then let us set sail for treason!'

'Ah,' Lemon said cheerfully, 'I'm sure it's not treason if
it's for a good cause.'

# PART II

# TEN

'Landfall by sundown. Be ready.' With that, Loveless strode back across the deck to resume her argument.

Chel could scarcely believe it. They'd been at sea for what seemed like an age, changing boats twice already – it wasn't, after all, a wise move to approach the Vistirlari coast in a Horvaun raiding vessel – but no one save Loveless and Rennic had been ashore since they left Ruumi's harbour. Chel's sea legs were well and truly bedded in, and he suspected that he'd pitch sideways the moment his foot touched solid earth.

Raised voices from the cargo ship's stern did little to draw his attention. The pattern was a familiar one by now: Loveless or Rennic proposed something, the other argued, terse words were exchanged before Whisper stepped in and either mollified or separated them, at least until the next flashpoint. They argued over everything: tactics, strategy – two distinct items, as Chel was by now exhaustingly aware – the wording on any communications sent ahead, even what to have for their evening meals.

'What do you suppose it is this time?' Chel asked Lemon, who sat beside Foss, dozing against some sacks.

'Ah,' she muttered, 'who the fuck cares. Maybe he's beating you too hard for her liking. Or not hard enough.'

Chel smiled without mirth. The fresh bruise on his cheek gave a gentle thrum in the salt air, a memento from yesterday's sparring session.

'Are they . . . I mean, have they been like this before? At each other so much?'

'I suppose we were due another turn of the wheel.' At his blank look, Lemon rubbed a hand through her matted braids. 'Ah, I forget your relative novelty, young bear.'

'Eh?'

'You've not been with us that long. I'm afraid this is a semi-regular occurrence for our golden couple. Once we've been cooped up on hoof or under sail for too long, they each get, you know, what's the word? When dogs run around widdling on each other?'

'Territorial?'

'Aye, that's the one. Like a pair of yappy wee bastards, each gobbing off to show how little each needs the other. And the rest of us get doused in the arcs of their piss.'

'So it's happened before? It'll blow over?'

She shrugged. 'Always has before. She'll threaten to go her own way, he'll dare her to do so, Whisp will drag them round by the scruff until they calm down – ancestors know she's the only one who can summon the energy these days – and it'll be kittens and birdsong come the thaw. Probably.'

'It sounds like our voyage might soon be over, at least.'

Lemon snorted. 'Aye, our voyage might be, wee bear, but I fancy our troubles may yet be near their beginning.'

Kosh bustled up from her work area below decks, carrying something bulky in her arms. She went straight toward Whisper, who squatted near the stern with one practised eye on the bickering; her nimble fingers were fletching a bundle of new bolts and arrows. Chel noticed coloured streaks in the Nort's dark hair, thin stripes bleached and dyed the same flame-red as Loveless. He wondered if they'd exchanged alchemical recipes.

'It is ready. We must test it!'

Lemon looked up. 'Oh, aye, what's ready? What are we testing?'

The Nort shot her a derisive look. '*We* are testing my latest improvements to that dreadful tool you people call a crossbow.'

'Is that so? As it happens, I have a few ideas for an alternative mechanism—'

'And I'm sure they are very . . . *optimistic*, for someone of your intellectual capacity. Please leave this to people who know what they are doing.'

'Now just a moment—'

Whisper stood, graceful as ever, and offered Lemon an apologetic shrug, before scooping up a handful of the new bolts and shouldering her bow. She followed Kosh across the deck, to the fore mast where the Nort had assembled some rough targets. The vessel's crew kept a wide and wary distance as they passed.

Lemon watched them go. 'You know what, fuck her. She's a splinter in the sphincter, that one. Why in hells do we keep her around anyway?'

'Same as the rest of us, my friend,' Foss said sleepily, roused from his doze. 'She's occasionally useful. And it's not like she has anywhere else to go.'

143

'We could fling her over the side. That'd provide a fresh direction of travel.'

Chel rolled his stiff shoulder around in its socket. The thought of landfall, and the magnitude of what faced them, weighed on him with great suddenness, and he was feeling a sympathetic ache. 'Do you think . . .' he began. 'Do you think we can do it?'

'Do what?' Lemon scratched at her mound of hair, sending up a puff of dust into the breeze. 'Which part?'

'All of it. Defeat Corvel and his army of confessors. Put Tarfel on the throne. Save the kingdom. We tried to gather forces and overthrow a corrupt ruler once already, and look how that turned out.'

'Ah, but that was the Rau Rel and all their baggage. This time, *we're* in charge.'

Chel shot a glance back at the stern, where the argument had moved on to words spoken at some stage two years before. 'Good thing there's no baggage here.'

\* \* \*

'Pay attention to this, or we're doom-fucked from the off.' Loveless glared at each of them in turn, silencing even Lemon, pre-quip. Chel sighed inwardly. He much preferred Loveless when she wasn't trying to out-general Rennic, and vice versa. But then, he supposed, it really wasn't up to him, and the better the generalling, generally the better.

'Princeling, give them the summary,' she continued, with a flick of her head in Tarfel's direction. They had the stern to themselves now, the force of the latest altercation sending the crew to the ship's opposite end. Rennic watched from the rail, arms folded, eyes narrowed beneath thunderous brows.

Tarfel cleared his throat. His mood seemed a little brighter today, despite the bite of the winter breeze blowing over the ship. His cheeks were rosy and his lips chapped, but Chel hoped the voyage had gone some way to hardening the prince along his path. Shepherd knew, he'd need it.

'By now we're all aware of what we face. My brother yearns to restore the empire of our Taneru forebears, which he may well believe is his birthright. Thanks to the events of last autumn, he has already pacified the more troublesome parts of the north. He now sets his gaze upon the south – the free cities, the unruly lordlings, and the disputed territories. From there, he will make war upon our neighbours, the former imperial vassals: Shenak, Amistreb, Tokemia, and then across the sea. The Taneru spread their borders wide, and Corvel believes only equivalent conquest can return Vistirlar to its once glorious station.'

Loveless stepped forward again, acknowledging the prince with a nod. 'Corvel's strengths are obvious: the armies of religious fanatics that Vassad assembled, cheaper and more zealous than any comparable force; total control over the kingdom's hierarchy, again care of Vassad and the Rau Rel's cack-handed attempts to unseat him; and . . .' She flicked a glance up-deck, to where Kosh was worrying at her invention as she rearranged her targets. '. . . Rumours of new weapons, something that can change the face of warfare across the continent at a stroke.'

'But?' said Lemon. 'I mean, there's a but coming, eh? Cos if there wasn't, we'd all be hauling on the tiller right now and swinging this fucker around for places new.'

With a half-smile, Loveless unrolled a sheet of canvas,

by the look of it cut from excess sailcloth, and laid it out on the misty deck. It was the victim of much charcoal-marking and rubbing-out. Chel saw Rennic's jaw flex at its arrival.

'We expected him to spend the winter consolidating his forces, then begin his march at the first thaw. Thanks to nearly-queen Ruumi, we know he's already begun disbanding and absorbing the mercenary companies in the north, under pretext of redundancy or illegality. We also know that, come the first moon of spring, she will land a war-band in the south-west and sow chaos. That gives us just enough time to enact our strategy.'

'Aye, which is?'

'Corvel's forces are mighty but they're concentrated and poorly trained. And, as the princeling said, with too many opposing forces pulling him in all directions at the same time, he'll disintegrate. We're going to stoke some fires.'

She gestured to the canvas, on which Chel was almost able to discern meaning. 'First we go to the southern companies. The latest news from shore suggests they're not blind to this threat. They're holding an extraordinary council, and we're going to join it.'

'Let's hope it goes better than the last conclave we attended.'

'Lemon, don't make me punch your eye out the back of its socket.'

Chel raised a hand, then felt foolish. 'How are we going to join a mercenary council? They're not going to . . . Well, they're not going to let us in, are they?'

'They'll let me in,' Rennic growled from the rail. 'The bloated bastards owe me that much, and they know it.'

Loveless offered a smile as bright as it was artificial. 'Our friend Gar has served alongside, ridden with, crossed paths with or drunk in the same alehouse as just about every company man in existence. He knows everyone in question, whether he'd admit it or not. You see? Problem solved. Next, we rouse the free cities. I have contacts we can use. Some coordinated whispers, the right motivation, they'll do what we need.'

'Poppy-merchants and leaf-peddlers,' Rennic muttered.

'Contacts,' Loveless reiterated. 'Useful, important contacts. From there, we move east, via Tenailen. When Corvel's forces cross the Kharin river to come south, they'll have to travel over Lord Shirin's lands. He'll be itching to confront them.'

'The man's a weapons-grade imbecile.'

'That may well be in our favour. And he's not alone, there are other minor lords who just need the right push to fall into line.' Loveless brushed back her vivid hair. 'At last, we reach the territories. The tribes will be gathered at Finica for the festival, where our prince will make them an offer.'

Foss stirred. 'What kind of offer? The tribes aren't renowned for dealing much with outsiders . . . beyond raiding them, of course.' He made the sign of the crook.

Tarfel cleared his throat. 'Autonomy.'

'Are you serious, friend?'

He nodded. 'Every spring, the tribal peoples come storming out of their mountain redoubts in dribs and drabs in their raiding parties, and every year the border lords send mercenary companies back to pacify them. The cycle has repeated for a generation, and it's a pointless waste. Their tax base is virtually negligible as it is so why not recognize it officially?'

Loveless nodded. 'When they hear the free companies are no longer defending the foothills and that independence is on the table, they'll rise as one and come storming out of the mountains . . . just as Ruumi's reavers begin their action in the south-west. Uproar in the west, sedition in the south, rebellion in the east, and no mercenary support. Corvel will have to split his forces, then our turbulent lords and errant free companies can cut their lines and squeeze them to paste.'

She stood back, defiant, hopeful. Chel stared at the canvas. 'It sounds like it could work.'

He heard a soft *plink*, then the sound of splitting wood. He turned to see Kosh and Whisper up-deck. Whisper strode over to the fore mast to inspect something, then looked back with a giant grin and a big thumbs up. It seemed the improved crossbow was a success.

'And what of the north?' Rennic was off the rail, approaching them with heavy steps. 'Without pressure in the north, he can sit back, let our factions play themselves out. He must feel true panic for this to work.'

Another *plink* from behind. A tinny thunk, then the same split of wood. The experiments were proceeding well. Chel just hoped they weren't damaging the mast; the vessel's crew seemed to loathe their passengers more than enough already.

Loveless's eyes were on the Nort. 'There is another ally in waiting, when things erupt in the south. Denirnas lies fallow, the black ships yet choking its bay, blockading the north. If we can make the trip, skirt north as our enemies turn south, and return that little monster to her people . . . threaten witchfire at Corvel's defenders. Imagine the fresh panic across the north, across the wetlands, all the way to

Roniaman. And as the panic takes hold, we enter the capital with a select force, and this time we make no mistakes.' Chel saw her sharp look toward Rennic, its unstated meaning: *This time, you don't leave me outside.*

'You know the Norts aren't who I mean.'

Loveless's face became stone. 'I will not go to that place, not in wrath and never in supplication.'

Chel blinked. 'What? Where?'

'A renowned army and impregnable fortifications, Ell,' Rennic said, his eyes burning with intent. In Chel's experience, he only called Loveless 'Ell' when he was trying to be persuasive. 'No love lost between Corvel and the regime. As likely to feel threatened as any neighbour, as likely to raise arms. How can we not?'

'I *will* not go there.'

'How can you still be afraid—'

'You're the only coward here, Gar, to even think to—'

'Where are they talking about?' Chel mouthed to Lemon. She made a face, waved a hand. *Later.*

Rennic remained emphatic. 'We need something concrete in the north, Ell. Too much is in the balance here – if one faction falls, or fails to rise when we need them, the whole plan shakes apart. We'll be entering Roniaman in chains, our heads next for the pike road. Then Corvel and his confessors sweep the south, eradicate resistance, roll over the east on their way to the next conquest.'

The east. Barva. Suddenly Chel felt the tightness return to his chest, a squeezing of his ribcage. The confessor army would travel through his home. Would Sab be there, fists raised at their oncoming, crying defiance with her own partisans at her back? He shut his eyes against the thought.

'You all right, little man? Something you want to add?'

149

Everyone was looking at him. He swallowed, shook his head. 'Just . . . Just that we need to see this through. We need to do what's right.'

Loveless met his gaze. 'We will.'

Rennic cracked a weak grin. 'Or we don't get paid.'

'You know,' Lemon said, 'it's almost enough to make you miss friend Spider. Always reckoned he could get to anyone, that fella, with a plague beggar if necessary. Fancy we could have set him on Corvel and retired, eh?'

'Fuck Spider,' Rennic snarled.

'This is about more than just the man,' Loveless said, her eyes still on Chel. 'This is about the system, the engine. We have to pull it apart, or the next henchman down will simply pick up the reins.'

Tarfel coughed. 'What about those new weapons you mentioned? Do we have anything to worry about?'

Another *plink* from behind, followed by a great metal boom. A moment later, a small Nort's cheer.

Chel felt himself smile. 'Maybe we'll have some new weapons of our own.'

\* \* \*

It loomed over the river, sheets of pale stone, topped with delicate crenellations, wrapped around an elegant cylinder of gleaming masonry, its circumference dotted with evenly spaced towers. Most of the pennants flying overhead boasted the sigil of a pair of crossed keys; over the gatehouse at the bridge's end, a black flag flew. The whole thing struck Chel as more palace than stronghold, but the sheer number of curving walls that circled the rising mound on the far bank reassured him that for all its gaudiness, the building had at least once been planned with defence in mind.

He squinted at the black pennant over the distant gate-house, fluttering against the undulating silver sky. 'Black flag? Truce?'

'Aye, all welcome at the Gracechurch on this chilly morning,' Lemon muttered from beside him, where she worried at the packs on one of the new mules. 'Official fortress-residence of the Company of Keys.'

'Gracechurch? Are the Keys a religious order?'

She sniggered. 'Hardly. They just had the coin to buy the place off the nuns years ago, liked the name enough to keep it. Makes them feel all grand and special, the danglers. They love to host the other companies, rub their faces in it.'

'The other companies don't have fortress-residences?'

'Oh, aye, any company of charter size has a wee stack of stonework somewhere to call home, but few are as splendid as this. Most try to maximize their time in the field, after all – if you're not burning, you're not earning, as the saying goes.'

Chel's gaze slipped back to the bridge, busy with small knots of people heading into the fortress, some on foot, some mounted, all seemingly armed and armoured. Most were coming from the north road. Chel and his party were the only group approaching from the south. 'Looks like quite a turnout.'

'It's an Extraordinary Council of the Companies, wee bear, a chance to meet and greet and quaff with toffs. You'll have your free companies, your agencies, freelancers and contract folk, hunters and quiet'ners—'

'What are they?'

Lemon paused to bundle something into her arms. 'Well, the hunters find things, or people, right?'

'Yeah . . .'

'And the quiet'ners, well, make them go quiet.'

'I see.'

'Friend Spider did a lot of work in that vein before taking up with the company, I believe. Ah, there we go.' Lemon stepped away from the mule, arms draped with layered fabric, her boots crunching on the loose and broken stone of the road beneath the thin crust of churned snow.

'Lemon!' Loveless's voice rose sharp and angry from the mule's far side. 'Where the fuck is my sword?'

'All right, all right, got everything here.' Lemon peeled off the top few layers and held them out to the approaching Loveless. They were bundled over a short, flat scabbard. Loveless snatched back the weapon, and the fabric with it, cradling it to her chest like a lost child.

'Here you go, wee bear, get this on.'

'What is all this?'

'New gear! Boss let me use a bit of our southern windfall to spring for some replacements for our losses in previous misadventures. Need to look the part today: got to impress the movers and shakers within with our call to arms, get them on-side before Corvel turns up to squish them to goo. We'll be best received if we're nice and shiny, eh?'

He lifted the rest of the bundle from her arms. It was heavier than he expected, rings of riveted mail jingling hidden within the folds. He set it down on a guano-streaked rock and braced himself to change in the sharp wind.

'Hold on, *pièce de résistance*.' Lemon passed him a shining silk shirt, and held another out to Loveless.

'What's this for?'

'Stick it on underneath your gear, bearling, and hope you won't need it.'

'Eh? Why not?'

'Cos it's for making it easier to pull arrows out of you, should such occasion arise.'

'Oh.'

Loveless was staring at Lemon's proffer with undisguised suspicion.

'Where's it from?'

'It's come out the saddlebags, you just saw me fetch it.'

'You know what I mean, Lemon. What's its origin?'

'Aye, well, there's no way to be certain for sure—'

'Don't fucking lie to me, Lemon.'

'Ah, come on, just put the bugger on, will you? It's for your own good.'

Loveless stalked away, pulling the mail shirt over her head, leaving Lemon standing.

'Ah, fucken *hells*. Every time.'

'What's her problem?'

'For that, wee bear, we lack the hours in a day. She takes issue with northern silk is the summary.'

'Serican silk? Wait, was it Serica she was raging against on the boat?'

'Well, Arowan in particular, but aye, the Serican capital.'

'What does she have against it?'

Lemon scratched at her cheek, running a hand over her jaw as she pulled her mouth aside in thought. 'Well, you know I'm not one for intimating another's intimates . . .'

'So you've said. Repeatedly.'

'. . . but it strikes me that there's some history there the lady herself has no hunger to revisit.'

'You don't. Say.'

'Aye, no doubt she thinks she has her reasons. Great shame, though; Arowan's a real hub of industry and, er, scientific enquiry.' From somewhere beyond the mule came a derisive snort with a Nortish accent. '*Not* to mention the creative arts. Lots of your favourite songs probably came from there. Now get dressed, will you? Do your Lemon a favour.'

Shaking his head at the continued uselessness of Lemon's answers, Chel pulled on the shirt. The silk was sleek and cold against his shivering skin. He laced as fast as he could before his fingers began to numb, then threw on the padded linen overcoat and Lemon's fancy new mail over the top. He was at least warmer with his new layers, especially once he got his cloak back around his shoulders, although he felt mule-wide and no less cumbersome. The mule gave him a quick side-eye, as if registering his presence for the first time, then flicked an ear and went back to staring into the middle distance.

'Everyone ready?'

Rennic looked edgy, eyes darting, feet jittering. It took Chel a moment to realize that he was excited. His gaze kept returning to the bridge and the waiting fortress, its black flag snapping in the breeze.

'How's the gear?'

'Yeah, pretty good, I think.'

'Good, good. Looks good.' Rennic drifted off, turning his staff in his hands. 'Loveless put hers on?'

'She wouldn't wear the silk, but—'

He threw up a hand like this was expected. 'Let's get moving.'

Chel fell into step with Lemon as they crunched down

the narrow road toward the bridge. He gazed again at the shining fortress, shielding his eyes from the cloud-washed glare. 'It's a hell of a structure, isn't it?'

'Aye, well, they've added to it as they've gone, of course.'

'Of course.'

'But you're right, there's a lot of coin to be made in the contract market.' Lemon flicked a glance toward Rennic, who walked beside Whisper with his shoulders hunched. 'Or at least there should be.'

Chel rubbed at one eye, watering in the day's grey glare. The closer they got, the more ornate the pale stonework became, the more intricate the carvings on every visible pillar and block. 'I get it, I just . . . I didn't think there was *that* much coin.'

'Depends on your outlook, cub.' Loveless was beside him, new mail belted beneath a fetching cloak. 'Economically speaking, maintaining a standing army is for chumps. All those fighting types, kept away from land and loom, needing to be fed, armoured and housed all year round, whether there's fighting work to be done or not. Makes more sense to rent a few hundred spears when the occasion dictates, no?' She paused, her gaze slipping away down the river's curve, and ran a hand through her lively pink hair. 'Until recently, anyway.'

'Assuming your opponent isn't offering a smidge more for the same forces, of course,' Lemon chipped in, still leading the mule with one hand while she gestured with the other. 'May present occasion for embarrassment there.'

'At that stage, we're talking a different kind of forces, Lem.'

'Oh, aye?'

'*Market* forces.'

Chel struggled to keep up. 'So, we alert the companies that Corvel is coming for them, they join our side and fight against the confessors when they arrive?'

'Tipping the companies is about more than just manpower, cub,' Loveless said, shortening her stride to fall back in step with him. 'Their primary purpose, these days at least, is policing the more unruly parts of the kingdom, those places where the crown or the local Names struggle to keep their grip.' Her eyes crinkled with a wicked smile. 'Remove the companies, and there's a lot of bottled chaos just bursting to get out into the world: free cities, rebel lords, hill tribes. Our next ports of call after today.'

'Might other companies not step in? New ones?'

Lemon waved a dismissive hand. 'Upstarting a new company is no idle stroll, wee bear, take it from me. Recruitment, training, overheads, equipment investment, then of course there's securing the gigs, which are at risk themselves. Now, I can see the merit of operating a smaller scale, perhaps temporarily, perhaps over the longer term, agency level you might say. Specialized, boutique. It's all about how you position yourself in the market. Of course, I pitched it to the big man,' she waved a hand toward the head of their column, 'but he's more of a, uh, solid concepts kind of fella.' She shook her head, sending her hair waving. 'I'm saying there's merit in serving a niche, that's all.'

'Lemon,' came Foss's rumble from behind them, 'what in His name are you talking about?'

'Aye, right, never mind.'

Whisper and Rennic had reached the grand pillars that marked the start of the bridge's span, Tarfel a pace behind, his new boots already splashed with slush-mud. The river churned some way below them, its flow still fast and white despite the snow streaking the steep banks, its rush blanketing the surroundings with a subtle hiss. It looked very, very cold.

A handful of heavily armoured guards stood at the bridge pillars, the crossed keys motif embossed on their breastplates gleaming in the pale winter sun. Before them, a liveried flunky raised a hand. 'Affiliation?'

Rennic didn't hesitate. 'Black Hawk Company.'

From over Chel's shoulder came Lemon's muttering to Foss. 'All I'm saying, big man, is that there's something to be said for reputation management.'

The flunky gave his list a cursory glance. 'Never heard of you.'

'We're new.'

'Affiliated?'

Rennic rubbed at his bearded chin with a clenched fist. 'Affiliation status, uh, pending. We're awaiting confirmation.'

The flunky raised an eyebrow. 'Then you can *await* out here.'

Whisper sighed, put a hand on Rennic's arm then signalled something in a flash of her hands. With visible reluctance, Rennic rolled up the sleeve of his new mail, revealing the prodigious tattoos that coated his upper arm. 'Previous affiliations withstanding?' he growled.

The flunky's other eyebrow shot up. 'What did you say your name was?'

'Rennic.'

'I'll add you to the list, Master Rennic. Welcome back to the Gracechurch.'

Rennic only grunted as he rolled down his sleeve, then went to step past. The flunky's gaze shifted to Whisper and Tarfel. 'Affiliation?' he said.

Rennic stepped back. From Chel's vantage, he was beginning to steam. 'They're with me.'

'And as you're no doubt aware, Master Rennic, and for obvious reasons, each recognized affiliate may send two representatives to the council, each with an assistant. Which of these is your assistant?'

Chel quickened his pace, reaching them just as Whisper was near hauling Rennic back from the man. 'You said they'd let you in,' Chel snapped, his tone midway between scorn and accusation.

'And they will, little man. That's not the fucking problem. Me and one more does us no good.'

Tarfel raised a nervous hand. 'I could declare myself? Under the Treaty of Kelsuus, they—'

Loveless had joined them. 'Won't matter a perfumed shit, your highness – they're an armoured risk pool, not a sovereign power. And declaring yourself out here might be inviting unhealthy scrutiny of the bladed variety.'

Chel shot her an anxious glance. 'And declaring himself at the council won't?'

She returned his look with a disarming grin. 'Different rules. Once he's across the bridge, he's a guest of the council. They're bound by both the black flag and professional etiquette, for as long as the council lasts.'

'So he's safe across the bridge.'

She nodded.

'But not here.'

The prince met his gaze with watery eyes. 'I'm willing to take the risk, Vedren. I'll have to present myself to potential hostility before long, and it might as well be at a time that I can do some good.'

'Then we'd better get you across that bridge, Tarf. You may have to be Rennic's assistance.'

Whisper signed something to the others, her eyes upon them patient but insistent. Chel missed most of it, and didn't dare request a repetition.

'She's right,' Loveless murmured. 'The two of you can qualify under former affiliations. The Gracechurch remembers its own.'

'That only gets four of us in,' Rennic replied. He shot frequent looks toward the flunky, who was conspicuously studying his list a few paces away. Chel estimated the big man's mood at only one or two notches above wanton bloodshed.

'What about you, Foss and Lemon?' he asked Loveless. 'You're all professionals, right? Don't you count for this affiliation thing?'

This time, her smile was sad. 'I'm afraid my professional affiliations have been less than public, cub. I won't be on any list of theirs, and my arms are bare. I can't speak for the other two, but four is all they'll permit, so four will have to do.'

'Who's the . . .' Chel began, then found all eyes on him. 'Oh. Right.'

She patted him on the arm. 'You'd only whine like a spurned pup if he went in without you.'

'I resent that!'

'Resent it from the other side of the bridge. Get moving.'

Rennic muscled his way between them. 'This remains a shitty turn,' he said, one finger wagging. 'We all need to

159

cross the river to reach Merenghi. The next crossing could be days north of here.'

Loveless offered a brilliant smile in reply. 'They said it was for the duration of the council, yes? We'll come across the minute it finishes. Or, worst case, we'll meet you at the next crossing in a couple of days. Worried about fucking it all up without my supervision, Gar?'

Rennic took a long breath, his attention on the rough bank beside the road. Small, dirty green flashes of growth were visible between the snow-strewn mud. 'We don't have time to dick about, spring is around the corner.' He rubbed at one eye. 'You know the plan, I know the plan. We'll cover this side of the river; you and the others do what's necessary on the other. Meet outside the Bridge House in time for the first moon, then we'll cross the Kharin together before the south goes up like that so-called brandy barrel in Black Rock.'

Loveless pursed her lips. 'Fine. But you'd better not be late. We won't wait.'

'Likewise,' he growled back, then cuffed Chel around the bad shoulder. 'Gird yourself, little man, you're about to experience the apotheosis of the free company experience.'

'The what?'

'Enough horseshit to fill an ocean. Foss, Lemon! Stick with Ell, keep an eye on the Nort, and we'll meet up at the Bridge House. Foss! Hoy!'

Foss ambled over, brows drawn low. Behind him, Lemon was moaning about missing out on showing off her new gear. 'Sorry, boss. I thought I saw something, up on that ridge.'

'What?' Rennic had grabbed one of the mules and was rummaging through its packs.

'A rider.'

'Lots of riders around today, Fossy.'

'I know, boss. Just this one . . . this one looked a little . . . red.'

Rennic's rummaging ceased, and he straightened slowly. 'Take the others and get back to high ground. Stay off the roads for now. We'll see you before the first moon.'

'Evil days, boss.'

Rennic yanked the mule's rope. 'Little man, get your prince across that bridge *now*.'

# ELEVEN

Whisper strode across the bridge, Rennic leading the mule behind her, while Tarfel trotted alongside. They were the last people on the bridge now. The weak sun was high somewhere in the leaden northern sky, although the vicious wind that blew across the bridge robbed it of any warmth it might otherwise have offered. Chel quickened his steps again, telling himself that the thudding of his pulse in his ears was only from the speed at which they were crossing the foaming river, and nothing to do with the sharp, fluttery feeling in his gut.

'Do you think there really was a rider?' He kept his voice low as he caught up with Rennic, working hard not to look back over his shoulder at the dwindling bank.

'Maybe. Maybe not. Nothing we can do about it now except get inside.'

'Are they going to be all right?'

'They'll be fine.' He didn't look back either.

'Are you s—'

'Shepherd's tits, little man, they'll be just grand, understand?

162

They'll be exemplary. They're professionals. Despite whatever lists that ink-fucker on the bridge might keep.'

Hushed but not reassured, Chel followed the others into the sumptuous might of the gatehouse.

\*\*\*

'Four Wars! Eastern Eagle! You're really still alive.'

A broad man in a long, dark coat was approaching them across the stable-yard, a powerful dappled horse tied up behind him. Three spearmen waited beside it, weapons loose against their shoulders but angles precise. Their livery was mottled with stars. He was northern, a decent size, passing Rennic's shoulder in height, his girth wrapped in a thick belt beneath the long coat. His beard and hair were short, wiry and more salt than pepper, his smile wide and seemingly genuine.

Rennic grunted. 'Fest. It's been a while.'

The two men clasped hands, although Chel detected reserve on Rennic's side. The newcomer's exposed arm boasted almost as many regimental tattoos as Rennic's.

'You got fat, I see.'

'Ah, the perils of a well-run company.' Fest grinned again, this time his eyes not quite so sparkly. 'You've kept your narrow bones though, eh?'

'Most of them.'

'Heard you'd struck out on your own,' Fest said, scanning the three others. 'Is this your company?'

Rennic bared his teeth. 'Plenty more waiting across the river. You're here for the council?'

Fest affected surprise. 'There's a council here? Today?' He smiled again, and this time Chel watched closely to see if it reached his eyes. 'Of course, of course. They couldn't start the thrice-damned thing without me. You coming inside?'

'Of course. Little man, tie up the mule.'

\*\*\*

The great hall of the Gracechurch more than matched its exterior for opulence. The distant ceiling was vaulted and panelled, rich paintwork vying with thick bands of gilt. The high walls around boasted frescoes and statues of what Chel guessed were past company captains. There seemed to be more than he'd expected. He was at least grateful for the fires burning in each of the room's great hearths, even if the central fire-pit did rather obscure his view of the raised dais at the hall's end.

The room was busy. As Lemon had suggested, the place was packed with armed and armoured types, sitting and standing in knots or apart in ones and twos. Boisterous laughter echoed from the thick stone walls, but the louder it got, the more Chel detected its false edge. Even the affiliates affecting the most jovial greetings were keeping their distance from each other, and the room reeked of mistrust.

'Where do we go?' he hissed to Whisper. Rennic had forged ahead with Fest and his men, and Chel had lost sight of him in the press. He was keeping Tarfel pinned to his side. 'How do we ensure the prince can speak?'

She signed back, the room's volume at least not impeding their communication. *Don't worry. Follow me.*

Chel did as he was told, dragging the cloaked and hooded figure of Tarfel behind him. He found himself wondering, as they slipped through the press of rich and dangerous figures to the hall's far side, what was Whisper's history? Rennic wore his on his sleeves and in his rage, but Whisper seemed to have both more to say and less inclination to say it, her lack of speech notwithstanding. She'd had no problems at the bridge, she knew her way around a mercenary council, and she alone seemed able to mediate between Rennic and Loveless in their rich and varied disputes. He resolved to find out more about her, just as soon as he got a moment. Lemon had said that each company's business was their own, but he was willing to risk at least asking some questions.

Rennic found them just as the room began to quiet, in that self-reinforcing way a pre-event hubbub ends. People were taking seats where they could find them. 'Agenda's tight,' Rennic muttered as he reached them, 'but I've twisted some arms. Princeling will speak.'

Chel looked from Rennic to Tarfel and back. The young prince seemed even paler in the flickering light of the hall, his skin damp with sweat in the firelight. 'Did you announce him?'

'Not exactly.'

Chel met Tarfel's eye. 'Are you ready to speak, Tarf?'

The prince nodded, but said nothing.

The council began. Chel was immediately struck by both the similarities to and the differences from the conclave of the Rau Rel. It was organized and polite, perhaps kept civil by the weight of the history in the walls around them, or the fact that nearly everyone in the room bar Chel and his companions was very heavily armed. At least there was no chance of Spider gate-crashing this one.

During the opening formalities, Chel did his best to look around without betraying himself too obviously. As Lemon had said, there was clearly a lot of coin to be made in professional soldiery, but from the look of those gathered in the hall it was far from evenly distributed. On the dais, their host, the grey-bearded captain-general of the Company of Keys was speaking, dressed in glittering formal robes with a jewelled scabbard belted at his waist. Beyond him sat the other council members, most in armour, and most of the amour exquisite. The first of them to speak was a woman of around Rennic's age, well-kept and mirthless, her mail dark, breastplate and bracers black and glossy. Her black hair was cut in the coastal fashion, cropped short on one side and tightly bound with small golden rings. Her visible ear bristled with more gold, a jewelled choker peeking from the rise of her breastplate at her neck. The breastplate, Chel noted, was embossed with the image of a radiant sun.

'Saleh,' Rennic murmured from beside him. 'Captain of the Black Suns.'

Chel kept his voice low. 'Who's that one at the end? The shabby looking one?' The woman was slouched in her chair, legs extended and boots crossed in open indifference to the pronouncements of the other council members. She was small and narrow, far younger than the others; the tribal scarring on her cheeks, split like grasping fingers, marked her as Bakani. She seemed more representative of the other half of the room, those without the gleaming armour or bejewelled weaponry. Perhaps that explained the fury in her eyes.

'Don't know.' Uncertainty entered his voice. 'But she's wearing the sigil of Gold Peak. What the fuck happened to Lucky Pel?'

Chel was about to make a comment about luck running out when the young woman was called on and pushed herself to her feet. There was a large man standing behind her, another Bakani at first glance. He had the look of a strong, silent type, his hard eyes looking out over the hall for any hint of a challenge.

'Nadej, I speak for the Peak,' the young woman growled. Her eyes had an unstable, trembling quality, as if the effort of keeping them still and focused were greater than anyone should have to bear. Her fingers twitched at her belt, which, Chel noted, sported an impressive Rennic-esque array of knives. 'Can we get the fuck on with this?'

Rennic chuckled. 'A woman after my own heart.'

Whisper made a little snort of laughter. *Be careful what you wish for.*

The captain-general of the Keys, with a disapproving glance at the re-slouching Nadej, announced the first item on the agenda: The Situation in the North, and Are We at Risk? To hear the mercenary captains tell of it, their former rivals, the northern companies, had outlived their usefulness now that hostilities in the north were concluded, and been forcibly disbanded before they turned to structured banditry. There seemed to be a general nodding around the hall at this.

Saleh of the Black Suns added that the northern companies had been a vulgar, treacherous lot, more interested in plunder than steady income and contractual stability, and had long darkened the name of professional soldiery in that part of the kingdom. There was a reason, she added, with a pointed look at Nadej, that every northern company tried to come south the moment they could scrape together the wherewithal.

Nadej's response was not recorded in the official account. Chel waited for the counterpoint, assuming this was a matter to be debated. Instead, the next speaker merely agreed. The situation in the south was completely different, and come the thaw the southern tribes would still come rampaging from their mountain holds, certain barons would decide their tax burden was too heavy, and the rebel cities of the south would overstep their pretence of independence. Not to mention, nodded another, that some of those rebel cities were using their newfound wealth handsomely in maintaining that independent pretence. One by one, the captains and affiliates gave themselves reasons to avoid concern.

'What is this?' Chel murmured to the others, trying to keep Tarfel from hearing. 'What's going on?'

Whisper shook her head with a wry grimace.

'An exercise in reassuring themselves,' Rennic muttered.

The captain-general cleared his throat and looked out over the hall. 'Fest tells me we have had a request for a special address. Normally there would be a place for this kind of thing but I feel—'

Rennic stood forward from the wall. 'Princeling, this is your moment. You ready?'

'Um, well—'

'Good.' Rennic pushed Tarfel forward and into the glare of the hall's attention. 'Prince Tarfel Merimonsun,' Rennic bellowed, silencing the hall at a stroke. In the quiet, Chel heard the small, significant sounds of a hundred hands being placed delicately on a hundred weapons.

'Fuck off,' came Nadej's voice from the dais. 'The runt prince is twice-dead.'

Tarfel looked suddenly small, hunched and alone. Chel swallowed. Then the prince straightened and pulled back his hood. His gaze was clear-eyed and defiant.

'I assure you, I am very much alive, and I come to you with a warning.' With a flash of his signet, he began walking around the hall toward the dais, his voice initially scratchy but carrying over the murmurs that had begun in all corners. 'You believe you are safe from the fate that befell your northern comrades.'

He reached the dais and stepped up.

'You are wrong.'

Nadej went to speak again, but was waved to silence by the captain-general. Tarfel was on the dais now, before the chairs, facing out over the hall. 'My brother the king,' he called out, his voice echoing over Chel's head, 'intends to replace you, each and every one. The only barrier is time.'

'Horseshit!' Nadej could control herself no longer. 'If this bleached bastard really is the prince, we should carve him here and now and send the strips to his brother. That ought to guarantee some contracts!'

'Nadej, be silent,' snapped Saleh of Black Suns, she of the glossy armour. 'All in attendance are safe within these walls.' She turned to Tarfel. 'Please continue, but don't dawdle. Your highness.'

'I shall be direct. My brother pretends to empire, a union of church and crown and a conquest to restore the borders of Taneru times. The existence of the free companies is an obstacle to this. You have seen him remove the northern companies, absorb them into his army of churchmen. Now that the north is under his control, he will turn his attention to the south, and one by one, you will fall.'

Chel was impressed with his demeanour, his ability to address this hostile and sceptical collection of mercenary captains without becoming flustered or overawed. Perhaps this was the sort of thing that being a prince prepared you for.

'The situation in the south is completely—' began one voice from the hall.

'Not to him,' Tarfel shot back. 'You are looking for logic where none exists. He dreams of empire, and in the service of this dream you must all be consumed.'

He's enjoying this, Chel thought. Despite their murderous reputations, none of the mercenaries has ever seen him weeping and afraid, only as the strutting young man before them, and he knows it. Already he could feel doubt in the room.

Saleh's hand rested on her chin. 'You speak of our replacement. This is the fabled army of red confessors? Farmyard bullies, ill-trained and equipped, a rabble of sackcloth fanatics. Look around you, Prince Tarfel Merimonsun. You address the cream of professional soldiery—' Chel covered Rennic's snort of derision with a cough '—and our capabilities are second to none. Even with a few of our former northern sistren to swell their ranks, their numbers will not touch ours.'

Tarfel stood his ground. 'Only if they are combined. Each company alone cannot stand. And for each company absorbed, their numbers grow.'

'This is preposterous. Why would a professional of good standing choose servitude in—'

'Because it is not a choice!' Tarfel was pink-cheeked now, glowing in the firelight. 'Despite what you may have heard, the crown is not making contractual offerings. The companies are disbanding because the alternative is anni-hilation. They are joining his ranks because they would otherwise face ruin or death.'

Saleh's brow was furrowed deep, and a hush fell in the hall. 'How can this be so? Have the bullies cavalry, have they steel armour and sword-craft? Will they learn the crossbow? The free companies are free because we choose to be so, because we work beyond simple ties of oaths and servitude. We are honed like—'

Tarfel fixed her with a baleful glare, and to Chel's astonishment she fell silent. 'Times have changed, company captains. You must open your eyes to what is coming. My brother has already begun his work, and he will not stop. Why would he stop? Because you wish him to?' He swept around, his cloak swinging dramatically as he turned. 'Many of you will already have received overtures, couched in familiar language, promising a new way of working. Do not be deceived. You will be absorbed, and your lives as you know them will be no more.'

This prompted some armoured shuffling from those around Chel. Muttered conversations sprang up; someone nearby him murmured, 'I did hear the northern lot were offered terms . . . the first ones, anyway . . .'

'—had an offer, via an intermediary, but you know, it all looked—'

'—thought it was just us, made it sound—'

Saleh had risen to her feet. By now she looked deeply disturbed, lines etched hard around her face. 'If you speak truly, Tarfel Merimonsun, you speak of abomination. We have long-term contracts—'

'He will void them.' Tarfel spoke quietly now, and the hall hushed once more to listen. 'He will call you marauders and parasites, outlaws and rebels, and one by one you will be eliminated. No one will come out to fight for you, not jealous lords, nor loyal subjects. Who, after all, will mourn your passing?'

Nadej was still slouched in her chair. 'Why tell us all this, ghost prince? Assuming there's truth to your ravings, which I doubt. What's your margin?'

Tarfel tried the baleful gaze on her, but her twitching stare more than matched his. The muscles on her jaw were pronounced. 'No one will fight for you,' he repeated, 'unless you fight for each other. You must agree a common strategy now, and act in concert when he comes.'

'We *must* do whatever the fuck we want,' Nadej snarled back. 'I did not take control of the Peak to have some floppy-haired sap give me commands.'

'Then I suggest you coordinate your plans with your fellow captains, because worse commands than mine are coming your way.'

Rennic chuckled at that. 'Doing well, our princeling, eh? Didn't think he had it in him.'

Chel offered a nod and a weak smile. His palms were sweating. He still had no idea which way the hall would go.

Saleh looked to be wavering. 'And what would you have us do? Rise up, march on Roniaman before winter's end?'

Tarfel shook his head. 'The reverse. Withdraw. Abandon your posts, retreat to your strongholds. Let the crown face what follows. And when you see its back, strike as one.'

'Void our own contracts?'

'They are already void; you merely await the paperwork.'

'Then attack the king's army?'

Tarfel met Saleh's gaze and held it. 'You will not be alone when you do. Which is more than can be said for the alternative.'

Chel nudged Rennic. 'I think she's going for it. That's good, right?'

He nodded. 'If Saleh swings, she'll carry a lot with her. Black Suns are huge.'

Nadej was getting to her feet. 'Where's the fucking—'

A flunky rushed to the dais – not the same one as had been at the bridge, Chel noted – and whispered something urgent to the captain-general of the Keys. He stiffened. 'Captains!' he bellowed across the hall. 'An armoured host approaches.'

The hall fell into uproar, both Saleh and the captain-general shouting for quiet. 'A *modest* host,' he added when the volume had dropped a notch, 'but clad in red robes.' He finished with a meaningful glance at Tarfel.

At once, the hall began to empty, the mercenaries streaming out through the wide doors. 'What's happening? Chel asked. 'Where are they going?'

Rennic's gaze was distant, his brows lowered. 'Battlements. Grab the princeling. Seems the Foss might have been right about that rider after all.'

\* \* \*

Not everyone was heading for the battlements. The stable-yard was teeming with activity as dozens of figures dragged their horses clear, mounted and made for the bridge. Chel hurried along beside the prince. 'Well done, Tarf. That was . . . that was really good.'

Tarfel's cheeks were flushed, his breath coming hard, but his eyes were wide with elation. 'Do you think so, Vedren? Do you think they believed me?'

'Even if they weren't all the way convinced, whatever

is across the bridge may well have nudged things our way.'

'Four Wars!' As they crossed the yard, Fest appeared once more, as if he'd been waiting in the shadows. 'Looks like someone tipped the big bad king to our little gathering of southern captains. Wasn't you, was it?'

Rennic grunted and shook his head, continuing his path toward the stairway at the yard's end. Chel and the others followed, although Chel stepped a little closer to the prince.

'Not joining us in riding out? Facing down our foe, or running to the hills?' Fest tapped the side of his nose. 'Although I understand the back gate is open, if you put a spurt on.' He diverted to his dappled mount and swung himself into the saddle. 'Be seeing you, Four Wars. Happy campaigning!' With that, he rode for the gate, his spearmen in formation riding after.

Rennic turned to watch him go. 'Prick,' he muttered. 'Let's see what's out there.'

\* \* \*

Shafts of sunlight had cracked the silver canopy of cloud, narrow streaks of gold drifting across the snow-streaked landscape. The battlements were busy, but not packed; it triggered memories of Denirnas Port for Chel, of the arrival of the black ships of the Norts all those months before, and the witchfire assault that had followed. His fingers trembled with familiar foreboding.

The new force was approaching over the ridge that Foss had marked, coming from the north-east. A narrow column, maybe a few hundred in number, marching on foot, with heavy wagons at their rear. At the head of the column came two riders, one huge on a plodding beast that looked better suited to dray work than battle, the second smaller, but astride a magnificent charger, and dressed from head to foot in gleaming golden armour.

Tarfel gasped. 'It's Corvel. He's here.'

'And he brought Brother Hurkel and friends,' Chel added, feeling the trembling reach his jaw. 'How did they find us?'

Whisper was beside them, hands moving, gesturing to Tarfel. The prince nodded. 'I don't think they were looking for us, but they reached the same conclusion we did. The free companies are a risk.'

'Have they come to negotiate? Surely that's too small a force to take on "the cream of professional soldiery".'

Rennic grunted. 'Depends what else is over that ridge.'

Riders were crossing the bridge, supported by liveried infantry in the colours of the Keys. Most of the riders, on reaching the gatehouse, took to the north road and rode hard out of view. Chel was shocked.

'They're running? They're not heading out to face the confessors?'

Rennic grimaced. 'To their mind, it's not their fight, not if they can get away from it. Nothing a mercenary hates more than unfunded violence.'

'Do we head for the bridge too? The others are still on the far bank, we could catch them up, bring them across.'

Whisper pointed to where a group in shabby armour loitered near the bridge's end, just outside the stronghold. *Look. Not friends.*

'Nadej.' Chel peered down. 'And the rest of the Gold Peak delegation, presumably. What are they doing there?'

Whisper gestured again. *Waiting for Tarfel.*

'Five hells,' Chel breathed. 'You mean . . .'

Rennic nodded. 'The moment we step back on the bridge, our hospitality is at an end. I'd say there's a good chance that Nadej intends to collect our princeling to take to his brother.' He sucked air through his teeth. 'Can't blame her for direct thinking.'

'What do we do? If we try to cross the bridge, we end up tangling with Nadej and anyone else who fancies following her lead. And if Corvel isn't here to parley . . . Modest force or otherwise, if he lays siege and we're stuck here, our plan withers on the vine.'

Rennic's teeth were bared. 'We're missing something. Corvel's blade-sharp, we've learnt that the hard way. He would not be here in person if he didn't feel he had the force to make his point to his audience.'

'And what's that?'

Rennic's gnarled fingers gripped the stone of the battlement. 'I'm not sure, but it seems fair hazard he's here to put the waking fear into every mercenary company that might otherwise have thought to face him. And if that motley bunch of confessors looks *modest* to us, it's because he knows something we don't.' He pushed back from the wall. 'We need to get out of here. Immediately.'

Chel swallowed. 'The back gate that Fest mentioned? Can we get out that way?'

The big man's gaze flicked to Whisper, who gave a soft nod.

'Let's go.'

* * *

The men were waiting for them at the rear gate, the pair tucked in behind two ornate pillars with their knives drawn.

Unfortunately for their attempt, Rennic had been more than expecting them. As the first stepped out, he was carried from his feet by a roaring charge, his helmeted head smashed back against the gleaming flagstones. Two arrows punched through his companion as he lunged to intercede. The first man's throat was cut before he knew what had hit him.

Rennic was getting to his feet as Chel and Tarfel crept around the corner, Chel still leading the mule. He nodded at the second man, from whom Whisper was removing her arrows. 'Thanks, Whisp. Don't know what I'd do without you.'

Chel now rarely voiced his disapproval of the big man's cavalier attitude to taking lives, but his feelings must nonetheless have been evident from his expression.

'Yes, little man, that was necessary,' Rennic growled, wiping his knife clean. 'So hammer down that gas-hole.'

Chel gave the fresh corpses a sad look. They were not well turned out, one mail shirt between them, rusted and part-rotted. 'Nadej's people?'

'Maybe. Or enterprising freelancers.' He paused. 'Or something else.'

A clatter of armour echoed from the hallway's end. 'We'd better get out of here before the guards show. I'm pretty sure you just broke the rules of hospitality.'

'What? They started it.'

'Let's *go*.'

\* \* \*

They ran, Tarfel bobbing white-knuckled on the mule, until they were many hills away and out of sight of the Gracechurch. Only then did Whisper slow her pace and allow them to catch their breath. Rennic used most of his to let out a howl at the silvery sky.

'What, what is it?' Chel slapped at his arm, still bent double in recover. 'Are you trying to bring the wolves on us? Lemon's not here to brain them with her hammer.'

'The plan's fucked, little man,' Rennic roared, kicking at a heap of loose earth, sending it spraying down the hillside. 'King Corvel of Fuck-Town has come west already, our band are split either side of the river, the wrong people in the wrong places, and we've got barely three weeks before Ruumi lands her reavers. We can't get everywhere in that time!'

Whisper had one hand raised, then placed it slowly on his shoulder. She followed it with a quick set of signs. Chel was fairly sure he saw 'trust' in there.

Rennic took a long breath. 'Right. Right. They know what they're doing. We do our part, they do theirs.'

Tarfel was looking back, his nose wrinkled. 'Can anyone smell burning?'

The sun was already getting low in the north-western sky, but the eastern horizon behind them had a curious glow to it. They stood in silence for a moment, ears cocked against the wind's soft moan. It sounded a little like . . . screaming.

Chel shivered. 'Let's keep moving'.

# TWELVE

The walls of the city rose like teal tombstones from a pallid landscape, its snow-coat torn and bristling with brown, stubby growth, parts worn clean away in great ugly stripes. A handful of peasants tilled in the fields before the walls, a couple trying to drive an ox-plough over the rocky ground, others spreading fresh muck and marl from a steaming cart, their flimsy shovels bending with each stinking load. Unseen animals lowed and stamped in the shack-like barns that nestled at the feet of the looming walls, while poultry pecked at the crusty earth in pens surrounding them. Occasional guards, watchmen most likely, paced the ramparts between blocky turrets, the steam of their breath rising into the silver morning, merging and lost. A knot of mail-coated heavies, their dark colours emblazoned with a silver many-petalled flower, stood before the great gatehouse, jostling and menacing any who tried to enter or leave the city. The same silver flower adorned the long pennants that fluttered from the turrets, their points curling and snapping in the cold breeze.

'Merenghi is the closest thing to a free city left in this

179

part of the world,' Rennic said as if reading Chel's thoughts as he gazed down at the city across the hollow. 'Loveless reckons there are people here who could be of use.'

Over the city wall, a looming blue curtain of dark stone, poked a dark, corrugated church, seeming oddly squat from their hillside elevation, its angles diminished. Around it lay slums, heaving and smoking, and beyond the other districts of the city, rooflines and construction varying by area, punctuated by the great erections of blue-grey stone that littered the city, the towers, the temples, the blocks. It dawned on Chel that nowhere did he see any of that pale, northern stone so prized by their Taneru forebears. Merenghi was its own.

Chel looked beyond the walls, at the distant hill that rose behind the dark block of the city, wreathed in swirls of morning mist and the shimmer of the city's emissions. Through the haze, he picked out tiered stockade walls and terraced gardens, dotted with domed buildings, grander structures at the hill's summit lost in low cloud. It seemed both part of the city and apart from it, overlooking it and distinct in appearance and construction . . . overseeing it.

'And what do you think?' he said.

'I think our options are sorely fucking limited. There are three other townships on the list after this place, all smaller, all colder, and I don't know a bastard in any of them.'

'How do we get in? The gate guards take a pretty friendly interest in the passing traffic.' He watched as one of the mailed heavies at the gate emptied out a trader's hand-cart and kicked the contents through the frozen slush of the roadway. Beyond them, a group of robe-clad pilgrims of some kind were remonstrating with another guard as he pored over what seemed to be a blackened tree trunk lashed to a donkey cart.

'Don't fret, little man, there's a system. The right words in the right ears, a greasing of palms, a little light off-market commerce and we'll be through with no questions asked.'

Chel's mouth pulled to one side in an expression of wry scepticism. 'You sound like Lemon. Does that mean you don't know what you're doing?'

Rennic bristled. 'Get fucked. See that cluster of huts over there, round the wall? We go there, ask for a specific name, exchange some of our remaining coin for a little leaf, do the handshake on the guards at the gate and gambol through like lambs. Understand?'

'We bribe the guards with leaf? Why not just give them the coin?'

Rennic shook his head, a little light in his eyes. 'Bribing an agent of the city is a capital offence, little man. But if they were to discover contraband and confiscate it in performance of their duties, well, they'd simply be doing their job, wouldn't they?'

Chel groaned. 'And I suppose the leaf makes its way back to the folk in the huts in fairly short order, ready for another go-around?'

Rennic cuffed his shoulder. 'Count yourself lucky, little man. If the stuff were fresh, we could be strung from the battlements for bumping the wrong person. The City Wards come down pretty hard on anyone engaging in the medicinal trade within the walls.'

'The who?'

'The Wards.' He nodded at the settlement on the hill overlooking the city. 'Merenghi's proprietors. Now can we get moving? I'm freezing my tits off.' He turned in the direction of the huts, some hundred strides around the span of the walls from the gatehouse. Chel saw odd shuffles of movement within them, a suggestion of lean and hungry figures inside. The more he stared, the less he liked them.

Tarfel tapped at Rennic's shoulder. 'Is it safe? Where we're going.'

The big man's eyes were wide and incredulous. 'Safe, princeling? I doubt there's a square foot in this corner of the kingdom you could call safe. Maybe if we dug a pit deep enough, but then the water would get in . . .'

'If it's not *safe*,' Chel said, 'should we really be bringing Tarfel along? I'm guessing there's no mercenary law of hospitality in play down there.'

Rennic nodded. 'That'd be a fair guess.'

'So you and Whisper go and sort this leaf out, the prince and I stay out here?'

'Fuck that, little man, the two of you'd be fatally mauled by rogue marmots the moment my back was turned. If anyone stays out with him, it's Whisp. At least then he'd be in safe hands.'

Whisper offered an apologetic shrug.

'Hey!' Chel could hear the pitch of his voice rising like the traitor it was. 'I can handle myself, and I've kept him more alive than any of you!'

Rennic simply stared at him, eyes narrow and crinkled at the corners, then stood. 'Coming then, fuck-stick?'

Chel felt cornered by his own bravado. He turned to the prince. 'Will you be—'

Tarfel nodded, although the smile he managed was narrow and drawn at the corners. 'As the man says, Vedren, I'll be in safe hands. Just don't . . . don't take too long.'

\* \* \*

'Remember, little man, this is a free city. It's not part of the kingdom, at least as far as those living here are concerned. They have their own way of doing things, and they don't like people like us.'

'Rebels?'

'Mercenaries. Officially they're not allowed within the walls, along with visible weapons and armour. So once we're in, keep that cloak tight and your head down, and don't start any shit with anyone who looks at you cross-wise, understand?'

'You worry about yourself,' Chel grumped. He was already feeling like a fool and a traitor for abandoning Tarfel, and had to keep reassuring himself that the prince was indeed safe with Whisper. 'Who are we going to see in the city?'

'Some old friends of Loveless's. People in the trade.'

'Ah. The "leaf-merchants and poppy-peddlers" you mentioned.'

'It's "poppy-merchants and leaf-peddlers", dick-head, and yes. Our beloved Loveless has a long and varied association with colourful characters in many walks of life, and she seems to think this bunch can be of use. As she tells it, they exert a rotten if extensive influence over the region, not just in the free cities and townships but into the winter garrisons as well. If they get even a fraction to declare openly against the crown, others will follow, then we've got a corridor from the south all the way through to the capital. Corvel will shit his breeches at the very thought.'

'And they'll help us out?'

'If we promise them that princeling will relax some of the prohibitions when he's king, they might.'

Chel came up short, mouth open in protest, and Rennic

cuffed him along. 'We can work out the details when the time comes, little man, but first of all we have to get into this stinking city, and for that we need some leafy gate-tokens. So, head down and up shut for time being, yes?'

Chel did as ordered, muttering in silence, until they reached the ring of huts, tucked beneath the looming blue-grey stone of the walls. The sounds of the city beyond drifted over them, the ringing of bells and bustling of crowds around the outer thoroughfares despite the early hour. Somewhere a chicken squawked, fluttering and panicked by the pursuit of unseen children. The place smelled strongly of dung.

The hut Rennic led him to was low, unremarkable and severe, nestled between a row of similar constructions and backing directly on to the city wall. Rennic consulted the note in his hand one final time then advanced, and Chel followed. The smell hit him a pace from the door: thick, cloying sweetness, that stench of sickness curled within it like poison. 'This is a poppy den!' he hissed.

'We need leaf for the gate guards, princess, and this is where we get it. Else we're not getting in, no meetings, no southern corridor of breech-shittery.' Rennic kept his voice low. 'You can wait outside if your delicate sensibilities are offended.'

Chel stepped back, well clear of the door and its drifting stink. The smell revolted him, and now he could hear little moans and murmurs from within, delirious and disturbing. The void of the doorway had taken on new depths, suggesting the interior was far larger than its external frame implied; perhaps it tunnelled back into the city wall, or down into the hard earth below. 'Just . . . be quick.'

'Don't wander off,' the big man muttered, then hunched

to squeeze beneath the doorway and into the darkness beyond.

Chel waited, uncomfortable, counting his heartbeats in the cold. The longer he waited, the faster his counting became. Heartbeats became minutes, and Chel started to sweat.

At last, Rennic emerged from the gloom, hands empty, brows low. Chel felt his relief like a hot rush, and almost skipped over to meet the big man as he came ducking through the doorway. Rennic's eyes were distant, and Chel noticed spots of blood on the big man's fists.

'What happened in there? Did you get what we need?'

'You know,' Rennic said, his tone devoid of its customary hard edge, 'just once . . . if I could have a way to make people tell the fucking *truth* about their intentions, or just do what they said they would.' He looked out over the broken fields, flexing his bloodied knuckles. 'Do you think the Nort could make something like that?'

Chel tried to follow his gaze, seeing nothing but snow-streaked mud. 'That's what an oath is. That's the whole point.'

Rennic snorted, the hard light returning to his eyes. 'To the weak-minded, maybe. No words professed, even with great eagerness, can ever focus a man's actions like physical coercion.'

'My father always said we could be better. We could make our word as strong as steel, as solid as rock. You say you'll do something, you do it. No matter what.'

Rennic turned and gestured back through the open doorway to where a figure lay in half-light, its gurgling indistinct. 'There's your better, little man. Wonder how rock-solid her intentions were this morning. There's a reason they say never make promises to children or kings, you know,' he continued, hands stuffed back into his coat. 'Eventually the world will make you break one. And when you do, you break yourself in their eyes. No coming back from that.'

'Rennic, are you all right?'

'Fine.'

'Did you get the leaf?'

Rennic patted the breast of his coat. 'Let's get inside this wretched place and do what needs doing. The sooner we're away from this hole, the better. We've got other stops to make.'

With relief, Chel turned his back on the poppy den and took careful steps into what passed for the fresh air of Merenghi's shadow, anxious to flush the syrupy stench from his lungs, and with it the concomitant edge of nausea. He took a couple of deep, dung-flavoured breaths as they reached the edge of the hut-row. Movement caught his eye, a small boy crouched in the mud between the opposite huts, digging at the old mortar with a pair of short sticks. The child looked up and froze in utter terror on seeing him, then scrambled back between the huts, his trembling gaze locked on Chel.

Nonplussed, Chel raised his palms. 'What's up with this kid?' he muttered over his shoulder to Rennic. Rennic made no reply.

Upset at the notion a child might fear him, Chel walked slowly toward the boy, attempting a calming motion, but the boy shied as if he were about to strike.

'Hey, relax, kid, I'm not going to hurt you.'

The boy's eyes were impossibly wide, his voice tiny.

'You always say that.'

His gaze flicked over Chel's shoulder, then he bolted, scrambling away through the narrow gap between the banked mud walls. Chel called after the boy, then turned in baffled frustration, hearing the crunch of Rennic's footsteps behind.

Rennic was not there.

A beast of a man stood before him, no taller than Chel but twice the width, his jutting chest draped in a dark, gold-trimmed cloak, emblazoned with a single golden flower. A long baton, silver-tipped, hung from his belt on the cloak's open side. It was his face that drew Chel's attention, however; the two of them stared at each other in surprise. The man had long, straight black hair, bound tight at the nape of his neck and interwoven with gold filigree, and he stared at Chel from above a broken nose with eyes of blue-flecked grey. The same grey as Chel's own.

'Who in hells are you?' Chel said, then started as another man, almost identical, sidled into view behind the first. They could have been brothers. They could all have been brothers.

The man said something Chel didn't understand. He repeated it, his growing frown matching Chel's own, then finally said something Chel caught.

'Come with us, please.' His accent was thick but oddly familiar.

He reached out a heavy hand and clamped down on Chel's shoulder. There was no sign of Rennic, the row empty behind the two new arrivals. His options seemed limited.

The man pulled, and Chel followed.

# THIRTEEN

The hood was plucked from his head, and he could see again.

'Remove your armour, please.'

Beneath the grey-eyed gaze of the bull-like man who'd kidnapped him, Chel did so. They stood in what he took to be a library or reading room, a stone-walled room decked with low shelves, packed with more books than he'd ever seen in a single location, including his time in Black Rock. Long benches spread in bands from a central hearth, lamp tables spaced evenly between them, the combined heat of which did little to raise the room's temperature above chilly. It got chillier as he drew the mail shirt over his head, wincing as the movement aggravated his bad shoulder. They already had his mace, of course.

'Where am I?'

They'd taken him, hooded, in a cart or wagon, something horse-drawn, the smell and clop of the beast in front unmistakable. He'd been packed in between the two barrel-chested men, rocked against them, crushed at each bump, barely able to breathe let alone squirm. He'd thought he'd heard Rennic shouting somewhere, muffled by the hood and the sounds of the vehicle's travel, but he was far from certain. There was no sign of the mercenary now, only the cuboid man watching him. Another Andriz, another desert bloom like him. The first of his people he'd seen since Sab, and since he'd left home before that.

'I said, where am I?'

He knew where he was. He'd felt the climb around the hillside, heard the groan of a gate and echoes of enclosure. He'd heard animals, voices. He was in the settlement that overlooked the city. He'd been taken by the Wards. They truly didn't care for the medicinal trade.

'Remove the jacket too, please.'

Grimacing, he did so, his shoulder grumbling. The Andriz watched with steady eyes, hands clasped behind his wide back. The heavy baton at his belt clunked as he shifted position, and Chel's mind clicked. No wonder the boy was so terrified, he thought. Dark cloak, something like a mace, and Andriz features. I look just like them.

He stood at last in only his breeches and silk shirt. 'Where is my—'

'Follow, please.'

This one was not a talker.

A panelled hallway, warmer than the library, led them to a wider, octagonal area, a receiving room of sorts, the blaze of snow-mirrored daylight cracking through slot-like windows high overhead. His escort strode directly up the weave-draped stairs at the chamber's far side, nodding to the guard who stood beside the wide doors. Needless to say, the guard was another Andriz, not quite as bulky as the first, but clearly a man who could carry a pig under

each arm up a steep hill without breaking sweat. Chel
looked closer as he approached, meeting the guard's curious
gaze. His features were quite distinct from his escort's, but
the same hairstyle, same outfits, even the same posture,
made them all seem cast from the same mould.

He waggled an eyebrow at the guard as he passed, as
he imagined Lemon might, and then he was inside. The
room beyond the doors had the same high ceiling as the
receiving room before it, the same slants of white and
watery light from high windows, casting diagonal shafts of
drifting motes through the room's upper gloom. Four fires
burned in wide, stylized hearths at opposing corners, and
oil-wick lamps glowed from alcoves along the walls. A wide
table dominated the room's centre, dark-wood and
burnished, half an octagon to match the surroundings. The
four chairs at the table's far side were tall, imposing and
occupied.

He could make out little of the occupants beyond
silhouettes, their faces cast in shadow by the lights behind
and the slanted light above, but he noticed one of the
squarish men from outside the poppy den standing beside
one of the central chairs, his head bowed in conference
with the chair's owner. He now wasn't sure which of the
two had been the one to grab and hood him, which had
been the one behind, but he supposed it didn't matter.
He was among his people now. His mother would be so
pleased.

His escort put a thick hand on his arm, then steered him
before the table's flat side. He could by now discern more
of the people sitting opposite, detecting familiar dark hair
and grey eyes on each. Quite the enclave, this place. His
people hailed from the plains and deserts of the arid west,

far, far from Vistirlar and its provinces, and he'd assumed that he was one of only a handful of travelling curiosities within their borders.

'What's your name, boy?'

The speaker was a woman, her age indeterminate, her skin appearing smooth but her hair a wall of silver sheen. Gold gleamed in the braids of her hair, at her throat, and at her fingers and wrist as she raised a hand to beckon him forward. In the same motion she waved away the lump hovering behind her. Her accent matched that of his escort, nigglingly familiar, something from long ago. He didn't answer. Two could play silly buggers.

The man in the chair next to hers, short and no less silver, leaned forward over table and said something, but the words had no meaning. He was a child again, hearing angry foreign words echo from the walls of the manor while he and his sisters supposedly slept above, his mother's angry growl, his father's placations, robbed of meaning and left purely as tone. Seeing once more the black door, the door unopened, while his father lay dying beyond and would speak through it to his mother only in those meaningless words, her anguish and rage voiceless for the children but screaming behind her eyes.

Emotion roiled within him, a great surge of physical pain like burning, like impalement. Of course, he recognized their accents. They spoke like his father.

He gasped and rocked on his heels, one hand going to his chest. The woman leaned forward, affecting concern. 'Heavens, boy. We only asked you your name.'

He swallowed. The burning was receding, but every in-breath felt sharp.

'Chel.'

'Your family name, if it please you.' Her words were polite, the tone anything but.

'That is my family name.'

Muttering, again in the tongue he recognized but could not parse. It was so strange to hear it again, to hear tones and syllables that had surrounded him as a child, his attempts to learn and understand stymied by first his parents' intent to keep their disputes impenetrable, and then by his mother's refusal to speak the language again. After she had no one to speak it to.

'That is not a name of our people, boy. What is the name given to your mother, your father?'

One eye narrowed. 'I couldn't tell you, that is all the name I have. Now, perhaps you might like to fill me in on a few things in return? I've been forthcoming.'

One of the other men said something and the others laughed. Chel guessed it was at his expense, but let their laughter wash over him.

'One more time, then,' he said, his irritation damping whatever nostalgic embers still lurked. 'My name is Vedren Chel, of Barva, first son to Justina and Antonin.'

'Those are not names of our people.'

He shrugged. 'Well, there you go, maybe I'm not your people after all. Now who the fuck are you and why have you kidnapped me?'

The woman beckoned back the bull-man, irritation lining her face, and spoke terse, low words to him. He nodded and left the chamber, heading back toward the library.

'So,' the woman said as he left, sitting back and steepling her fingers. Jewelled golden bangles clattered at her slender arms. 'Your parents took local names. We will find them; our archives are most comprehensive.'

'And then what?'

'Then we will know where you fit.'

'Where I fit?'

'Indeed.'

'How about you just let me go about my business instead? How about you return my belongings and my . . . friend.'

The woman pursed her lips, the corners of her mouth rising in curt amusement. 'I'm afraid we have a duty of care, Vedren Chel of Barva. Deny it all you like, but you are one of us, and your state is . . . Well. You might be wearing Serican silk, but your company is questionable, and I cannot believe your parents would be delighted to hear of your entanglements.'

Frustration burned within him, white-hot and rising. 'My father's dead, and my mother is in the thrall of some fat fucking southerner.'

'Your language is also improper.'

'My language is my own fucking concern.'

'It's no surprise, I suppose. You've grown up beyond our protection, our guidance, who knows what you've been exposed to. The good news is that you're still young, and your wanderings in darkness have ended.'

Chel could no longer control his rage. 'What the fuck are you talking about?'

The woman nodded to Chel's left, and the meathead beside him cracked him across the back with his baton. The pain was sharp and staggering, sending him lunging forward onto the table, both hands planted. A second rap of the baton against his knuckles made him yowl, dragging his hand back and cradling it beneath his arm.

'As I said,' the woman continued, 'your wanderings in darkness have ended. Your path back to the light begins today.'

'Who are you?' he hissed, mentally inserting '*the fuck*'.

'My name is Haranali Laralim.' She smiled, this time with unexpected warmth. 'But you may call me Auntie.'

\* \* \*

Chel walked beside Laralim out into the brisk air of the terraced gardens, paying close attention to his foot placement lest he step on the swishing train of her bright silken dress. Behind them lurked the squat bruiser, named by Laralim as Urbu. The baton remained in his hand.

'Why have you brought me here?'

She tilted her head, awaiting something.

'*Auntie*,' he added through gritted teeth.

She smiled. In the silvery light of the gardens, he could see the layers of make-up that caked her face, applied with expert hands but cracked and flaking nonetheless. He realized that the shadows were long, the absent sun descending in the north-western sky, soon to be lost behind the wall of smoky peaks that loomed over them. They'd left him bound and hooded for hours. He had places to be, and people to find.

'We are the Wards,' she said. 'The Wardens. We are the keepers of our people. This is our enclave.'

'Oh. I've heard of you.'

She nodded, still smiling, more to herself than to him. 'As well you might.' They walked along a covered path around the faceted edge of a building, the occasional drip of meltwater plopping from roof to the puckered earth below. The gardens bloomed beyond them, a regimented array of brilliant colour, reds, pinks, and lilac, stacked in terraces down the hillside toward the grey walls encircling them. Directly before and beneath them sat the gloomy bulk of Merenghi, steaming and huffing in the afternoon light. In the other directions, he saw little; curls of drab, rolling plains, pockets of scrubby trees, another distant run of hills, the barren rise where they'd parted from Whisper and Tarfel, empty now. The gardens were a splash of vivid colour in a sea of dinge.

'You have a pretty garden,' he ventured, hoping a little flattery might earn him some answers.

'We do. It is well-tended and carefully nurtured, like our family.'

He sighed inwardly.

'My friend, where is he? Why are you keeping him? Keeping us both?'

The path diverged at the wall's end, and she directed them out along the edge of the terrace, under the pale shade of thin and barren trees, moulded into arches. Urbu stomped behind them, quietly seething.

'You are here, Vedren of Barva, because you concern us. Which is to say, you are of interest, rather than you are a source of worry, although perhaps both may yet apply.'

He stayed tight-lipped.

'You see, dear boy, we take great interest in the comings and goings of visitors to our city.' Ah. There it was. She crinkled one corner of her mouth at the stiffness of his reaction. 'You thought you'd slip in undetected, did you? Let me guess, some manner of exchange with the guards at the gates, some unpleasantness within the walls.'

They stopped at a wooden railing, hewn from the same narrow wood as the bent trees behind them. Laralim leaned on it, looking out over the estate, the rising columns of steam and smoke from the huts and gatehouses at the hill's foot, the fiery orange gleam of evening sun searing the horizon.

'There was a time, long before your birth, when our people left the heartland in great numbers.' Presumably she meant the plains, somewhere far, far to the north-west, from which his people had apparently sprung. 'It was a sad time, a hard time, of great upheaval and greater strife. Many of us perished, but some of us flourished.'

She gave a little smile, the evening light rich on the deep furrows of skin around her mouth. 'Our people acquired a reputation for achieving tasks that others would not, or could not, and we were rewarded in turn, first with coin, then later with land and titles. In turn, more of us came, and for a while, at least, we continued dispatching the flower of our youth to expand our legacy.'

Laralim paused, and the smile ebbed away so fast it was hard to imagine it had ever been. 'Times have changed. But some legacies remain. As I'm sure you have surmised, Merenghi, vile as it is, is ours. Think of it as an unpleasant but dutiful inheritance, say a nasty old uncle. The hut-folk and their confederates within the walls come with the territory, and as long as they keep to their business and keep their business discreet, we tolerate them.'

She sighed, her breath misting orange in the dying rays of the vainly resurgent sun. Laughter drifted up from the terrace below, a gaggle of no doubt grey-eyed children racing between twisting trunks. 'Sadly, people like that are a fungus, an infection. They never stay where they're put, always looking to seep and spread. Hence, as I said, we maintain an interest. The slum-dogs might claim to have the constables in their pocket, but they know who pays their wages.'

She turned to face him. 'The sudden arrival of a ruthless hireling and one of our own? You can see it would have piqued our interest. Whatever the slum-dogs were planning, we will not permit it.'

Chel leaned back next to her. The fading sun was almost warm as the air temperature dropped. Already small lights were sparkling around the squat, domed buildings above them, the smoke from two dozen hearths blending with the darkening sky. 'Well, now you've met us. You can see we're nothing to worry about. Why not let us be on our way?'

'You have, perhaps, somewhere you need to go?'

'Yes. Some people we need to see, in other cities. About . . . a festival.'

Her look was half reproach, half maternal indulgence, her eyebrows rising high enough to crack her pristine maquillage. 'Dear boy, please do not take me or my peers for fools. We have steered this family for a generation, against the machinations of better liars than you. I have already made it plain, you will be staying with us, at least until we can send word to your mother that you are in our care. After that, we will see.'

He was no longer listening, his heart sinking through his gut like a lead fist. He was being held prisoner, little better than the cells of Black Rock. Rennic was somewhere within the walls, no less caged. If their visit to Merenghi was a bust, they needed to move on as fast as possible. As Rennic had said, there were other stops to make before they hauled east to the river crossing. Take too long about it and they'd miss the first moon, and the rest of the company with it. He offered up a silent prayer that the others were faring better than he was.

'At least . . . At least release my friend, let him continue our journey. He is of no concern to you. He's a northerner. I think.'

She shook her head. 'Your associate will remain with us for the time being, until we understand his motives, and he ours. The trouble with the kind of people in his profession,' she said, her silver-fluted eyes boring into him, 'is that they can say one thing to your face, yet do something entirely different the moment they are out of view. It's best to keep them where you can see them, I find.' She moved off down the path again. 'This way.'

She led him back indoors, Urbu still dogging their every step, up a wide, wood-finished staircase to a room on the upper floor. The shutters were already drawn and bolted, a small fire kindling in the hearth, a candle on a narrow table. 'This will be your room for the time being. I don't think you are ready to eat with the rest of us yet; I will have your meal sent up.'

She went to leave, the door half-closed before she paused. 'Dear boy,' she said, 'why didn't you come straight to us in the first place? However bad things might be, there was no need to approach the filth-traders. We could have helped you out. We're family after all.' With that she pulled the door closed. After a moment, he heard the key clanking in the lock.

He sat down on the straw-packed mattress, watching the woven, patterned blankets rise in response. The pattern featured a lot of many-petalled flowers, interwoven with keys. It seemed a lot like a taunt.

'Fuck,' he muttered.

\* \* \*

The clank of the lock roused him from his doze, sending him bouncing up from the bed. Finding nowhere else to stand, he sat back down on the bed as the door swung inwards. Shadows filled the doorway, giggling silhouettes in the lamplight beyond. He peered into the mass.

'Who's there?'

One of the shapes entered, carrying a steaming tray. For a moment, he thought it was Sab, then his brain caught up with his blinking eyes and rendered an Andriz girl, somewhere around his own age, dressed plainly but well, placing the tray on his table. Another girl followed, carrying a silver pitcher, which she laid down beside the tray. They turned in unison, eyes lowered but peeking upwards.

'Who are you?' he said.

The girls cast nervous, mischievous looks back toward the door, where their presumed chaperon lurked. Chel watched them, seeing them both as young adults like himself, but also as cosseted children, who'd seen nothing of his own rich experiences. He felt himself adjust his stance, affecting a somewhat world-weary slouch, knees spread. The girl who'd brought the tray was really rather pretty.

'Are you the mercenary?' said the one on the right, the water-carrier.

'The ruthless killer?' the other added, flashing wide, oyster-coloured eyes at him. She reminded him of someone, although he couldn't think who.

He drank in their curiosity. 'I may be ruthless,' he said, rubbing one hand over his less-than-stubbly chin, 'but I'm no killer.'

An angry shout came from down the hallway. Urbu, or one like him.

They almost squealed, hurrying from the room. The tray girl gave one backward glance, and he caught it.

'Wait. What's your name?'

'Rasha,' she said, cheeks darkening, and then she was gone from the room. Chel stood to follow, but Urbu filled the doorway as he reached it.

'You,' he said, from beneath thick and lowered brows. 'Stay in here. Do. Nothing.'

Chel let him slam the door, his thoughts already drifting back to the adoring gaze of the departed Rasha. Perhaps his confinement wouldn't be the end of the world.

He sat down to eat and his thoughts drifted, trying to place the memory the girl had jogged. Someone darkly pretty, friendly, a nervous smile shared.

The spoon dropped from his hand, clattering back against the tray. The hunter's daughter, the girl on the Raven-Hill. The girl Brecki had murdered, thanks to his inattention, his complacency.

He no longer felt hungry. He had to get out.

'Fuck,' he whispered in the growing darkness.

# FOURTEEN

It was late morning before Chel was allowed back outside, and only in the company of one of Urbu's clones, a wide-faced man with a thin beard and shoulders like hay bales. He seemed unable or unwilling to speak, but his disapproving gaze followed Chel everywhere.

Chel had seen little more of the girls who'd brought him supper; breakfast had been delivered by one of the Urbunites, and he was anxious for any human contact he could get. The sun was bright that morning, casting warm amber rays beneath a muddy expanse of turgid cloud, its climb in the north-eastern sky a reminder that time was moving on, even if he wasn't.

Laralim met him at the top of the terrace. 'Good morning, dear boy.'

He didn't miss a beat. 'Good morning, Auntie.' He'd fast decided that absolute compliance was the order of the day. Only by giving them mastery over him would he gain trust, leeway, a measure of independence. He needed all of these things if he was to escape the compound, and take Rennic along with him. By his own guess, he had only a few days to get back on the road east and ride hard before they would arrive too late for the first moon. If they missed the others at the river crossing, they'd be stuck, isolated, the wrong side of the kingdom as warfare erupted around them. If he was lucky.

'You will be pleased to hear that we believe we have found your parents in the archives.' He nodded, waiting for her to continue. In truth he gave not a shit, but couldn't risk informing her of that. 'Tell me,' she went on, 'did your father have an elder brother? He would have died before your birth.'

'I don't know.' And really, he didn't.

'No matter. Would you like to hear of your parentage now? We will be gathering the archivists for a reading shortly.'

A tinkle of familiar laughter reached him from the lower terrace. He saw movement among the blooms: Rasha and her friend, along with a handful of other girls, mostly younger.

'If I may, Auntie, would it be all right if I took a walk in the gardens first? I've spent too much time indoors recently.'

She raised an eyebrow, in two minds, and he added, 'Of course, you'd be welcome to accompany me and my friend here.' He gestured at the Urbu, who glared back in mute antipathy.

She smiled then, that same mixture of indulgence and motherly reproach. 'Very well, Vedren. Stretch your legs, and come and join us when you are ready.'

He watched her depart, then nodded to the Urbu. 'Come on then, Chuckles. Let's go for a walk.'

He made his approach to the terrace railing carefully, seemingly aimless, coming to rest just above where Rasha was digging in the fresh earth. The Urbu remained watchful, but at a distance, and Chel made a show of looking in every direction but down, angling his head away before hissing a greeting.

She looked up, then up again; her face brightened, then creased with worry at the sight of him.

'Hey,' he whispered, keeping his jaw as still as he could, speaking almost through gritted teeth. 'Keep as quiet as you can.'

She nodded, casting looks over her shoulders at the other girls. If they had noticed her budding conversation, they were keeping it to themselves. She looked up at him, morning sunlight burnishing her tightly coiled hair, the thick linen of her work clothes.

'You're outside.'

'I am.'

'I wanted to . . . We weren't allowed to—'

'I understand. It's fine. Really, though, I'm nothing to be afraid of.'

'Oh.' She actually looked disappointed. He felt himself flushing, tried to steel himself.

'Listen, there's another man here, who arrived with me. Do you know where he is?'

'The *hajamin*?'

There it was, another gust of past aches thought long forgotten. A word he knew, one he'd not heard in over a decade. A word meaning outsider, foreigner, one who does not – cannot – belong, delivered as a guileless punch to the gut by an oblivious teenager.

'Yes.'

'He's in a hut, down by the stables.' She chewed her lip. 'They told us not to approach him.'

'That's good advice. He's dangerous.'

Her eyes widened, and she edged involuntarily back. He immediately regretted his words and tried to repair their intimacy.

'He's not so bad when you get to know him. Mostly.'

She smiled, then dropped her head in a flash, reabsorbed in her planting. Chel frowned, then felt the thick presence at his elbow. His friendly Urbu was staring at him, at the girl, then back at him, frown deeper than ever. He grunted, and nodded back toward the main building, and Chel walked. He risked one last look over his shoulder at the terrace below as he went, and she was looking back. He winked, then strode from sight, feeling an odd, hot tingling in his chest.

\* \* \*

The chamber was busy, the benches loaded with petitioners or supplicants or merely those interested in the results of whatever occasion this was. Chel counted heads as he slid behind the Urbu along the side walls, guessing at the number of Andriz who lived on the estate. Most seemed older, their hair the same colour as their eyes, some very frail and ancient types near the front. He saw few children beyond a couple of babes in arms, guessing that the young of the Wards were either working in fields or gardens, like the girls outside, or undergoing some level of education. He wondered where his fate would lie, should he prove unable to extricate himself from Laralim's schemes.

The Urbu went straight to her, bending to whisper or

grunt into her ear, just as his namesake had on the day of Chel's arrival. The elder woman nodded, her eyes still on the sheaf of thick, genuine paper notes before her, then she looked up at him, locking eyes across the wide table. Her expression was neither angry nor disapproving, more appraising, a hint of calculation behind those faded silver eyes. Chel shifted, defensive. He'd done nothing wrong, after all; nobody had forbidden him to talk to anyone else. If anyone had the right to be angry, it was him.

The reader standing before the table completed her oration, closed a heavy book and, tucking it beneath her arm, nodded in acknowledgement to both the folk in the high-backed chairs behind the table and the audience on the benches. Conversational hubbub rose around the chamber as the reader departed, and Laralim signalled for Chel to approach.

'Did you enjoy your walk?'

'I did, Auntie.'

She smiled, a quick twitch of one corner of her puckered mouth.

'I'm afraid you missed the reading, but I can summarize things for you, unless you'd care to read them yourself?' She pushed one of the thick sheets toward him, its scribblings arcane and impenetrable.

He shook his head. 'Not my letters.'

She nodded as if this had confirmed a long-held, and disappointing, suspicion, then lifted the paper, squinting just a little as she read.

'Only one entry even mentions Barva. Your mother was born Hurania of Pasaj, hailing from the heartland. She was promised union to Lorash of Aratesh, local to these parts, as part of an arrangement contingent on the acquisition of certain new lands.'

'That's my father?'

She didn't answer directly. 'The archives, at least those we have within the walls, specify only that the arrangement was agreed, and that these lands would be entering his family's possession in return for what was recorded as "Service to the Lord".'

'Was that church or king?'

'Uncertain, and unimportant. It's dated twenty-four years ago, so although the archives are somewhat dry after that, it's all too obvious what happened.'

He shifted, irritated. 'Which was what?'

'Lorash met his end in the course of his service, and the lands he was promised passed to his brother, as did the planned union to Hurania. We have no name for the brother, whom I take to be your father, but his presence is clearly implied. The two of them would have moved with their household to take up their stewardship of the manor of Barva, which must have been quite the journey. Especially given the novelty of their acquaintance.'

'What are you saying? My parents were never supposed to marry?'

'As it would seem. The lack of records on your father suggests he absconded, or was cast out; nobody seems to remember him. Wherever he was, he was called back and sent off to fulfil his brother's obligations.'

Her words set things clicking in his head, his family dynamic recast, his father's words and actions reversed in motivation. 'He . . . he was in Roniaman. Training to be a minister.'

'Ah, ever the lot of the second son. What a stroke of

fortune for him that he was diverted, if you'll pardon the expression. He and his new bride took a local name, and followed suit for their children.' She finished with a smile that was not entirely manufactured. 'Isn't it better to know where you came from?'

He stood unsteady on his feet, legs trembling. On some level, he'd always assumed that his parents had a bond, a great attraction, a friendship at least, from which their disputes had flared. His father's attempts to win the affections of the local populace, what Chel had taken for noble obligation, pronouncements of duty were, instead, the desperate attempts of a man destined for a life of priestly solitude to achieve some measure of substance, away from the fury of a wife who hated him as a stranger. His ministrations, his sermons, his deliveries of alms, quite unheard of for a local liege, even to plague houses . . .

'Fuck,' he whispered, swaying on his feet, something hot and burning like acid in his chest.

Laralim hadn't heard. She dipped her pen and hovered it above the foot of her notes. 'Now, I'm sure you mentioned other siblings. Perhaps you could supply their names and details for the archives?'

He wiped one hand across his forehead, feeling its slick clamminess despite the cool in the chamber.

'I think,' he began, then steadied himself and tried again. 'I think I would like to speak to my friend.'

She glanced up at him then, silvery eyes peering from beneath silvery brows. She said nothing for a moment.

'Very well.'

\* \* \*

Rennic was lodged in a fat-walled wooden shack at the back of the stables, built right up to the outer wall, its windows barred and door securely bolted. Two men stood guard, little more than stable-hands from their appearance; at Chel's approach they were seated on upturned wooden buckets, pouring steaming tea from a kettle. They jumped to their feet as Chel reached them, the original Urbu a pace ahead of him. Urbu spoke low words to them and they made a show of retrieving the spears they had left propped against the shack wall. One still reached for his tea the moment Urbu turned his back.

Chel stood before the door in expectation, but Urbu nodded at the barred window.

'Window.'

'Seriously?'

'Window.'

'You're all heart, Urbu.'

He rapped on the round-logged wall, peering into the gloom within.

'Rennic?'

'That you, little man?'

Chel's eyes focused, and found him, upside down against the far wall, pushing himself up and down on his hands just as he had in the cells of Black Rock.

'Old habits, eh, old man?'

Rennic sprang down and back, then rose from his crouch and came to the window, reaching knotted, gnarled knuckles around the bars. Chel doubted he'd ever seen the man's hands so clearly. He looked dirty and tired, a little hollow from the isolation.

'You all right?'

'Had worse. They're feeding me, and they change the

shit-bucket regularly, so mustn't grumble.' He looked at Chel through the bars, eyes black beneath his thick brows. 'And you, little man? You look rough. Thought they'd be giving you the treatment, one of their golden folk.' He spat through the bars, the gobbet sailing past Chel's shoulder and splattering on the grey mud of the stable-yard.

'Had some, I dunno, news, I supposed you'd call it. Two decades old, but new to me.'

'Something bad?'

Chel slumped against the wall beside the window. 'Only that my parents never cared for each other, and it's probably what drove my father to devote himself to charity, which is what killed him.'

'Sounds heavy.'

'Yeah.'

'I was born in a whorehouse, never knew my dad, and watched my mother cut her own throat, rather than be taken by looting soldiers.'

Chel's mouth hung open. He was wordless.

'If we're sharing,' Rennic added. He seemed dispassionate, staring vacantly out into the stable.

'That must . . .' Chel tried, but he had nothing to say.

'I tried to fight them, tried to make a stand, give myself so she could escape with her friends. They batted me aside, left me in the mud, just went on past. Didn't even bother to kill me.'

'How . . . How old were you?'

'Fourteen, fifteen or so. Probably a little before your parents were first getting to hate each other.' He blinked. 'I never told anyone that before. No one who wasn't there, anyway. Suppose I'm not accustomed to having time for reflection.'

'Did you, did you get revenge? Hunt the soldiers down?'

Rennic shook his head, as if clearing cobwebs from his mind. 'No, what? No. How? A bunch of mercenaries, beneath the king's pennant? How would I find them? It's not like they killed her either, she took care of that herself. Who's going to shed a tear for the grief of a whoreson?'

Chel's troubles seemed abruptly small.

'I'm sorry.'

'Yeah, and likewise for your sad parents.' Rennic flexed his grip against the bars, straightening, shaking off his reverie. 'Have you found out what the fuck we're doing here, and why the fuck I'm locked in a box that smells of horseshit?'

Chel leaned in close. 'They're watching the traders in the huts, saw us going in and grabbed us on the way out.'

'Then what do they want from us?'

'You, as a mercenary, they don't trust, and apparently they don't like to let the leaf-traders talk to anyone outside their existing circle, especially "ruthless hirelings". Me being one of them, looks like it surprised them. The one in charge, Laralim, who wants me to call her "Auntie", she's talking about, well, adopting me. They want to keep me here with them, make me one of them.'

'Huh.' Rennic's indifference surprised him. He'd been expecting outrage, or ridicule. 'Can see why,' he said. 'How many you reckon there are here? In this bastion of purity? Can only have another generation or two before they're as inbred as ancient royalty.'

'What do you mean?'

'They want you for breeding stock, little man. Stop their chins disappearing. See if you can use that to get us out.'

Chel nodded. 'They might yet let you out, you know. Maybe we just need to be patient.'

'Princeling would pitch a fit if I turned up without you. Besides, we stay here much longer, we won't even make the Bridge House before the first moon, never mind hitting any townships on the way. Let's hope Lemon and the others are having an easier time of things, eh?'

He shot a look at the barn opposite, indicating the small door at its side. 'They stowed our gear in there. If they start going through it, we'd better hope that leaf I bought wasn't too fresh or we'll be wearing our arseholes as hats.'

Urbu was coming, his slow mouth already forming the word, 'Enough.'

Chel raised his hands. 'I'm going, I'm going.' To Rennic, 'Stay strong.'

'Me? I've got my own bucket. I'll be happy as a nun weeding asparagus.'

# FIFTEEN

'Tomorrow,' Chel said, chasing a spongy lump around his platter with a hunk of hard, dark bread, 'might I do some work in the gardens?'

Laralim looked up from her reading. The light in her chamber was low, a scattering of candles supplementing the stick at the small table's centre, and she was squinting more than normal. She mulled his request, and he could almost hear the ticking of her calculations.

'An unusual request,' she said. 'Most boys your age are engaged in field-work or training. I'd have thought the latter more in your interest.' The corner of her mouth twitched, a fleeting half-smile. 'Was there any reason in particular?'

*Concentrate, react correctly.* He fidgeted and looked away, down at his food, then up at the candles on the high tables by the door, doing his best to manufacture a blush. His thoughts jumped inexorably to Rasha, her plump cheeks, her nervous smile, and he found the heat rising in his cheeks was anything but affected.

'I would like to, er, get my hands dirty.' *Too much?*

Her smile returned, reinforced, that familiar look of indulgence lighting her tired face. 'I will speak to Banu, see what can be done.' She shuffled the thick papers, holding the uppermost closer to the candlelight.

'Thank you, Auntie.'

'It will do you good to make some friends,' she said, eyes still on the paper, her smile undimmed.

\*\*\*

Rasha's look of surprised delight at his appearance was almost reward enough. She stood with a clutch of other girls of varying ages, the morning's planting laid out on canvas before them in the slanting and dappled early sunlight. Chel recognized the other girl who'd brought him water that first night, whispering with Rasha behind a cupped hand, their faces alive with giggling gossip. He felt immediately ridiculous, his cheeks burning anew in the frosty morning air, chiding himself for his stupidity in thinking this would be a good idea. Is this my undoing, he thought, the defeat that derails our great scheme? A dearth of nerve in the face of the judgement of teenage girls?

It was the Urbu behind him, since named as Mero, who bumped him forward and drove him to his fate. Too nervous to speak, he nodded silent greeting to the girls, whose reactions varied from excited grins to outright alarm. Mero kept him to one side, away from the others, as Banu the overseer gave them their directions for the day's efforts and left them to it. Chel nodded along, collected a wooden trowel and a small sack of plantings, and followed the others. Nobody spoke to him directly, not even Mero, who offered nothing in the way of help and guidance.

As the sun crept upwards through the cobalt sky, bathing the gardens in a long-missed amber warmth, Chel dropped to his knees and began to dig.

\*\*\*

'You're not going deep enough.'

He'd not even seen her approach, working her way along the line toward him while he dug, oblivious.

'You need to go down further, or it won't flower in the summer. May I show you?'

He looked around for Mero, but his slab-faced guardian had wandered away, seemingly bored of supervising drudge-work. She was beside him now, close enough to feel the gentle heat of her body, warmed by both sun and exertion. She reached across, steering his hand out of the way, shuffling round, scooping at the hard earth with her own trowel.

'You need a deeper hole, you see?' Then, quieter, direct to his ear. 'Why are you here?' A pause, then, 'Is it for me?'

He could feel the flush rising, somewhere around the top of his chest and heading for his face. On some level he found himself ridiculous, which just made it worse. He'd faced red confessors, mercenaries, wolves, reavers, threats to life and limb. But there was something so much more unsettling about this.

She was looking away, disappointed, and an electric surge in his gut drove his mouth.

'Yes. Maybe a little.'

She smiled, tucking a loose strand of hair behind her ear, her attention still on the growing hole before them.

'Is it true you come from the east?'

'Yes.'

214

'And that you're an outlaw?'

He frowned at that. 'I suppose so.'

'Are you staying with us? For a long time?'

She wasn't looking at him, but he could feel the force of her attention, her apprehension of his answer. He kept his eyes on her hands, watching her gouge and scoop the earth, thinking of Rennic's words. Three days gone already, the year's first moon racing toward them, their chance to alert the south before Ruumi's war-band arrived, slipping away. He wondered how the others were faring, taking their plan to disaffected lordlings, fierce hill tribes, agents of foreign influence. How had things ended at the Gracechurch? Would the southern mercenaries heed their warning? They had to get back on the road. They had to.

He couldn't meet her eye. 'I think so. Yes.'

She grinned and looked up at him, her copper-flecked eyes radiating genuine joy. 'I'm pleased to hear that. There aren't many boys my age.' She coughed, catching herself, knowing she'd said too much. 'It's always good to make new friends.'

Chel wondered where she'd heard that.

\*\*\*

It took another morning's planting before he felt ready to push forward, confident of Rasha's interest, and the indulgence of their supervisors. He'd caught Mero watching them, his cliff-side face studiously blank, making no move to intervene. Rennic had been right. Laralim wanted to keep him, and had concluded that his motives toward Rasha would act in her favour. Alone in his room the night before, his thoughts wandering, he wondered if she might know better after all. He was certainly looking forward to seeing her, a slight tightening in his chest when he saw her look up and smile.

'Could we meet? Later?'

She kept her attention on returning her tools to the canvas as they stopped for the morning, but he heard the change in her breathing. Her friends hovered to one side, waiting for her to join them, not wanting to approach while she and Chel spoke. 'What did you have in mind?' she asked at length, her gaze still low.

He chose his words carefully. 'Maybe a walk later, after evening prayers? There's so much of the estate I've not yet seen, I could use a good guide.'

She straightened, looking over his shoulder to where Mero lurked. 'And Mero can't take you?'

He smiled, biting down on his unease. 'I'm sure Mero has far better things to do.'

Rasha gazed at him, considering, and he felt his heart thumping against his ribcage. He couldn't be sure of the exact cause of his anxiety.

'If you can get out alone, I'll meet you behind the chapel.'

\* \* \*

He sat through the prayers, habitual boredom at the drone of proceedings aggravated by his jitters of what was to come. If Laralim, seated beside him on one of the good benches, noticed his fretting, she made no comment. At the final bell as the assembly filed out into the darkening evening, torches lit along the pathways and the vanishing sky the colour of an old bruise, he rolled his dice.

'Auntie, might I make my own way back to the chamber?'

Her guard was up immediately, her eyes on him cold, calculating. *Too soon, too much.* His stomach turned over, sinking fast, and with it his plan's chances. 'I have a question for you, Vedren of Barva.' She ushered him to one side, away from the departing congregation.

'Vedren,' she said as they stood in the relative seclusion of the terrace, 'do you believe I wish you harm?' She gave him no chance to answer. 'It is quite the reverse. You must realize by now, you are not the first stray we've had to take in. Tell me, have you ever lived somewhere you felt you truly belonged?'

The question caught him off guard, and his reaction betrayed him. The lines around Laralim's eyes deepened with satisfaction. 'For a time, our people took noble roles in these lands without noble history. We were neither of the ruling class, nor the ruled. Some adapted better than others, but for many the harvest has been bitter. Too many were left isolated and lost, yearning to be among their own, to be called home. Were you happy, growing up? Since you left your childhood behind, have you felt at peace?'

He didn't know where to look, what expression to hold. The thoughts that rattled his brain made it impossible to concentrate on something as mundane as his face. How could she know? Could she know? Was this a wild guess, or was his predicament more common than he realized?

She was watching him, her eyes glowing silver pools in the gloom.

'You can be at peace here, Vedren.'

Then her gaze lifted, focusing on something behind him, and her indulgent smile returned. 'As long as you have a friend with you, and you are both back where you should be by next bell, you may make your own way back.'

217

Relief washed through him like returning blood, bringing with it uncomfortable tinglings, but his disquiet at Laralim's words remained beneath. Was he so transparent? Was she telling the truth? He took a breath, tried to concentrate. He had a mission. He had a duty.

'Thank you, Auntie. Good night, Auntie.'

Rasha was on the path behind him, waiting patiently, her friends and family shuffling away into the gathering night. Laralim had endorsed their inevitable union. Let no one intervene.

'Where would you like to see? There's not much light left.'

Despite the coming spring, the night's air was chill, their breath fogging in the torchlight. Chel watched their clouds plume and merge, mingling and fading. They were alone on the upper terrace, the low wind rustling the washed-out blooms beneath them, stirring the freshly turned earth where they'd planted.

'What's at the bottom of the terraces?'

Her nose wrinkled in the twilight. Clearly not what she'd expected. 'The barns, the low barracks, the stables.' Then her expression shifted, hardening, and she seemed to age before his eyes, becoming at once the young woman she might have been beyond the walls of the estate. 'Where your friend is.'

'Do you think, perhaps, we might take a wander that way?'

Her mood had darkened, the playfulness gone from her speech. *Too soon, too much.* 'They won't let you see him, not without an escort. And I'm afraid there I wouldn't count.'

He had to salvage this, rescue the situation. He was

218

surprised at how bad he felt already. His thoughts began to creep. Would it really be so bad to take a stroll down to the grove in the incipient moonlight, hold hands, lock arms, who knew what else? The whole affair was something of a closed book to him. In the years since he'd been sent from home, his encounters with members of the opposite sex his own age could be counted on the fingers of one hand, and one notable example had ended in tragedy. How rare it was to meet someone . . . suitable.

Her eyes were on him, but they were no longer affectionate.

'I don't have to talk to him or anything.' He could hear the plaintive panic in his voice. 'Just to see that he's still there, still healthy. Please. He's my friend.'

An eyebrow still arched. 'I thought he was dangerous?'

'He is. Extremely. But that doesn't make him any less my responsibility.' He paused, gulping a quick breath, mental wheels spinning. 'It'll be quick, and afterwards we can have our walk. Properly.'

'Well,' she said with a sigh of exaggerated weight, 'if it'll set you at ease, I suppose it can't do any harm . . .'

\* \* \*

The first plops of rain dropped as they neared the stables, bouncing from the cold earth in small puffs in the dying light. A single youth stood guard over Rennic's shack in the gloom, his stool pulled under the awning of the barn opposite, his small fire hissing with the reflected splash of raindrops. He was making tea, and looking miserable.

Rasha drew the shawl up from her shoulders and over her head. 'How close do you want to get?' She peered upwards at the black carpet overhead, and was rewarded with a direct hit on the forehead. Spluttering, she added, 'I don't much fancy staying out if it's going to piss down.'

Chel nodded in dim agreement. His heart was pounding again, but he remained uncertain of the exact reason. 'I can't see him from here, maybe I could get a little closer?'

She frowned at him from beneath the shawl, the suspicion returned to her eyes. 'He's in a dark room in a dark night, outlaw. Unless he pokes his head out of his own accord, you're not going to see him short of pressing a torch against the window. And I'm going no closer – if Hesso sees us, he's going to say something, and we both know we're not supposed to be here.'

The rain was thickening, fat drops thudding in greater numbers, their sounds melding from patter to rush. Rasha ducked under the narrow overhang of the nearest stable and Chel followed, pressed against the slatted wall beside her as the rain thundered down. A chewing mule, head jutting through a notch in the stable door, glanced in their direction, registered and disregarded them, and went back to staring vacantly into the rain.

He could feel her body, warm beside him, her breath fogging in the dim and filtered light of the stable-boy's struggling fire. He almost jumped when he felt her cool hand reach for his, her fingers twining his own, drawing him closer. She said nothing, staring ahead just like the mule, but when he took half a step sideways after his hand, she rested her shawled head against his shoulder.

'There's something soothing about spring rain, don't you think?'

*Spring. We really don't have long.* 'Do you think it's spring already?'

She puffed a half-chuckle, oblivious of his concern. 'It's raining and not snowing. That's usually how we measure it around here.'

He swallowed. He could feel her presence, her warmth, her openness. He was more conscious of it than he'd ever been conscious of anything in his young adult life. And he had a duty.

'I think it's easing off. Listen, I'm really sorry about it, but I still need to check on my friend. There's no point us both getting into trouble – why don't you head back? If Hesso sees me, it's just me who gets it. I can claim I didn't hear the bell in the rain.'

She lifted her head from his shoulder, her hand still in his but withdrawing inch by inch. 'Go back? What?'

Her hand was gone, and she was facing him, eyes wide, incredulous in the misting murk. He gambled, desperate. 'The rain's ruined our chances of a good walk anyway. We can try again tomorrow. Do it properly. Assuming I'm not confined to my room again.'

'Tomorrow?'

'Tomorrow. For sure.'

A small smile then, a measure of indulgence, and for a moment he saw a startling echo of Laralim. Could they be related? The question seemed ludicrous, given Rennic's words on the shallowness of their breeding pool.

She reached up with one cold hand, laying her fingers against his cheek.

'You'd better not get caught then, had you?'

He nodded. 'For sure.' She had no idea how right she was.

# SIXTEEN

The rain eased but did not desist, maintaining an even thrum as Chel edged around the stable buildings, his eyes on Hesso and his sorry fire. The rain provided excellent cover, masking the sounds of his movement and obscuring visibility. Chel made sterling progress, but Hesso was a lousy watchman. He seemed to be incapable of keeping his fire dry, his tea a long way from ready.

Chel reached Hesso's barn, diverting down the narrow mud alley to its side. There was the small door that Rennic had indicated, unlocked. He crept inside, into dry darkness, dripping on straw-covered floor. Even with only the light from Hesso's feeble fire through the barn's open main door, it didn't take long to locate their confiscated gear, stacked next to animal feed and barrels of salted goods: Chel's armour, Rennic's coat. Chel felt inside the coat, finding a small, wrapped bundle.

He crept back toward the open doorway where Hesso sat. He'd been blowing on the fire and finally had a decent flame heating his kettle. The tea wouldn't be long now.

Chel looked around, then picked up a loose clod of grey earth, dislodged from some hoof. He snaked his way to the doorway, watching Hesso carefully, then as the young man bent forward to give the fire one more blow, he flung the clod.

It sailed through the drizzle and thumped against the wall of the shack opposite, exploding into dirty mist. Hesso reared in shock, eyes searching.

'Who's there?' he called. 'You'd better not be trying to escape, sell-sword!'

He snatched up a thin spear from the ground beside him, threw up his hood and strode into the rain to investigate, his shoulders hunched tense as if expecting a blow. Chel darted forward in his absence, lifted the kettle lid and, peeling off one, two, three leaves, dropped them in. He paused, considering, then dropped in the rest of the bundle. Rennic had said it probably wasn't fresh. It was best to be sure.

He ducked back inside and hunkered down. Hesso returned a moment later, muttering to himself, apparently satisfied that he had quelled whatever rebellion Rennic was plotting. He settled back down on his rickety stool, shaking drops from his cloak, then poured himself a mug of steaming, well-earned tea.

Chel sat anxious in the barn's darkness, listening to the drumming of the rain on the roof and to Hesso's stretches and grumbles. He poured himself another mug in short order, and his grumbles began to shift, becoming erratic, then interspersed with giggles. Chel smiled. The tea was working.

The giggles became more frequent, Hesso's monologue now loud and gabbling, then he stood in a rush, pacing around the fire, gesticulating, ranting, screeching with laughter. Chel had a sudden cold, sick feeling, the growing sense that he might well have overdone it. He peeked around the door, seeing Hesso pause mid-chatter to pour himself another tea, then down it in a single swallow. He resumed his pacing, now apparently having a full-on conversation with himself, muttering and gesticulating with pointed looks toward the top of the hill.

Hesso tugged at his cloak, throwing it from his shoulders, pulling at his collar. Still not satisfied, he strode out into the rain, walking in small circles in the yard, gabbling and steaming. He marched up to the shack, shouted something at the window, then doubled over, retched and vomited. He stood, swaying, tried to say something else, then bent again, losing another tranche of his dinner. He looked around, dazed, then slowly collapsed into the thickening mud.

Chel counted to ten, but Hesso didn't move. His unease became panic, and he scampered across the yard, finding the young man lying on his side, a fresh puddle of vomit beside his mouth, diluting in the persistent rain.

'Fuck, oh fuck, I'm sorry, Hesso, I'm so sorry,' he whispered, reaching out a hand to the boy's neck, checking for a pulse.

'Get over yourself, little man. He's fine.'

Rennic's face filled the window, cut into slices by the bars, an incomplete apparition.

'He's going to have one skull-fucker of a headache tomorrow, but he'll live. Puking his guts out was the best thing for him.'

Runnels of rainwater ran down Chel's brow, dripping from his nose. 'I can't leave him here. Not like this.'

'And you won't. But he can sit there for a moment longer.'

The shack key was on Hesso's belt, and a moment later the door was open. Rennic was still sitting by the window, perched on an upturned bucket. Chel wasn't sure if that was the only bucket in the room.

'Come on, let's go.'

The big man nodded, but he was still staring out of the window, pale snatches of moonlight washing over his skin. He looked thin, unkempt, but somehow different. Chel realized that there was a stillness to him, an absence of edge, the eternal restlessness that seemed to animate him through each day. Chel wondered if he'd ever have noticed it, had he not witnessed it gone.

'You came back, then.'

'Of course I did. Did you think I wouldn't?'

Still Rennic hadn't moved. 'Got to admit, I wondered. Can't be a bad life here. Long way from anywhere.'

'Are you all right? We should leave.'

'You know,' Rennic said, his gaze still somewhere in the drizzling night sky, 'I rode once with a terrible old bastard, a man called Gamarveb Klesien. Ever hear of him? Fought in half a dozen wars, back when it was a ransomer's game. His lot dropped a bollock in one of those battles, I forget which, Lemon could tell you, and he was captured. Spent nine months in a cell somewhere over the Shenakar border, hoping his lot back home would raise the coin to free him. Eventually, the front shifted, and loyalists overran wherever the hells he was stuck, and he was free.'

'And? So?'

'You know what he said to me? When he saw the pennants flying through the bars, heard the clank of his cell door opening?'

225

'What?'

'Said he felt disappointed. Lost. Regretful. Said those nine months were the most peaceful of his life, and he knew in that moment that he'd never know peace again.'

'Why are you telling me this now? You want to stay here, is that it?' Already Chel's mind was racing away, imagining a course of events where they stayed. Where Rennic was contented in his shack, where Hesso's episode was explained as illness, where he and Rasha finally took their evening walk together . . . Where he found peace . . .

'No, fuck no, imbecile. I'm merely commenting that I can finally see where he was coming from. It's a simpler existence, and no mistake.'

'And you didn't have this epiphany during our time in Black Rock?'

'We were about to be murdered by twats. It was not much of a time for peaceful reflection.'

'Well good, then.' Chel felt hot around his throat, an urge to snipe. 'I'm delighted. You must be sure to tell Gamarbollocks that you can finally sympathize with him.'

'I'd love to, but he took a bolt to the eye the week after he told me that story. Stupid old bastard, never did learn to keep his helmet on. Shall we get a move on?'

They propped Hesso back beside his fire and retrieved their gear, Chel stripping back down to his silk undershirt, glad to be out of the damp clothes Laralim had given him. He stared at them a moment, crumpled and soggy, feeling a sharp pang for what could have been.

'Nice move with the leaf, by the way,' Rennic said, belting his jacket. 'Course, I'd just have cut the poor fucker's throat, but you love a bit of righteousness, eh? How many did you slip in there, three, four?'

226

Chel coughed. 'Dropped the whole bundle in.'

'Nine hells, no wonder he puked. That could have killed him three times over.' He laughed, a sneering chuckle, his old edge reasserting itself. 'And there I was thinking it was the revolting sight of a couple of mooning teenagers that had brought on all that heaving.'

'You *saw* that?' Chel's cheeks were burning. 'What did you see?'

'Enough to know you've done well, little man. Now let's get the fuck out of this place.' He hefted a staff he'd found in the barn and nodded toward the door. Somewhere a lone bell tolled, sad and final. 'What's the plan for getting through the gate?'

Chel paused. 'I was going to save some of the leaf, but I wasn't sure—'

'Shepherd's piss-pipe, seriously? Is this the curse of your family? An inability to get past stage one of any plan?'

'We can salvage the tea, maybe if I take it down to them—'

'I might as well walk back in there and bolt the door myself, save some time. Fucking *hells*!' Rennic went to put down the staff, then froze, his eyes locked on the barn's open doorway.

'Company,' he said, very quietly.

Chel gripped his retrieved mace, fingers tight, wrist loose, and turned with deliberate slowness, coiled to strike.

A figure stood before them, cowled and dripping, flinching as if expecting a blow. One shaking hand reached up, pulling back the shawl that covered her head.

'Rasha?'

'I wondered . . .' she said, voice unsteady, her fear obvious. Chel slid his mace hand behind his back. 'I wondered what you'd do. If I should trust you.'

227

From the corner of his eye, Chel saw Rennic rest his staff against a barrel and slip one hand to his belt. He raised his empty hand, calming, placatory.

'I know this looks—'

'What did you do to Hesso? Is he dead?'

She might have been crying, he couldn't tell. She was soaked through.

Chel shook his head, emphatic, sheer willpower keeping his movements sure, his tone even. 'He's fine. He'll have—' he shot Rennic a look, '—a bad headache tomorrow, but he'll be fine.'

'And you. You and your dangerous friend. You're leaving?'

He took a long breath, closing his eyes. He could hear Rennic shifting behind him, hear the subtle slip of a knife from its sheath, clean over the pounding of blood in his ears.

'There is a war coming, and we need to stop it. Or, if we can't stop it, at least fight it well. Because otherwise it's a massacre. Every day that Laralim holds us here, that war comes a day closer.'

She frowned, upset, uncertain. 'Truly?'

'Truly. I'm first sworn to Prince Tarfel of Vistirlar. He's the only one who can stop his brother.'

'This war, would it come here?'

'It's possible.'

'So . . .' She tilted her head back, working over the thoughts. 'So if you were to prevent it, you'd be saving people here from harm?'

'Yes, I suppose so.'

'And if I helped you, I'd really be helping my own people?'

Chel felt a grin pulling at his mouth, a warm tingle of

relief spreading outwards from his core. He tried to keep his face serious. 'Absolutely. You'd be a hero. Secretly.'

She was smiling now, a sad, nervous smile, bedraggled but proud. 'I always wanted to do something heroic.' She pulled the shawl back over her head. 'You'd better follow me.'

They followed. As they walked, Rennic leaned in to whisper, 'Who the fuck is this girl?'

Chel only smiled. Somewhere, another bell tolled.

\* \* \*

'I'll sound the alarm over poor Hesso, then say I saw someone running off the other way. You must have ditched me in the gardens, lost in the rain, poor me.' Chel smiled, but something sharp and regretful needled his innards. 'Wait behind there until the gate guards come running past, then run for it. There are three of them. Don't get seen, whatever you do – if it looks like you made it to the river, they won't bother pulling the dogs from the kennels. Get it?'

They nodded.

'Good luck, then, sell-swords.'

Rennic ducked his head in acknowledgement, then scrambled through the rain and down beside the muddy track that led down to the gate. Chel was left before her, fumbling for suitable words.

'Rasha, I don't—'

She took his elbow and pulled him to one side, behind a chicken coop and out of sight of the track's far side.

'What is it? What's wrong?'

She stood before him in the drizzle, dampslick, her eyes shining up in the dim glimmer of distant lamps. 'Take care of yourself, outlaw,' she said, her arm still on his. 'When this is over, once you've stopped your war, come this way again, and we'll take our walk.'

She kissed him then, before he could speak, pulling him down to her, her lips cold and soft, their faces slippery with rain. She pressed against him, the cool of her hands on his cheeks at first startling, then soothing, their warmth growing. He felt dizzy, breathless, enraptured by the sudden inexplicability of it all. And then she broke away, her hands leaving his cheeks, her breath steaming before them. Chel's lips were numb, bereft, her warmth on him already fading.

'Stay safe,' she said, then turned and hurried away into the soggy night. Chel stood, rolling his lips against each other, marvelling at the lingering tingles that shivered over him. He thought about calling after her. *Wait. Come back. I want to do that again.*

A fat slug of rain slopped from the edge of the coop and down the back of his neck. The spell broken, he made for the ditch where Rennic lay, just as her first cries of counterfeit alarm drifted over the rain.

\* \* \*

They stomped down terraced fields in the darkness, Rennic hissing and cursing at every slurping mud pocket, damning the hill and those who built upon it. Chel concentrated on keeping his footing, the dark near absolute despite the rain's abatement. He strained his ears at the shouts and bells from above them, softened by mist and distance, the tell-tale barking of hounds so far little more than excited accompaniment to the buzz of activity. But in his head, her voice spoke again and again. *When this is over . . .*

'What's the plan . . .' Rennic muttered, his breath coming

hard as he crested another of the rugged humps of earth,
'. . . for the outer wall?'

The outer wall. Chel had forgotten about the outer wall.
He could see it now, through the misting gloom, a black
stockade stretching along the extremes of their vision, the
dark mass of the city rising beyond it. Not hugely tall or
thick, but a serious obstacle for two bedraggled mercenaries
lugging a box of contraband in the dark.

'Where's the outer gate from here? It won't be manned
overnight, will it?'

He could feel the force of Rennic's glare, even without
seeing it.

'That a chance you want to take, little man? Piss this
magnificent escape away on a hunch?'

They made for the wall's nearest section. The tolling of
the bell up on the hill had ceased, but still occasional shouts
drifted over. Chel wondered how Laralim was taking the
news of his escape. His betrayal.

'I can probably shin it, if I climb on your back?'

'What?' Chel started, already lost in a spiral of worries
of Rasha, punished for her collaboration. His hand was at
his mouth again, without him even being aware, his finger
running over his lip, reliving the feel of her.

'Wake up, little man! The fuck's got into you? I said, I
can shin it, you're my mounting block. And fuck knows if
I can pull you up after me, especially after slogging through
all this shit.'

The thick carpet of cloud cracked overhead, thin streams
of moonlight slipping through as if through water. A silver
sliver washed over them, hazy and meandering, bathing the
stout logs of the stockade in a heartbeat's pale radiance
before vanishing.

Something caught Chel's eye. A flutter at the crest of the wall, a little further down by a cluster of thin trees. 'What's that? It looks like . . .' He squinted in the moonlight. 'A ribbon?'

Rennic was by his side immediately, one hand heavy on his shoulder, peering past. 'It's not . . .' he began, then, 'it can't be!' At once he barked a sudden laugh that seemed to echo from the hillside, and clamped a grimy hand over his mouth.

Chel was whirling between hope and terror like a wind-driver in a gale. 'What, what is it?'

Rennic only waved to follow. 'Come on.' He loped toward the fluttering object with long, sure strides, his mud-dogged slouch forgotten. Chel was a few steps behind him, arriving in time to see Rennic reach up with his staff and poke at the fluttering object above them, jabbing and teasing.

Something flashed between them, squirming and half-formed, then slapped against the wooden palisade, rebounding once before hanging still. Chel shied back, heart thudding, before his eyes processed what had fallen: a rope.

He looked up to the wall's summit as another glimmer of moonlight rode over them. There, jammed into the wood, stood a black-shafted arrow, its fletching stripped. Instead, a set of long, fabric tassels of various colours flowed from it, dancing on the wind.

'What in hells is that?'

Rennic was already hauling on the rope, one foot against the palisade, testing its strength. To Chel's relief, it was evidently not anchored on the slim arrow.

'A wind marker,' Rennic replied, unable to keep the glee from his voice. 'Here, hold my staff.'

Chel did as he was told as Rennic began to heave himself up the wall, his breath sharp and heavy in the night's sudden stillness.

'It marks the wind? What's it doing here? Why is there a rope with it?' He paused. 'Not that I'm complaining.'

Rennic reached the wall's summit and threw one leg over, straddling it. He reached out a hand. 'The staff, gormless.' He was grinning in the silvery moonlight. He took the staff and Chel began his own climb. It was much harder than he'd anticipated. 'One of Whisper's tricks, if she was setting a trap or ambush without trees or similar. Shows you when the wind's blowing, from where and how strong.'

'Are . . . we . . . going to be . . . ambushed?'

'No, little man, nine hells no. It just means she was here.' He let out a contented breath. 'She left this for us.' He grabbed Chel and dragged him up alongside him, and for a moment the two of them sat, legs dangling, catching their breath as the black clouds rolled overhead. For all the moment's peace, it was extremely uncomfortable.

'Stroke of luck, us stumbling over it,' Chel said at length. Rennic stared at him, dark brows crashed together in withering disdain.

'Use your brain, little man. How many of these do you think she set?'

'Ah.'

'Yeah, ah. Now let's get moving. This fucking wall is giving me splinters.'

\* \* \*

They found packs beneath the trees, artfully covered but, as Rennic declared, easy enough to find if you knew what you were looking for. He was of the opinion that Whisper, presumably with Tarfel alongside, had tracked their capture and been confident enough of their eventual escape to leave means and provisions. Chel had to admit that his theory bore weight.

'Do you think they're still around, waiting for us?'

Rennic shook his head. 'Whisp knows the plan, and she's more professional than any. She'll have set this and made for the meeting point. She wasn't going to waste days waiting for us.'

'She and Tarfel went cross-country, alone?'

The big man held his gaze. 'Safest hands there could be.'

'What about us, what now?'

Rennic shouldered one of the packs. 'We're miles behind where we should have been. We abandon the other stops and make for the Bridge House directly – if we get our pace up, we can still meet the others and cross the river together.' He tightened a strap. 'Let's hope they've accomplished more than us.'

'You think we can make it in time?'

Rennic swung the other pack up into him.

'How fast can you run?'

# SEVENTEEN

It stood on a wide, solid outcrop of dark rock, proud from the churning waters around it, at the joining of two rivers: one wide and sweeping, the second narrower, eager. It was a rising, many-tiered thing, alive with lamplight in the waning silver of the afternoon. Steam billowed from a dozen chimneys on its structure, twisting and curling until it melded with the cloud above. It seemed both elegant and sturdy, thick blocks of dark stone blended with older pale crenellations and slender turrets, myriad silken pennants drooping in the still air.

Two great bridges arced from the outcrop at the water's centre, one to each bank, wide and walled and dotted with lights and squatting substructures. Each ended in a mighty gatehouse, ringed by stakes and torches, and beyond them shanties of hawkers, traders and supplicants had sprung, secondary settlements, parasitic and expanding.

'So that's the Bridge House.' Chel took in the imposing gatehouse looming over the huddled staging inns, the peaked arc of the thick bridge beyond, the sprawling, towering structure at its end. 'I heard of it. Never thought I'd visit.'

'Don't stand there gawping, you fucking hayseed,' Rennic muttered from beside him, his eyes roving the structures at the muddy roadside. All around them, the auxiliaries called their wares and services, stabling and storage, coin exchange and covert fencing, knock-down companionship for the more frugal traveller. 'Help me look. If we've missed them, I swear to God, I'll cross that river floating on your bloated corpse.'

The third staging inn proved the right one, and it was the noise that guided Chel and Rennic – exhausted, mud-caked and farcically travel-sore – to their target. Voices rose from behind a wooden partition at the edge of the churned and puddle-washed stable-yard, the first with a strong Nortish accent.

'Stop making that noise.'

'What noise?'

'That disgusting honking sound.'

'I'm just fucken *breathing*!'

'You are wheezing like a punctured bellows.'

'I've got a cold, all right? It's cold around here, we're wet all the fucken time, I've waded more waterways in the last few weeks than I thought I'd see in a year. It happens.'

Chel almost collapsed as his doubt and anxiety evaporated. *Lemon. We've found Lemon.*

'Ah, I cannot wait to get shot of you, you shirty wee bollocks. The sooner we dump you back on your lot in Denirnas, the better.'

'The only thing that could rival my delight at returning to my people would be my joy at escaping the stench of your undergarments. Do you have some kind of mortal aversion to bodily hygiene?'

'*You want to hear what I've got a fucken aversion to—?*'

Rennic was ahead of him, his stride reinvigorated by the confirmation of their journey's end. 'Lemon!' he bellowed. 'Get out here.'

A wild and orange head popped over the partition. 'Boss? That you? Fucken hells, man, where have yous two been? Whisp and princey showed up ages back. You're lucky we didn't cross without you.'

Chel rested himself against the partition's rough wood and squinted up at Lemon, her head haloed copper in the watery afternoon light. His legs were numb, which was for the best as the blisters on his feet had long since passed through all known realms of discomfort and arrived at a new place of agony. 'Why didn't you? We missed the first moon, didn't we? We were counting days . . .' He rubbed at one eye and regretted it as flakes of mud clung to his lashes. 'I lost count a bit.'

Rennic clapped a hand up to where Lemon's presumed shoulder lay, a look of near affection cracking the grime around his eyes. 'They wouldn't have gone without us, they hung on to the last. Reckless, Lem, but I can't say I'm not a little touched.'

Lemon offered a tight, unconvincing smile, cleared her throat and dropped from view. A moment later, she wandered around the side of the partition, brushing straw from her boots. 'Aye, well, truth be told we would have crossed last night were it not for a touch of, ah, indelicacy around our travel arrangements.'

'What?' Rennic and Chel said in unison, with markedly different inflections.

Lemon kept her eyes on anything but them. 'Spot of trouble with negotiating our transit, the securing of certain approvals, and the, uh, wherewithal to acquire said.'

'What?' Chel repeated, this time in genuine confusion.

Rennic let out a long breath. 'She means they didn't have enough coin for all the bribes. Nine hells, Lemon, what happened to planning ahead?'

'Ah, don't blame me! I was in charge of nothing more than keeping arse-bastard the alchemist on a tight lead, income and expenditure was Loveless's remit.'

Chel's head was now resting against the partition. He could feel his eyes trying to close against his will. 'You and our Nortish visitor not getting on, Lem?'

She tried to smile again but managed only a murderous leer. 'That salty wee fuck-spoon? If it were up to me—'

Rennic cut her off. 'Where are the others now? How did you get on with your tasks?' He swallowed and a touch of his nervous edge returned, the lines deepening beneath his eyes. 'Does the plan hold?'

Lemon waved a hand toward the grand bridge that rose beyond the walls of the stable-yard. 'Back with the gate clerks. I believe we, uh, unlocked some new funding since the last attempt.'

'And the plan?'

'Ach, don't ask me, man, I'm just the fucken babysitter.'

A needling voice came from the partition's far side. 'You are welcome to seek other duties, savage, assuming you can find any worthy of your abilities. Perhaps a privy requires brushing with something coarse and wiry?'

Lemon jerked a thumb, her round eyes wide. 'You see what I have to put up with? This fucken—'

'Where's the prince now, Lem?' Chel asked, near poleaxed by a sudden remembrance of his oath and duty. 'Where's Tarfel?'

She nodded her head at the yard's far side. 'Yonder. Don't

worry, Fossy's keeping an eye. We both drew the jobbie-fla-voured ends of the stick this time round.'

Chel nodded his thanks and began a slow limp across the squelching yard, while Rennic set off in the direction of the privy. 'No bother, boys, nice to see you,' Lemon called after them. 'I suppose.' Then: 'Oh, first moon was last night – you'd have seen it if it weren't for the shite-sheet of cloud. You were only a day behind.'

Only a day, Chel thought as he crossed the yard. Turns out I can run pretty fast after all.

\* \* \*

Foss was resting against a stack of mottled crates, eyes half-closed, when he saw Chel's approach. He leapt up, a beaming smile across his broad face and a look of great relief in his eyes. 'My friend! You are returned to us. Is the boss with you?'

Chel nodded, returning the smile. 'Availing himself of the facilities. Where's Tarfel?'

A crash came from an open stable door beside them, followed by the sound of splintering wood. They were followed by a muffled hammering sound, as if someone were ineffec-tually beating a piece of wood against a plaster wall.

Foss's smile diminished. He was already edging away, Chel noticed, back into the yard. Perhaps that relief in his eyes hadn't been entirely from seeing Chel alive and whole. 'Taking out his frustrations within.'

'His frustrations?'

'He can explain it better than I, friend. It's good to see you so well!' With that, Foss was off, lumbering across the muddy yard to where Lemon lurked sulking.

Another crash issued from within the stable, although it sounded as though it was losing steam.

Chel peered inside. 'Tarfel? Your highness?'

'Vedren? Vedren, is that you?' Tarfel came trotting into the doorway's grey light, a broken length of rotten wood in one hand. He looked like he'd been crying, but was otherwise healthy. Thinner, if anything. 'Shepherd be praised, you're alive!'

'I am, high— Tarf. I am. I'm glad to see you're well, but . . .' Chel gestured to the wood in the prince's hand. His eyes were adjusting, and he could now see the stack of rotting crates against the far wall, the ragged pile of broken wood at one end. '. . . Is everything all right?'

The prince took in a long breath through his nose and pulled himself straight. 'If I am to be honest with you, Vedren, and I believe I should always be honest with my first sworn,' Chel nodded along, feeling his trail-aches creeping back with renewed vigour, 'then no, everything is not all right. I have been . . . ill-used, Vedren, and certainly ill-served.'

'How so? Do you mind if I sit, Tarf, it's been quite a trip.'

'What? Yes, by all means, although not on those boxes, they're a little, ah, unsteady. Perhaps outside?' They emerged, blinking, as Tarfel continued. 'Ill-served, Vedren, for the duration of your absence. When first we witnessed your abduction outside the walls of Merenghi, I demanded the mercenary intercede but she refused. I commanded her to rescue you, and she refused again. Instead she kept me huddled in a hedge while she went off and planted little flags. Then!' He was beginning to pace, the soft mud of the yard smearing his boots. 'Then, instead of awaiting your escape, she force-marched me across the countryside, made me hide in trees, in ditches – ditches, Vedren! Cold, icy, slimy ditches! – avoiding anything that could be considered civilization until we reached this place.'

He stopped and waved a regal arm around him, before leaning forward to meet Chel's drooping eyeline. 'Now, Vedren, I realize that I must travel incognito, to keep my royal status under our collective bonnet, but I am still a prince beneath my simple garb and I am still in command of this expedition, this great endeavour, the salvation of our kingdom. Yet since finding the rest of our company, every one of them has done little more than ignore me, or worse, give me orders. Orders, Vedren! I'm the prince!'

Chel tried to offer a smile that was both sympathetic and calming. He was very tired, and the prince's cheeks were getting redder by the moment. 'And if that weren't enough,' the prince continued, his voice now what passed for a low growl, 'do you know what day it is, Vedren?'

'Not enough?' Chel shook his head. 'The first day after the spring moon, I think.'

'Exactly,' Tarfel replied. 'The spring festival is upon us.' He took a long, shuddering breath, and Chel saw tears glisten in the corners of his pale eyes. 'We have missed my birthday.'

Chel felt the silence stretch, and summoned what strength he had left. 'Your birthday?'

'It's a week before the new light festival. I was . . . I'm eighteen now.'

Chel swallowed. 'Happy . . . belated birthday.'

'Father always said that you became a man, a true man, at eighteen. My brother received new titles, had a lavish feast that went on for days. All the vassals came, bringing gifts, tokens, offers of marriage . . .'

'I'm so sorry you missed it, Tarf.'

'Of course, Father would have been dead by then, and Mendel too. Vassad must have arranged the whole thing, while Corvel faked his way through it. Who would have arranged my birthday feast? Does my brother even know I'm still alive? Does he care?'

'I'm sure he cares.'

'If he does, then it's only because I'm a threat.' Tarfel stood tall, white fists clenched by his side. 'I'm a man now, a prince of the realm with a claim to the throne. My brother cannot be allowed to drive this nation further into the mire! People need to listen to me!'

Chel could only offer a weak nod. To his relief, he saw Foss wandering back across the yard toward them. He'd attained new understanding of the look the big man had given him on his arrival. 'Foss?'

'The others are back. There's news.'

# EIGHTEEN

Loveless and Whisper had entered the inn's main structure, but Foss suggested the others wait for them by the door. Chel was too tired to argue, and simply lay down in the straw where Lemon and Kosh were sheltered. Rennic was already snoring in the corner while Tarfel continued to pace in the yard. The downside to the straw, of course, was suffering another bout of international bickering.

'What in hells are you making, anyway? Are those wings?'

'Nothing you would understand.'

'You always say that. I understand plenty, missy.'

'Do you understand the essence that permeates all things, that flows through every material, every object? The essence that must be respected, embraced, shaped and entwined?'

'You do talk a lot of bollocks, don't you?'

'You see, you have no understanding of such things. Balance and harmony. The correct measures of earth salts, the correct strike of a hammer on steel, the incantations and ceremonies for all things.'

243

'Aye, right. Steel is steel, stumpy. Doesn't need a song to get it to bend.'

'Perhaps not to a cave-dweller. It is a marvel to me that your people, such as they are, have even achieved its production, however crudely.'

'I can show you fucken crude, pal.'

'This is my most surprised face. Do you understand it?'

'Ha, yeah, ha. You can talk all you like, midge, chatter on about your inanimate spirits there, but you see, I'm a *rationalist*. A thinker. Where I come from, we don't go in for all this superstition.'

'Really? What do you worship, where you are from? I imagine something burning, perhaps a giant pig made of bark and dung.'

'Ha. Worship nothing, we do. The Clyde is beholden to no man or god, you see, no spirit or pictsie.'

'Indeed. Each an individual, then, alone in the world? No sense of a whole, no belonging?'

'Bollocks again. We're tight as anything, where I'm from. Great sense of history, of family.'

'Yet here you are, far from all—'

'*Wisdom* of ancestors, passed down generation to generation, ever expanding. No daughter of Clyden is going to repeat any ancestor's mistake. We're all part of a great whole, a giant one.'

'It certainly sounds like it. You must consider yourselves fortunate, I suppose, that your people are born with strong and lustful animal urges, or you would no doubt have died out years ago.'

'I don't have to listen to this blather. I'm going to find Fossy.'

'Watch out for gods and spirits.'

'Fuck off.'

'For a rationalist, you're showing a great deal of emotion.'

'Fuck *off*!'

A crest of faded pink hair appeared around the partition. 'Everything all right in here, ladies? Not disturbing an intimate moment, am I?'

'You can fuck off an' all,' Lemon muttered.

Loveless flashed her a malicious grin, which softened when her gaze fell on Chel. 'You made it, cub. Good to see you.'

He could only stammer a reply, his tired brain flashing straight to thoughts of Rasha in the rain, and a sudden burst of guilt. He felt his cheeks darkening and tried to cover his face with his hands in a feeble pretence at cleaning off some of the filth, but she had already moved on. His relief must have shown too clear on his face, as he turned to find Lemon giving him an appraising look, one eyebrow raised.

Rennic was upright and awake. 'On your feet, little man.'

Chel tried to follow. His aching body was protesting seriously. Eventually, Lemon launched him from the straw-pile, and Foss kept him upright on landing. He was too sore to be grateful.

\* \* \*

'God's bollocks, we thought we'd finally cut you loose, Gar.' Loveless's smile was playful, but something simmered in her eyes. Apparently, their arguments had not been forgotten in their time apart. In the fading afternoon light she looked tired, paler than Chel remembered. Perhaps she'd had a tough trip too. 'You had the decency to be late by only a day, I suppose. Did you keep your heads down on the way in? This place is crawling with small-timers, and there's word of more on the road. Did anyone see you? Did you see anyone you recognized?'

Rennic was gazing up at the darkening sky, wearing a look of uncharacteristic stoic patience. Chel wasn't sure if it was affected or not, thinking back to his time in captivity in the Andriz enclave and the calm that had settled on the big man before their escape. While their trip had been hard and exhausting, it hadn't been . . . angry. Perhaps Rennic had gained a new perspective in his time alone, perhaps some of the rage had left him. It seemed a lot to hope for.

'Don't think so,' he mumbled at last. 'Little man and I were focused on finding you lot.'

'Whisp told us you made some unplanned friends in Merenghi. Does this mean you shat the bed when it came to meeting my contacts?'

'Yeah, we fucked it,' Rennic said with a sigh. 'By the time little man busted us out, we had no time to get anywhere but here. And like you said, a day late.'

'Lucky we had to wait, eh?'

'Who needs luck when you've got the little man along.'

Chel waved a half-hearted arm. 'Can we not dredge that up, please? Andriz are no luckier than anyone else. Seriously.'

'So you say, cub, yet here we are. No good news to report, then, Gar?'

Rennic shook his head. 'We went cross-country, hit the river and followed it east. Could hardly have told you what month it was. Although little man did turn his back on a lifetime of studding the young fillies of Merenghi's Wards.'

This time there was no disguising the blush. Even Loveless couldn't keep the incredulous mirth from her face. 'Come again?'

Rennic's grin was savage. 'Did you know the Wards were all Andriz? They wanted to keep him as a sire for their stock, could have seen out the rest of his days doing little more than covering their maidens.'

Chel gritted his teeth, stared at the floor and tried not to think of Rasha. So much for a new perspective.

Rennic's levity departed without warning. 'We failed, then. What about you? Do we still have a chance?'

This time Loveless's smile was bright and genuine. 'We did well. Maybe we should have left you to one side earlier.'

Rennic didn't rise to it. 'How well?'

She reeled off a string of accomplishments, from enlisting the enthusiastic support of a number of minor lords, some with connections to kingdoms abroad, to the exuberant reaction of the tribal emissaries at the news that the free companies that usually kept them in check would be holding fast in their strongholds. Foss sighed heavily at the mention of the lords, and muttered something about parties. 'Come the thaw in the high places,' Loveless finished, 'our tribal friends will likely come rampaging down with greater force than ever. They have particular enmity for the church forces, it seems; it rather sounds like they have a new religion up there.'

From the corner of his eye, Chel saw Foss make the sign of the crook.

Rennic let out a long breath. 'That's good. That's really good. We may have snarled the free cities, but if all else starts to roll our way . . .'

'Exactly.' Loveless finished the thought. 'They won't want

to be left out, especially if they fear their rivals will be taking advantage.'

'Then a lot rides on the decisions of the free companies. At the Gracechurch I thought we had the balance, before Corvel arrived and made our point for us. What happened after?'

Lemon cleared her throat. 'Aye, right, we legged it on their arrival, same as you, but the tales since, weeell, they suggest there was something of a set-to.'

Rennic gazed at her from beneath lowering brows. 'A set-to?'

'A fracas. A ruckus. A brouhaha.'

'Nine fucking hells, Lemon, spit it out!'

'Aye, well the wildest tales suggest that during the afore-mentioned altercation, the Gracechurch was somewhat . . . levelled.'

'Horseshit.'

'I did describe said tales as the wildest of their ilk.'

'There's no chance, the place is . . . You'd have to grind the walls down with engines for months, they'd still be chipping away at the curtain wall even now—'

'Aye, all right, all right, I only know what I heard, boss.'

Chel thought of the smell of burning on the wind the day they fled the Gracechurch, and wondered.

'Irrespective,' Loveless said over Lemon's protestations, 'for every gambit failed, a gambit won – and vice versa. We're on the blade's edge here. Our next stop can sink us, or save us.' She was leaning against the piebald wall of the staging inn, and for a moment Chel thought she looked as tired as he felt. He spotted that Whisper was keeping close to her, within easy reach. She must be as concerned as Chel.

'Denirnas,' Rennic said, fast enough to remind everyone he was in command.

'Denirnas,' Loveless repeated, as if crediting Rennic with the correct answer to a question she'd asked. 'Alliance with the Norts. We bring Kosh's people on-side, Corvel and his forces will quickly feel the noose begin to tighten.'

Chel stared down at his hands. Back to Denirnas. Back to where it had all begun. Unprompted, his shoulder began to throb.

'If you ask me,' Lemon said, 'we can't get rid of the wee shite fast enough. She's toxic, that one, just like her nasty brews.'

'Funny, Lemon,' Loveless shot back, 'she says the same about you.'

'Now listen here—'

'Keep yourself together, Lem, just a little while longer. We need them to like us when we propose alliance, remember?'

'I'm being fucken nice! I'm being a fuck-sight nicer than her behaviour—'

'Just a little longer, Lemon. Take deep breaths.'

'Do you all see that? She's fucken *smirking* at me! She's—'

'It still might not be enough.' Rennic's eyes were on Kosh but his words were for Loveless. 'We have to consider—'

'No.'

'You know people there, important people.'

'No.'

He swung to face her. 'If just one of the pieces of our plan doesn't fall into place, especially after our failure with the free cities—'

'No! The Norts will be enough, they'll be the key you wanted, the dagger in Corvel's back. Pressure in the north.

His forces split, nowhere safe – he'll be begging for parley before the crops begin to turn.'

She turned to face the others, leaving Rennic standing. 'Once we cross, we make for the coast, full-speed.' Chel thought he caught a slight waver in her voice at the last. 'Ruumi's reavers may already have landed, all we need do is stay ahead of the news. Denirnas, Norts, victory.'

'It may not—' Rennic began.

'Whisp and I have got the passes sorted,' she ploughed over him, 'and we'll cross tonight. There are far too many unfriendly faces around here for my liking, too many people with the sniff of a contract about them. So, we'll cross in darkness, disguised as merchants.' She gestured to a wagon across the yard. 'That's us there, cloaks, hoods, and packs aboard. Gar, Fossy, and Whisp will be the guards, Lem and I the drivers.'

Chel put up a tired hand. 'What about the rest of us? Me, Kosh, and the prince?'

'In the back. You're our cargo. Out of sight, under canvas.'

He considered being offended, but the thought of lying down in the back of a wagon for a while was an appealing one.

'Huh,' came a voice from behind them. Chel turned to see Tarfel stalking off across the yard, back in the direction of his stable of rotten wood.

All eyes were on Chel. 'Fuck's wrong with princeling?' Rennic said.

'Cares not to be cargo?' Lemon enquired.

'We, er . . . He missed his birthday.'

Rennic's glare carried more heat than the midday sun. 'The fuck you say?'

'. . . And you've all been mean to him! He is a prince, remember? He's supposed to be in command. He's the reason we're doing all this.'

Rennic seemed to grow before Chel's eyes, swelling with charged outrage, and he steeled himself for the onslaught.

'See if you can talk him round, cub,' Loveless murmured before Rennic could burst. 'Shepherd knows there's worse to come than this.' She circled a hand. 'Let's get packed for the road, fellow merchants.'

# NINETEEN

'Feels a bit sad,' Chel said from under his canvas, as they peered up at the glowing glory of the Bridge House from their dismal perch in the back of the wagon. They were through the giant gatehouse now and rolling up the gentle slope of the first bridge, the churn of white water against its piers quickly drowning the calls and cries from the bank as they climbed. The bridge was busy, people travelling in both directions, some mounted or with carts or wagons, others on foot in groups or alone. Chel thought he could tell the through-traffic like them from patrons of the House itself; they seemed to walk with their gaze downcast, never making eye-contact with anyone. He knew how they felt. 'Getting so close to so grand a place, then not going in.'

Kosh was huddled beside him, peeping through the canvas gap while trying to affect indifference. Her excitement at the coming reunion with her compatriots had mutated into an irritable impatience, making her marginally less pleasant to be around than usual. 'What is this place, that floods your gussets so?'

'A meeting place, you might call it,' Foss murmured from beside them. He was pacing alongside the wagon, a pretend guard, swathed in acres of rough cloak and the drooping brim of a hat too big for him. 'You see that river, the big one? The province of Banut ends at the river. And you see the small one? That marks the start of Piaunu Province. But between them, that chunk of rock? Technically neither. It's a black spot, a floater. Bound to no one.'

'What does that mean?'

'No tax or levies, as I hear it. They set their own rules over there. And they maintain the bridges, a major thoroughfare, for which they collect a no-doubt reasonable toll.'

'Nobody has tried to take it by force?'

'Look at it. I'm sure they've tried, but it's still here, eh?'

'What happens inside?'

Foss looked uncomfortable beneath the appalling hat. 'A lot of things. People come here from all over, not always as themselves. It's said that what happens there, stays there, according to popular convention at least.'

'How charmlessly banal.'

'Indeed.'

Up close, the house was even more imposing. It loomed over them, a soaring stack of nested blocks, lamplight burning from countless gauzy windows. Statues stood in its forecourt, lions and bears and other great beasts, carved from dark stone and capped with bronze and steel. A great archway marked the forecourt's entrance; beside and beyond, the second bridge began to the far bank, the disappointing destination for their trundling wagon.

'It's majestic,' Chel said, neck craned to make out the

summit of the structure, wreathed in drifting steam overhead. The canvas was peeled back now, and he knew he risked a sharp rebuke from the drivers if they spotted it.

'It is gauche,' Kosh muttered from beside him. 'Artless. The spiral towers of Astrum in Serasthana are majestic; this is a child's rendering of majesty. A stupid child at that.'

'Then forgive my artlessness but I like it. Maybe we can come back one day, once all this is over. Would make a fine location for a belated birthday party, eh, Tarf?' He looked back beneath the canvas, across the wagon bed. 'Tarf?'

He stuck his head in deeper.

'Shit.'

\*\*\*

'How the fuck did you lose him?' Rennic hissed from the wagon's far side. 'He was right there next to you!'

'How could you miss him?' Chel hissed back. 'He must have slipped right past you!'

'Aye, right, where's friend princey now, anyone?' Lemon called over her shoulder.

'I told you: you all needed to be kinder to him!'

'That boy needs to cope with a bruised ego a fuck-sight better than this if he has any hope of holding a throne someday,' Loveless snapped.

Whisper signalled urgently. *There he is!*

'He's going into the courtyard!'

'Of course he is, cub. Shepherd's tits, he's probably going to wail to them about his birthday.'

'Little man, grab him!'

'You grab him! I'm supposed to be cargo, remember?'

'Whisp, you—'

Loveless threw up a furious hand. 'If anyone tries to grab him and drag him back here, he's going to squeal like a horny piglet. And we are going to attract a *lot* of unwanted attention.' She looked up and down the bridge through narrowed eyes, torchlight flickering in the crosswind. 'We're already too much of a spectacle.'

Lemon cleared her throat. 'Folks, no rush but we're coming up on the turning here. Any danger of a plan?'

Loveless looked very tired. 'Someone needs to go in after him, and coax him out.'

'Little man, you're up.'

'Thrilled as I am to be upgraded from the status of baggage, how the fuck am I meant to find him in there on my own?'

'Wee bear makes a good point, to which I'd add, exactly what do the rest of us do in the meantime? Park up the wagon on the bridge-side here? Pretend we've bust an axle?'

Whisper signalled again. *And if there's trouble inside?*

Rennic let out a long, low growl. 'Nine eternal goat-fucking hells!'

Loveless gave a sour chuckle. 'Better steer for the archway, Lem. There are courtyards we can park up inside. Did anyone bring party clothes?'

\* \* \*

'Do you see him?' Chel pointed ahead. 'Up by the door. Seems to be talking to someone there.'

Loveless strode past. 'With any luck they'll delay him long enough for us to catch up.' She offered Chel a bright, brittle smile. 'Let's hope it's nobody nefarious. Now all of you play along with the next bit, or none of us gets in.'

Burly guards in gleaming breastplates stood at the internal gate, behind them a squat structure with very thick walls. An administrator looked up at their approach.

'Party of how many?'

Loveless counted. 'Seven. Plus one already inside.'

'Weapons?'

'Plenty.'

'Together or separately?'

Loveless unstrapped her precious sword, balanced it scabbarded in her hand.

'Separately, I think.'

'Very well.'

When Chel's turn came, he passed the mace through a boxy window in the stonework to a clerk on the far side. The man placed it in a box, then looked up. 'That all? Any knives, daggers, knuckles, small implements, anything that could be used to do harm?'

Chel surrendered his good knife. It went in the box with the mace.

The man in the window sniffed, wiped his nose on his sleeve. 'You hereby declare this collection as the sum of your ordnance, and consent to a search of your person prior to entry as well as at any point during your stay with us. Any breaches of policy will be dealt with in the harshest terms. Yes?'

A little unnerved, Chel nodded. 'Yes.'

'Wait here.'

A narrow door opened in the wall behind the man, and for a moment Chel caught a glimpse of a glittering armoury, row after row of boxes groaning with weapons mundane and exotic. His own box disappeared through the door, and it slammed shut.

'Here.' The man was proffering something, a wooden token, smooth with use, engraved with a symbol Chel didn't recognize. 'Don't lose it. Lost tokens are your own responsibility, unclaimed effects will be adopted by the estate after a lunar cycle. Next!'

Chel shuffled away, feeling somehow robbed. Lemon was waiting beyond the door, staring at her own token. She looked diminished without her tools.

'Aye, now these boys know their business. Weapons at the door, keep it simple.' She looked over at his token. 'What did you get?'

'No idea. Looks like . . . a drunk bird, falling into a pond?'

She reached over and turned it in his hand, righting it, apparently. 'It's the unshattered anvil. Very auspicious.'

'For who?'

She shrugged. 'Whoever runs this place, presumably.'

They looked up at a shout. A grim-faced Rennic was trudging back from the line of gate guards, a short, pointed dagger dangling guilty in his hand.

'They catch you out, boss?'

'Forgot one,' he muttered as he passed.

'Should be grateful, eh? Shows they're thorough!'

\* \* \*

A silk-wrapped major-domo met them at the top of the wide, ornate stairway to the main door, her face as smooth and gleaming as her robe. 'Good evening, masters, and welcome to the Bridge House. Have you visited before?'

Loveless shot a quick look at the rest of them, then nodded. 'Yes.'

If the major-domo was repelled by their ragged appearance, she gave no sign. 'What can we offer for your visit? Do you have need of our conference chambers? Accommodation for a prolonged stay? Companionship? I can—'

Tarfel appeared over her shoulder, eyes wide and nostrils flared, although Chel couldn't tell if it was anger or excitement that animated the prince. 'Ah, here they are!'

'These are your company, master?'

'Indeed, indeed. This lady is company treasurer, and will see to the collateral. Remember, your finest service!'

'Of course, master, the Pearl Terrace awaits.' The major-domo turned back to Loveless. 'You may present your collateral to my colleague.' With a measured tilt of her head, she indicated a woman behind a tall wooden desk inside the door, then withdrew, ready for the next approaching group.

'We could grab him now and make a run for it,' Rennic growled. 'Let's hear him squeal with my boot in his teeth.'

'You heard the lady, the Pearl Terrace awaits,' Loveless said, jingling her remaining coin. 'On the bright side, Gar, we're unlikely to meet anyone we know up there.' She strode inside without a backward glance.

'Normally we scumbags are confined to the lower terraces,' Rennic replied to Chel's questioning look, then went up the steps after Loveless, shoulders hunched and fuming.

'There goes our contingency,' Foss sighed as the rest of them walked after him.

'Cost of living, innit, Fossy?' Lemon chuckled. 'Everything you earn.'

With one last neck-cricking look at the looming structure, Chel followed.

\*\*\*

'This place,' Kosh said, from his elbow as they walked, 'is disgusting.'

Happy noises echoed from the polished wood floors and wall-panels, their Serican silk coverings lilting in the wind of their passing. Not the delirious whimpers of the poppy den, but genuine mirth, a genial hubbub, the clink and clatter of drink and fare. Distant sounds echoed from the galleries that opened above them, the muted roar and closer splash of water, the occasional moan or cry from somewhere in the dark recesses above. More guards stood at every corner, perfumed, oiled, and bulging with muscle. Chel tried to avoid their gaze.

'This place is honest,' Loveless said over her shoulder. 'It makes no secret of its purpose, and no apology either. More than can be said for most great institutions.'

'You seem very at home here,' the Nort replied. 'You've visited before?'

A tall, elegant woman passed them, dressed only in wisps of silk, a bulbous man with a beaming smile bobbing in her wake. Chel, Tarfel, and Kosh paused to watch them pass.

'Or perhaps you worked here?' Kosh said with an eyebrow raised.

'Is *that* why you don't like silk?' Lemon added.

Loveless offered only a half-smile of her own. 'Stairs are this way.'

Rennic still radiated fury, wrath coming off him in waves.

'We're inside and he's in grasping distance, let's slug the little fucker and carry him out like a drunkard.'

'The damage is done, Gar – we've paid our share, and we might as well try to enjoy ourselves while we're here. God knows we deserve a break.' Again, the light revealed the tight lines around her eyes, the dark smudges beneath. No wonder she was pushing for a rest, Chel thought, she looked more tired than any of them.

As they approached the winding stairway up to the galleries, a well-dressed man sauntering the other way came to a sudden halt before Foss, staring openly. He was in early middle age, thick dark hair gone silver at the temples, and the cut of his robes suggested both wealth and access to exclusive tailors.

'I say, I know you, don't I?'

Foss froze. The man turned to Loveless, who had been walking a pace ahead. It seemed he'd taken Foss as her bodyguard. 'My apologies, my lady. Sam Sayad, once of Qazvizd – before it fell to the Red Hand – at your service. Your man here, I've seen him before, haven't I?'

Loveless's gaze flicked from the new man to Foss and back, eyes narrow. 'That seems . . . unlikely.'

'Out east, years ago, easily a decade, maybe fifteen. I was touring then, lending assistance as it was required – as was done back then.'

Loveless flashed a flattering grin, but her eyes returned to Foss, sharp and urgent. *Who is this and what does he know?* Foss was sweating under his thrice-wrapped cloak.

'You were king of the pit, weren't you? In Marichan. We stayed to watch the whole tournament, quite incredible stuff. Missed the battle of Metten as a result, which didn't go down too well!' He shrugged in mock apology, then slapped Foss on the arm. 'I must say, I've never seen a man, before or since, with such command of the environment. Stellar stuff. Obviously, we've all put on a bit of timber over the years—' he patted his belly, which remained utterly flat, '—but you've made an excellent pick here, my lady. This man is a born champion.'

Loveless was still staring at Foss, but her expression had become one of mirthful surprise, tinged, perhaps, with a dash of admiration. Foss was still sweating, but for once his cheeks were dimpled with unfamiliar pride.

'Thank you, my lord.'

'What was it they called you? The Bridge . . . no, the Wall!'

'Back then, they did.'

'A title earned, good sir. I'm delighted to see you're doing well for yourself, Master Wall, with such a charming employer. Good fortune to you all.'

With a cheerful wave, Sam Sayad passed on from them and was lost in the merry traffic on the outer hallway. Loveless watched him go, then turned with great deliberation to face the stairs.

'That was interesting, wasn't it? How about no more surprise visitors from anyone's past this evening?'

\* \* \*

Chel watched the décor change as they climbed, from the wood and silk of the lower floors, past the polished stone and solid furniture of the floor marked with steel plates, the wool-covered flooring and furs of the floor marked with ivory, all the way up to the wide, closed door, on the floor above, emblazoned with a sun of gleaming pearls. His excitement growing, Chel tried to peer through the lattice window, catching a glimpse of reflected lamplight glittering golden beyond. Music drifted through the door, something stringed, and laughter. It all sounded beautifully expensive.

A woman stood beside the door, another of the simpering silk-robed staff. She bowed at their approach and unlatched the door. 'All are friends beneath this roof. Please, friends, enjoy your evening.'

'Aye, no fear on that score,' Lemon cackled as she piled through the doorway, 'consider it a devout imperative . . .'

# TWENTY

'This,' Lemon said, raising an exquisite cage cup that glittered in the candlelight, 'is fucken brilliant.'

They sat in a secluded, sunken booth on the Pearl Terrace, ensconced by tall screens, reclining around an octagonal table on cushions that were as plump and luxuriant as any Chel had ever seen. Even Rennic was able to raise a smile, turning his delicate drinking vessel in his calloused hands, allowing Lemon to refill it yet again with another splash of heavenly wine. The big man watched the liquid swirl around the cup, mesmerized, while strains of gentle music flowed over them from musicians unseen and undisturbed, and laughter echoed elsewhere on the terrace. On the booth's far side, Whisper dozed, long limbs stretched and her boots set neatly on the floor beside her.

Chel swallowed a grape, one of the few that Foss hadn't got to first. 'Is this . . . Are we . . . ?' The wine was getting to him. 'Tarfel's birthday?'

'A rest, cub. Princeling can celebrate himself if he wishes. Discreetly.'

263

Tarfel sat apart from the others, a wine pitcher to himself, drinking steadily and without pause, and occasionally toasting himself. He seemed both joyful and morose, which was quite an achievement. Chel determined to shuffle over and join the prince in his solitary revels, just as soon as he'd had a bit more fruit. And maybe some olives.

'Ancestors,' Lemon said, eyes glassy as she leered once more at her cup, 'this is the fucken good stuff.'

Loveless took a swig from her cup and made a face. 'Tastes off to me.'

'You're missing out, but more for the rest of us!'

A young couple slid into their booth, clean-limbed and dressed in wisps of silk, each equally smooth and beautiful. The boy smiled and said, 'Were you looking for any company? We have many friends.'

Rennic belched and pushed himself to his feet. 'I'm going to the privy.' He pushed past the young people without a second look.

'Oh, Gar, try to enjoy yourself,' Loveless called after him. She looked the new pair over, then muttered, 'Really going in for the silk thing around here, aren't you?'

The boy's polished brow creased, perplexed. 'I understand we have excellent relationships with many merchants who travel the Serican trail.'

'I'll bet you do.'

From her pitch in the depths of the booth, Kosh was staring at the friendly girl. She was tall, muscular, oiled or buttered from the sheen on her smooth skin. Her hair was braided with small silver rings that tinkled when she tilted her head. Kosh gazed, enraptured, then looked sharply away when the girl met her eye with a smile.

'You know . . .' The voice came from Tarfel, looking up

now, an empty wine pitcher lying flat across his knees. 'My birthday party. My proper one. Would have been like this. Bigger, though.'

Chel stirred himself. 'Well, Tarf, Loveless did say—'

'Courtesans!' said the prince emphatically. 'Concubines! Companions!'

The friendly girl offered the prince a beaming smile. 'Perhaps, master, you would enjoy a private party this evening?'

Tarfel stared up at her, purple-lipped, his bloodshot eyes offset against his ghastly pallor. 'You know what? I would!'

The smile widened. 'Very good, master. Please, take my hand and follow me. How many friends should attend?'

Tarfel disappeared from view, arm-in-arm with the friendly girl. 'I think . . .' came his voice as he skipped away, 'at least four.' Kosh watched them go, her face very still. After a moment, she got up and followed.

Chel wanted to go too. An image of Rasha fluttered into his mind, Rasha in the rain, Rasha's lips on his. He very much wanted to make the most of the Bridge House's hospitality. All he had to do was stand and walk, something he did countless times a day.

Instead he sat and watched the others vanish from view, his mouth twisted and sullen. A suppressed belch resurfaced. 'You're sure it's safe to, you know, let them go off on their own?'

Lemon and Loveless offered flat stares. 'We're all friends here, remember?' Loveless said. 'The scumbags and vaga- bonds are downstairs.'

'Fewer guards up here, too,' Lemon added, her speech slurring. 'Cos we're all trusted folk, see? Those of good stature. Standing. Stature.'

The friendly boy hovered still. 'Would anyone else care for a celebration? Perhaps you, master?' He rested one gentle hand on Foss's shoulder. The big man swallowed and, with great care, removed the hand.

'Thank you, friend, but I am just fine.'

The boy smiled, nodded, and excused himself.

'How . . .' Foss sighed, then paused, face clouded.

'How the fuck do you think, Foss-bot?' Loveless chuckled. 'They're professionals, no different from us.'

'Aye, well, they're a *little* different, though,' Lemon said.

'Admittedly, I imagine they get less blood in their hair. I'd certainly hope so, anyway.'

'You know,' Lemon said, then paused to drain the last of her wine. 'I'm surprised you're not taking them up on their offers.'

Loveless scoffed. 'I don't pay for it.'

'It's all-inclusive tonight, Ell! Quids in!'

'You know what I mean.'

Lemon poured out another cup. 'Not sure I do, honestly. I mean, you generally hop aboard anything with a winkle and a heartbeat, eh?'

Chel expected Loveless to anger, to snipe, but she seemed to keep her humour. 'Like to think I'm a *little* choosier than that.'

'You get your pick, though, eh? Any fella you fancy?' Chel felt suddenly uncomfortable.

'I'd rather break noses than hearts.'

Lemon chuckled and sucked air through her teeth in mock-pain. 'Still, those looks of yours have opened doors for you over the years, right?'

'Maybe. Doesn't mean I've liked what's come through them.' Loveless took another sip of the wine, then put down her cup, frowning. 'And you, Lemming? You're not shopping in the market yourself, this evening? I understand Brother Foss's reluctance— No, scratch that, I'm aware of it, but I can't understand it. But how about you, Lem? Nothing on the menu whetting your appetite?'

Lemon concentrated on her cup, her eyes glossy with booze. 'Aye, well, y'see, it's just not that interesting to me.'

'What is? Isn't?'

'You know . . . The *act*.'

'The—? Sex?'

'Yeah, all that, I dunno, squelching. Proximity. Smells and . . .' She shuddered. '. . . secretions.'

'You are joking, yes? This is a famous Lemon joke.'

Lemon put up one hand, the other balancing her newly refilled wine cup. 'Now, I'm not averse to the odd knuckle shuffle, of course, I'm as human as the rest of you. Shut it, Fossy. No, no, if you've got it, use it, and all that. But, well, other people, eh? They're the worst bit.'

Loveless nodded, eyebrows arched. 'Ain't they just?'

\* \* \*

'How can you keep drinking this? It's off. Definitely. What's wrong with you?'

'Aye, what's wrong with *you*? It's magnificent.'

'Maybe try the brandy, my friend, if the wine doesn't agree.'

'If they've spiced dodgy wine and expected nobody to notice, I can't see the brandy being any better.' Loveless poured herself a small cup and swilled it around her mouth.

'Aye, you were moaning about that stuff we lifted from

the cellars in Tenailen and all. You sure you're not coming down with something?'

She swallowed, made a face, grunted. 'Huh. Maybe I just need to drink through it.' She poured another, then swivelled on Chel with terrible focus.

'How about you, cub? Got your eye on anything this evening? Planning to avail yourself of the facilities?'

Chel had been dreading this. He shifted, looked anywhere but her, feigned interest in the decorative frieze that ran along the top of the luxuriant walling. 'I'm, er . . . worried about Rennic.'

Lemon hiccupped. 'Boss-man has been at the privy a while, eh? Hard rations on your little trek east, was it? I told him, told him I did, you don't get the pickling right, you're looking at a downstairs deluge—'

'That's, um, not what I meant.'

Loveless's gaze hadn't left him, sharp and piercing. 'What did you mean, cub? Something happen on the road?'

He shook his head. The room wobbled. 'Not on the road. With the Andriz. He was locked up, on his own, for days. I think . . . I think he was on his own for too long.' He tapped at the side of his head, nearly managing it. 'Too much time with his thoughts.'

Lemon waved a dismissive hand. 'He gets moody, it happens. Same as this one,' she added, jerking a thumb at Loveless, who flared her nostrils in response. 'Whispie can talk him down, *if she ever wakes up*!' Lemon threw a leftover grape at the sleeping scout, who flicked up a hand and caught it with a smile. Her eyes remained closed throughout.

Chel chuckled, marvelling at the catch, then turned back to find Loveless's gaze still pinning him.

'I note, cub, you have yet to answer my question. Nothing here tonight tickling your fancy?'

'Ha, yon wee bear has appetites that cannot be sated by tonight's menu.'

He shot Lemon a fierce glare, which set her off in a fit of giggles.

Loveless sipped at her brandy and looked around, puzzled. 'I doubt that. If there's one place to serve all desires, it's this wine-piddling establishment. How unusual could your proclivities be, cub? What sort of heinous shit are you into?'

'I fear,' Lemon said between giggles, in defiance of Chel's warning look, 'that it's not so much a *what* as a *whom* . . .'

'What? Oh!' Loveless turned on him, one eyebrow raised, a pleased and mischievous smile pulling at the corner of her mouth. '*Oh.*'

'Thrice-damn you, Lemon,' Chel growled, feeling the flush ripple up his face from his throat.

'I'm trying to save your life, wee bear! Poor wee thing like you, she'd break you in half!' Foss's gentle chuckles underpinned her cackles, huh, huh, huh.

Loveless was staring at him, amused, undecided, the way a cat stares at a cornered mouse.

He stood, rocking on his feet at the sudden rush. 'I'm . . . privy,' he managed, head spinning.

'You are, mate, you are. See if you can find out what happened to the boss, eh? Check he didn't fall in.'

He focused. 'He's there, at the doorway. Hey, isn't that . . . that . . . ?'

Sure enough, there Rennic stood at the terrace's end, bathed amber in the light of the many-candled chandeliers overhead. A smaller figure stood before him, tan and gilded, great stacks of glossy black hair coiled and bound. She had a hand on his arm.

Lemon leaned out of the booth, peering past him. 'I'll be fucked. What are the odds?'

Loveless pushed her out of the way, and her smile calcified. 'Grassi of the Mawn. What in hells is she doing here?'

'Not mixing with the scumbags?' Chel supplied. Last time he'd seen the Mawnish mercenary, they'd been in a mountain gully of blood-pinked snow, Brother Hurkel their beaten prisoner. Beneath a black flag, Grassi had let them go, on condition that the good brother did not survive.

He had survived.

'Aye, looks like they're getting well reacquainted and all. Guess the boss won't be back any time soon, eh?'

Loveless only stared, her brows low and furrowed. 'But what is she doing here?'

'Ah, relax, Ell. They're having fun. You did tell him to go off and enjoy himself, right? We should all try and get some jollies?'

'Yes. I did say that, didn't I?'

Loveless turned her back, downed the end of her brandy and poured another. Chel took the opportunity to slip out of the booth, and make unsteady progress in the direction of the now empty doorway.

\* \* \*

The music changed as Chel passed the musicians' nook, the last delicate notes of *When Come the Black Doves* fading into the merry buzz of the background, followed without delay by the clear strums of an opening he recognized. A moment of cold shock punctured his drunken fug.

'Please don't play that one.'

The musicians were a good-looking lot, their polished instruments almost glowing in the burnished light of their nook. The nearest glanced up at the sudden appearance of Chel's head in their space and broke off what would have been the opening bars.

'You have no love for the *Ballad of the White Widow*, master?'

Chel thought of the extreme reactions he'd witnessed from Rennic on previous occasions to hearing the song, and Foss's words in explanation: *If one of the company has an issue with a thing, then all in the company do – that's how it works, my friend.* Given the instability of the big man's mood, the last thing he wanted was another violent scene in such beautiful surroundings.

'One of my party prefers not to hear it. If that's all right.'

'Of course, master. We are all friends here.'

He ducked out as they started up *Qish Baymul and Joy*, a seasonal favourite, and went on his way feeling like he'd done something rather good.

\* \* \*

She was waiting for him in the hallway on his return, framed in the doorway by the soft glow beyond, a silhouette from his every dream.

'What—?'

Loveless silenced him with a kiss, grabbing him by the hair with one hand, the other soft against his cheek. She mashed her lips against his, hot, fierce, furious, her tongue already pressing against him, licking at his teeth, pushing inside his mouth. She reeked of brandy, tasted of liquid flame. He was against the wall before he realized, light-headed, reeling, its thump against the back of his head an odd and unwelcome intrusion from the rest of the world. A small voice somewhere in his head was comparing the kiss to Rasha, the cool softness of her lips in the rain, her gentle embrace. Loveless was a firestorm, her body rammed against his, her chest flattened against him, her thigh already rising between his. Her heat astonished him.

*I can't believe this is happening. I can't believe this is happening.*

She broke the kiss. 'Room.'

Half-dragged by the hair, she pulled him down the hallway, trying each door until one opened. The chamber within was dark, cool blue moonlight creeping through a lattice window in the corner. She hauled him inside, the door barely swung closed before she was on him again, hands on his belt, one hand already past it, inside, reaching. He gasped, shuddered, aware his own hands were waving empty and useless in the air. Another kiss knocked him back against the wall while she worked on him, hands expert, while his befuddled brain tried to suggest actions beyond pawing at her back and moaning.

*This is happening. This is really happening.*

Her kiss faltered, then broke. She staggered back from him, one hand to her mouth, eyes wide, searching. Then she lurched for the chamber pot, dropped to her knees and vomited. Chel watched, stunned, still laid against the wall like meat, feeling his lips cooling in the room's fireless air. It took him three attempts to speak.

'Are you . . . all right?'

Her response was another heave, wet splashes from the pot.

*Was it me? Did I do this?*

He said nothing.

She retched and puked twice more, then it subsided, and she fell back, one hand wiping at her mouth. Even in the bleached moonlight, she looked pale, sweating, shaking.

'God's cock,' she croaked, 'what's wrong with me?'

\*\*\*

'Y'see . . .' Lemon said, then trailed off. 'Fuckballs.'

Foss started, belched, then sat back in the booth. 'Yup.'

Chel was supporting Loveless under one arm, edging back to the booth in a desperate attempt to avoid attention. It appeared to be working; they were two paces away, and Lemon and Foss had yet to notice them.

'The thing about that wee Nort, right, she's not . . . She hasn't . . . She's a wanker, that's what.'

'Nothing wrong with that, right, friend?'

'No, right, exactly. That's my point. She's *not* a wanker. But she *should* be. Might fix her fucken . . . attitude. There any brandy left?'

Foss belched again.

They reached the booth, and Lemon spotted them at last through her booze-fug.

'All right, lovers? Go well, did it?' she sniggered. 'Don't look like a man just shot his bolt, wee bear. Not so much walking on air as last march to plague-pits, eh?'

'We didn't—' he started as they slid into the booth. Loveless raised a trembling finger, staring at Lemon with bloodshot eyes.

'Shut. The fuck. Up.'

Lemon fell quiet, then perked up as she saw Kosh

273

approaching the booth, brow creased and jaw set in the appearance of great ponderings. 'Alright, squirt, did you get your—'

A commotion from the archway drew their attention, cries and thumps. A moment later, a half-dressed man came haring around the corner, hopping to pull on one boot, shirt and jacket bundled beneath an elbow, scattering punters in his path.

Lemon half-rose. 'Boss?'

Chel still had Loveless's arm over his shoulder, and was loath to relinquish it. 'Rennic? What in hells—?'

The shirt went over his head as he reached them, the jacket dropped to the table. 'Where is he?'

'Who?'

'The fucking prince! Where?'

Lemon was stammering, seeing the look in the big man's eyes. 'H-h-he went with the company! Back that way.' She spied the friendly boy who'd offered his services, still milling serenely between knots of drinkers. 'Him, he'll know!'

The boy was face-first to the wall before he could react, Rennic screaming in his ear. Chel staggered up in pursuit, Lemon right behind him, sending platters crashing. 'Rennic! Rennic, what are you doing?'

The boy spilled his guts before they could catch up, and Rennic was off again, crashing off down a hallway, loose shirt flying, boots slapping against the rich wood. Chel and Lemon followed, stumble-footed, the walls a blur. Ahead of them, Rennic stopped, turned, then smashed in a nameless door with a ferocious kick, darting inside without a breath.

Shouts came from within, surprised and angry cries that became shrieks and squeals. A moment later, Rennic re-emerged into the hallway, dragging behind him, by the hair, a kicking, screeching and entirely naked prince of the realm, pallid flesh flapping in the candlelight. His hands were locked on Rennic's wrist, struggling in vain to release the grip and the pressure on his scalp.

'Unhand me! Unhand me!'

'Rennic!' Chel bawled. 'What are you doing?'

Rennic gave them a dead-eyed stare as he dragged the thrashing prince past. 'Get his clothes.'

'Aye, right.'

Lemon ducked inside, through the splintered door, past the upset furniture and alarmed professionals. Chel followed, trying to ignore the musky reek in the air. 'Apologies, folks,' said Lemon. 'Which of these are his?'

By the time they caught up, Rennic had driven the others out of the booth and to their feet, and most of the other punters had cleared out of the open terrace. The friendly boy was nowhere to be seen. The prince was now wrapped, shivering and cursing, in Foss's long coat. Chel charged at the big man, his arms full of Tarfel's clothes.

'The fuck is going on, Rennic?'

'How fucking dare you!' the prince spat, rubbing at his battered pate and reaching for his crumpled garments. 'How fucking *dare* you!'

'They are *coming*, dumbshit!' Rennic's hands were claws, imploring, anguished. 'They are coming for you!'

Chel interposed himself between Rennic and the huffing prince. 'Who is?'

'*Everyone!*'

\* \* \*

275

Rennic threw on his jacket, casting a frantic look around the now-empty terrace. 'We need to leave immediately! We have to keep him safe, remember? He's the reason we're doing all this!'

Over Rennic's shoulder, a figure strode onto the terrace. A small figure, in a long, flowing robe, unbelted, and nothing else, walking with icy confidence. Her hair rolled down her back like a waterfall. Rennic caught Chel's look, turned and came up short.

'Grassi—'

She said nothing, only gazed at Rennic with a look of irritation, of disappointment. She extended her hands from the sleeves of her robe. In each glittered a *shunoul*, a needle-like stabbing dagger, silver-bright and deadly.

'Aye, how the f—'

'Grassi, come on, now—'

She looked from Rennic to the others and back, her expression unchanging.

'Come on, Grassi, this is a place of friendship, remember? You still don't know the job details, it might be anything.'

Her gaze swung back to him. Chel stared at the little woman, shorter than any of them save perhaps the Nort, a slip of a thing and virtually nude. How could she seem so terrifyingly dangerous?

Rennic swallowed. 'A head start, at least . . .'

Without breaking her gaze, Grassi reached her hands up behind her head, then began to twist and wrap her mane of hair. She stared at Rennic the whole time, until it was piled and bunched at the back of her head, held with one hand, then with great precision she slid the daggers, one after the other, into the mass, pinning it there. She folded her hands back into her sleeves.

'You bad for business, Rennic.'

'I know. I'm sorry.'

'Get out of here.'

Thumps and jangles came from the stairway, suggesting the imminent arrival of Bridge House security.

'I don't fancy explaining this mess to the guards, do you?' Loveless had pushed herself to her feet, her brow gleaming with cold sweat. 'Service stairway, back there.'

Grassi remained still as they hurried past, making for the stairs beyond, watching Rennic the whole time.

'Listen,' he said, 'next time—'

'Won't be next time, Rennic. Professionals from here.'

He nodded. 'Professionals it is.'

'Run, Rennic. Run!'

# TWENTY-ONE

They pounded down the back stairway, polished wood creaking beneath their feet, rich panelling flashing past. The back ways of the Bridge House were a labyrinth, each turn of the stairs offering a glance of another corridor of identical, ornate doors, the symbols above indistinguishable as he galloped by. The smell of oil and incense permeated everything, but at least the thump of footsteps covered the gasps and moans that seemed to leak from the walls around him.

Blood thundered in Chel's ears, but all he could think of was Loveless, Loveless kissing him, her hands on him, the heat of her in the cold room. Loveless retching, vomiting, their chance gone, Rennic shouting, raving. What had he said? Everyone was coming. Coming for the prince?

Loveless beat him to it, her pallor lifting as her cheeks flushed from their run. 'What the fuck happened back there, Gar? You were supposed to be scratching an itch, not setting a fucking hunter on us!'

Foss's breath was coming heavy, his cloak long-gone,

sweat staining his clothing beneath. 'What's going on, boss? Who's coming?'

Ahead of Chel, Tarfel was running, bandy-legged and reeling. 'The gall, Vedren!' he spat as he stumbled down the stairs. 'The shame and the . . . the . . . impertinence!'

Rennic had run fast to catch them, his still half-fastened clothes streaming behind him as they rattled down the stairs. 'Word's out, there's an open contract. Everyone is looking for us,' he barked back. 'Him, princeling, and his entourage: us!'

Loveless slowed to let him draw level. 'Then why the fuck didn't she shiv you with one of those hairpins the moment she laid eyes on you, instead of taking you out for a gallop?'

'Because she didn't know we were the entourage!' Rennic's breath rasped at his words. 'You know she doesn't hold with affiliation. They only just arrived from the north.'

'So what tipped her off, Gar? What changed her mind?'

Rennic didn't reply immediately as they heaved around another twist in the stairway.

'Well,' he said, 'I mean, it's not really important *how* she found out. . .'

'Gar, you fucking idiot.'

'I never know what to say afterward! It was awkward!'

'Who did you mean by "they", boss?' came Foss's anxious huff.

'Just keep running, she gave us a headstart, right? That was fair of her!'

A loud whistle sounded from above, piercing the air and echoing through the floors.

Foss's steps were getting heavy. 'I'd say that headstart just expired, my friends.'

Ahead of them, a door flew open and two burly figures

burst onto the stairs, draped in tan leather, edged with fur. Mawn, but not like the hunters Chel had seen on the mountain. These were broad and stocky, and they took one look at the fleeing company and charged.

'Tarf, duck!'

Chel went to throw himself forward, but his drunken foot slipped on the polished stair and he crashed sideways, just as Foss and Rennic surged past him. They leapt at the Mawn, driving them back into the hallway beyond, while Chel staggered back from the wall nursing a fresh bruise to his temple. At least everyone inside is unarmed, he thought, one hand to his head.

Lemon bounded past him, still carrying a bottle from upstairs. 'We'll take care of these boys, wee bear. Follow Whispie, get princey out the back door, eh? See you at the wagon.' She tossed the bottle in her hand, caught it by the neck, then with a wild cry she charged toward the open doorway after Foss and Rennic just as another Mawn heavy appeared.

Loveless had Chel by the scruff. 'Go, go, go!'

Whisper leading, they ran, Kosh keeping a nervous and disapproving pace beside Chel and Tarfel, Loveless to their rear. Chel felt light-headed, fighting a rising tide of bile at the back of his throat. He was flying down the stairs, never faster on his feet, but his body was exacting a terrible price. He rubbed a sleeve over his face, mopping at a sudden, stinking sheen of sweat.

The walls had changed, they had reached the lower floors and now slabs of unpolished dark stone loomed alongside them. No more corridors, instead a wide hallway at the stairway's end, and across it, a heavy-timbered archway with a rolling double-door.

'There,' Loveless urged, pointing ahead. 'The courtyards are beyond. Shit!' She came up short, a look of panic in her eyes.

Chel crashed to a halt, the others with him, and fought back a revolting burp. 'What? What is it?'

'My sword. I need to get it back from the steel-room.'

Something thumped over their heads, hard enough to shake dust from the floorboards above.

Chel raised a sweat-slicked eyebrow. 'Seriously? Now?' He thought he could hear Lemon roaring overhead.

She met his eye with a look so fierce he released the noxious burp.

'Give me your tokens. I'll get everything I can, meet you at the wagon. Whisp, get the horses hitched and be ready to go.' She gestured to the door. 'It's one-way, once you're through, you can't get back. If the rest of us don't appear by the time you've hitched the team, make for the bridge and we'll meet you there.'

Chel found his legs were trembling; it had to be from the run down the stairs. 'And what if you don't show there, either?'

She flicked her eyes back to him. 'Stick with Whisp. She'll look after you, cub.' Then she was away down the hallway, around the corner and gone from sight.

Whisper put one hand on his arm. *Time to go.*

They made for the door.

\* \* \*

Chel stared blankly around the torchlit courtyard. 'Where did Lemon park the wagon? Did anyone see?'

'Don't ask me,' Tarfel huffed. 'I was nowhere nearby.'

'Indeed,' Chel replied through gritted teeth. They were somewhere around the back of the main building, its stacked tiers towering overhead, yet still well within its complex of walls and outbuildings. The courtyard itself was grand if functional, wide gates at the far end and parked wagons suggesting a loading zone for the cellars. A low retaining wall and short run of steps separated the entryway where they stood from the main courtyard itself. Braziers burned at the fringes, but much of the courtyard's centre was lost to the murky steam that issued from vents somewhere beneath them.

'Kosh, did you— Ah, where the fuck's she got to? Come on, Akoshtiranarayan!'

'The mechanism is not so complex as it appears, simply a ratchet and a spindle, allowing foot traffic to exit the building but not return. Of course, reversing it would only be a matter of—'

'Leave the fucking door alone! Find the wagon!'

Chel scanned the gloomy courtyard, one hand pressed to his temple, which had developed a menacing throb. People were moving around the fringes, their voices muffled by the surroundings, loading or unloading, carrying and clinking their cargo. There were far more wagons and carts than he'd been expecting, and this might not even be the right courtyard. His throat felt very dry.

Whisper pointed, and Chel spotted the wagon beneath a canvas canopy by the courtyard's far wall, lurking in near-darkness beside another, heavier wagon stacked with kegs and crates.

'Thank the Shepherd. Come on!'

He raced forward, Whisper marshalling the others along behind him. No horses, of course, but a quick check over the side confirmed that everything else was where it was supposed to be. The wagon beside theirs sat very low on reinforced axles, and its sides were plated with steel. Something about the kegs poking from its summit was naggingly familiar, a delivery of brandy, most likely. 'Whisper, can you get things untied? I'll track down the horses. I can certainly smell the stables from here. Kosh, Tarf, jump aboard and get under cover!'

The prince hadn't moved, hunched against the wagon-side and huffing his displeasure. As the immediate panic of their descent passed, Tarfel had wrapped himself in self-pity like a cloak. 'How dare he, Vedren? How *dare* he! How can I command the respect of my subjects if I'm dragged naked through a whorehouse?' He kicked at a wheel, scuffing a boot, and yelped.

Chel slid back down, attempting a calming voice despite the hammering in his head and chest. 'You were officially incognito, Tarf. And I think they prefer "House of Friendship" here.'

Whisper looked over, pausing in her task, concern in her eyes. Chel waved her back, out of the prince's eyeline. *I'll handle it.*

'Not the point, Vedren! Not the point! Am I being unreasonable? He could have knocked, warned me in good order – instead he smashed in the door and dragged me out in the all-together. These people, Vedren, they're not like us. Their only recourse is violence. Honestly, I don't know what I'd do without you here to look after me. And once again, I'm denied my birthday feast!'

'I'm sure once you're king—'

'People need to start listening to me, taking me seriously!'

Chel rested a tired hand on the steel-sided wagon beside them as the prince began to pace. 'I quite understand, Tarf.

You've every right to feel aggrieved. But do you think, perhaps,' he swallowed, 'we could get the wagon hitched and get things moving? For all his, uh, impertinence, Rennic did seem mightily concerned that we get out of here without delay.'

The prince paused, one finger raised, recollection interrupting his pity-procession. 'Why did he say that was?'

'People are coming, he said. For us. For you.'

'For me? Here?'

Chel nodded, his fingers on the cold metal of the keg's band. There was something so familiar about them. 'Have I seen these kegs somewhere before?'

The prince turned and squinted in the gloom, as if noticing the heavy wagon he'd been pacing beside for the first time.

'Saints' breath,' he whispered.

'What? What is it?'

Tarfel was ghost-white in the distant firelight, sweat popping from his sallow brow. 'From . . . from Black Rock. The keg your sister placed at the wall, for the d-diversion.'

Chel whipped his hand back and stepped away from the wagon. 'The one that exploded and blasted a hole in the citadel wall?'

Tarfel nodded, his throat bobbing like a raft in a storm.

'But there are . . . dozens of them here.' Chel took a step around the wagon, peering over its side. 'And these crates? What are these?'

'Don't touch them!'

Kosh's head poked up from the canvas behind them. 'What is all this wittering? I thought we were to depart without— What is that?'

Chel couldn't help himself. He levered up a loose lid,

exposing a nest of packed straw inside, and within it, a handful of strange objects. They were metallic, a dull grey in the low light of the courtyard, and roundish, about as big as two fists. Short, uneven, jutting prongs covered them, like spikes. They looked heavy and unpleasant.

'What in hells do you think these are?'

'Great spirits!'

Kosh was beside him, descended from their wagon, her eyes wide and white-rimmed in the gloom, flares of distant torchlight reflected in the onyx gleam of her irises.

'This is bad, right?'

'Get back!'

'What are they?'

She was backing away from the wagon, her mouth working, eyes trembling, beads of sweat clear on her brow. 'We must get away from here. We must flee this place immediately. *Immediately!*'

Tarfel was already moving away from the wagon, back in the direction of the one-way door. 'You know, Vedren,' he called softly, 'you were quite right, we really must be going now.'

'But what are they?' Chel insisted.

'*Ajagarandan,*' came Kosh's reply. 'Demon eggs.'

Chel stepped back from the wagon as Whisper reached them. *What is it? Are you all right?*

He nodded at the heavy wagon. 'I think,' he said, finding his voice harder to work than normal, 'I think this wagon is loaded with witchfire.'

She stared at him, then at the wagon, then back to him. *Why is it here?*

'I don't know, and I don't want to know. Let's get out of here. Fast.'

*I'll get the horses.*

'No, there's no time. Grab what we need from the wagon and run for the gate.' Chel put out a hand. 'Wait. The others could come charging out here any moment. Someone needs to warn them.'

Tarfel looked back in naked horror. 'You want us to loiter here until we're incinerated?'

Chel looked past him. 'Kosh, did you say you could get back through the door?'

She swallowed. 'I have no wish to return to—'

'I'll go,' Chel snapped, 'just do what you must to get me inside. Go!'

She went, scrabbling away across the courtyard, visibly relieved to put distance between herself and the wagon of witchfire. 'Whisper, you and the prince take what you can from the wagon, then get him and Kosh round the front. I'll warn the others, we can all meet there. If we're lucky.' He offered her a nervous grin, which she returned.

*Got it.*

'Then let's—'

Light flickered from the wagon's far side, casting sudden dancing shadows at their feet. Whisper put up an urgent hand and they froze but Tarfel continued making a tiny whimpering noise.

Voices followed the light. 'Keep those torches back, Shepherd's tits! Have you forgotten it all already? Yes, yes, you'll have passes once your watches are over. On the Steel Terrace. Oh, stop moaning, at least you get to go inside, you worthless fucks. Think the rest of the legions would be allowed within a mile of this place, let alone inside?'

That voice, had he heard it before? A woman's voice, sharp-edged, one accustomed to command. He'd certainly heard a few of those over the last year or so. Not to mention his mother, come to think of it . . .

'New plan: let's back up to the door,' Chel whispered, edging into the deep shadow between the wagons and the wall. 'Either we all get through, or you two skirt round the far side and we meet out the front, right? Remember, the place is busy, and we could be anyone. Chances are, nobody will recognize us anyway. Let's look like we belong here, draw no attention, then get gone.'

They nodded, Tarfel whey-faced, Whisper calm but focused.

'Let's go.'

Chel took a deep breath, steeled himself against the shiver of the night air, and stepped out from behind the wagon to find himself face to face with Nadej.

\*\*\*

The leaf-chewing Bakani captain of Gold Peak Company wasn't looking at him. She was looking straight at Tarfel, one pace behind, who seemed to glow waxen in the torch-light.

'Fuck me, the runt prince. Jaul, it's the fucking runt prince. He just . . . walked right into us.'

The enormous man behind her grunted in appropriate astonishment.

'Nadej,' Chel said, then realized he had nothing to add. Rennic's words upstairs had acquired deeper meaning. *They are coming for you. Everyone.* That's what Grassi had told him. Had all the mercenaries made their choice?

Nadej twitched a look at him, her head snapping around like a bird's. 'That's Captain Nadej to you, commander of the 11th Legion of the Merciful Shepherd. Or at least I will be, when I hand them this quivering quim. Who the fuck are you?' Her eyes moved fast in the darkness, never still, taking in Chel and Whisper, now standing protectively in front of the prince. 'You were at the Gracechurch. Both of you. The runt's minders. Hand him over and you walk away with all your parts still attached.'

'It *was* you. Tipped off the confessors about the extraordinary council.'

She scoffed. 'Fuck, no. That was Fest, the sleazy prick. Always one to hedge his bets, old Fest. Not that you can blame him.'

Chel balled his fists. 'What are you doing here? Why are you hunting him? The tide is about to turn, in another few weeks the confessors will be on the run. You should be fighting beside us!'

'Horseshit,' Nadej snarled. 'There's one game left in town, and it wears red robes. Those tome-fuckers made it abundantly clear that we go their way or go the way of the Keys.'

'And which way was that?'

'*Immo-fucking-lation.* Hard to keep a company together after an offer like that. Most of my people deserted straight to them, took up the confessor's cloth in a heartbeat. The others fled. Those of us left, we take what's offered, and we keep our eyes open. I'll tell you one thing, there's a damned sight better chance of ascension if we come bearing gifts than when they reel in our chain. And they will.'

'What are you doing with all that witchfire? Ascending?'

'It's called black powder, you ape. And we're doing what we're told, something you might care to try.'

'You don't understand, Nadej. The south is about to

erupt. Reavers, tribes, free city rebellions – the church army will be torn apart.'

Nadej raised her hands, exasperated. 'You fucking people. Who cares? Reavers pillaging the south-west, tribes the south-east, good fucking luck to them. They'll all be ash come summer.'

'That's not all, the Norts in Denirnas Port will come to our aid—'

Her laughter battered the courtyard walls. 'The Norts? The Norts are gone, little boy.'

'Gone? Gone where?' He swallowed. From the very corner of his eye, he could see Kosh at the courtyard door, hunched over the mechanism, apparently engrossed in her task. He tried not to draw Nadej's attention to her. 'Sailed away?'

The mercenary's voice was rasping and low, jagged-edged. 'Scoured. Seared. Blasted into the sea by the forces of divine unification.'

'What?' Chel blinked and stammered. Behind him, he heard Tarfel's sharp in-breath.

Nadej took a sharp step forward, and Whisper shifted to block her path to the prince, but she went no further. 'They said it was like a storm,' she whispered, round eyes bulging, mouth pulled wide in malicious delight, torchlight gleaming from her tapered teeth, 'a maelstrom of lightning and flame, a tempest of terror, the mother of nightmares. Razed the port and sunk the Norts, did in one day what the cowardly northern lords never could. The peoples of the north would be rejoicing if they hadn't already starved or fled.' The smile faded, leaving only a wide-eyed grimace. 'That's what's coming. That's what's coming for all of us. Denirnas is only the start. There's no one left but the confessors, and it's him they want, you dog-fucking half-wit.

They *want* the *prince*. And ascension awaits for she who brings him.'

'No.' Chel's voice was raw, hoarse. 'We can stop this. We can stop them.'

'Who the fuck do you think you are, little boy?' she said with a trembling shake of her head, the corners of her mouth tweaking upwards once more. 'No one can stop us. Jaul, bring me the ghost. If the other two get in the way, rip their arms off.'

The big man nodded, and lumbered forward.

'Not just a figure of speech,' Nadej added, her grin fully restored.

Chel pushed himself beside Whisper, blocking the big man's path to the prince. He was shaking all over, his wrecked body surfing one last blast of adrenaline. 'Highness, run for the door, get through with Kosh. Whisper and I will hold them up.'

Hold them up, not off. His slip of the tongue betrayed his pessimism. The only bright spot was that they were within the grounds of the Bridge House, and weapons were forbidden. He glanced down at the advancing Jaul's enormous fists. Being pummelled to death suddenly didn't seem very bright after all.

'Wait,' Nadej grunted, her gaze over her shoulder and one hand raised. 'What's that grimy little pig-dog doing over there? One of yours, runt?' She whistled through her teeth, hard and piercing. From the gloom beyond the heavy wagon to Chel's left, four figures emerged into the courtyard's misty murk. They might have been unarmed, but they were evidently well-armoured, and held themselves like professional soldiers. The sigil of Gold Peak still emblazoned a couple of breastplates.

'Captain?' said one. 'We were in the middle of a game of—'

'Boys,' Nadej called, her voice loud with cruelty, 'fuck these apes up, but bring me the pale one. Enough of him to be recognizable. Jaul, get the little one by the door.'

Chel stopped dead. They were trapped at the courtyard's edge, hemmed in by the wagons, Nadej and Jaul between them and Kosh at the door, the new men between them and the far gate to the night beyond. Jaul had turned, and was making for the door where Kosh crouched, oblivious of anything but her work. She was muttering to herself, Chel could hear her clearly over the crunch of footsteps on the courtyard's loose stone. How could she be unaware of what was happening behind her?

'Kosh!' he bawled. 'Is that door open yet? Getting urgent!'

Finally she looked around, her irritation melting into surprise, then alarm as she took in the scene in the courtyard.

'Jaul,' Nadej called, 'hurry it up! Boys, bring me that bleached bastard.'

Jaul broke into a jog. Whisper stepped ahead of him, dodged a meaty swing from the big man and lashed a kick at his knee. He shuffled back, shielding himself, and she followed with two sharp blows to his kidney then, as he turned to take another swipe at her, drove a forearm into his throat. Gasping, Jaul collapsed backward, thudding to the courtyard floor in front of the incandescent Nadej.

Whisper looked back to Chel and Tarfel. *Run.*

They did, sprinting across the courtyard toward where Kosh hunched, her movements frantic. 'Kosh, door!' Chel yelled as they closed.

'It's not . . . I can't make it . . .' she gasped back, voice cracked with desperation and no small embarrassment.

'Fuck.' Chel pulled up short of the steps from the courtyard.

The prince skidded to a halt beside him. 'Vedren, why have we stopped? Why have we stopped?'

Chel swallowed. 'There's no point leading them right to her if we can't get through.' Sweat was dripping from his forehead, despite the bite of the cooling night, and he had to blink it away. The breath in his lungs felt hot enough to scorch his throat. 'We need to draw them away, give her time.'

Jaul, spluttering and wheezing, was regaining his feet. He looked vexed. The four newcomers were closing, skirting around the courtyard toward Chel and the prince, well wide of where Whisper faced down their captain. Chel's empty fingers twitched. Six against three. There had to be some way to even the odds.

To their right stood a line of wagons, the nearest loaded with what looked like pottery. With a yell to Tarfel to follow him, he lunged for it and scrabbled up, just as the Gold Peak mercenaries began to close.

'I think we'll struggle to ride this wagon out of here, Vedren,' came the prince's panicky squeak as Chel hauled him aboard. 'There aren't any horses!'

Chel grabbed the nearest piece of earthenware, a stout vase around half his height, and hoisted it upwards. 'Start throwing things, highness!'

The first man to reach their wagon took the vase straight to his chest, hurled by Chel two-handed with all the force he could muster. To his disappointment, it didn't shatter, but the man was knocked backward and left winded in the dirt. Chel grabbed another pot this one smaller, and flung it at the next mercenary, who shied away with arms raised. The third pot did shatter, carving a dark line down one mercenary's cheek as he stumbled.

'They're coming, Vedren, they're coming!'

'Kick them off and hit them over the head!'

Whisper, meanwhile, had ripped a torch from its mooring and was swinging it like a flaming quarterstaff, keeping Nadej and Jaul at arm's length. Jaul tried and failed to grab the haft, scorching his palm in the process. He now looked sorely vexed.

'Kosh, the door?'

'Nearly, nearly – there is something—'

Behind Chel, Tarfel smashed a pot and squealed.

'Tarfel! Are you hurt?'

'I, uh, cut my finger, Vedren. Some of these edges are rather sharp.'

From his vantage aboard the wagon, Chel looked around the courtyard. Their situation was not improving – the door remained closed to them, they were a long way from the far gate, and while three of the four mercenaries chasing them were nursing bumps and cuts, they were far from defeated. Whisper, meanwhile, was hemmed in, keeping Nadej and Jaul from passing her to get to Kosh but not much more. The courtyard seemed otherwise deserted. Their cries for help had done nothing more than send those nearby fleeing for cover.

'Kosh!'

'Almost!'

He kicked at a clambering mercenary, dragged his foot clear as the man tried to grab it, then smashed a small, ornate vase over his head. It wouldn't be long before they ran out of earthenware, either. He looked up to see Whisper being driven back by another lunge from Jaul. She was running out of room before the low wall.

'Tarf! Pass me a smallish pot, Whisper's in trouble.'

'Don't worry, I've got it— Whoops, butterfingers.'

The prince heaved, sending a glazed water-jug arcing through the air with a stripe of bright blood down its side from his wounded finger. It shattered beside Jaul's right boot, and for a moment, he looked down, distracted. Whisper pressed her advantage, batting Nadej to one side with her torch, then driving her elbow into the side of Jaul's head. He dropped like a stone, and did not move.

'Yes!' Chel cried, then aimed a kick at the last mercenary, who had paused mid-climb to watch the scene beyond. The man grunted as Chel's boot connected with him and dropped from the wagon-side, although the sharp pain that lanced up Chel's leg suggested that, should he live to see the morning, walking comfortably was unlikely to feature in it.

'I have it!' came Kosh's victorious squeal from the door. Beside her, the door clunked, then began to turn. Then, with a juddering thunk that echoed from the courtyard walls, it stopped.

'Ah,' said Kosh.

Her foes at bay, Whisper turned to the door. Chel saw movement behind her, a smear in the drifting mist, then Nadej was there, one arm wrapped around Whisper's neck, her other hand rising and falling in a blur. Five, six, seven times, faster than Chel could blink. Whisper gasped, flexed and threw her clear, then dropped to her knees, one hand on the torch, the other clutching her side. A long shard of broken pottery dropped to the earth before her, one end splattered dark.

Chel hadn't even realized he was running. 'Whisper!' he bellowed, crossing the courtyard on numb legs as Tarfel strained to keep pace behind him. 'Whisper!'

Nadej was still there, clambering to her feet, her eyes searching for her improvised weapon, and Chel hit her like a runaway cart. One fist caught her jaw, the other somewhere on her upper arm, and the two crashed back to the dirt. He landed another two flailing punches before she rolled clear and scrambled away, one hand pressed to her cheek, back to where her battered mercenary crew were regrouping.

Chel dropped to his knees beside Whisper, trying to ignore the terrible pulsing of his knuckles. 'Are you hurt? How bad is it?'

Tarfel was crouched behind them, burbling apologies about the pot. Chel tried to hush him but couldn't think how.

Whisper looked up at him, took a sharp, pained breath, and, with a tight, tearful smile, shook her head. Her arm was clutched close around her middle but the torch's dancing light caught the cascade of dark blood that pumped over it.

'We'll . . .' He swallowed. 'We'll get help. The others will be coming through any moment. You'll be all right. Kosh! Where's the fucking door! Get it open, one way or the other!'

The Nort sounded on the verge of tears. 'I can't . . . It is stuck! Something is blocking it!'

In the background, on another register of his brain, he heard Nadej order her crew to break out the weapons, heard their protestations about losing access to the Bridge House, heard her angry snarls that the head of a prince was worth more than a lifetime's access to the house's upper floors. He looked up to see them heading back to the heavy, keg-laden wagon, which it seemed smuggled weapons as well.

Whisper pressed the torch gently into his hand, then met his eyes and began to sign one-handed. *Go to door. I stay. You go to door.*

Chel shook his head. 'We'll get you out of here, the others will be here soon, we just have to hold on—'

She shook her head again, and a single tear tracked down her cheek. *Watch. Remember.*

Then she signed three words, only two of which he recognized. In the distance he heard the clatter and clang of the Gold Peak mercenaries retrieving their contraband ordnance.

He tried to protest that he didn't understand, but she stilled him. *Remember. Yes?*

'Yes.'

She began to push herself to her feet, and he helped her stand. He could see the Gold Peak crew now, pulling spears and axes clear of a compartment beneath the heavy wagon's axle. The Bridge House needed to improve its cargo scrutiny.

Standing with a wince, she took the torch back from him, her fingers cool and smooth, then nodded toward the door. Chel stood there for a moment, unable to speak, unable to breathe, feeling tears forming thick in his eyes. She leant forward and kissed his forehead, then gave him a gentle push with her shoulder.

'Don't—'

She met his eyes and he fell silent. She held his gaze for a moment, her own eyes full of tears, then turned and began a slow limp toward the wagon, one hand clutched to her body, the other holding the torch aloft, leaving bloody footsteps in the courtyard's grey dirt.

The Gold Peak crew began to notice. A shout went up, followed by another, warning then confusion as they watched her approach. She limped faster, then broke into a halting jog, then a stumbling run, and too late they realized her intent. Weapons went up, first to challenge her, then in a panicked attempt to get clear. Nadej stepped forward, a long spear in her hand, trying to block Whisper's path, but the lanky scout vaulted her – one foot to her midriff, the next on her shoulder – and flung herself onto the wagon.

The straw went up in an instant, hissing smoke merging with the drifting steam from the courtyard's vents, then Chel was running, fleeing behind Tarfel as they made for the low wall by the steps. 'Kosh,' he screamed, 'get down!'

They were five strides from the wall before the first flash came from behind. Immediately the courtyard seemed lighter, new shadows growing from their pounding feet as a delicate glow rose behind them. Chel could see the lip of the wall ahead, a shrinking line of shadow, seeming ever darker as the orange light lit the walls. Ahead of him, Tarfel stumbled, dropping to his hands two strides short of the wall as Kosh scuttled back from the door and behind it.

Chel seized Tarf by the collar and dragged him up and on, hauling him over the lip of the wall, when around them the courtyard went white. Something popped in the air, then the wave hit as they threw themselves down past the stone, a wall of sound like the smashing of a thousand pots, the beating of a thousand gongs. The heat followed, a flame-tongued shock that blasted over their heads like the wash of a furnace as big as a city.

Chel felt the air leave his lungs, incredible heat, and then he was chewing dust, the loose stone of the courtyard floor pressed to his singed face. Rain was falling, cold and distant against his battered back, trickling down his neck.

He sat up, feeling the groans and cracks of his body, the raw patches of skin and smouldering hair. His eyes were still gummy with tears. The courtyard was transformed. The wagons were gone, the canopy gone, the wall behind a blackened smear, its remaining stones marked by a scatter of lingering flames. The other wagons had been blasted off their axles, thrown into a shattered mass on the courtyard's far side. Thick black smoke boiled up into the night. And behind them, the grand embossed door of the archway had buckled inwards, the fine lacquer visibly scorched.

There was no sign of Nadej, or Jaul, or any of the Gold Peak mercenaries, in any form Chel could recognize in the smoking crater where the wagon had stood. There was no sign of Whisper.

Kosh was hunched beside him, huddled in her cloak, still but breathing. Tarfel was crying, snivelling in the rain, whimpering over and over that he was sorry, that the pot had slipped from his hands, that he should never have sneaked off in the first place. His voice sounded distant to Chel's numbed and ringing ears, irrelevant, useless.

Behind them, the archway door clanked and lurched, its bolts dangling loose, its mechanism wrecked. Then it fell open. An orange-girdled head emerged from within, grazed and battered but otherwise whole. 'Aye, right, finally! That's got it, just needed a big old bang. Ah, there you are, you wee pricks.'

She took a moment to absorb the scene, her eyes distant, still fuddled with booze. 'What in the name of galloping fuck happened out here?'

Another pause. 'Where's Whispie?'

Chel couldn't speak, but the desolation of his gaze must have told its own story. Her face fell.

'Oh, no. Oh . . . oh, no.'

# TWENTY-TWO

They fled through rain and darkness. Chel was hardly aware of the rest of the company's arrival, of their hurried exit into the pouring night beyond. His legs were used up, his body beaten and aching, his gut weighed with leaden despair. He faded in and out of wakefulness, finding Foss first supporting him, then carrying him as they jogged, slung over the bigger man's shoulder in an unwelcome echo of their first flight from Denirnas.

Denirnas. He'd forgotten it in the flashing horror of Whisper's loss, but the thought bubbled uncontrollably back. Had Nadej been truthful? Denirnas Port destroyed, the Nort fleet sunk, after months of blockade? What did that mean for their grand plan? Had the chance for victory dropped beneath the waves along with the black ships of the Norts? Could the church armies be so fierce? She'd said they were coming, coming for Tarfel, an echo of Rennic's words on the terrace. The confessors were hunting them, and at least some of the free companies had flocked to their pennant. And over and over he replayed his final images of Whisper, her soft kiss, her sad smile, her halting walk toward the wagon. It had all been so fast. It shouldn't have happened at all. He should have stopped it, done something different. Done something right.

His innards roiled with hot spikes of hopelessness, his fractured mind dropping in and out of coherence, and eventually, head bobbing from Foss's broad back, he slept.

He awoke soon after dawn, silvery light creeping northeast beneath a slate wall of cloud. Chel found himself laid on a grubby verge beside what would have been called a road before spring rain and heavy traffic had churned it into a rolling mire, thick with gloopy ridges of red river-mud, the deepest ruts maroon canals. Behind him on the matted grass, Tarfel lay huddled beneath what must have been Lemon's cloak. His eyes were open, hollow and staring, and for a moment Chel thought the prince too was dead, but then he whimpered and shuddered. It did not look like sleep had come easily to him.

The slow squelch of footsteps drew Chel's attention to the road. Rennic stood a few paces away, clear of the tree canopy and soaked to the skin, his long coat draped sodden against his frame. He was staring out into the grey distance, back toward the foaming waters of the river. They had made it to the north bank then. Chel tried to sit up, and his gasp at the attempt made Rennic turn. He just stared, saying nothing, his black eyes boring into Chel where he lay. He clearly hadn't slept, and his stance and loose movement suggested that he might still be drunk from the night before. The pain in Chel's own head was merely one voice in a chorus. Needless to say, his shoulder ached.

'Where's everyone else?' Chel said, pushing himself up a

second time, teeth gritted against the throbbing across his body. Every muscle felt tenderized. Even his hips ached.

Rennic stood motionless, rain dripping from his brows, his hawk-like nose, running in streams down the hollows of his cheeks into his beard. He seemed to sway, a gentle movement, as if moved by a summer breeze. The memory of Whisper in the courtyard hit Chel once more, a fist to his gut, and with it the thought that it would be so much worse for Rennic. He could think of nothing to say, nothing that could possibly convey his regret, his guilt, his shame.

He managed to stand, although he was sure he'd broken at least one toe. They were on a wooded curve, the distant rush of the river just audible over the patter of the rain on the trees overhead. Spring rain or not, the wind remained bitingly cold against his damp frame, and the earth of the verge beneath him felt solid enough to leave a dent in his hip.

'Shelter,' Rennic rumbled. 'Transport. Seeing as we lost our wagon.' He gestured back down the road, where through the drifting rain Chel thought he could make out a low huddle of buildings at a crossroads, possibly a staging inn. 'She thought it better I stay away from other people,' Rennic went on. He seemed to be chewing the words around before spitting them out. 'In my state.'

'Listen, Rennic. I'm sorry . . .'

'Wasn't your fault.' The gaze snapped back on him, and Chel took half a step back. 'Right?'

Chel couldn't answer, but the rustle of a damp cloak behind him signalled Tarfel's rise from his stupor. He looked dreadful, hunched and sallow, eyes rheumy from sickness or grief. He tried to look up at them, flinched away, then with hands twisted in supplication he managed to speak.

'I'm . . . I'm so sorry. It's my fault, it's all my fault. I should never have run—'

Rennic's razored eyes hadn't left Chel's.

'See? It was his.'

Tarfel nodded, swallowing rainwater. 'And I'm so, so sorry—'

The blow took him off his feet, a thunderous backhand that loosened the prince's teeth and sent him sprawling back to the mud. He gasped in shock, one muddied hand going to his face, but Rennic was on him before he could cry out, driving him down into the oozing sludge, striking again and again with closed fist as the prince waved a feeble hand, trying in vain to ward off the blows.

'Rennic!' Chel forced himself to move, stumbling forward, trying to catch the arm that rained punches on the stricken youth. 'Rennic, stop!'

He got a tenuous grip on the wrist, then an elbow crashed between his eyes, sending him reeling. Bright spots of colour danced before him as a numbness spread across his face, blood thumping around his head. Frantic blinking cleared his vision in time to see Rennic clear the knife from its sheath, drawing it back to slice. Chel lunged, throwing himself at the bigger man, taking him sideways, splashing the pair of them into the quagmire swirling around them. He grabbed at Rennic's arms, at his wrist, trying to capture the knife-hand, trying to pin him in the slick muck. The whole time he was shouting, screaming, hoarse. 'Stop! Stop! Stop!'

Strength, size, and a lifetime of dirty fighting shook him off, another blunt thump to the nose his reward. Then he was on his back in the mud, Rennic's foot on his neck, struggling with both hands against the boot on his windpipe.

Thick wet earth oozed around him, splattering his face, engulfing his struggles, as the life was crushed from his throat. With Chel still anchored, Rennic reached out and grabbed Tarfel up by the scruff, dragging him up from his scuttling crouch. Rennic yanked the prince back by the hair with a snarl, and another knife cleared its sheath.

'Rennic . . .' Chel struggled to breathe, to speak. 'It wasn't his fault . . . He wasn't to know . . .' He fought against the boot, sliding and slapping in the oily mud, rain still speckling his face. He changed tack. 'We need him, remember . . . ?'

Rennic paused, his breath coming in great snorts. He'd not spoken during the assault, producing only grunts and snarls. The boot lifted from his neck a fraction, and Chel sensed an opening.

'Think about it . . . We need him for the kingdom . . . She knew that, gave her life to save us.'

Rennic had the blade at the whimpering prince's neck, his knuckles creaking as his grip clenched and flexed. 'He did this,' he rumbled. 'He did this.'

'She . . . saved . . . him.'

Still Rennic didn't move, the boot on Chel's neck as immobile as a tombstone. 'Rennic . . . we need him . . . alive,' Chel gasped from the mud. 'He's our only shot at . . . peace. We have to do . . . what's . . . right . . .'

'Twelve hells, boss, what are you doing?' came Foss's voice from somewhere above.

Rennic released Tarfel as if he had forgotten he ever held him, then walked with heavy steps through the rain to the road's far side. Chel breathed long and deep as his neck re-inflated, as Tarfel slumped beside him in the mud and sobbed.

Lemon appeared overhead, her hair a sodden orange halo around her freckled face.

'Lemon,' Chel croaked, one hand on his neck, the other exploring the throbbing damage to his face. 'He thinks . . . He blames Tarfel . . . for what happened.'

'Oh, aye?' she said, and only then did he see the circles beneath her bloodshot eyes, the lines in her face. 'Maybe he's not the only one. Best keep him the fuck away from the rest of us, eh?'

Then she was gone, leaving only a weeping sky the colour of bruises.

\* \* \*

Foss and the others had secured a cart, at least, along with an appropriately dismal-looking mule, but shelter was harder to come by – no inn would admit them in their current state, the momentary cleanliness of the Bridge House lost with so much else in the rain. They packed up what little they had into the cart and rolled off along the forest road, hunched under the persistent drizzle. Chel and Tarfel walked a long way behind, their battered faces a pulsing reminder of the company's division.

All exhausted, they made meagre progress. Someone called a halt well before the wan light began to ebb, most likely Loveless, and as the rain finally eased they built a camp of sorts in a scrubby clearing not far from the roadside. Chel helped collect firewood, doing his best to find un-sodden branches, while Tarfel cowered beneath his cloak in the lee of the cart. Kosh and Lemon between them raised a fire, and for a moment, things seemed back to normal. Then Rennic absently called for Whisper to bag them some dinner, and the gloom descended like new rain. Eventually Loveless hefted Kosh's augmented crossbow and strode out into the woods. Chel watched her go, feeling he should follow. They'd had no chance to speak since their moment the previous evening, and in light of what had happened since, it seemed ridiculous to dwell on.

And yet.

He met her on her return, lingering at the clearing's edge like a smell. She met his gaze, saw the hesitation, the unease. Neither spoke, then both did:

'Hey, about—' 'I wanted to—'

'Sorry, you—' 'What did—'

Another silence, awkward, excruciating. Chel gritted his teeth, still not looking at her, and let it stretch until finally she spoke alone.

'I'm sorry, cub. About last night.'

'You don't need to apologize. Lemon knows, we all have our digestive troubles, sometimes.'

'No, cub. Listen.' She put one hand on his arm, triggering memories of the night, her hands on him, her mouth on his. He shuddered, felt foolish, struggled to meet her gaze. 'I'm sorry I did that to you. It was irresponsible. I don't shit where I eat.'

'What? But what about you and Rennic?'

'That's an arrangement, nothing more. And this isn't about that.'

'Hey, you don't—'

'Cub, listen. Please. I took advantage, I . . . I need to be better than this.'

Hurt bloomed somewhere within, cold bitter rage. 'Better? Better than me?'

He met her eye and his juvenile anger withered under

the ferocity of her gaze. 'Don't for a moment think that this is about you, cub. You are, in the kindest possible sense, incidental.'

'Fine. Understood.' He wanted this conversation finished, wanted himself away. 'Never again, right?'

'Never say never, cub,' she said, a glimmer of old mischief in her eye. 'Perhaps on the eve of our execution, eh? Come on, let's get this poor creature dressed and cooking.'

\* \* \*

Fire, food, and the last red dregs of spring light brought some measure of equilibrium, and then finally Loveless walked to the cart and retrieved a small brandy keg, purchased or pilfered from somewhere along the way. It brought back all too many memories of the armoured kegs of the night before, the little barrels of horror on the back of the reinforced wagon. She thumped the keg down on the soft earth, not far from the fire, and announced it was time for the circle.

'No,' Rennic said, not looking up.

'It's time, Gar.'

'No. Not yet.'

She looked at him sidelong, then turned and put one hand on his cheek, tilting his face up to look at her. 'Gar. You'll never be ready. None of us will. If we don't do it now, it will never be done. And that would be worse, wouldn't it?'

His eyes were ice and fire, rage and heartbreak. Then he nodded, pulling back from her, and waved a hand with a grunt.

Foss approached Chel and Tarfel. 'Would you like to join us for the circle? It would be appreciated.'

Chel nodded and stood. Tarfel cleared his throat. His bruises had bloomed and his face was badly swollen; his nose was unquestionably more bent than it had been before. 'Perhaps I should sit this one out,' he said. Nobody disagreed.

Chel knelt beside Foss as they formed a narrow circle around the fire, Kosh on his other side, Rennic, Lemon, and Loveless beyond. Loveless cracked open the keg and passed it to Foss, who sipped from it, then said the opening prayers. Chel marvelled at his level tone, his controlled delivery, as he could clearly see the leak of tears from the big man's closed eyes as he spoke.

Foss finished the prayers, then picked up the brandy and passed it to Chel. 'You can start, friend.'

'Me? But I—'

'It's fine. There's no wrong thing to say.'

Chel thought of the circle after the conclave, of Eka's words on her brother, of the tales of Palo and the others. He realized he'd not thought of his sister in weeks, and her journey back with the hunters to Barva. He felt a great surge of guilt and grief. He took a swig of the brandy to cover it, almost choking on the fiery spirit, holding it burning in his mouth, swallowing it with his shame.

'There was a woman, Whisper,' he said, fighting down a cough.

*There was a woman, Whisper*, they repeated.

'She was . . . I only knew her as a hunter, a scout . . . a presence. In truth, I barely knew her at all.' He looked around in apology, but nobody chided him, ordered him to stop. Rennic watched with hooded eyes, no expression or focus.

'She saved my life,' Chel said. 'Several times. She was

always there when I needed her. And she seemed, I don't know, fun. Nice. Er . . . I'm sorry.'

'Her name was Whisper,' Foss intoned beside him, 'and she was there for us when we needed her.'

The others repeated, and Chel passed the brandy to Kosh, relieved and abashed. The Nort took a small sip, made a face, then without prompting recounted a story of Whisper teaching her how to shoot straight, how to read wind and elevation, how to fine-tune the construction of her crossbow, all through signs and gestures. Chel listened in growing surprise and embarrassment at Kosh's story.

'Her name was Whisper, and she was a teacher.'

Loveless talked of her humour, her practical jokes. She skipped the brandy, the previous night evidently still weighing on her. Rennic said nothing, and the brandy passed to Lemon, who also deferred. Foss told a story of her roaming walks across entire kingdoms, her boundless stamina, her determination. Lemon summoned enough of herself to speak of Whisper's protective instincts, her willingness to endure hardship for those she cared for, her gentle, silent chidings. She placed the brandy back before Rennic.

To Chel's surprise, the big man roused himself, leaning forward, elbows on knees, firelight glimmering in his eyes.

'There was a woman, Kwayedza of the Kundai. She was a soldier, a leader, a friend. She was loyal and she was stoic, tireless, professional, purposeful.' He looked up, tears prickling at the corners of his eyes. 'You know how old she was? Nor do I. Older than me for sure; she lived lifetimes before us. She found me, took me under her wing when I was a drunken stripling. She kept me alive, through one doomed venture after another. Saved me from myself, from staying with bad company. She made me, moulded me, managed me – and the rest of you, don't pretend different – and I owe her more than I could ever say. She was a sister to me, hells, she was a mother.' He took a long breath, then another, and a swig of the brandy to go with it.

'Where did she come from?' Chel felt their reactions, their surprise, irritation at his speaking out of turn. Rennic didn't seem to object.

'Deep east. Don't know where. It's hard to be precise when you've got a language and a speech barrier, eh?' He sighed, all his rage spent, his tears yet to come. 'She was a leader, a general, but her side lost. I know that much. She was banished, sent to wander, mutilated, humiliated. But she overcame. She always overcame.'

He took another swig, deep and burning, then offered it to Loveless. She demurred again, looking pained, and Rennic took another swallow. Their rolling arguments had passed like a storm in the night. Whisper's loss had sucked the air from their fire, but in its absence neither seemed to know how to look at the other.

'Someone once told me,' Rennic said, 'growing up is watching your heroes die, and trying to live up to their image once they're gone. Thought at my time of life, I was done with that. I was wrong.'

He raised the brandy in toast.

'Her name was Kwayedza, and she was a hero.'

*Her name was Kwayedza, and she was a hero.*

Foss said the prayers and the final refrain.

*While we speak their names, they ride with us still.*

'She said something,' Chel said, his gaze lost in the fire, the memory returning with a sudden sting. 'You know, at the end. Told me to remember.'

Rennic looked up, resharpened. 'What? What did she say?'

Chel made the series of gestures, slow and clumsy with unpractised fingers. 'The first two, I know – *look, mine* . . .'

'Are you sure? Are you certain? Do it again.'

Chel nodded, and repeated the gestures. 'What? What did she say?'

Loveless looked over at him, uncertainty and discomfort warring against grief across her face. 'She said, "find my children".'

Rennic stared back into the fire. 'Then once this is over, that is what we will do.' With that, he stood and marched to the clearing's edge, resuming his solitary contemplation, his clinging clothes still only half-dried. Loveless watched him go, brows narrowed, tight lines beneath her eyes.

Chel looked around the fire. 'Should we . . . I don't know, be mourning?'

'We don't mourn.' Loveless didn't even look at him. 'We give the circle. We add the tales to our stock. We move on. We don't have the time. The luxury.' She paused, then met his gaze with a look of unexpected tenderness. 'Cub,' she said in a low voice, 'what did happen? In the courtyard?'

Chel clutched his knees to his chest and shuffled closer to the fire, still feeling the evening's chill despite the grumbling glow of his burns. He knew he must have told them something in their flight from the Bridge House, gabbled an explanation, but his memories were sketchy, and he'd clearly fallen short. He clenched his eyes shut. It was too soon to relive it all. He opted to summarize.

'We ran into the remains of Gold Peak Company. They've

taken up with the church after all. They had a wagon, they were guarding it, loaded with kegs like the one we saw at the citadel, the one that cracked the wall.'

'A wagonful of witchfire,' Lemon breathed. 'Fucken hells. So that's what went up.'

'Black powder, Nadej called it.' Chel tried not to think of it, tried not to remember, concentrating only on the Before. 'That wasn't all. There were crates, straw-packed, with these spiky metal balls inside.'

'Maces?'

'No, bigger.' Chel gestured. 'With thin prongs, like this. What did you call them, Kosh? Devilled eggs?'

'*Ajagarandan*. Demon eggs.' Kosh rubbed at her eyes. Her voice was an anguished whisper. 'How did they make so much, so quickly?'

Loveless had her head on one side. 'I'm guessing from the name these things are bad news. What else does it mean?'

'What *I'd* like to know, more than that . . .' Lemon said, her round eyes narrowed to crinkled lines. 'I'd like to know where those red bastards learnt how to make witchfire. Only time we ever saw anything like this, well, was the day those black ships hauled into Denirnas and cremated half the Ducal Guard.' Kosh was staring back, guarded, tense. 'See, what I could never work out was why those fellows came knocking that day, what it was they wanted. But I think I'm beginning to put it together now, eh?'

Chel looked from one to the other. 'What do you mean?'

Kosh only scratched at her hair, tugging at the frayed, dyed ends.

Lemon went on, warming to her topic, now addressing the others around the fire. 'Now let's say we have an alchemist, proud, a bit stupid but capable.' Behind her, Kosh sniffed in indignation. 'Knows a bit about making things go whoosh and boom. Word gets out to people with motives, let's say secret rulers of a corrupt church by way of example. They seize said alchemist, drag her – or him – away and lock in a dungeon, demand all the secrets. In the meantime, alchemist's fellows take umbrage, come knocking, blockade the entire north of a kingdom, but, well, secret ruler doesn't care, does he? He's got what he wanted. The stick to beat all sticks. The stick to secure his empire. Only question left is . . .' She turned to Kosh, looking her dead in the eye, her gaze burning like witchfire. 'How much did you tell them?'

'I told them nothing!'

'Oh, aye? You were down there a long time, not a mark on you!'

'Nothing, I say!'

'Then how in royal fuck did they master the great burning wrath of hellfire? They fucken *guessed*?'

'I . . . It was . . .'

'Spill it, you wee shite. You come clean now, you can help us fix this fuck-up of yours before things get any worse.'

'*Fuck-up?*' Kosh was looking back, hot tears streaming down her cheeks. 'How *dare* you! You think I was the only one they took? You think I learnt what I know from the air, from the skies? I had a family! I had parents, a sister, a brother! They took us all!'

Lemon raised a hand, her fire quenched, horror dawning in her eyes. 'What I meant was—'

'They killed us, one by one, drawing the words from us like guts. My father held, my mother too, my elder sister, despite the privations, the atrocities. They gave them nothing but trifles, child's tricks. But they knew, they knew they were teased, so they cut deeper and longer. Until it was me and my brother, all that was left. I was next. So, *yes*! I told them things. I couldn't watch my little brother die, watch myself be cut and scoured away like my elders, and for what? For your miserable little kingdom? Your mad king's pretence of empire? This place, this wretched place is a *sink*, a bog of ruined, lost peoples, drowning in their own filth. You are a joke to us, your stupid, isolated little country, backward, worthless. A plague-soaked, damnable pit.'

Nobody spoke. Foss extended a slow hand, reaching for little Nort's shoulder, but Kosh turned hard away from him, pressed her face into her hands and sobbed, great heaving gasps and wails, her tears dripping from her chin and splashing onto the grass beneath her. At last, as the others sat in awkward silence, she subsided, wiping at her eyes with sodden sleeves.

'The flotilla . . . The blockade,' Chel murmured. 'It was all for you. You and your . . . family.' His voice was tight and scratchy. 'Your brother, what happened to him?'

'What happened?' She sniffed, rattling fluid around her head. She pointed an accusatory finger at Tarfel, who still huddled alone by the cart. '*His* brother happened to my brother. A plague upon you all.'

She stood suddenly, turning this way and that, an escape with no direction.

'Whoa, friend,' Foss called, moving to stand alongside her. 'Hold a moment, please.'

'Just let me go home! Take me back to your accursed port, let me see my people again, let them take me away from this horror, this savagery.' Tears brimmed anew in her eyes. 'I just want to go home, and I have no home to go to.'

Chel swallowed hard. 'You didn't hear? They . . . they didn't tell you?' The eyes around the fire swung to him. '*I* didn't tell you, last night?'

Loveless was watching him, firelight sparkling in her eyes like embers. 'What is it, cub? What else?'

He swallowed again, his throat suddenly dry, and wondered who had the last of the brandy. 'Denirnas is . . . gone. Corvel's forces. The other news from Nadej.'

'Gone?'

He jerked a nod, feeling his fingers starting to shake, seeing the growing dread in the young Nort's eyes. 'She said . . . she said it was like a storm. Of flame, and terror. It levelled the port.' A memory bubbled at the back of his mind, a box-preacher with scarred arms and wild eyes, standing in the empty plaza of Denirnas lowport. *A great storm will come*, she'd said. *The Mother has shown me. The Mother of Storms. The mother of nightmares.* He shivered. Was this what she'd meant?

Kosh's lip was trembling. 'And my people? The black ships?'

*Scoured. Seared. Blasted into the sea.*

His voice was a hoarse whisper. 'Gone. Sunk.'

The Nort was shaking her head, too hard, too fast. 'Impossible, impossible. Our vessels are the pinnacle of naval engineering, impervious to inferior concoctions, built to withstand—'

'I only know what she told me.'

315

'Then she *lied*! It cannot be!' Already tears sprung fresh from her eyes, her voice choked with a returning sob. 'Even if it were true, more ships would come. More ships will come!'

Foss reached out his hand again, and this time took her into his arms, cradling her like a weeping child. 'Hush, my friend,' he murmured. 'Of course they will.'

'Not soon enough for us.' Rennic had rejoined them at some point during the outbursts, and stood at the edge of the firelight. His voice was low, grim. 'Storm season in the north could last another month or more, assuming they'd risk the crossing again. In the meantime, we have to face Corvel and his armies, plus Grassi's people and any other freelances taking the hunting contract . . .' He explicitly didn't look at Tarfel.

Loveless had her head in her hands. 'Get the prince, cub. This concerns him as much as any of us.'

Chel looked to Rennic. 'You and Tarfel, you're . . . all right? You're not going to, you know . . . ?' Rennic had made no mention of their altercation in the mud, no apology, no acknowledgement beyond sparse words to Chel. Whether he bought Chel's pleadings on Tarfel's behalf was unclear, but he'd made no move toward the prince since, murderous or otherwise. Perhaps, Chel hoped, he'd genuinely seen sense, but Rennic's mood was impossible to read. He'd always been distant and moody, but now his natural inclinations were starkly amplified. Whatever passing epiphany he'd experienced in his wood shack was long gone, replaced by something darker.

Rennic met his gaze with a look that did absolutely nothing to reassure.

'We do what's right.'

Somehow it didn't sound right coming from him. Chel went to get the prince.

\* \* \*

Tarfel was sitting behind the wagon, still wrapped in Lemon's cloak. His expression was neutral, gazing out into the deepening evening. The bruises on his face were not improved by the twilight.

'Ah, Vedren. I was, I'm afraid, listening in. How is the little one taking the news?'

'As well as you'd expect. I think she'll be with us a while longer, if only because she has nowhere else to go.'

He nodded. 'I can sympathize. Vedren, I'd like to ask you something.'

'Anything, Tarf. I'm still your sworn, after all. Can't exactly refuse.' He offered a smile to blunt the statement, but it made it no less true.

'Quite so, quite so. From now on, I'd like you to stay at my side. Not leave me alone with, well, the others, or anyone else.'

'But—'

'What if . . .' He tailed off, swallowed, lowered his voice. 'What if they decide they don't want to support me any more? I have no hold over them, they've sworn no oath.'

'You have nothing to fear from them, Tarf, really.' As he said the words, Chel wondered if he meant them.

'You're so sure? God knows they blame me for . . . you know.'

'That wasn't your fault. Truly. They know that. Even Rennic knows that, even if he won't acknowledge it. And even if they did take a dislike to you, they need you, remember? We all do. You're the claim, the rallying pennant. You're the reason for all this.'

The prince nodded, his laugh a mirthless snort. 'Now you're just being mean.'

\* \* \*

'Do you think we can outrun Grassi and her kin, Lemon, or any of the hundred other coin-eyed dagger-fuckers that will follow? Without . . . Without a pathfinder? We need allies, strong allies.'

Rennic's words were hard, but his tone lacked its customary edge. Lemon sat back down nonetheless. Chel and Tarfel came to a shuffling stop behind her. Chel's mind kept drifting back, to Rennic's words, to Whisper, to the Bridge House, to Loveless, to Rasha, to the Andriz enclave. To Laralim's revelations about his parents, his father. Everything his father had told him had been true, hadn't it? But it hadn't been everything. It hadn't been *all-true*.

What if his father had been wrong about some things?
*Are we doing the right thing?*

'They removed the Nort armada,' Lemon grumbled, half to herself, 'those fuck-off floating blocks of black iron, lobbed jets of fire like a teenage boy lobs his relish. Is nobody else just a little perturbed by that?'

'I'm a little perturbed by your imagery,' Foss replied, brows pinched as if in pain. 'And we don't know that it's true – Nadej had every reason to lie. Perhaps they simply grew tired of their blockade and sailed home?'

'Either way,' Rennic said, his words to Foss but his eyes on Loveless, 'we cannot count on the Norts for aid.'

Loveless had dropped her gaze to the fire, shaking her head softly. 'Then there's only one place left to go.'

'It's been a time,' Rennic said, his voice almost gentle. The two of them were struggling to rekindle the heat of their previous disputes. 'They might not even know—'

'They *always* know,' she spat. 'If we travel, we push through and out, go to the plains.'

'Make for a vast expanse of baked nothing? For what? Princeling can call in treaties. We'll fight them, push them back into their own southern chaos. Pressure in the north.'

'If we stay there, that place will be our tomb, one way or another.'

Rennic offered her a flash of a grin. 'Beats dying alone down here, right?'

She didn't match it. 'Time will tell. I will do this for you, Gar, but I fear this will be the end of us.'

Chel looked from one to the other. 'Where are we going?'

Loveless looked up from the fire, flames dancing in her eyes. She looked more grieved than he'd ever seen her.

'Arowan.'

# PART III

# TWENTY-THREE

The fortress was the mountain, the mountain the fortress. Only with the greatest effort could Chel spot where one ended and the other began. The construction squatted in the pass, filling it, choking it like a boulder, the monstrous gatehouse at its centre a consuming maw. Humanity thronged before it, a torrent of people funnelled by the pass into its jaws, shuffling slow and fearful. From the tiered ramparts above, rank after rank of impassive archers gazed down, armour glittering in the fierce sun.

'I thought this place was supposed to sit on a gorge. Where's the gorge?' Chel squinted against the glare, peering beyond those ahead at the rugged structure rising over them.

'Arowan sits on the gorge, my friend. This is Korowan. Gateway to the great beyond.'

Lemon leaned across. 'They call it the Stop.'

'In what sense?'

'At a guess, all of them.'

Chel looked over the banked walls, the rising crenellated tiers. The colour of the stone varied, the style and ornamentation, even down to the decorative carvings. 'Bit of a mixture, isn't it? Who built it?'

Foss sniffed and rubbed at his nose. Pale road dust clogged the air, drifting in clouds from the thumping passage of the crowd. 'The Sericans. Word is, any time it was breached, they'd rebuild it bigger, plug whatever the weakness was, and then some.'

'How old is it?'

'The oldest bit? Hundreds of years.'

'And the newest? When was it last breached?' Chel squinted up. Suddenly the massive structure seemed all the more imposing. Long, silken pennants snapped from a dozen mounts along its upper tiers.

'Not in our lifetime, friend. Generations.'

'Arowan itself? Did it ever fall?'

Loveless approached from the direction of the gatehouse, head low and hooded, keeping to the shaded part of the road. She'd slept in the cart for the early part of the morning, and seemed a little restored. In fact, she'd spent almost more time in the cart than out of it in their frenetic cross-country journey to the Serican border, joined by a rotating cast of whoever was struggling most with the brutal pace that Rennic had set: Tarfel, Kosh, and on one occasion, Lemon, although she blamed an underdone breakfast for that episode. Chel was as glad as any of them that their journey's end was in sight – his legs and feet were almost as sore as his shoulder – but the knowledge that they were hunted kept any thought of relaxation at bay. They knew Corvel's agents pursued them – several times they'd had to change their path at the last to avoid sure ambushes, and had more than once taken it in turns to haul the cart beside the mule to keep up their pace – but they'd at least skirted direct confrontation in their frantic journey. 'Wake the prince,' she said.

A moment later, a bleary Tarfel was beside them, descended from the wagon, dust-streaked and blinking. Momentary confusion was swiftly replaced with habitual anxiety. 'Can we pass through? Our enemies are on our heels!'

'They'll see you. You'd better impress them.'

'What are all these people waiting for? Why do they shamble like corpses?' Tarfel looked up and down the road, at the dusty throng, the evenly spaced pairs of spearmen keeping idle watch on the shuffling crowd. Hawkers moved up and down the shifting line, crying their wares. The smoke from a handful of food stalls drifted over, mingling with the dust. Somewhere a group of pilgrims was singing, discordant and jarring over the sound of distant bird cries. Traffic was sparse in the other direction, barely a handful travelling south-east on the silk road.

'Each is vetted at the gateway, highness,' Foss said, maintaining a measure of deference in his speech that had long since fled that of the others. 'Their means and motives assessed. It takes time. The Sericans are a careful people.'

'They're avaricious arseholes,' Loveless replied. 'With me, princeling. You too, cub.'

The slope steepened and the gloom of the fortress's shadow enveloped them, then they entered the blissfully cool darkness of the gatehouse. Loveless, her hood kept low despite the relative cool and quiet beneath the first of the massive gates, gestured to one of the gild-armoured guards. He was taller than those around him, his armour finely wrought, his silken surcoat emblazoned with a shape of a winged shadow. He sported a long, droopy moustache, as did many of the other guards. In Korowan, moustaches were in.

'The captain.'

Tarfel approached the man. 'Captain! I am Tarfel Merimonsun—'

The guard stared at him blankly.

Loveless slid beside him, still hooded. She said something in a language that Chel didn't recognize that seemed to feature a lot of long vowels, and she sounded fluent doing so.

'Of course,' Tarfel muttered. 'Our imperial forebears never made it through the pass, did they? Are you announcing me?'

'Your name carries little weight up here,' she murmured, 'but I'm doing what I can. We may be better off—'

He shook his head in irritation. 'My name, dear girl, is all I have left. And if it carries no weight, we may as well turn around and march back to meet my brother's minions. What, after all, is the point of me? What am I for? If I can't command a modicum of respect, then our every effort is wasted.'

Loveless stared at the prince from beneath her hood, calculating. Those in the shadow of the gate were watching their hushed, if unintelligible, exchange: guards, clerks, traders, and pilgrims all. The tall guard with the long moustache gazed from one to the other, brow lowered, then waved a hand to a knot of his companions, his indulgence expired. The men began to approach, spears loose in their hands.

Loveless spoke, fast and clear, again in the language Chel took to be Serican, or whatever they called the tongue. The faint lilt of her accent slotted against her words, and he realized at last that she was a native. Whatever she said, the guards paused their advance, and as one their attention swung back to Tarfel.

'I announced you, like you wanted. Now it's your turn. Do something royally mag-fucking-nificent.'

'Right,' he said, looking flushed beneath his dust-coat. 'Right.'

It was suddenly very quiet in the gloom beneath the gatehouse. The guards shifted in expectation, their mail jingling. Their gear really was of intimidating quality.

Tarfel introduced himself, trotting out his full name and titles as Loveless translated. He spoke with sudden, unexpected confidence, and brandished his signet with a flourish at the peak of his words. One of the guard captain's eyebrows rose.

'Under the terms of the treaty of Kelsuus,' Tarfel said, 'as a visiting head of state I request an audience with the Keeper, and the hospitality and protection of the city.'

Loveless translated. The guard captain's other eyebrow rose. He spoke, and Loveless repeated his words.

'Head of state? What head? What state?'

'I am king-in-exile, disputing my brother's claim to the throne of Vistirlar. As Arowan has no active alliance, under the terms of the treaty I must be recognized as a sovereign.'

The guard captain listened to the translation, then stood for a moment, tugging at the ends of his moustache. 'Here. Wait.' He muttered something to his men then walked away, into the darkness of the inner structure. Chel shuffled up to Tarfel and Loveless, flanked by the guards, and nodded in acknowledgement. Tarfel was maintaining his regal bearing, despite the obvious scepticism of those around them and his entirely un-regal appearance.

A liveried rider came galloping into the gatehouse from the road, flushed and dust-stained, dismounted and ran into the darkness after the guard captain. A moment later, a groom appeared and led the foaming horse away.

As they waited, Chel looked at the brutal yards-thick walls, the etching and carving around the second gateway, set off from the outer. Beyond, in the gathering gloom, he saw the flicker of torches marking the passageway to the third and final gate, and a sliver of light that might have been the open air on the far side. For a gatehouse, Korowan was enormous; for a fortress, it was dense, tightly packed, its sole aim to block the pass to the lands beyond. Three huge gates, portcullises and deployable blockades between them, arrow-slits and trenches overhead: any invading force would be shredded in its depths.

Chel felt some part of him unclench, wavering on the point of relaxation. Corvel's agents could not follow. None could pass the Stop. As long as Tarfel could get them in.

The guard captain returned, one hand fidgeting with his moustache. He marched to Tarfel, stopped, then bowed. Chel let out a breath he didn't know he was holding.

'Come.'

'Wait, my retinue. Loveless, tell him!'

'Retinue? Are you—'

'Tell him!'

She rattled off a translation, and the guard waved a hand in impatient acknowledgement. She turned to Chel. 'Get the others. Fast.'

'What's wrong?'

'That rider was a messenger. Something's happening. Go, now!'

By the time he returned, a long, upholstered wagon had appeared beneath the gate, drawn from some hidden stable and pulled by two fine-looking horses with ornate collars. Mutters from the queue of traffic behind them had turned to angry shouts, especially when they had pulled the cart onto the roadside and driven up the slope, kicking up ever more of the arid dust.

Loveless met them at the long wagon, her hood still pulled low. 'Leave the cart, they'll bring it. Get on board. Fast as you can.' Tarfel was already seated on the wagon, on one of the two facing benches that ran along its length. Two of the guards sat beyond him, apathetic, their spears couched between their knees.

'Aye, right, what kind of wagon is this then?'

'Troop transport. Ferrying bodies to and from the city.'

'And they'll be bringing our gear, will they?'

'Get a fucking move on, Lemon!'

The shouts from the roadway were growing, an ugly unrest uncowed by the lowering spears of the roadside guards. The guards themselves had begun a slow withdrawal, steady backward footsteps moving them up the hill and back to the fortress.

Chel peered through the heat haze, over the surly crowd. 'What's going on back there?'

The cries were mounting, the displeased shouts of those overtaken by the wagon now overlaid with cries of rising alarm. Movement drew his eye through the wobbling air, a torrent of rising dust from beyond the dip of the mountain road. Something was coming.

'Cub! Move your arse!'

The others aboard, Chel pulled himself up into the wagon. It started forward without delay, as another pair

329

of guards jogged beside it then hauled themselves up alongside him. One of them had a moustache.

As the wagon pulled away into the cool darkness beneath the fortress, Chel heard the rumble of the outer gate beginning to close.

# TWENTY-FOUR

The heat of the day hit them like a wave as the wagon rumbled out from beneath the fortress and into the blazing daylight beyond. Reddish stone and rock surrounded them as they climbed the widening roadway, the horse-team foaming and champing as they pulled. Then the slope eased and the mountain walls opened up, and Chel got his first sight of Arowan.

The city sat on a plateau, an odd, flat depression in the mountainous surroundings, stretching for several miles in each direction. As they rode the road's bumps, Chel saw flashes of the gorge that split the plateau, a winding chasm as if the two sides had slowly been pulled apart over centuries. The walls of the city rose from the giant standing pillars of rock that remained in the gorge's centre, a towering cascade of domes and towers, jumbled over the sheer drops into nothingness below. In the strong, persistent headwind, pennants lashed from spires jostling between the glimmering silken sails of countless windmills, their varied revolutions somehow lazy and frantic. Sunlight

331

gleamed from tiled roofs, bright blues and reds over white and sandy stone, the dazzling ribs of a giant central dome too bright to regard.

'To answer your earlier question, friend,' Foss called over the wagon's racket, 'never.'

'What?'

'Arowan has never fallen. It's supposedly God's chosen city.'

'Supposedly?'

He shifted as the wagon bounced. 'There's some, er, difference of opinion on the matter.'

'On the choice of city?'

'On the god.'

Two rows of riders fell in alongside the wagon, their strides in unison, silvered armour brilliant in the sunlight. Neither riders nor guards aboard the wagon gave any acknowledgement, all attention fixed dead ahead. Lemon cast an eye over the riders and gave a nod, their manner apparently meeting her approval.

'Let's hope we break our streak here, eh, boys?'

'What do you mean, friend?'

'Aye, well, just thinking how the last couple of places we've sojourned with a reputation for clement neutrality have come to a, you know, somewhat explosive denouement.'

'Evil days, Lemon.'

'Evil days, Fossy.'

The plateau unfolded before them, and with it, the camps: a spread of tents and semi-permanent dwellings, organized in rows and clusters with clear roads and pathways cut between. They carpeted the plateau from the drop of the peaks on either side, all the way to near the lip of the gorge.

Chel counted standards and improvised pennants, the milling denizens matched by the determined progress of riders and carts along the thoroughfares.

'What is all this? Army camp?'

Foss squinted through the glare. 'Doubtful, friend. These are pilgrims and refugees.'

Chel thought of the squalor of the Shanties beyond Roniaman, the incinerated remains of the slums that had ringed Denirnas. 'They're very well organized.'

'They got through the fortress. They must have had some coin to their names. Probably bought a better class of camp.'

'But they're not allowed inside the city?'

'Guess space is limited to the citizenry, friend. Connections or coin only get you so far.'

Chel peered over the ordered rows, shimmering in the haze of the day's heat. 'At least they're safe here.'

Foss nodded, but did not comment. The riders either side of them pulled in as another procession approached, a thundering column of burnished cavalry riding two-by-two, then a stream of half a dozen wagons, each loaded to the gills with guardsmen, their elevated spears waving as they trundled over the rocky road. Chel turned to watch as they passed, the jangle of mail and tack barely audible over the sound of hooves and steel-rimmed wheels. Foss followed his gaze, then made the sign of the crook.

'What's wrong, Foss?'

'Something is occurring, back at the fortress. They closed the gate behind us. Those folks were in a hurry.'

Chel nodded, unsettled. At least they were safe behind the fortress. Assuming Tarfel could say the right things to those who ran the city, ensure they weren't thrown straight out. He looked back, watched the column begin their descent down the slope toward the fortress, dropping out of sight beneath the tips of the still-visible tower-tops. Unusual flags decked the top-most tower, facing inwards, toward the city, huge and patterned, he guessed as signals. Of the three on view, red featured predominantly.

He turned back and caught a lungful of road-dust, displaced by the column's passage, blown straight into his mouth by a capricious swirl of the ever-present wind. Spitting grit, he cursed the wind and all who sailed on her. 'Is it always so fucking windy here?'

Foss shrugged, Lemon likewise. Kosh, beyond them, leaned over. 'What do your own eyes tell you?'

'My eyes are full of this piss-cursed dust.'

'Look around. The open plain beyond, the narrow gully of these mountains, the shape of the plateau.'

Chel spat the last of the mouth-dirt over the wagon-side. 'I'm no student of terrain.'

'Evidently. Then look at the features of the city, the stupid little flags—'

'They're called pennants.'

'—the wind-drivers. The fixed constructions. All clear indications of the prevalence of this "piss-cursed" gale. The land around funnels it, and its denizens harness it. Effective, if uninspired.'

'It's always windy here?'

'Best learn to keep your mouth closed, perhaps.'

He offered Kosh a sour, close-mouthed smile, and sat back against the wagon-side. She hadn't exactly been amiable company since the news of Denirnas's destruction – her usual self, except more so, as Chel thought of her – he was sympathetic to her directionless, miserable anger. Sympathetic, but not impervious.

Their re-expanded cortege rode down into the plateau, rumbling over its undulating surface, weaving down the cleared roadways of the expansive camp. It was huge, a city before a city. It seemed to have districts, regions, lines of demarcation between arrivals of differing origins. He recognized standards of the south, the east, the wetlands, some from along the coast, the pennants brought north by the refugees as mementos of home.

A great congregation stood gathered at the edge of one of the camp divisions, spilling into the roadway. The lead riders bellowed for them to clear the way and they shuffled back beneath the spindly shade of a blackened, withered tree, set apart from the dwellings around it. Chel stared at the tree as they rolled past, the gathering beneath it, the expectant expressions, glassy-eyed with wonder, their arms painted like spreading roots. So the message of the Mother of Storms had made it to Serica ahead of him. Then they were gone, lost behind the skeleton of a half-built structure adjoining the road, bedecked by a team of southern craftsmen hammering away beneath the hot sun.

They were close to the city now, close enough to see the ring of small towers that marked the camp's end and the clear scrub before the gorge's cleft, close enough to slip between the long shadows of the tallest towers crowding over the walls above like eager children. One tower in particular stood out, a narrow, twisted construction of sand-coloured stone, its lines gently spiralled, garlanded with slow-turning wind-drivers like pale flowers, rising from the heart of the city into the pastel sky.

A giant bridge awaited them, wide enough for half a dozen wagons to travel abreast with room between for stretching. Hewn from curving blocks of the sand-coloured stone, it rose in a smooth arc over the sheer drop below, its surface worn by the passage of decades, if not centuries of traffic. At its end stood the boxy gatehouse, projecting from the sheer walls, its wide-open gates a flat, dark arch. Another, smaller gateway lay beside it, some way around the sweep of the walls. A stunted, orphaned thing, Chel traced its line back to the ruins of another bridge, now little more than broken spars and a severed stub of stone, jutting from the craggy edge of the gorge opposite.

The wind did not relent, carrying strong, exotic tangs from the waiting city: spice and saffron, woodsmoke and burning oil, cured meats and leather. White birds turned lazy circles overhead, riding the incessant gusts, occasionally swooping into the gorge or erupting from it like angels reborn.

Kosh watched the birds, her entire body juddering to the shakes of the wagon on the road. She gazed at them, jaw loose, her eyes as absent as the folk before the tree. Chel reached to prod her, to check she was well, then with a clatter of bumps the wagon mounted the long bridge, and Chel found himself staring past her into the depths of the gorge. At first he saw only darkness, a numb emptiness beside the glare of sun from pale stone, then he found he could pick out the curve of the vast rocky pillars through the blurred gaps in the bridge-side, the variegated strata of millennia stacked from lightless canyon floor to the creeping foundations of the city's walls. Water flowed somewhere beneath, and fast; the spray from its emission drifted within the wind-sheltered gorge, sparkling like rainbows where it met the piercing shafts of light that angled within the clasp of the ravine. Chel squinted, seeing flashes of what could be waterfalls, or waterwheels, fixed against the rocky walls below, silver strips of water flushed over them and away by narrow aqueducts, into the shadow of the monstrous rock pillar on which the city sat. Could there be tunnels beneath? The angle of his view was poor, his window closing. Already they were nearly at the bridge's end, and the city's shadow had embraced them.

The riders drove them through several gatehouses and into the twining narrow streets of the city, cleared by the bellow of their approach. The city lived vertically, buildings stacked and nestled, ramps and curling stairs leading ever upward toward the sunlit upper reaches. Bridges and covered passageways passed overhead, strung between tilting structures, and everywhere hung bright and fluttering silk, stretches, tassels, and strips, pulled flat against the whistling wind. Chel gathered snatches of greater edifices rising between the narrow loom of the twisting streets, the glittering domes he'd seen from the plateau, the gnarled spire topped with swooping wind-sails. At the roadsides, beneath raised colonnades, citizens went about their business in the cool of the shade, long-robed and serious, unperturbed by the rumble of the wagon and its escort.

The spectacle of it all washed over Chel, his eyes unfocused, unable to choose any one thing to rest on amidst the flickering splashes of coloured silk and mind-muddling architecture. Around the wagon, all seemed similarly overwhelmed, all bar Loveless; she kept her gaze down, her hood still pulled low. Even Kosh seemed impressed with what she saw, although she was evidently trying not to show it.

They rolled past a tall, narrow building as they climbed, pressed against the roadside, its stone ancient and pitted compared with its creeping neighbours. Its windows to the street were as tall and narrow as the building itself, almost pointed slots in its facade, its doorway a dark arch to a candlelit interior. An inverted triangle of bronze marked the yellow stone above the door, greened and darkened by the years, but polished and free of tarnish. Foss stared at it as they passed, staring at the triangle, the walls and windows, what little of the re-tiled roof they could see from beneath. He sat back as they rounded the next curve and mounted a well-worn stone ramp, unconsciously making the sign of the crook with one hand.

'You all right, Fossy?' Lemon had one eye on him, the other on the dancing strings of hanging silks.

'Hmm? Yes. Well.'

'Aye, right. What is it?'

He rubbed one eye, clearing a patch of his gentle patina of road-dust. 'That place back there.'

'The little chapel?'

'Yes. The little chapel.'

Chel leaned against the wagon-side, gripping with one hand to stop him sliding as they climbed. 'Something wrong with it? Thought that was your sort of thing?'

He raised an eyebrow, but his heart wasn't in it. 'It was an old chapel. Very old.'

'Seemed like they were taking care of it though, eh?'

'Yes. Exactly.' He sighed and rubbed at his eyes again. 'There aren't supposed to be any old chapels here.'

'There aren't?'

'No. It's . . . The teaching of the True Church, the reason for its foundation . . . This was the seat of the Church, the Old Church. But they abandoned it, turned their backs to God, spurned the Shepherd. They . . . According to the Articles . . . They tore down their chapels, desecrated them.

338

The seat of the Church was lost, the city and its region were deemed Godless. The New Church arose from the ruins, a church for the people, the true believers, who would never again . . .' He tailed off, looking miserable.

'But if there's an old chapel here . . .' Chel said, eyes on Foss, waiting for him to complete the thought.

Lemon did it for him. '. . . Then the old foundation story ain't quite so pure and virtuous, eh? Oh, chin up, Fossy, it's not like the current bunch are a particularly fine exponent of the Shepherd's ethics, is it?'

Kosh sniffed. 'Your people's need to invent mythical figures of worship appears to be some kind of tribal failing, and should long ago have been stamped out. The inbreeding of your continent presents many lingering issues.'

'Hoy,' Lemon said, 'I'll have you know—'

'Yes, yes, "No Clyde is beholden to any God", very bold. I'm sure you find other ways to be subverted by intercessors.'

'What do you mean by that?'

'In this uncultured south, you are a fearful, uneducated people, ripe for prescription. Tell the mud-dwellers that an invisible sky-demon wants their labour or land, or that perhaps a man with a golden crown has the backing of the so-called Almighty and must be obeyed, and they fall over themselves to do as they're told. The ignorant masses just want to feel like they're on the right side, after all.'

Foss was staring at her, nostrils flared. 'You say too much, young lady.'

'I say nothing less obvious than the nose on your face. Power structures that claim authority from things unseen are exploitative by definition, especially when such claims are enforced with fear of a conveniently unverifiable afterlife. Any student of history, anyone with half-a-day's learning, will see this. Unless, of course, their position in said structure defines their worth.'

'Meaning?' Chel said.

'Meaning that nobody wants to look too closely at the contents of the pie they are selling, and that, paradoxically, those with the power to change affairs have the least incentive to do so. It can require an outside influence to effect change, as we say in my country.'

'No gods in your country, Nort?'

They turned toward the front of the wagon. Rennic was watching, eyes intent, ignoring the wagon's rock. Chel had had no idea the big man had been listening.

Kosh made a moue. 'The true spirits are those in material things, in the wood and the water. The spirit of the ore, ground and fired and rolled as steel, honed and hammered and pressed into service, respected, venerated. The partnership of craftsman and element.'

'And who leads you?'

'Leads? We lead ourselves, mercenary. Ours is a meritocracy, where those of ability and education may vie for local administration, and those of the greatest ability rise to serve at the level of canton, or even on the federated assembly.'

'Administration? That open to anyone?'

'Of course, anyone from the appropriate classes.'

'The appropriate classes?'

'It would not do to inflict the burdens of duty and administration on those ill-equipped to perform such functions. We have our own mud-farmers in our country, after all.'

'But if they had ability, could one of your *mud-farmers* serve?'

'Had I the wings of a bird, could I soar like an eagle?'

Rennic narrowed his eyes. 'No gods or kings, yet still some rule.'

Kosh shrugged. 'It is nature's law.'

'Shame nature isn't around to corroborate. Still,' the big man stretched his arms as the wagon's climb levelled off and the vehicle began to slow, 'you've got one thing right. If you want people to do what you want, make them afraid. Make them think they're under attack.'

The wagon came to a halt on a wide, incongruous plaza, a network of fountains at its centre, fully a hundred feet above the gate through which they'd entered the city. Still towers and spires clustered around its circumference, including the great twisted spire Chel had seen from beyond the walls, but before them stood the great gilded dome Chel had seen from afar.

'The House of the Keeper,' Loveless said, motioning them to dismount. 'Keep your fucking mouths shut in there, or so help me I will flay you all.'

# TWENTY-FIVE

They waited in the Butterfly Room, and it was no challenge to work out its name. Bright creatures flitted between giant silken facsimiles of the same, fashioned from curls of filigree and decorated with glittering jewels, suspended by threads from the distant domed ceiling, itself a masterwork of tile and coloured glass. Kosh peered at the nearest silk butterfly, sniffed, and pushed it with a finger, watching it swing and sway. She tutted.

A chamberlain announced them as a wide set of curtains parted, revealing the rest of the chamber, its swirling columns and rows of prismic windows, pulsing in the afternoon's light. A cluster of musicians in the far corner played gentle, teasing harmonies on instruments that Chel didn't recognize.

'We're announced as Tarfel of Vistirlar and his retainers,' Loveless hissed from beneath her hood, 'so look retaining.' She stepped forward to meet the oncoming group, and the others followed.

Three figures approached, a pair of the gleaming house

guards led by a tall, angular woman, dressed not in silk but in rich, soft leather, a long sabre at her belt. Her breast-plate was ornate but functional; Chel guessed her to be a captain of the guard, perhaps some level of overseer. Loveless came to a stop as they met, bowed, still hooded, then stepped aside, clearing the way for Tarfel with a flourish.

Chel watched Tarfel and the tall woman converse, watched the prince attempting to mask his nerves with bombast, the woman's impassive expression, the mirror of the glazed archers staring out from the fortress in the pass. Lemon was beside him, chewing at one thumbnail, her attention matching his.

'What's with all the butterflies in here?'

'National symbol, innit? Serican butterfly and all that.'

'Any idea why?'

Lemon paused, chewing a tiny piece of nail-grit. 'Butterflies look impressive but are fucken useless?' she offered. Chel let the matter drop.

'Who's the prince talking to?'

'No idea. The Keeper's keeper, perhaps?'

'Very good, Lemon. That's not the Keeper, then?'

'Her, fuck no, wee bear. Word is, the Keeper's ruled the city for eighty years, so the old girl will be showing a few creases I expect.'

'Eighty years? That's not possible.'

'Who am I to say? I am merely a simple Clydish wench.'

'Do you think he's making an impression?'

The tall woman's lip had curled in a small but perceptible sneer. She inclined her head in a formal but dismissive bow, then turned on her heel.

'Ah, bugger-burps,' Lemon said.

Something bright and shimmering arced over her head, swooping like a diving bird then rising, soaring up into the rainbow gleam of the windowed gallery. It was butterfly shaped, yet far bigger than any of the creatures that flitted around the chamber, its wings fixed and stiff. At last, it dipped again, following the bend of the wall in a lazy curve, before skidding over the polished marble floor to a skittering stop. The tall woman stared at it, mesmerized, then at Kosh, who with casual strides walked to where the object had come to rest, scooped it up, and fussed over the dents of its impact. She turned, ostensibly oblivious to her audience, revealing one of the oversized silken butterflies in her arms, the filigree of its wings reshaped into something altogether more birdlike.

The tall woman approached, gaze intent on the butterfly and the woman holding it, eyes burning with questions. Kosh looked up, then away. If her modesty was affected, Chel thought, she was giving a masterful performance.

Whatever words they were to exchange were interrupted by Loveless, still hooded, inserting herself between them like a chaperone. Her words were fast and urgent, playing on both the witnessed feat of engineering and the promise of more to come if Prince Tarfel were to receive a full and proper hearing. Tarfel himself nodded along, as if his life depended on it. Perhaps, Chel considered, it did.

The tall woman nodded, distracted, her eyes still on Kosh and her butterfly, then signalled to one of her guards. The man turned and marched out of sight beyond the curtain, and Chel felt himself unwind a notch, relaxing a sliver of the tension in his aching shoulder.

'Again?' the tall woman asked, over Loveless's shoulder to Kosh. The Nort fussed with the butterfly a touch more, then straightened, turned, and cast it into the air with a supple roll of her arm. The vessel soared from her hand over their heads, turning gently in line with the contour of the walls, then bobbed and dipped, sending some of its mortal brethren fluttering up in an iridescent cloud. It came to rest on the chamber's far side, skidding over the marble, just as a new procession came into view.

The group flowed with silken finery and dripped with jewels, with the exception of the mailed and rigid house guards. At its head came the Keeper herself, haughty and upright, her long train carried by a trio of scuttling waifs. They skirted the fallen butterfly precisely, all the while giving the impression that it didn't exist. From either side, the assembled attendants and nobility near-threw themselves prostrate with deep and conspicuous bows, some pushing bodily in front of others. The tall woman broke away from Kosh and strode to meet the group, saluted with pole-arm stiffness, then stood to one side, fixed as a statue.

Loveless, maintaining her role as herald, bowed deeply with her hood pulled low, then stepped aside once more. Tarfel took a step then inclined himself in courtly greeting, a calculated gesture, indicating he felt he was greeting an equal in stature.

The Keeper paused for a moment, then bowed her head but not her body. Chel saw Tarfel grit his teeth. His gambit had failed. Formalities complete, the two approached each other, coming close enough to speak. Loveless hovered in Tarfel's shadow, head bowed and still hooded, translating with the manner of someone who'd rather be spending their time in any of the five to twelve hells.

Chel watched them talk, watched the Keeper's face for

signs of her intent. A thin, strong-featured woman in later years, her eyes sunken into dark hollows over drawn cheeks, the white of her hair bundled and bound into an ornate head-dress, she gave nothing away. She barely seemed to blink, her stare like a lizard's.

'Look at her.' Lemon was gazing at the Keeper with something approaching awe. 'Buried three husbands and countless offspring, yet still here she is.'

'You sound like a fan.'

'Pff, three husbands more than I'd fancy, but you've got to admire the old girl's staying power.'

'Any idea what they're saying?'

'The usual, no doubt. Princeling will be doing his best to enkindle her affections in search of protection, alliance and mutual beneficence, and she'll be working the angle to see what's in it for her. Blah blah, fate of nations et cetera.'

'Affections? Is he going to try to marry her?'

'Her? Come on, wee bear, keep up. Friend Keeper still has one living daughter. Last living scion of the dynasty, never married. If our man can secure her hand, we're nailed on for alliance and reconquest. For the time being, at least. The winds of courtly favour blow fast and capricious in these parts.'

'How do you know all this? You studied Serican politics?'

'Told you, man, I'm educated! May not have *hattended* a fancy *hacademy*, but I know things. I know many things. The only shame in learning is confining your horizons.'

'How do you think it's going?'

Lemon furrowed her brow, squinting as if reading the micro-expressions of the involved parties. 'I would say . . .'

The Keeper took a step away from Tarfel, her expression soured and impatient, face pinched like a raisin.

'. . . Not well.'

'Maybe if Kosh throws her butterfly again?'

'Tall order, wee bear, tall order.'

Tarfel took a step forward, one arm out in entreaty, but the Keeper raised a hand to still him. Instead, she turned toward Loveless, who skulked at the prince's side.

'Is there perhaps,' she said clearly, in a voice like rustling parchment, 'something you wish to say for yourself?'

Loveless froze.

'Remove that hood. Did you think I would not recognize you?'

With glacial slowness, Loveless reached up a hand and pulled back her hood, revealing her travel-stained and glowering visage beneath, the faded lilac of her hair revitalized beneath the vivid light of the glowing dome. Once more her beauty hit Chel in the gut, his ardour for her carving a streak through his innards. She looked sidelong toward Rennic, her eyes radiating both fury and deep unhappiness.

'You see,' she muttered toward him, 'they always know. They always know.'

'That is better. Perhaps now we can speak without veils.' She murmured something to a flunky, then turned back to the prince, who regarded her through narrowed eyes but said nothing. 'Shall we start again, your highness?'

Tarfel gave a slow nod, his gaze flicking to Loveless, then back to the Keeper. The tall woman remained beside and behind the Keeper, resolutely still, gaze distant, but Chel thought he saw distaste in her expression. To what, it wasn't clear. In the background, the musicians started up a new tune, something both alien and maddeningly familiar. He looked back to Loveless, and wondered exactly what the Keeper had meant.

'Exalted Hayal,' Tarfel said, his voice carrying over the music, 'forgive my ignorance. I wasn't aware you conversed in my native tongue.'

The Keeper merely inclined her head in acknowledgement. Apologies only travelled in one direction in these parts, it seemed.

'I come to you with an appeal, and an offer,' Tarfel continued, 'at a time of great peril for us all. You will be aware of the ructions in my kingdom, of the wars and rebellions. You may not be aware that my brother, who calls himself king, wishes also to call himself emperor. He wishes to unite church and throne beneath him, then convert or subdue all within our borders and without. I am raising an army to fight him, to repel his madness, and we come to you with an offer of alliance. Your city has stood firm in the face of aggression from the south for generations, and as king-in-waiting I ask for your strength to buttress my own.'

The Keeper nodded, slowly, in comprehension if not in acquiescence. Her eyes were still on Loveless, whose own gaze searched the whirls in the marble beneath.

'I offer a coalition of mutual benefit. I have many allies, both inside the kingdom and at its borders, and with your cavalry—'

'That is enough, thank you, your highness. There will be no alliance. Arowan does not take sides in the squabbles of the lordlings of the Sink.'

Tarfel started forward again. 'Exalted, I think perhaps you do not realize what is at stake. My brother has acquired alchemy, stolen from the Norts across the sea, and means to conquer—'

'I believe you have said enough, your highness. In deference to your station and those with whom you travel, you and your retinue may rest here for a few days. After this, you must return south.'

Her words hit Chel like a gut-punch. Tarfel stood bereft, his jaw working, producing no sound.

A messenger arrived at speed from an outer door, rushing to the tall woman's side. She bent for his whisper, then relayed the message into the Keeper's ear. The old woman nodded. 'Your brother, it seems, has come to collect you himself. An armoured host sits before the Stop. They are . . . *demanding* you.'

Tarfel blanched, blue and ghostly in the dome's filtered light. 'Corvel's here? In person?'

Chel felt the cold grip of an old fear, thought banished, and tried to calm himself. His heartbeat thrummed against his ribcage, sweat cold on his back. An armoured host? That sounded like more than the ragged remains of some free companies. And Corvel himself? How could things have turned so fast? He thought again of Nadej's words. *They said it was like a storm. Razed the port and sank the Norts.* He needed to sit down.

The Keeper sniffed. 'Arowan does not accede to . . . *demands*. We will inform his delegates that you are currently our guest, and invite them to return through the pass.'

'And . . . and if they refuse?'

'They shall be coerced. Korowan does not suffer the unwelcome.'

'Exalted, what I said before, about the alchemy – the like of which—'

'You have borne witness to these alchemical weapons, highness? Faced them in battle? Can speak of their measure?'

'Well, no, not in so many words. But we've seen their effects, and the stories—'

'Korowan has been breached three times in its history, and never in my lifetime. No army has passed it in a century. They shall depart or they shall be destroyed.'

'That's what you'll tell them?'

'If it's what they must hear. Once they depart, so must you, but for now will you remain as guests.' She turned back toward Loveless. 'Even you, my daughter.'

Relief washed over Chel like a tingling wave.

*Wait.*

*Daughter?*

Loveless met her gaze, staring back with onyx-hard eyes. 'I am not your daughter.'

'You were the wife of my son.'

'We were not married, and he had many others.'

'Yet still you carry something of his.' Chel followed the old woman's gaze, seeing the prized blade that hung from Loveless's belt, peeking from the folds of her cloak.

'This,' Loveless said, her eyes never leaving the Keeper's, 'is *mine*.'

'You carried his child, for a time. You were my daughter then, you remain so now, no matter the intervening.'

'Not for long, and never since.'

The Keeper inclined her head, her smile small, supercilious. 'We will talk again later, when you have rested. There is much we should discuss.' She turned back to Tarfel. 'Your rooms will be prepared. Your highness, I will notify you when your brother has left our lands.' She swept away from them, trailing courtiers and retainers. The tall woman remained, her antipathy aimed firmly at Loveless.

'You said you'd never come back.'

'How are you, Matil?'

'You said you'd never come back.'

'And I meant not to. Yet here we are, so let's grin and bear it, shall we?'

'Don't expect me to smile, Rai.'

Lemon was chewing at her fingers, eyes locked on the women in front. 'Brother of shite, that's Matil. That's the last scion.'

Chel stared, trying to process everything that had happened. 'She doesn't look much inclined to marry Tarfel,' he managed.

'No, indeedy.'

The music finished, and as Loveless stalked away from Matil, Chel ran the melody back through his head and it all clicked into place.

'God's balls,' he said as she passed him. 'You're the White Widow.'

The ferocity of her glare could have punctured his skull. 'You're mistaken. That's some bint in a song.'

'They played it . . . She told them to play it when she saw you. That's your song?'

'It's nothing to do with me.'

'That's why Rennic won't let anyone play it – because you don't like it? Come on, isn't it flattering? A beauty who so adored her lost love that her hair turned white overnight when he died?' He stared at her hair as he said it, its constant changing of colour taking on new meaning.

'I prefer "ash blonde",' she said, voice controlled but eyes burning.

'But—'

'That song is *propaganda*. And the truth of it, cub . . . The truth is . . . sordid, and vile. Let a song be a song, but don't confuse it with a life.'

351

For once, Chel ignored Lemon's cautions on the pursuit of intimates. 'What really happened, then?'

The slightest softness entered her eyes as they drifted, then her gaze hardened once more. 'You want the true story? Here it is: when I was young, all my choices were made for me, until one day I made one of my own.' Two fingers traced the scar at her temple. 'Now leave me the fuck alone.'

She marched from the room, leaving the others standing around, staring at each other in bafflement. Matil's mood seemed improved by her exit, and she turned to Kosh.

'It looks like you will be staying with us for a time after all,' she said. 'Now, what other tricks do you have?'

# TWENTY-SIX

Officially, the tour was for Tarfel's benefit, but it was to Kosh that Matil directed her words.

'Our workshops are the envy of the civilized world, as you can see. From the wind-drivers above and the water mills below, we combine the power of the elements with the latest in machinery—'

Even over the hiss of steam and clanging of metal, Chel heard Kosh's disdainful sniff.

'—to produce fine-milled steel, here within the city. Our cavalry, house guards and archers are the finest-equipped force across the mountains and the plains. With our steel and stonework, we have kept the tribal raiders long at bay, allowing ever-more intensive farming across the expanse and the formal protection of the trade roads. And you have seen Korowan, our jaws on the throat of the southern pass. Arowan controls the trade for six regions and provides protection to an ever-growing area of the expanse. We have the finest artisans, the greatest merchants, the most advanced production of arms and armour.'

Kosh sniffed again. Matil noticed, but instead of irked, she seemed amused. She ran a finger over her fine-wrought breastplate, picking out the detail of the rearing swan in dark metal. 'You would not consider this well-made?'

The Nort pursed her mouth in equivocation, her gaze following the path of Matil's finger. 'Well-made, of course. Advanced, well . . .' She moved to the gantry rail, surveying the steam-obscured activity beneath. It was very, very hot within the workshop, the channelled breeze from the vented windows on high doing little to disperse the warmth of the forges into the blaze of the day outside. Chel felt the sweat dripping from him, and from Tarfel's pallor he suspected the prince was devoting all of his energies to staying upright.

'What's down there?' Tarfel was doing his best to maintain the fiction that the tour was of some benefit to him. He gestured to a menacing-looking set of double-doors at the workshop's end, flanked by a pair of sturdy house guards dressed in far too much armour for the room's heat.

Matil started, as if surprised to find the prince still there. 'The looms, highness, and access to the waterways below the city. I'm afraid they are off-limits to outsiders.'

Tarfel pouted. 'Surely—'

'You can understand, highness, that our peerless silk production is the source of Arowan's wealth, the seat of its power. We wouldn't wish to put the city's lifeblood at risk, would we?'

'Ah, no, quite so, quite so.'

Kosh had approached a rack of mail shirts. 'I can see your people are doing their best. This is reasonable stuff, if a little antiquated. Tell me, are you rolling the steel hot or cold? What is its proportion of *kaarban*?'

Matil wrinkled her nose, still amused, her eyes narrowed

354

to their crinkling corners. She was older than Chel had first thought, perhaps even Rennic's age, although she moved with none of his creaking force. She was light on her feet, languid, rarely seeming to move without purpose. Chel guessed it was too hot in Arowan to waste energy on excess movement.

'I could not tell you.'

'Who can? Who is in charge here?'

Matil despatched one of her attendants, a seneschal she called Mira who struck Chel as having kind eyes, to summon the chief artificer. The artificer duly appeared, a hunched, shrivelled woman in singed robes, her thick head of curls bound in a waving tower from the top of her scalp. She met Kosh's interrogation with terse and defensive answers, translated via the ever-more amused Matil. Kosh herself became increasingly condescending with each retort; had Chel not witnessed it, he would not have thought it possible.

Smirking to herself, the Nort paused at a long workbench containing crossbows in various states of assembly. 'How far can one of your bows shoot?'

'More than three hundred and fifty strides,' came the proud reply.

'And what is the lethal range?'

'Greater than seventy strides.'

'Against armour? Say, that breastplate of yours?'

Matil and the bent woman conferred for a moment. 'Depending on the quality of manufacture, still lethal at twenty-five strides.'

Kosh's smirk was uncontainable. 'Have our effects been brought up, yet? I would like to show you something.'

\* \* \*

With the crossbow and sundries from the cart came Lemon, Foss ambling in her wake, as curious and amused as Matil. Chel was glad to be back on the plaza, the fierce breeze cooling his cheeks and blowing the sweat from his neck.

'Oh, aye, crossbows, is it?'

Kosh ignored her, collecting only her exhibition piece. Lemon continued to chatter, following along. 'As it happens, I have an invention of my own, a highly-functional piece for the warrior outnumbered in the field. It uses two—'

'Thank you, that will be all.' Matil waved a hand, her attention solely on Kosh. 'Your servant is quite outspoken. My mother would have her whipped.'

Kosh's smirk broadened, but she said nothing. Eyes wide and nostrils flared, Lemon stomped over to Chel and Foss, making a sort of hissing sound.

'That steam coming off you, friend?'

'Servant? *Servant?* Fucken hells, man.'

Matil summoned a house guard, who then paced out twenty-five strides. Kosh gestured, and he paced five more. Then another ten. Then another ten, with increasing disbelief. From the workshop's darkened arch, the chief artificer watched proceedings through scrunched eyes of deep distrust.

The house guard stopped at sixty-eight strides, only because he had run out of room. The pillared balustrade pressed against his back, the only barrier to the drop to the winding streets below. The man set down a marker, then stood, looking nervous.

Kosh nodded to herself, pleased. 'Who is the best bowshot in the city?'

'Perhaps I am,' Matil said with a mischievous smile.

'Perhaps you are. Your breastplate, please?'

Matil looked down in surprise, one hand on the armour, protective.

'Come, what do you have to fear at that range?'

The tall woman hesitated a moment, then started on the straps. 'What indeed?'

The relieved house guard propped the breastplate on two stacked barrels at the balustrade, then withdrew. Matil raised one of the bows from the workshop, aimed, and held, waiting for the wind to drop. After several moments, it did, the constant whisper of the distant trees and snap of the city's silken trails falling suddenly quiet.

Matil fired. The bolt streaked from her bow, whistling in a flattening arc across the plaza. It struck the base of the breastplate with a clang, rocking it on its perch. It teetered for a moment, then fell back against the barrel, little to show for the impact bar a faint smudge. With a rueful shrug, Matil passed the weapon back to a guard, who relayed it past the glowering chief artificer.

'A good shot,' Kosh said with affected indifference.

'Wasn't it? Your turn, I believe.'

'One moment.' Kosh called back the guard, who approached only after Matil's nod. She muttered to him and passed him something, then bent to unbundle her own weapon.

'May I see?'

'Afterwards.'

The guard had reached the stacked barrels. He thumped a bolt into the topmost, its fletching stripped. Instead, a set of long, fabric tassels of various colours flowed from it, dancing on the wind.

Foss stirred. 'I'll be.'

Chel stared at the flapping tassels, mesmerized. 'A wind-marker. Like Whisper.'

Kosh had extracted her crossbow and was kneeling, fiddling with something on its upper edge.

'I forget she spent time with the old girl,' Foss said, his voice tinged with melancholy. For a moment, they rested in silence, each ambushed by their own memories of their departed friend.

Kosh lifted, sighted and fired. The bolt was a blur, a black smear over the plaza. It struck the breastplate with a crunch, slamming it back against the barrel, the dark fletching jutting from the ragged hole in the neck of the swan.

Matil's mouth was open. 'Gods . . .'

Kosh stood, beaming, her cheeks flushed, the crossbow cradled in her arms. She looked almost girlish in her proud delight. 'You see,' she said, to Matil or to the world, 'it has an adjustable sight, placed over the prod, which allows the shooter to see their target even at flatter elevations.'

'Gods . . .'

'The mechanism can't really be improved from here, but I'd like to concentrate on the construction, test out lighter materials and try to reduce the carry weight without sacrificing power. Efficient and robust construction is really the key, and I was thinking of separation into modules, so it could be stowed in the wet, or better yet some kind of replaceable—'

'My armour!'

The house guard had separated the breastplate from the barrel and approached, funereal, the stricken plate in his hands.

'My . . . armour . . .' Slowly, Matil's gaze returned to

Kosh. If before it had been curious, now it was reverent. 'You made this?'

'This? Yes. Yes, I did. Of course, the skeleton was canni-balized from other—'

'Can you make more like it?'

'Like it? This is a mere prototype, not something to replicate. My *new* design—'

'*How fast can you make more?*'

'Very fast. I am extremely efficient. I could make as many as three or four in a week.'

Matil's smile was tinged with mania. 'Can you instruct others? If you had the run of the workshops, and our artificers, could you instruct them?'

'You must understand, increasing those under instruction is lost production time, and I could really be—'

'We have twenty artificers in these workshops, and more across the city. Would, of course, that we had more. How fast can you build bows?'

'Assuming the availability of materials, I could probably oversee up to ten in a week. The assistants would have to be excellent though, good listeners, able to do exactly as they are told. I have no time for egocentrism.'

Lemon snorted at that. 'Aye, right, now you know me,' she said, swaggering back into the plaza, 'I don't want to widdle on any parades, but . . . Splendid as that little twangy-stick is, you may yet be staring down a world of witchfire in the none-too-distant, and I'm not sure how much difference a dozen more twangers will make . . .'

Matil gave no sign of being aware of her existence. She held her ruined breastplate up to the light, inspecting the jagged rent the bolt had made. 'You owe me a new breast-plate, engineer. Can you afford to buy me a replacement?'

Kosh met her eye, bold, teasing. 'I will *make* you a replacement.'

Matil grinned like a tiger. Chel looked to Foss and Lemon. 'What's going on with those two?'

Foss only chuckled, while Lemon wrinkled her nose. 'I dunno, maybe it's for the best. Could be getting her velvet tipped might make her less of a pain in the wossname.'

'What?'

'Never mind, wee bear, never mind.'

\*\*\*

They heard the raised voices, anger through dark wood, long before Mira the seneschal stopped at the door to the rotunda.

'Your chambers. Her radiance, Exalted Hayal bids you rest while she resolves the matter of the southern force. Please await a summons.'

Loveless and Rennic stood on opposite sides of the circular antechamber, bristling like alley-cats. They froze when the others entered, the atmosphere in the room frigid despite the day's warmth.

'Everything all right?' Tarfel asked, calculatedly blasé.

Loveless ignored him, switching her focus to Lemon and Foss, and to a lesser extent, Chel.

'We need to leave this place.'

'What? We only just arrived.' Lemon flopped down on a bloated cushion; silken, of course.

'And staying here is poison. It will consume us, one way or another.'

'What are you talking about, friend?'

'I'm talking about the fucking army at the threshold, the

one that wants yon princeling's blood. I'm talking about
the venomous lizard that rules this place, and her sow of
a daughter.' Kosh stirred at this, ready to dissent, but
Loveless left no space. 'I'm talking about this vile,
constricting place, its scheming lords and poisoners. It will
choke us all if we stay more than a breath.'

'Lot of snake imagery there, friend.'

'I can't think why.'

Rennic stepped around the cushion pile, into the patterned
light of the upper windows, their blinds like frozen spider-
webs. 'Why the hurry, Ell? Why the desperation?'

Her gaze fixed him with cold fire. 'You should know
that better than anyone what this place is to me.'

His hands were up, palms down, his approach slow as
if to a cornered animal. 'For the first time in as long as I
can remember, for a while at least, we are safe. Does that
count for nothing?'

'No true safety exists in this city.'

'Corvel and his confessors will be held, maybe even
routed. Things in the south will escalate. And even if they're
not—'

'For the last time, Gar, this is not our problem to solve!'
She waved a hand at Tarfel without looking at him. 'Even
princeling himself isn't certain he wants to challenge his
brother, it's written in the sweat of his pallor. Maybe
"safety" is good enough for him. But this place isn't safety,
it's a trap, a pit. They will scheme and they will plot and
they will *use* us then throw our husks to the wolves at the
gate. Did we learn nothing? What happened to Whisper
can happen to any of us, and the closer to this insanity we
are, the closer to alchemy and witchfire, posture and plotting, the greater the chances.'

'You're saying "us", but—'

She wheeled on Rennic. 'You *want* to face the confessors, don't you? Kill Corvel, save the kingdom.' She threw up her hands. 'What are you trying to prove, Gar?'

Rennic's placatory demeanour vanished. 'We'll fix nothing by running away. We're staying, that's final.'

'I'll make my own choices, Gar Rennic.'

'We're. Staying.'

A throat cleared at the doorway. A different seneschal stood there, a study in precise uninterest. 'At his earliest convenience, the Exalted Keeper requests the presence of Prince Tarfel and his retainers in the upper gallery.' The seneschal filed away before she could hear anything that might incriminate her.

'Aye, well, that didn't take long, eh? The matter must be resolved already.'

Loveless hadn't moved, and when she spoke it was with the growl of a feral beast. 'You stay if you want, old man. But don't count on me sticking around.'

# TWENTY-SEVEN

Kosh was already on the upper tier, in huddled, whispered conversation with Matil in the shadow of a wide stone archway leading onto the gantry, long curtains curling at their feet in the reflected breeze. She barely acknowledged their presence when the seneschal led them out from the stairway, although the scowl that rode Matil's features at her sight of Loveless was unmissable.

Chel caught up with Tarfel as he hovered uncertain, awaiting the Keeper's arrival. 'Tarf, was it true what Loveless said back there? About not being sure you want to challenge your brother?'

Guilt overrode the prince's expression, his cheeks flushed, and he swallowed. 'Ah, well, Vedren, if I were completely honest . . .'

'Of course you can be honest with me, Tarf.'

'. . . then I would say that, on some level, I have some doubts about our course of action.'

'What do you mean?'

'Well . . .' he swallowed again, looked up at the rainbow-lit

363

ceiling far above. 'Am I fit to rule? I've tried to be decisive, assert myself, and that disaster at the Bridge House was the result. How can I challenge my brother for a kingdom I couldn't summon the strength to master?'

'One mistake, one accident, Tarf—'

'I've sold the southern coast to a pack of reavers, pushed the free cities into chaos and insurrection, and come within a gnat's chuff of surrendering dominion over the territories. Half the kingdom is in uproar while my brother chases after me with his armies, leaving ruin in his wake. Might it . . .' He squinted, rubbed at one eye, and his voice dropped. 'Might it not be simpler if we just let him win? Surely it would be a more peaceful outcome than what's ahead?'

Chel moved himself into the prince's eyeline, met his wavering, watery gaze. 'We're doing the right thing, highness. We do it because we must. You know Corvel won't stop unless someone makes him. That someone is you.'

The prince nodded, a faint smile on his lips. 'Yes, yes. Right you are, Vedren. The right thing. Thank you.' He seemed to stand a little taller.

'I'll be with you all the way, Tarf. Father always said a problem shared is a problem halved.'

'How true.' The prince's smile crinkled. 'Reckon we could find forty or fifty thousand others to share this one with?'

A crack and groan from the gallery's far end signalled the opening of the grand doors and the Keeper's imminent arrival. Matil's face lost all expression, and she stood tall and stiff, leaving Kosh gabbling to her chest. She had eyes only for her mother, as the Keeper swept into the room in a torrent of swishing silk, flanked by flunkies and censer-swinging ascetics.

Lemon was at the back of the assembly, looking uncomfortable. Chel joined her. 'Loveless had plenty to say on this place,' he murmured.

'Aye, I was right, wasn't I? There's history there.'

'What dark scheming do you think she was referring to?'

'Aye, well, probably relating to the current political cloud in this here juncture, vis-a-vis succession.'

'What?'

Lemon sighed in expansive disappointment, although Chel saw the corners of her mouth lift as she did so. 'Her radiance, Exalted Hayal, has yet to name a successor for the Keeper-ship. Keeper-dom? Keeper-age. Hence a substantial volume of political jockeying for her favour.' She indicated the assembled worthies who bowed and scraped at the Keeper's approach.

'Surely Matil is in line for succession? Is that not how it works here?'

'Yes and no, wee bear. While she's indeed currently on the hook for it, she's more of a – what's the word? – a place-holder.'

'She'd refuse it, or something?'

'Oh no, she won't be offered, come the time of naming. Sounds like the old girl is just dragging the whole thing out for the spectacle, loves to see the body politic scrap and connive.'

Chel clicked his tongue. 'Another succession drama looms? We're getting to be connoisseurs.'

'Aye, well, hardly a surprise, is it? You go round basing your systems of government on who fell out of whose bits, you're going to come a cropper sooner or later. The whole notion's inherently precarious. Now, if it's good breeding you want, come the season in Clyden—'

'You think Loveless is worried she'll be dragged into it?'

They watched one long-moustached lord elbow another discreetly out of the way as the Keeper approached, then present an ostentatious bow as she passed.

'Aye, I'd say so. Ach, I've no patience for more of this, wee bear. Catch me up later, I'm off to find some grub.' With that she swaggered for the door.

The head seneschal bade the prince recline on a cushion-packed dais, while the Keeper arranged herself neatly opposite. The retinues stood behind their principals, hovering uneasy. Platters of fruit appeared before them, apricots, plums, pomegranates, and grapes, borne past by indifferent servants with fixed and dark expressions. A third space remained clear to the Keeper's right, and she scanned the assembled group, looking for someone. Chel saw Loveless slide behind Foss and out of the old woman's eyeline. The place remained empty. Matil was not invited to sit.

The Keeper did not eat, it seemed, but she stared hard at Tarfel until he caved in and picked up a plum to chew. It was far too juicy for polite consumption, and all present pretended to ignore the squirting dribbles of syrup that soon coated the prince's hands and chin.

'The message is delivered,' the Keeper said. 'The rabble at the Stop will now either depart, or be destroyed.'

'Exalted Hayal,' Tarfel said through a mouthful of plum, 'I must once more impress caution – the forces that pursue us are of singular construction, an amalgam of church and crown, mercenary and fanatic. My brother is building armies for conquest, for empire. They have stolen the alchemy of the Norts, as our own alchemist can attest—'

From the corner came a quiet hiss: '*Engineer!*'

'—and I'd not be surprised if half the folk on your doorstep weren't victims of this latest aggression in one form or another.'

The Keeper watched, aloof, cold as marble. 'Do you fear war, highness?'

'Do I . . . Well, yes, I suppose I do. The provinces have suffered two decades of it, on and off. I think we could all do with some peace, eh?' He offered a weak smile, but the Keeper made no acknowledgement. Instead, she nodded, once, as if marking off a task completed.

'Indeed, a ruler should care for her people. What is a ruler, after all, but a custodian? Am I not the Keeper of my people, their lands and possessions?'

Tarfel paused, trying to judge the question's rhetoricity. 'You are,' he said at length.

'But you must not fear war, highness. War is the cleansing fire, scouring the dead wood, leaving the ground clear for fresh growth. It is a judgement on the righteous, on the worth of a kingdom, a people, a ruler.'

'I'm not sure I—'

'Highness, if you cannot win a war, then what can you offer your people?'

'Isn't there more to—'

'Your father, Gods rest him, as example. *His* father, Gods rest him, had won the wars in the south, made himself king, but it was your father who made the lands his own. He saw what he wanted, what he needed, and what the kingdom needed with it. And he took it. He was not afraid of war.'

'Exalted, what do you mean? What did he and the kingdom need?'

She paused to take a small sip of rosewater, and Chel

noticed the slightest tremble in her hand. 'Heirs, highness. Without succession, a ruler is . . . precarious. The people deserve clarity, expectation. Uncertainty breeds . . .' She paused again. 'Bad thinking.'

Tarfel said nothing, waiting for her to continue. The plum juice was a sticky glaze on his hand.

'Your father ruled, but without successors, or prospects, even to his middle years. When the gods showed him his chance, he took it. He did what was necessary.'

'Are you talking about . . . ?'

'Your mother, yes. She was already married to another, a lord of the eastern province, but when he saw her, he knew she was the answer. She was of Horvaun blood, like him – how else would you and your brother be such pale and golden lions? – and of fertile age. Your father and Vassad made a pact, and a day later the lord of the east was denounced as a heretic, his lands and titles forfeit. When he resisted, he was put down. Your father had no fear of war, and the kingdom was stronger for his actions.'

Tarfel was staring at the old woman, fibrous plum stone held immobile in one hand. 'How do you know all this? Exalted.'

Her eyes were dark pools in the shade of the gallery. 'Because I witnessed it. Arowan was party to the pact, if only as a neutral observer. We would not intervene, but would defend our lands with tenacity. That pact has held to this day, although it seems your brother has forgotten it.'

A skivvy signalled something from the gantry, and the old woman fussed herself to her feet, waving away the offers of assistance. Tarfel stared at the hollow cushions where she'd been sitting.

'Wait, Exalted, wait. My mother,' he said, voice tight, 'was she content in her marriage? To the eastern lord? Was she happy to marry my father instead?'

The Keeper paused, two swishing steps toward the gantry. 'I cannot speak for her thoughts, Gods rest her, but her suicide would suggest that she was not.'

Tarfel rocked in his seat, as if with a roll of muscular spasm. 'My mother died in childbirth—'

'Your mother died three summers after your birth, in a fall from her tower window. Surely you have some memory of her?' Tarfel stared back, mute, blank. 'I understand that this information was suppressed – her servants went to the tomb alongside her – but you must have heard rumours since? Mine were not the only spies in your father's court.' The Keeper shuffled on toward the gantry, leaving the prince stricken on the cushions, his eyes filling with tears.

'You see?' Chel heard Loveless mutter to Foss. 'It was about sex. It's always about sex.' She turned to leave, and Foss went with her.

On the gantry, at the balustrade, stood an odd device, a long, wide tube of brass or burnished metal on a multi-legged stand, pointing out over the plateau toward the mountain pass. Kosh was on it immediately, inspecting, scrutinising. Matil was beside her, murmuring something of rock crystals and convex ground glass, before the Keeper swept her away with a fierce glance. She barked at the flunky beside the device, who responded with stammering unease.

'Your brother's army has refused our request to depart,' the Keeper announced. Matil looked pained at the news. 'They are, once again, demanding you, highness. Have you a wish to go to them?'

Tarfel stood, alone, in the archway, eyes red and stung with tears, hand still sticky with fruit juice. He shook his head.

The Keeper nodded, then barked another command at the flunkies. Matil took a step toward her mother, then stopped and turned away, shame-faced. Above them, signalling flags rolled from the tower, great splashes of coloured silk, bold and patterned. Red had primacy once more. Beyond the balustrade, over the lower buildings of the city, the walls, the gorge, the camp-stuffed plateau, Chel could make out the hazy tips of the fortress towers, their own signal flags bare specks against the sun-washed stone.

Chel sidled close to the prince, mindful of his fragility.

'Don't worry, Tarf,' he said, 'she might be old but she has no way of knowing—'

'I remember her, Vedren.' He was still holding the plum stone, turning it over and over in his palm. 'I remember . . . love. Kindness. Sadness. A presence, golden and wonderful. Then a terrible absence. I remember it, but until now I had no measure, no means. I remember her.' He looked up, meeting Chel's gaze with fearful melancholy, a raw longing that made Chel's soul ache. 'What do I do? What can I do?' He swallowed. 'Does my brother know? Why did he never tell me? Am I so little a part of my family?'

Chel had nothing to offer. He opened and closed his mouth, chewed at his lip, and the prince's gaze fell back to the plum stone. Chel's joined it. In the distance came the sound of drums and discordant horns, fighting valiantly against the wind across the plateau.

The earth shook. Chel thought he heard a crack over the rush of the wind, a sound like something huge snapping

in half. Another tremor followed, then another, a gentle
rumble beneath their feet, the slightest rattle from the platters of fruit on the low table beyond the arch. Chel and
Tarfel exchanged anxious looks, the prince's pain forgotten,
each turning to the balcony.

'Could it be—'

'Witchfire!'

Kosh was already at the rail, Matil at her side. 'Smoke!'

The Keeper had not moved, although deep lines furrowed
her paper-thin brow. She muttered something to an attendant, who fussed his way to Matil's side and to the tubular
device at the rail. Chel could see the smoke now, black and
rising, and a wafting pale cloud that intertwined its base.
It came from the pass.

'What in hells—?'

On the plateau, awareness was spreading like flame. Chel
could see the eddies of hurrying figures, little more than
dark blurs through the haze, stripped of sound by the flap
of the wind. Spurts of activity flared around the camps,
small at first, then spreading outwards until a full-fledged
stampede was in progress. The gleam of armour drew Chel's
attention to the ring of watchtowers before the gorge; the
guards were abandoning their posts, making for the great
bridge over the divide.

The Keeper barked again, and the flunky at the tube
yelled something back over the growing murmurs on the
gallery. Chel could hear bells tolling around the city,
increasing in number, and felt a familiar sick panic swelling
in his chest. This had happened too many times.

'What's happening?' he called toward Kosh and Matil.
Was that screaming from the plateau? 'What's he saying?'

The smoke was thick now, a dark column like a wedged

shaft of night, around it a blooming yellowish fog, spreading out from the pass, clogging the neck of the plateau. Matil turned toward him, but her gaze was still toward the pass, toward the smog obscuring the fortress.

'He can't see the signals from the fort. The smoke and dust are too thick.'

Urgent bells were all around them now, panic had taken the city and its towers. The passage to the bridge was choked with fleeing guards and those escaping the camps, fighting to get across toward the sanctuary of the city.

Messengers appeared at the gallery's arch, first a couple, then half a dozen, each panting and wide-eyed. They clamoured their indecipherable reports over each other, struggling to be heard. The Keeper remained unmoved, the lines on her face the ancient furrows of a petrified tree. Then she spoke a single command. From the hush that followed, Chel read shock on the faces of those present, then the messengers bolted, disappearing back into the darkness whence they'd come.

He and the prince turned back toward Matil and Kosh, eyes searching for explanation. Matil stood as stiff as her mother, one hand on the rail.

'What—'

'To close the city gates,' she said.

Already the cries and bellows from beneath were reaching them, their passion and fury carrying them above the wind. Traffic on the bridge had stalled, with half the camps yet to reach it, struggling away from whatever lurked in the pass.

'That's madness! They'll crush each other! You can't just shut them out!'

'The Keeper has spoken.'

The man at the tube yelled again, his eye pressed to its aperture.

'*Still I cannot see the signals,*' Matil translated automatically.

Chel squinted out toward the bleached bulk of the mountain pass. 'The dust is clearing, even if the smoke lingers. Surely they're visible now?'

The man yelled again, his voice ragged with hysteria.

'*I cannot see the signals. I cannot see the towers.*

'*The towers are gone.*

'*The fortress is gone.*'

The balcony exploded in shouts as retainers and stewards blustered and screeched, while Matil stood very still at the rail. Chel felt numb, noticing only very distantly Kosh's hand on the tall woman's arm, the look of concern in her wide black eyes. He turned back toward Tarfel, whose ghostly pallor had returned, then in the midst of the chaos, from the corner of his eye he saw the Keeper falter. She took half a step to one side, staring at one of her hands in apparent disbelief, then her mouth began to droop in the most peculiar fashion. Despite the bedlam encircling her, Chel felt like he was the only person watching her as she wobbled on her feet, closed her eyes and collapsed to the stone.

# TWENTY-EIGHT

Chel sat at one edge of the rotunda, the late afternoon light streaming through the narrow windows casting thick bars of dancing motes before him, staring at the plum stone in his hand. If he concentrated on it, he could almost ignore the clamour of bells, shrieks, and cries from beyond the windows, the angry shouts echoing around the towers, the frantic jingle of hurrying troops. Behind it all, the wind was a constant, howling, moaning, a trapped and miserable animal.

The door flew open, and Lemon struggled into the rotunda, her arms piled with small boxes. Foss was right behind her, carrying a pair of crates that clinked and tinkled with each step.

'All right, wee bear, what's the crack up there? Place is in uproar.' She stomped to the low table at the room's centre and unloaded her cargo, spilling fruit and pastries. Foss placed his crates down beside the table with great care. 'Not that it didn't play into our hands.'

Chel stirred from his perch. 'What's all this? Where did you get that?'

'Did a bit of a tour, picked a few things up. Everyone's tear-arsing around, nobody minded us a jot.'

'You *stole* this?'

Loveless was in the doorway, a sack over one shoulder, a thick clay jug under the other arm. 'Fuck them. You can't rob snakes.' She kicked the door closed behind her and strode to the table, laying her contraband beside Lemon's. Something peeked from her jacket, a wrapped package, and she tucked it quickly back inside. 'Where are the others? What's the fuss? I thought I heard thunder.'

Chel rubbed his eyes and wondered where to start. 'I don't know where Rennic is. Kosh is still with Matil, and Tarfel is with them. In the gallery.'

'He let you out of his sight? You're his comfort blanket, aren't you?'

'I was . . . removed.'

Lemon was already devouring a fig. 'Removed? What magnificence did you perform, wee bear?'

'I demanded they reopen the city gates. Quite . . . strenuously.'

'The gates are closed?' Loveless had been halfway to sitting, but this brought her back to her feet. 'All of them? Why the fuck are the gates closed?'

'The main gate, the bridge to the plateau. I don't know about the plains side. They're closed to stop thousands of people fleeing into the city.'

'And why are they fleeing the plateau?'

'Because Corvel's accursed alchemists have levelled Korowan.' Rennic stood in the opening doorway, leaning heavily against the frame. 'They've destroyed it with witchfire.'

'How?' Loveless had spun to face the door, her words an accusation. 'It's a fucking mountain of stone!'

'Packed those kegs around the base and blew it in on itself? Battered the first gate and stacked them within? Either way, it's gone. Where's the Nort? She might be able to shed some light on this.'

'With her new friend, apparently,' Lemon said. 'Keeping a low profile, I imagine.'

'That's the other thing,' Chel said, eyes back on the plum stone. 'Matil is Keeper now, it seems. Acting, maybe. I don't know if Exalted Hayal herself is still alive, somewhere.'

'*What?*' The shout came from multiple directions.

'She . . . fell. Just after the fortress.' He turned to Rennic. 'You're sure? The fortress is really gone?'

He nodded. 'It's rubble and blood, the pass is blocked. They sent riders from the gatehouse, they just returned.' He saw Chel's look. 'What? I know a little Serican, enough for professional courtesy.'

'How did the riders get back in? The gates are closed.'

'They'll open to those who count.' He levelled his gaze on Loveless. 'Still want to leave?'

'Still want to stay? After the red confessors have flattened the greatest defensive structure in the known world? Think what they'll do to this place if they choose.'

Rennic walked down the steps from the door and flopped down beside the table, plucking a pomegranate from Lemon's hoard. 'They must have spent all they had on destroying the fortress – as you said, it was a mountain of stone. It'll take them days to clear the rubble from the pass. In the meantime, they're trapped in the gully as if the fortress was still there. Calculated attacks from the slopes, pin them with archers, can whittle their numbers before they can get clear. Sow enough panic in the ranks, they'll break, especially those who took the cloth unwillingly. In three days they'll be little more than a rabble of fanatics in muddy cloth, clawing at boulders with their hands. They might think they've demonstrated their power, but all they've done is hem themselves in.'

'And if you're wrong?'

'I'm not.'

'You could be. It's happened before. Then what?'

'There's only one bridge to the plateau. I'd like to see them try and stack kegs around the walls of this place, assuming they have any left. They'll need fucking wings.'

'Aye, right,' Lemon volunteered, 'and what about those little egg-things the wee bear mentioned, the spikey wee fuckers.'

'They'd need hundreds, maybe thousands. And what are they going to do, throw them across the gorge?'

Loveless's gaze hadn't left him. 'And what if they do?'

'Then we face them.'

'Face them? What, the four of us against the red tide?'

'You want to keep running? We've been running for months! They've hunted us the length of the country. They're not going to stop, unless we give them reason.'

'They're *not* hunting *us*. They're hunting *him*.'

'So you're back to abandoning him, our princeling? Our client?'

'Our client? Fuck me, Gar— When has he ever paid us?'

'He can pay when he's king.'

'When? You're talking fantasy!'

'You want to give up? Hand him over, or leave him to swing in the wind here?'

'Why not, Gar? Why in righteous fuck shouldn't we?'

'Because . . . Because then . . . What was it all for? What did she die for? What did we do any of it for?'

'What?' Loveless took half a step, paused, rubbed at the deep scar at her temple. 'We did it for coin, Gar. We did it because we are mercenaries, a free company, contractors.'

'Did we? You said it yourself, when did we last get paid? Isn't this about something more, now? About doing something . . . right?'

'Shepherd's tits, Gar, do you think if we eliminate Corvel and his cronies, that all will be brandy and roses? You think Prince Shit-for-brains will be wise and just and rule with fairness and equanimity? Oh, I'm sure he'd have the best intentions, but mark me, jobs like that have a way of changing people. You watch the Nort's new friend Matil, now she's holding the reins. See how long her compassion lasts in the face of the realities of power.'

'Then we shouldn't even try to change anything? Why even bother?'

Loveless nodded and sucked her lip, then grabbed a handful of fruit and one of Foss's bottles. 'You do what you want, Gar,' she said, heading up the steps toward the rooms on the upper gallery. 'You always do.'

Her door slammed a moment later.

Rennic stared after her, breathing hard, nostrils flared, but not angry. Chel stared at the big man, trying to puzzle his mood. He seemed . . . surprised?

'Ancestors' wisdom, boss, you sounded like the wee bear then.'

'Shut your fucking mouth, Lemon.'

'Righto.'

Rennic stalked up the steps to the outer door, and a moment later, it too slammed.

Chel, Lemon, and Foss were left alone, only the wail of the wind and the clanging of bells for company.

'Well,' Lemon said, but nothing more.

'It would be five,' Chel said, still sitting off to one side.

'What's that?'

'Five. Loveless said it would be four of you against the red tide, but I'd be there. There would be five of us.'

'You? You're still sworn to princeling, aren't you, wee bear? He says jump, you say what on?'

'He'd understand. He'd let me, if I asked him.'

'Oh, wee bear, stop, you're making me weepy. My poor heart can't take all this.'

Foss chuckled and lowered himself down to the table, and Lemon followed suit. Chel watched them, still turning the plum stone in his hand.

'What now? What do we do?'

Foss began pulling bottles from the crates, arranging them on the table beside the piled food. 'Well, friend, either an army masses on our doorstep, ready to crush us, or our hosts will grind them to powder in the gully. Either way, matters rest in God's hands for now.'

'Meaning?'

Lemon arranged gilded cups, produced from some hidden pocket in her clothes. 'Meaning, wee bear, we've got nothing to do but eat, drink, and be merry. Because we have no idea what tomorrow brings, so we might as well face it with a granny-fucker of a hangover.'

Foss started pouring from one of the bottles, then added a dash of another, then another. 'An occasion to merit Uncle Foss's Special Drink.'

'Evil days, Fossy.'

'Evil days, my friend.'

They clinked cups, and after a moment, Chel went to join them.

*** 

Things had become hazy. At some point Rennic had returned and begun drinking with them, but Loveless remained in her room above. Tarfel was still not back; Chel rather blithely assumed he'd turn up eventually. The daylight had gone, the room lit with candles and lamps kindled by unseen attendants, and the air had become chill. Chel handled this by increasing his intake of Special Drink, which tasted mostly of spiced fruit and smelled of alchemy. From somewhere beyond came the bells, the shouts, the incessant whine of the wind, the occasional rumble, like distant thunder, making the bottles jingle in their crates. Nobody seemed to pay it any heed, so Chel did his best to ignore it too.

'Which is why . . .' Lemon said, paused, drank, resumed. 'Which is why the wee bear remains as useful as a one-legged man at an arse-kicking contest.'

'Thank you?' Chel said, brow furrowed. He'd put the plum stone down somewhere, and couldn't remember where.

'Aye, right, so here's the thing, right. Why are you called "bear"? You're not exactly bearish, are you? You're more of a . . .'

'Faun,' Rennic said, then sniggered into his cup.

Chel coloured. 'I thought we didn't ask for intimates.'

'Aye, well, thing is, could be an army of red bastards rolls into town in a day or two and does for the bunch of us, and I'd hate to go into the beyond with this bugging me.'

Foss sipped at his cup, reclined, replete, eyes half-closed. 'It started with your sister, friend? That's what the prince said.'

'It did. But listen, tell you what: you tell me where your names come from, I'll tell you mine. Fair?'

'Oho, he's a tricksy one, this wee fella.'

'Deal,' said Foss.

'Deal,' Chel repeated. 'So what does "Foss" mean?'

Foss eased back against the cushions. 'It's an old word, this one. Very old.'

'It means "wall",' Lemon announced with a proud grin. 'Back from your pit days, right, Fossy? No bastard could touch him.'

Foss raised a hand, a pained look on his face, eyes open but downcast. 'No, friend. Not quite.'

'Eh?'

'It means 'ditch'. It means something that . . . lies down.' He rubbed at his beard, running his fingers over his jaw, feeling for something beneath. 'But I got it in my pit days, and I've kept it since. To keep me honest.'

Chel blinked, unsure of what had happened. 'Has it worked?'

Foss stared into the middle distance for a moment, then a slow smile spread across his face. 'Yes, friend. I think it has.'

Chel nodded, bemused, then switched to his neighbour. 'And what about Lemon?'

She shrugged. 'Nothing to it, no great story.'

'Really? *Really?* I find that a . . . *challenge* to believe.'

She spread her hands. 'My real name is Lennon. One of these pricks misheard, or pretended to, and that was that.'

'Lennon? Lennon of Clyden?'

'Aye.'

'That's the most ridiculous name I've ever heard.'

'My thanks, Bear of wherever the fuck you're from.'

'And what about you?' Rennic stirred under Chel's stare, but didn't flinch or fidget. 'Where does "Gar Rennic" come from?'

'My mother,' he said, black eyes unblinking in the lamplight, and Chel let his gaze fall away.

'Come on then, wee bear. Spill your guts. What makes you bearly?'

'Fine, fine. When Sabina, my sister – she's younger than me by a few years – was little, she couldn't say her Vs, couldn't pronounce my name.'

'Which is?'

'*Vedren*. Hells, Lemon, you knew that.'

'Aye, right you are.'

'She'd try to say "Vedren", but it would come out "Bedren", if even that. She was a lazy sow, only bothered with the first syllable most of the time, so mostly she called me "Bear". My f—' His throat caught, and he took another swig of Special Drink before continuing. 'My father . . . he was quite tickled by it, started calling me the same. His little bear. Even once my sister was grown, and had full control of her speech . . . for better or worse.'

'Well, that,' Rennic said, lip curled over his cup, 'was disappointingly anodyne.'

'You asked. I told you.' Chel took another swallow, emptying his cup. Something fizzed within him. 'Lennon of Clyden, eh?'

Across the table, Lemon shrugged. 'It's really quite a common name where I'm from.' She looked momentarily wistful. 'You know, when I thought maybe we might go back – to Clyden, that is – I had the strangest feeling. Like, like, I wanted to, but I didn't want to. Like I never expected to.'

'But you're a, what was it, *tourist*, right?' Chel paused. 'What *is* a tourist?'

She shuffled back in her cushions, assuming her posture of great lecturation. 'Ah, well, the tour is a grand tradition of the Clydish youth, especially among those at the upper end of the social dynamic.'

'You're a princess?'

'Am I fuck. Kind of the opposite, as it turns. My touring was . . . uncommon.'

'Wait, what's a common tour?'

'Aye, you know, go out, see the world, experience different peoples and places, enhance your linguistic acumen, expand your mind and horizons. Very standard stuff. Important part of attaining adulthood, course, but . . . basically a grand old adventure for a young up-and-comer, under careful chaperon. They head for the continent, pootle around Amistreb or Shenak, poke at the old buildings and imperial relics, buy up some souvenirs for the trip home, to show off how much they saw and how much they grew – or how many forgers they enriched on their travels.'

Chel leaned closer, the cup tight in his hands. 'What about family, though, duties? Obligations?'

She looked up at the patterned ceiling, her mouth pulled down in thought. 'Depending on your outlook, you could say it's part of your duties, but in the grand scheme, they're . . . paused. Idea is, you'll be better-placed to meet them on your return, grown up a bit, got some . . . perspective.'

'You, then? The uncommon.'

'Aye, right, not for Lennon of Clyden the standard and

well-trod. I wanted to see Vistirlar, seat of the Taneru, where all the history comes from. See the art, the culture . . . course, how was I to know you were all backward savages compared to the majesty of Clyden, eh?' She shook her head, tresses bouncing. 'All a bit grim round these parts. Still, I've hit the high notes. Worked on a whaling ship, woven fishing nets, made armour, built a bridge, plus all the mucking about with you bastards . . . Expanded horizons, all right. Not bad for a simple Clydish lass.'

'When does your tour end?'

She looked at him with sad, distant eyes. 'The average tour is a year, wee bear. I've been away for . . .' She counted on her fingers, getting to at least seven. 'I don't think I'm ever going home.'

'Won't that upset people, those waiting for you?'

Her gaze dropped and her voice with it, and Chel had to strain to hear. 'Nobody's waiting for me, bear. My unreturn was priced in from the start.'

Chel felt something prickle in his own chest, a feeling like his own thoughts were being drawn out of him into the light. *Going home . . . Where even is home for me now? Wouldn't it be something to strike out into the world, make a new life of my choosing?*

Lemon belched and the spell was broken. 'Aye, well, seems only fitting to be expectorating secrets on our last night in the corporeal realm.'

'You what?'

'You know, assuming the boss is talking as much bollocks as ever, and Corvel and his bastards come knocking for us in the morning. At least we'll have had . . .' Lemon waved her hands around, slopping the contents of her cup. She didn't seem to notice. '. . . This.'

*The eve of our execution.* The phrase stirred something inside Chel, a memory of a promise. He lurched to his feet. 'I'll be . . . Back.'

He was halfway up the stairs before he realized it, feet moving faster than his stumbling mind could have foreseen. Lemon or Rennic called something after him, but it was lost to the pounding of blood in his ears, the sudden roar of his own breath.

His feet stopped him outside Loveless's door. It was closed, but light shone from beneath it, flutters of shadow indicating movement from within. Eyes shut to still the latent whirling, he knocked.

She looked tired. If she'd been drinking in her room, he saw no sign of it.

'What, cub?'

'It's . . . It's the eve of our execution.'

'What?'

'You said. You said before, about what happened. How we'd . . . try again . . . the day before we died.'

Her eyes narrowed. 'Have you come looking for sex?'

He found he couldn't answer. No combination of words seemed right.

She took a long breath and swung the door open the rest of the way.

'You'd better come in.'

\*\*\*

The lamps in the room were low, but even by their gentle light he could see she'd been busy. A knapsack, bedroll, and several satchels lay on the bed, some of Foss and Lemon's pilfered fruit poking from within. She'd laid out clothes, hard travelling wear, along with some of the richer gear the Sericans had provided for them. Nestled among them was Ruumi's fat blue stone, peeking from a leather pouch, its delicate facets twinkling in the light.

She poured him a cup of water from a pitcher and nodded toward the chair in the room's corner. He sat, heart fluttering in his chest, still uncertain of what might happen.

'Did you know Lemon's real name was Lennon?'

She raised an eyebrow but said nothing, concentrating only on bundling the clothing to fit in a pair of conjoined sacks. At last he recognized them as saddlebags.

'So, when you said—'

'If you're about to ask if we're going to fuck, then no, cub, no we are not. Just sit there, drink water and be quiet for a while, will you? Shepherd knows you stink of booze.'

Inside him, something crumbled, perhaps hope. His eyes fell on the bed, forbidden territory, and the ordered effects that lay on it. His mind caught up.

'You're packing? You're leaving?'

She looked up at him, her mouth a thin line.

'Yes.'

'Why?'

Her eyes widened, perhaps in anger, perhaps amazement. 'More reasons than you could name.'

'You're leaving us?'

'You could come too.'

'But . . . But the—'

'Yes, exactly. Now hush. Drink the water.'

He drank the water. She packaged up the clothes, then paused, and at last shrugged off her shirt, bundling it and stuffing it in with the others. Beneath she wore only the strapping he remembered from Wavecrest, from tending her wound after her sparring with Dalim. He looked for a mark, a narrow scar below her chest, and as she turned in the amber lamplight he saw at last what had been escaping him for weeks.

'You're . . .' He swallowed, throat dry, swigged water. 'You're . . .'

She gazed at him, level and unhurried, making no move to hide or cover her thickening abdomen.

'Yes.'

'A b . . . baby?'

'Yes.'

'I thought . . . you couldn't?'

'So did I. Apparently God has a sense of humour after all.'

'Is this why you're leaving?'

'Nothing I said before is any less true for this.'

'Does Rennic know?'

'Why would he care?'

'It's not his?'

'*She* is *mine*.'

Chel nodded slowly and sipped water, ill-equipped to cope. 'Does he know you're leaving?'

'Cub . . .' She pulled a silken robe from the ornate screen in the room's corner, and pulled it on with a look of distaste. 'Listen to me. The world, the people in it, they try to *funnel* you. To push you the way you're supposed to go, the way they want you to go, need you to go. This place . . . this place reminds me of who I was, and to them I'll never be anything more. I can't stay here without falling back into the role they chose for me. They'll choose for you too, given the chance.'

Chel thought of the Andriz enclave, thought of Laralim

sizing him up for the breeding pool, thought of Rasha, thought of Loveless . . . He drank more water.

'The big man and I, we've been pushing back against that for years. It's what we've done together, in all the time I've known him. Push back against the world, dig in our heels and deliver a big *fuck you* to it all. Travel our own path.'

She fussed with the items on the bed, then stopped and sighed. 'But something's different in him now, and I'm not saying it's your fault, but he's been changing since our path crossed with yours. If he had his right mind today, we'd be saying fuck all of this, let's get gone. But here I am, the only one with one foot out the door. We used to discuss things, him, me, and Whisp, talk things out, decide together. Now he just does what he thinks . . . So you tell me, cub, what's changed? What's left Gar Rennic staring down the business end of a hero's valiant, *pointless* death, and not walking away?'

'I don't . . . I—'

'Yeah. Things change, nothing lasts. What do you want, cub? And don't say sex.'

'Huh?'

'Why are you here, in Arowan? What has brought you to this madness? God knows you've been riding this runaway horse for half a year, and sooner or later you're going to have to choose when to jump.'

'I swore an oath. I have to do my duty—'

'Answer the question. What do you want?'

Chel swallowed more water. 'I want . . . I want the prince to be safe. I want peace.'

'But for yourself? What are you yearning for, pining for? And again, don't say sex, or at least not sex here and now.'

'My sister asked me the same thing, before we parted. A little differently, of course.'

'And? What did you say?'

'To . . . do my duty.'

'Five hells, cub, you're exhausting. Why? Why this obsession with duty and obligation, beyond all sense and reason?'

'My father said—'

'Oh, saints preserve us, your dear dead dad. Let me guess, you miss him terribly, and don't much care for your mother now she's remarried.'

The flush that burned his cheeks cut straight through the booze-fug. 'I . . .'

'Guess what, cub, I doubt she had much choice. Your father is gone, before he had a chance to disappoint you beyond up and dying. Your mother remained, human and fallible, facing the world alone. You think that's easy? You think she remarried to spite you, you infant? Shepherd save us from the solipsism of youth.'

'The what?'

'Thinking you're at the centre of everything, cub, that every decision another makes has you at its heart. Your father is dead, Vedren, and his approval will never be forthcoming, no matter how nobly you hurl yourself into peril. There are plenty of people alive who care about you. So why this obsession? What is so absent in your existence that you drive yourself this way? What is it that you *want*?'

'I . . . I don't know. I want . . .' He could feel tears prickling in his eyes, running hot on his burning cheeks. 'I want this feeling to end.'

Her voice dropped, intent now, gentle. 'What feeling, cub?'

'Like . . . Like I'm weighed down. By what people expect

of me. Like I have no control over my life, I just have to do what's . . . expected. Demanded.'

She leaned back with a triumphant grin. 'Now you're getting it. We're closer than you might think.' She walked over, the robe trailing on the floor like a train, and refilled his cup. 'That feeling, my young friend, exists in your mind. You escape it by choosing to.'

She ruffled his hair, infuriatingly maternal. How fitting, a small, detached part of his brain observed. 'I wasn't kidding before. You could choose to leave. You could walk back down those steps now and tell Prince Gargleballs we're fleeing, and he'll go with it. You might be his sworn man but he's your puppy. The others would come too. You could save everyone.'

Chel's voice was cracked and hoarse. 'But not the rest of the kingdom.'

'You can't save a kingdom by yourself. You need to care for those around you first.'

'But you're leaving us.'

'Because I need to look out for myself most of all.'

He half-expected her to put a hand on her stomach, but she went back to fussing over her packing. His thoughts boiled, and the silence grew.

'I . . . I can't do it,' he said at last, eyes on the beautiful silk rug at the bed's foot. 'I can't walk away. Not with all this danger—'

'I know,' she said, not looking up. 'But maybe one day you will.' She tightened a bag-strap and stepped back. 'Time for bed, cub. There are no more answers to be had tonight.'

He stood, the rush leaving him wobbling on his feet.

'Just promise you won't go before . . . Say goodbye in the morning, tell the others.'

'Of course.'

She walked him to the door, one hand on his arm, supportive, intractable. She spoke quietly as they walked, her voice a murmur. 'You need to be very careful with Gar, cub. I called him a coward before, but I was wrong. He's innately cautious, or he was, but that's gone, scoured away . . . Once he gets an idea, he . . . hardens around it. He's set on his course now, and you'd better be thrice-damned sure you have the stomach to follow him to its end.'

She pushed him gently through the door and began to close it.

'Watch him for me.'

\* \* \*

When he returned to her room at dawn, ready to apologize and redouble his efforts to convince her to stay, she was gone.

# TWENTY-NINE

Foss, Lemon, and Chel stood in the doorway, staring at the empty room. The bed was made, blankets pressed flat, and on it lay a single bottle, one of the wines Lemon and Foss had pilfered. It was unopened.

'Guess she wasn't thirsty,' Foss said. 'Half-expected her to have left the sword.'

'You're joking, eh? She'd sooner part with an arm.'

Chel looked from one to the other, searching their faces for oncoming levity, a relieving break to the tension. None was forthcoming. 'She'll come back, though, right?'

'Hmm?'

'She's threatened to leave before. She'll come back, once the dust settles. Right?'

Lemon puffed her cheeks. 'Often said it. Never done it.'

'So?'

'So, I don't know, wee bear.'

'Will she be all right?'

'Her? Aye, she'll be grand, that one. All of nature's bounties.'

'What do you mean?'

Foss stirred. 'You know, if you break a bone, it heals thicker, stronger than before?'

'Yeah, I suppose.'

'If you break it again, it gets a little thicker? A little stronger?'

'If you say so. What are you getting at?'

He nodded, slowly, his gaze still on the bed, bright shafts of patterned sunlight dancing over it. 'I'm saying she'll be all right, friend.' He took a long breath. 'It's the rest of us we should worry about.'

Footsteps thumped up the hallway behind them. Rennic was almost at a run.

'Get to the gallery. Now.'

'What's the commotion, boss?'

'*Now.*'

Chel searched for words, thinking of how to phrase the news of Loveless's exit. Lemon overtook him, with a nod inside the door.

'Did you see—?'

'Yes. Now *move it!*'

\* \* \*

The dust cloud had gone, although dark smears of thick smoke still rose from the neck of the pass into the brilliant morning air.

'No,' Chel whispered, his hands on the gallery rail. 'Already?'

'How the fuckity . . .' Lemon murmured beside him. Foss just stood very still.

Before them the plateau had parted, the abandoned camp at its centre, the seething press of the unwelcomed refugees still choking the bridge and the guide towers. And at the plateau's far end, slithering into view like a steel-plated blood-snake, came the column. It widened as it advanced, spreading outwards, revealing thickening ranks of marching figures, little more than gleaming crimson blurs. Behind them, the first great engine rolled out of the pass, a giant armoured wagon on steel-rimmed wheels as tall as a man, hauled by a team of indistinct, lumbering beasts. Even at the extreme distance, the scale of the machine was breath-taking.

Chel stared, fighting the urge to rub his eyes. It was too much to take. 'There are so many of them. So many . . .' This was not the modest host of the Gracechurch. This was a horde. 'How could they have got through so fast?'

'By blasting.' Kosh was behind them, dark eyes wide, face solemn. She was wearing Serican clothes, a lot of silk, although she had kept her outfit practical. 'They have . . . far more powder than I could have imagined. An impossible volume.'

'You mean witchfire?'

Her brow furrowed, and her eyes flicked onto him, finding focus. 'What you call "witchfire" is many things, none of which I have the time or the inclination to distinguish for you. Rest assured, they have more of it than they should. Far, far more.'

She looked off over the rail for a moment, then her gaze snapped back to Chel. 'The Keeper has requested your presence.'

'Me?'

'All of you.'

'Aye, right, so the old dear came round, did she?'

'No.'

\* \* \*

394

Matil stood beneath the outer arch of the Butterfly Room, the Keeper's chain held loose in her hands. From the way her shoulders hung, it might have been made of deep lead. Kosh almost raced to her side, taking her hands and relieving some of the weight of the chain, metaphorical or otherwise. Behind her, at the chamber's centre, angry voices bellowed over each other as a knot of figures, some in robes, some in polished armour, jostled and jabbed at each other, their retainers encircling them in a sheepish ring.

Chel and the others hung back, uneasy at breaking whatever moment was passing between Kosh and the new Keeper.

'She's in charge now?' Rennic's voice was a growl, but hushed in the confines of the hallway. 'Why do you think she summoned us?'

'As it happens, she didn't, I'm afraid.' Tarfel stood to one side of the arch, also alone, peering round at the sound of their approach. 'Not directly, at least. It was me, really.' He looked a little abashed. 'Everyone else had a retinue; it was difficult to be taken seriously.'

'Where have you been?' Chel asked. 'You didn't return last night.'

The prince nodded. He looked tired beyond measure, purple hollows beneath dawn-red eyes. 'I was in attendance of our former Keeper, Shepherd rest her. Duties of state, you understand.'

Matil approached, the chain still dangling from her hand, no evident intention to wear it. Kosh trailed her like a puppy. 'Prince Tarfel, if you are ready,' she said, 'perhaps we should bring the council to order.'

'My condolences again, Exalted. I can sympathize, of course, my father was ill for a long time . . . probably.'

Matil ignored him. Her gaze rolled over them as she

turned back toward the council, then she paused. 'Where is Rai?' It took Chel a moment to realize she meant Loveless.

'Gone,' Rennic replied, voice stripped of emotion.

'Gone? Where?'

'Through the north-west gate and out into plains, some time before dawn. Bartered for a horse at the gatehouse. That's all I can tell you.'

Matil nodded, eyes narrow, her reaction controlled. Chel scanned her for emotion, struggling to read her thoughts. As she turned back to enter the chamber, he caught a flash of something he could have sworn was relief.

The commander of the house guards, and apparently, by extension, the defence of the city, was a slick, well-presented man of Rennic's age or thereabouts, whose gleaming breastplate was almost as ornate as Matil's had been. His long moustache was oiled and styled to points, and his smooth skin shone like wax. Chel disliked him immediately.

'In deference to the presence of our honoured guest,' Matil announced, her accent stronger as she raised her voice over the hubbub, 'we will conduct our affairs in his language.'

The commander bristled, his moustache twitching, but he offered no dissent. Chel hung back with the others in the outer circle of retainers, hoping they felt no less out of place, as Matil and Tarfel advanced to the tall, circular table at the council's centre. Kosh went with them, always a step behind Matil.

The new Keeper summarized the situation: the Church's forces had cleared the rubble of Korowan from their path far faster than anyone had expected, working through the night and detonating black powder – the rumbles that Chel had felt through the evening, no doubt. The confessors were streaming onto the plateau, dragging their engines and supplies, and looked to be forming up to lay siege.

'We should sally,' the commander said, his accent less thick than Chel had expected, his voice precisely as smug. 'They have marched, assaulted, dug through the night, and marched again. Their men will be exhausted. We have the finest cavalry at our disposal, ranks of seasoned spearmen. We advance to the towers, set ranks, and encircle them. They will try to flee, and we will have them, trapped by the neck of the pass.'

Matil rubbed at one eye with her free hand. She looked more tired than Tarfel, whose own complexion was grey in the room's gilded light. 'Thank you, Lord Ghiz, for your thought. I foresee a number of potential obstacles, however: first, their force is very much larger than we realized, encompassing a number of what appear to be former mercenary companies. Our lookouts report company pennants, overpainted with the symbol of the crook.' Rennic twitched at this, and Chel thought of Nadej's words, and Fest's treachery. 'There is no guarantee that the men who dug and laboured through the night are the same as those entering the plateau, especially given our intelligence on the nature of their alchemy.' There, a little look to Kosh, who responded with a tight smile of satisfaction. 'Second, we cannot attack in cold blood. They have raised a flag of truce.'

'Truce?' cried one of the robed types. 'They laid our fortress to waste!'

Matil nodded, jaw clenched. 'Which they may claim was in defence of an act of aggression from those manning it. We have no way to confirm, there being few left to us who can speak of the events, and under the treaties we have little alternative.'

Ghiz's moustache was trembling. 'Your mother would never have stood for this.'

'My mother,' Matil replied with a voice of ice, 'refused to treat with an army on our doorstep, dictated an aggressive ultimatum and triggered the destruction of our city's greatest defence beyond the gorge and the loss of hundreds of lives. I shall not make the same mistake. Keep your forces ready, Commander, but you will wait for orders.'

'Very well.' He turned to leave.

'Very well, *what*?'

He paused, exhaled through his nose. 'Very well, Exalted.'

'You are dismissed, Commander.'

The rest of the council filed away after him, muttering in their own language. The words might have been unknown to Chel, but the tone wasn't, nor the pointed looks at Matil and Kosh both.

Tarfel remained. 'You're going to treat with them? Is that wise, Exalted?'

'I understand your concerns, highness. But we risk little in hearing them out. Their position may be more flexible than was implied.'

'And if not?'

'I will not surrender you, highness. If they insist, I will refuse, and they will lay siege, as was perhaps always their intent.'

'You're not worried?'

'I am. But Arowan is the most defensible city in the known world. They must cross the gorge to reach us, along a wide, open bridge, to reach a triple gatehouse. And they cannot surround us – we will always have the water of the wells, the aqueducts, and two bridges out to the plains, allowing us to bring in food and evacuate people as we see fit. Arowan has never fallen, nor will she. Ever.'

Matil paused, one hand resting on the table before her. A brilliant blue butterfly descended onto her shoulder, resting there for a moment, slow wings shining in the shafts of coloured light from above. 'When we treat with them, highness, you will need—'

'Yes, quite, I shall attend.'

'No, absolutely not. If they have come for your head, I will not present it to them as a gift. You will need to nominate a second, someone to represent you and your interests.'

Tarfel nodded, relief bringing some colour back to his pallor, and with it, a small smile. 'What better second than my first sworn. Would you do the honour of representing me, Vedren?'

Chel swallowed, nodded, took a step then stopped. 'Of course, highness.'

'Chel has been my man for half-a-year, kept me alive with the kingdom against me. I couldn't have a better second.'

'Anything we should know, Chel sworn to Tarfel of Vistirlar?'

'You need to open the gates and let those people in.'

'I believe you said as much before.'

'And it's no less true now. If you care about those people—'

'They are not my people.'

'But they are *people*! And they will die on that bridge if you do not let them in. You said it yourself, the gates to the plains are open – they could cross the city and go straight out the far side, no bother to a soul.'

'I cannot allow unrestricted access to the city. For centuries we have controlled—'

'Leave them on the bridge, and you will have their blood on your hands. *Your* hands, Exalted.'

Matil gazed past him, off toward the slow-spinning silken butterflies. 'I will think about it, Chel of the South.'

She turned to leave, and Kosh went to follow. The engineer shot Chel an angry look as she did so.

'Wait,' he said. 'I want to talk to you.'

She frowned, but stayed as Matil strode away.

'What?'

Chel nodded her away from the others, toward where the silk butterflies dangled. His mind swirled along with them. 'I've been thinking.'

'You surprise me.'

'We need to prepare for the possibility that everything is about to go to shit.'

Kosh raised her eyebrows, but said nothing.

'You know better than anyone what those confessor bastards are lugging in those wagons. I've seen your alchemy—'

'I am an en—'

'*Engineer*, yes, but you know more than enough alchemy to get by, don't you? More than anyone in our wretched kingdom, I'd guess.'

She preened, but didn't disagree. 'What are these thoughts that pain you?'

'Why did you believe they'd have less than they do? You keep saying they should have exhausted their stores, yet here they are on the city's doorstep, and they seem in no hurry to conserve their alchemy.'

She folded her arms. 'In simple terms?'

400

'Why not.'

'The powder is difficult, time-intensive and dangerous to make, and the recipe I gave them was the hardest of all. They should have struggled to procure reagents in sufficient quantities, and lost many batches along the way.'

'Is there a chance you could have been wrong about the difficulty of, uh, procurement? Or could one of Corvel's own alchemists have experimented and refined the recipe?'

Kosh pulled at the end of a dyed and frayed tangle of hair, her lips pressed together. 'Maybe.' Her next words sounded like they were being dragged from her by a straining team. 'It's possible I may have miscalculated, in my duress.' The flash of her eyes dared him to make something of it. He did not.

'If they still have stores or witchfire, powder, whatever, they will be keeping it in those armoured wagons, yes? Well away from fire, out of the reach of anything we might try to lob at them.'

'Likely, yes.'

He turned to one of the silken butterflies, a miracle of gilded orange and green, rotating on the faint breeze from the upper window. He ran his finger along it, pulled it back, let it rock and spin on its thread.

'I was in Denirnas when your people's ships arrived,' he said, eyes fixed on the twirling artifice. 'And I saw something *significant* . . .'

# THIRTY

Chel watched the heaving mass from the rampart of the second gatehouse, the jostling flock fighting their way into the city, leaving the fearful plains and the bridge behind. The guards, resplendent nonetheless, jockeyed and bellowed at the incomers, directing and harrying them, keeping the flow moving, and occasionally intervening in a shove too far. The crowd felt at the edge of panic, but holding there, tingling with adrenaline but in sight of safety. Those behind, still shoving their way off the bridge, did so with wild eyes and frequent backward glances, but at last the warm yellow stone of the bridge shone through at its far end.

Chanting reached Chel's ears, a sudden, lurching shock, and he turned to see a column of drab-robed refugees thudding their way through to the next gate, eyes downcast, their rhythmic chant in time to their plodding. Many of them carried charred branches, or had marks like spreading tree roots adorning the visible skin of their arms. Most of the other refugees gave them a wide berth, but others joined them, taking up the chant, until they passed through the

402

second gate and out of his sight, their dour singing lost beneath the call of the wind. Their song disturbed Chel; it wasn't a church dirge, one of the confessors' threnodies, but something keen, yearning, undulating like the breath of the wind.

'Happy now, Chel of the South?'

Matil was there, mailed and gleaming in the slant of the sun. She wore a new breastplate, its reflected sunlight too scorching to scrutinize, and a tall, plumed helmet that framed her face with burnished steel.

Still unsettled from the odd singing of the refugees, he only nodded, eyes scrunched against the glare from her armour. She returned the nod, her face a slice of darkness in the halo of the helmet, then gestured to the stairway.

'Our mounts are being brought around. The gates will be clear enough to leave soon.' She turned to go, then paused. 'Have you, by any chance, seen Akoshtiranarayan recently?'

'She's taken herself off to the workshops, I think. Seemed, er, full of inspiration.'

Matil nodded again, distracted, her express lack of reaction revealing in its own right. He felt a pang of guilt.

'We should leave.'

\*\*\*

Tarfel was waiting with the horses, along with a cluster of house guards, Ghiz among them. Those already horsed turned and stamped, corralling their mounts into formation. Matil's charger stood to one side, a monstrous glossy black stallion, in the care of what looked like half a dozen grooms. Thick barding glittered from his withers, draped over him like a golden steel curtain.

'Are you sure this is all right, Vedren? You really don't have to go if you don't want to.'

'I'll be fine, Tarf. I'm lucky, remember?'

'Right, right you are.'

Ghiz dogged Matil's footsteps, his jabber impenetrable to Chel but clearly vexing to the new Keeper. She pulled herself up into the saddle with a face like thunder, then turned and called out something to those assembled, over Ghiz's head, to his consternation. As she finished speaking, all eyes in the courtyard turned on Tarfel.

He kept very still, unflinching but unnerved. 'What did she just say?' he said from the corner of his mouth. Chel shook his head, but Mira the seneschal, ever-present in Matil's attendance, leaned forward.

'She said that Prince Tarfel commands the city while she is outside. Not Lord Ghiz.'

Tarfel pulled at his collar. 'Can she do that?'

'It is unconventional, but legal.'

The commander was staring at the prince with utter contempt. His moustache twitched with a sneer, and then he turned and marched out of the courtyard, a dozen house guards at his heel. The remainder shuffled over to the prince, surrounding him in a manner that was less than comforting.

'They will protect you,' said the seneschal with a guileless smile.

'Right. Right you are.'

Matil spurred her horse over to them. 'Apologies, highness. I cannot abide that man, and in my absence he may try to depose me. It will be harder for him to try now.'

'If you say so, Exalted. Anything I should be doing, you know, until you get back?'

'Command the city. Marshal the defences, keep the lines,

prepare for the worst. Keep the refugees moving and out into the plains.' She flashed a quick, bright smile. 'Don't worry, highness, my staff are competent. They will help.'

'Indeed. Of course.'

'Come, Chel of the South. We must not be late for the parley.'

\*\*\*

The meeting site was beyond the gorge, but still just within theoretical bowshot of the city walls. Chel wondered if Kosh's special crossbow could still punch through armour at this range, and hoped he wouldn't need to find out. The outriders had staked out a small area of plateau and erected a wide awning, shielding a low table beneath from the sun's heat. They'd even brought out food and water jugs, before retreating past the lines and back to the safety of the city. Over the awning, a black pennant danced and snapped in the wind.

'They are late.' Matil had bidden Chel recline by the table, but seemed unable to relax herself, pacing in her mail, staring out to the blood- and rust-coloured lines forming up beyond the abandoned ruins of the refugee camp. The confessors were already cannibalising the former buildings for their materials. More of the giant engines had risen from the pass like dark demons, as big as houses and trailing ribbons of black smoke. A pall hung over the church lines, constantly renewed despite the wind's harrying, a haze of smouldering alchemy.

'There. At last.'

From within the lines and the smoke rose a plume of paler dust, and in time a wagon appeared, rocking over the roadway in their direction, a black sheet streaming from an improvised mast. It took Chel a moment to recognize it as one of the same troop transports that he and the others had ridden from the fortress into the city. They must have pulled it from the ruins, or found it abandoned. He cast a look back at their own escort, waiting beyond the stakes. A company of fine horse, long spears and bows held ready.

'We could shoot them now and be done with it,' he said. 'Back over the bridge before they know it.'

Matil cracked half a smile. 'We are not the animals, Chel of the South.'

Chel returned the half-smile, but he honestly wasn't sure if he'd been joking.

The wagon halted at the line, and its occupants disembarked. Grim-faced confessors, true believers to a man, their long red robes patchy from dust, were followed by plusher figures. The last to dismount wore a robe of cream and vermilion.

Chel started. It couldn't be.

Vashenda swept up to the awning, bright sunlight casting her silver crop to gold. She seemed older than when Chel had seen her last, somewhere beneath the citadel, and less belligerent than she'd been in Denirnas. There was a cold reserve to her gaze, a questioning that had not been there before, but she remained as imperious as ever.

Falling in behind her came another familiar face.

'Motherless horse-fucker,' Chel said, remembering himself, then repeated it under his breath.

Esen Basar, novel Grand Duke of Denirnas Port and Doromin province, his smug and handsome face still bearing the mark of Rennic's knife-throw, took a preening step beneath the awning and saw Chel. Immediately he blanched, his eyes and nostrils wide, one hand jumping to his scar.

'The traitorous sand-crab,' he hissed. 'I will not—'

'Wait in the wagon, your grace,' Vashenda snapped, and he stiffened, turned, and returned to the transport, passing the last of the party on his way in. Chel watched this last arrival with a sense of leaden disappointment.

Fest looked rumpled and off-kilter in his confessor's robes, but he grinned when he recognized Chel. His hair had been cropped short, his blessed armour seemingly no different from the wild-eyed young men escorting them, but he swaggered apart, confidence undimmed.

'The Eagle's totem! We must be in the right place.' He gave Vashenda a knowing grin, which she ignored.

'Sand-flower,' she said, stepping beneath the awning. She was sweating in the robes, clear beads proud on her brow, but she gave them no acknowledgement. 'You live. Does the prince?'

Matil took a step forward, jaw set. 'Perhaps some introductions would be polite?'

Chel rose to his feet beside her. 'Exalted Matil, this is Vashenda, sister of the Order of the Rose, executive prelate of Denirnas Port.'

Vashenda inclined her head, far less than the bow due to Arowan's Keeper. 'Please the Shepherd, Acting Herald of the Merciful Forces of Divine Unification.'

'The other one is Fest, a double-crossing piece of shit.'

The man's grin widened. 'As if the Eagle spoke through him, one hand up his arse, working the mouth with his grubby fingers.'

The corners of Vashenda's mouth twitched downwards. 'And you are Matil of Arowan. You speak for your mother?'

'I speak for myself.'

'Oho?'

'My mother is deceased, the city mourns. You may address me as Keeper.' Matil smiled, small, hard.

'Oho.'

Chel found his legs were trembling, his fingers tingling, fighting the urge to shiver. 'Shall we get to it? I'm sure Fest has graves to rob.'

Vashenda nodded at Matil, deeper this time, although still too shallow. 'With your permission, Exalted?'

'Speak.'

'First we must ask after the health of Prince Tarfel. His brother, our emperor-in-waiting, cares deeply for him, and wishes only to see him safe.'

'He is well. He is under the city's protection. Safe.'

Vashenda nodded. 'That would be a matter of opinion.'

Chel clenched his jaw, fighting its nascent chatter. 'What do you want, Vashenda?'

She looked straight at him, and he was back in the Denirnas lowport, transfixed by her cold fury. 'You've survived, sand-flower, but it seems you have not learnt. Now be quiet. The adults are talking.'

'I am here as the prince's second, to speak as he might.'

'Including your descriptions of Master Fest?' Matil asked, a tight smile pulling at one corner of her mouth.

'Let's assume so.'

'Very well,' Vashenda said with exasperation that seemed to transcend the events of the parley. 'We want only the prince. His safe return, to the loving arms of his family.'

'Horseshit! Corvel wants him dead.'

'Are you still speaking as the prince?'

'Let's assume so,' Matil murmured.

Vashenda took a step forward, and Chel flinched back, unable to stop himself. Still she had power over him. Fest laughed, too loud and too long.

'Then, ear of the prince, I suggest you listen carefully, if you can summon the wit. It is imperative that—'

A shout came from behind them, and Fest tapped her arm. They turned to see a rising plume of dust approaching from the direction of the army's camp, something dark and glinting at its head.

'No,' Vashenda whispered, soft enough that only Chel heard.

Matil had one hand on the hilt of her sword, relaxed but deliberate, one eye on her escort beyond the awning. 'What is this? What is coming?'

Fest puffed air from his cheeks, leaned over and spat in the dirt. He looked up with a cheeky grin that did not reach his eyes. 'The big lad, isn't it?'

Matil squinted at the oncoming cloud. 'Gods be damned . . . Is that a chariot?'

Fest's head was close to Vashenda's. 'Why would he come to negotiate?'

'He isn't going to negotiate.'

The chariot pulled right up to the awning, scattering the waiting confessor host. A barrel of black steel hauled by two powerful horses, it shone dark and hot in the sunshine. At its back stood a giant figure, cream-coloured cloak still billowing in the strong breeze. It waved an angry arm, and confessors ran forward to attend to it. Clanking came from the back of the chariot, the sound of metal drawn against metal, and then the figure thumped down to the dust, stomping stiff-legged under the awning, which bowed over its beetroot-red head, crested with a shock of blond hair.

*Hurkel*. Chel's eyes went immediately to the man's missing hand, the appendage removed by Loveless somewhere in the snows of the western mountains. A short, three-pronged fork, a miniature trident, jutted from his stump, fixed into a gleaming silver setting. It looked new, and reinforced. He moved slowly but with great power, angry red face snarling at the effort of dragging his legs. Chel saw the metal bands beneath his luxuriant robes, the rigid braces for the limbs. In his remaining hand, he held a long, grand staff, gilded and hooked. Chel had seen it before, in the private chambers of now-former Primarch Vassad.

The beady eyes seized on Chel immediately, widening with a mixture of astonishment and murderous glee. 'Sand-crab!'

'Oh, you just know *everyone*, don't you?' Matil said, incredulous, amused. 'And who is this, who joins us so late?'

'Brother Hurkel,' Chel kept his voice steady, trying to hold Hurkel's mad-eyed gaze. 'And he's a piece of shit too.'

'*Pentarch* Hurkel!' the giant roared, leaning forward on the staff, bending to Matil's level. 'Crowned with the fires of God's vengeance, and serving his divine will. This afterbirth—' Hurkel jabbed his trident-hand at Chel's chest, falling barely an inch short, '—I can thank for my unusual walk. Is that pretty piece with you, sand-crab? That vulgar harlot owes me a hand with interest, and I've a mind to collect.'

Chel shook his head. 'Gone.'

'We shall see, sand-crab. We shall see!'

Matil took half a step, interposing herself between Chel and Hurkel. 'And I am—'

'I know who you are. Where's the rancid old cow? I'm not here to bandy with withered fruit.'

Chel shot a glance to Vashenda. She remained silent, impassive, her face held tight and still, her gaze straight ahead.

'My mother is indisposed.' Matil's voice was calm, cold. 'I speak as Keeper.'

'She's fucking dead at last? Now? Hilarious. And in her place . . . you?' Hurkel burst into barks of rough, aggressive laughter. Matil watched him through narrowed eyes.

'Do you, perhaps, have a proposal?'

Hurkel fought down his laughter. For a moment, Chel thought he might wipe away a tear with his hand-fork, and was disappointed when Hurkel caught himself.

'I do. From the forces of the Chosen-Emperor-in-Waiting, Anointed by God, Ruler of Land, Sea and Sky, Commander of the Armies of the Merciful Shepherd, I give you this message: Give us the princeling.'

'Or?'

'OR BE DESTROYED.' Hurkel waved his stump. 'You have seen what our divine wrath did to your precious fortress. Your city is next. You have until dawn!'

'Let's save you the wait.' Matil turned to Chel. 'Our prince's response?'

Chel didn't hesitate. Perhaps he should have.

'The answer is no,' he growled.

'Now leave this place,' Matil said with a small smile, 'or be destroyed in turn.'

Hurkel smiled again, a hideous smile, then turned and stomped away, back to his chariot.

'Until dawn!'

The confessors began to withdraw, Fest and Vashenda

411

with them. Chel caught her eye as she turned to leave, and she paused.

'I'm surprised you're still going, sand-flower. Impressed, even.'

Hurkel bellowed for her, and her eyes narrowed. As she went to follow, Chel said, 'You're what, his *pet* now?'

'The Shepherd moves in mysterious ways,' Vashenda muttered as she departed. 'I hope we'll get to speak again.'

The confessors rolled away, the wind blowing their dust cloud after them. Chel and Matil stood alone beneath the awning, the Keeper chewing her lip and staring into the middle distance.

'I like you, Chel of the South,' she said at length. 'I hope you don't get us all killed.'

\*\*\*

He thought he saw it as they returned to the city, a delicate flutter of something above the looming towers. He made straight for the workshops, where the artificers within directed him up to a winding hexagonal spire, adorned with carvings of geometric patterns, that overlooked the plaza.

Kosh stood on a wooden gantry, a balcony extended with freshly hammered dark wood, the former chief artificer at her side. The two were poring over a boxy construction of rods and pale silk, great coils of thin rope around their feet, spilling over the gantry's side. They had affixed a pair of pulleys to the improvised wooden rail, wound with ratchets, torn from some crane in the works below.

'Is this it?' he asked, breathless, peering between them. 'Does it work?'

Kosh turned, irritation at the disturbance mixed with pride. 'It is. And it does. Of course.'

'What about the other half? The . . . rest?'

'A simple matter, for me at least. We need only charcoal, yellow-stench, and marsh salt. The easy recipe.' She turned to the chief artificer, who made a puzzled face. Kosh sighed, exasperated. 'I know the first two are in abundance here. As for the third . . . The silk caves, they are teeming with bats, yes?'

The artificer nodded, back on safer ground.

'Then all we need is an expedition to harvest their streaked excrement, and seas of urine. This can be arranged?'

The artificer nodded again. Her expression did not change, as if nothing Kosh said was unexpected. The Nort turned back to Chel.

'No problem is insurmountable, with knowledge and application.'

He grunted. 'Don't take too long, that's all.'

'What do you mean? The parley was unsuccessful?'

'You could say that.'

'How long do we have?'

'Until dawn.'

The answer displeased her, and she turned away with a scowl that said this was all Chel's fault. He wondered if the scowl was right.

He loitered for a moment on the gantry, ignored, then withdrew.

\* \* \*

The council was in full-flow on the upper gallery, raised voices carrying down the hallway beyond. Mira the seneschal directed him to Tarfel, who stood close enough to Matil to be using her as a shield. Opposite them were arrayed the usual suspects, Ghiz at their apex, his long moustache pulled back around his sneering mouth.

'Your mother would never have stood for such stupidity.'

Matil's temper was even but fraying.

'Once more, you forget yourself, Lord Ghiz. You address your Keeper.'

'A temporary accident. Once the mourning period is over, the council will settle this properly.'

'Mourning period? The army at our gates has come to make war, and they mean to prevail.'

'You could give them what they want. What is he to us?'

Behind Matil, Tarfel stiffened, but did not shy away.

'A commitment. But tell me, Ghiz, do you think if we presented our guest to his brother's forces, that they would immediately pack their wagons and depart without a word? Is that seriously your expectation?'

'There is a chance—'

'There is *no* chance, Ghiz! When they levelled Korowan, the die was cast. Corvel already calls himself emperor-in-waiting. How much clearer could this be? You call yourself a tactician? What would you be planning in their place?'

The commander stood silent for a moment, spear-stiff, moustache quivering. 'Then we must sally! Meet them on the plateau, crush them with our cavalry, torch their engines. We can rout them back to the pass before they begin their earthworks.'

'No.'

'They will not be expecting—'

'There is every chance that they are, and it is a pointless risk. If come at us they must, then come at us they will,

414

but I will not throw the lives of our troops away in a great gamble. The city can withstand them, we have the plains at our back, the gorge at our front, and a triple gatehouse at the bridge's end. Any army attempting to breach us will be shredded at our door.'

'It won't be enough.'

The group turned at the voice. Rennic leaned at the gallery rail, framed by the late afternoon sun, affecting casual indifference, cleaning a fingernail with a slim knife. Chel had no idea how long he'd been there, and was confident that the big man was feeling very pleased with himself.

'*Who*,' Ghiz said, meaning 'what', 'is this?'

Matil didn't miss a beat. 'This is one of Prince Tarfel's military advisers. Rumic, was it?'

Rennic smiled. 'Rennic, Exalted.'

'And why do you say it won't be enough, Master Rennic?'

He half-shrugged, as if it seemed too obvious to say aloud. 'You saw what they did to the fortress. All the gatehouses in the world won't stand up to that.'

'Korowan was undermined and collapsed from beneath,' Ghiz said, a dark flush building in his cheeks. 'Tell me, military adviser, how will they undermine the jaws of Arowan?'

'Undermined, you say? You're sure of that?'

'We have been unable to inspect the ruins, of course,' Ghiz declared, 'but how else could it be done?'

'How else indeed, commander.' Rennic offered a head-shake of synthetic wonder. 'How else indeed.'

Matil was humouring the big man, but her patience had limits. 'And what do you suggest, Master Rennic, in the service of Doing Enough?'

'Collapse the bridge.'

Ghiz's squawk of laughter was strangulated outrage. Matil stared very hard at Rennic.

'Do what?'

'Collapse it. Bring it down. Before they can even think of crossing. Before it's too late.'

'That bridge has stood for centuries, in one form or another. It is our lifeline to the south. As soon as the siege is broken, we will need it—'

Rennic put up his hands. 'You want the siege to end in your favour, you do it now. Because none of us here knows what's coming, but leaving the fold open for the wolf doesn't strike me as prudent. *Militarily.*'

'That bridge is the work of our ancestors, the greatest—'

'Then why the fuck didn't they put in a drawbridge?'

The council did not agree to collapse the bridge.

# THIRTY-ONE

The engines moved before dawn, the rumble and creak of their giant wheels audible in the predawn chill above the moan of the wind over the city. As the sun's first rays slid across the plateau, a detachment of armoured confessors stood ready at the bridge's end, black flag of truce fluttering above their heads. Behind them, a monstrous wagon stood, its entire front a wedge of black iron, a ploughshare as big as a cottage; behind it stood the lines of rust-coloured troops, their armour glinting in the early sun. Whatever was left of the refugees' camp lay trampled or stripped beneath their feet.

Chel watched from the ramparts of the second gatehouse, one more gawping face flanking the worthies on the raised platform. A buzz of constant argument surrounded Matil like a cloud of flies, waved away with no less resigned irritation. Tarfel hovered alongside, neither within the circle of dissent nor distinct from it, whatever allowances were made for his comprehension. Chel felt exhausted just being in their presence.

Matil caught his eye. 'Chel of the South,' the Keeper called, shouldering her way through protesting types to reach him. She looked tired. 'Have you seen the lady Akoshtiranarayan, by any chance?'

'She was here earlier, overseeing delivery of a batch of the new crossbows, fresh from the artificers' bench. She seemed very pleased with the work, and with herself.' He flexed an eyebrow. 'As ever.'

The intensity of Matil's gaze drained his feeble mirth. 'And where is she now?'

His throat was drier than he'd realized. 'Returned to the workshops, I believe. Said she had lots to do.'

'Of course. Tasks weigh upon us as never before. Tell me, is she well? I did not see her . . . last night.' Matil swallowed, her composure creaking.

'She's busy. I think that means . . . she's happy.'

'Of course. Perhaps, Chel of the South, if you were to see her, you could—'

A shout called her away, movement from the bridge's end. She strode away, their conversation unfinished. Chel found himself back beside the prince, unmoored. Mira, the kind-eyed seneschal was with them, unbidden.

'Exalted Matil has bidden me translate for you, high-ness,' she said, although she directed some of her words to Chel. Tarfel nodded, fingers worrying at his signet, gaze fixed on the scene below, the black pennant whipping in the morning wind.

Bold words in Serican drifted over from where the council gathered, Ghiz's strident tone unmoderated by the elegant tongue. Mira bowed her head. 'We should sally, now before they are entrenched,' she translated, her voice carrying some of his shrillness.

Matil responded, calm, firm. 'No,' Mira said in her voice.

A horn blew below, half-lost on the wind, then a bell tolled once from somewhere within the lead engine. Eyes on the rampart focused on the wedge of dark iron, and voices muttered as an uneasy hush descended. The seneschal's commentary dropped to a murmur with it.

'Do they mean to drive that thing at the gates? We'll burn it on the bridge. Ready the archers, light the braziers.'

A messenger streaked past them, dropping to one knee before the Keeper. 'Last chance to surrender the prince,' said Mira, eyes scrupulously averted. Tarfel cleared his throat, but did not look over.

A fresh messenger departed, and a moment later a great blast of a deep horn echoed from the walls.

'Exalted Matil has demurred.'

Down on the plateau, the black pennant dropped from view. In its place rose a new standard, a white pennant emblazoned with a golden star and crown. Tarfel stirred.

'The imperial standard. My brother has truly lost his mind.'

The confessors and their pennant fell back, lost behind the dark lump of the engine. Chel thought he saw Vashenda's silver crop among them, and thought back to her words at the parley. She'd been about to tell them something when Hurkel arrived, something important. Something the Pentarch's arrival had precluded.

'What happens now?' he asked the seneschal.

She offered an optimistic smile. 'They lay siege. They are repelled. Eventually our outriders will cut their supply lines, and they will starve, while we sit safe within the walls. Then we will treat again.'

A thin wisp of smoke rose from the lone engine, carried

back toward the mountains by the incessant wind. Chel's memories stirred.

'And just what kind of engine is that?'

Something whiffled out from the engine, a dark shape that fizzed up in an arc from behind the black iron shield, rising into the clear blue morning sky. The crowd on the walls held their breath, Chel among them, watching the object's passage. It flew wide of the gate, wide even of the walls, reaching an apex somewhere over the gorge, struggling against the headwind, then dropping into the darkness beneath. The jeering from the walls obscured whatever sound its distant impact made.

'It's not a ram, then.' Tarfel had drifted forward, one hand on his chin, the other on the pale stone of the rampart. 'Nor are they intending to come at us with their demon-kegs.'

Mira the seneschal was smiling. 'Lord Ghiz once again asking to sally. Exalted Matil has demurred. We have little to fear from such feeble engines.' It was unclear whether these were Matil's words or her own.

Chel looked over to where Matil stood, Ghiz at her side. The little man was pointing and jabbering with excitement, resplendent in gleaming mail and colours. Matil was in armour herself, her new breastplate burnished gold. Everyone wants to look the part, he thought, but will that be enough? Back on the plateau, figures were scuttling around the back of the engine, and after a moment it lurched forward, pulled by an invisible team.

'There are horses behind the shield,' Tarfel said, eyes narrowed, as if in answer to Chel's own thoughts. 'Vedren, could this be—'

The engine rocked to a halt, another wisp of smoke rising

from within, and after a heartbeat another object came fizzing out from its innards, this time at a flatter angle. It whooshed out over the gorge, trailing a drifting plume of black smoke, flying wide of the city once again. Already the jeers were rising in answer, but Chel followed its path, swivelling to track it out of sight. He raced to the rampart's far end, losing the projectile but tracing its path by its dissipating tail. It would have cleared much of the gorge that time, maybe even hitting the cliffs of the far side where the Martyrs' Bridge – one of the two structures connecting the city to the northern expanse – joined the plains.

The Martyrs' Bridge.

He fought his way back to Tarfel, heart thumping in his chest. 'Tarf! We have to warn Matil. They're not going for the city, they're aiming for one of the bridges to the plains!'

The prince turned, concern etching deep grooves in his young face. 'This is Denirnas all over again. The black ships! Nortish alchemy!'

The seneschal followed their words, her smile fading. 'But even if they could hit the bridge,' she said, 'how would they damage it with these smoking arrows? It is solid stone!'

'They're not arrows,' Chel said, urging Tarfel toward where the Keeper stood surrounded. 'They're loaded with witchfire.'

Tarfel called for Matil, Chel his ram, shouldering their way through the crowd of worthies toward her as another dark arrow hissed through the sky behind them. The seneschal followed, bobbing in their wake.

'Exalted!' Chel cried, hoping Tarfel was close enough to prevent him being tackled by house guards. 'You must get everyone off the Martyrs' Bridge! Clear the bridge!'

She heard him at the third cry, waving him and Tarfel

through. 'What are you saying, Chel of the South? We need to keep moving refugees out of the city.'

'They're trying to destroy it. Those arrows are packed with their black powder.'

She blinked, her eyes flicking back to the engine on the plains. 'Even if that is true, it will take many more such arrows to damage our bridge. At this rate, it will be days before they even stain it.'

'Exalted,' Tarfel said, his voice low and hard in the commotion. 'They are not yet firing to destroy. They are finding their range.' Shouts went up, signal flags and a horn. The black arrow had hit the bridge. 'And now they have it.'

Matil went very still. 'Clear the bridge.'

The shouts continued, orders and reports fighting each other, drowning each other in noise. A very large plume of dark smoke was rising from the engine on the plateau.

It took a moment for the hissing sound to reach them, over the wind and the upheaval on the rampart, a sound like water drops on hot stone, or a thousand angry snakes. The smoke rising from the engine went corpse-grey, billowing outwards and upwards on the wind, then streak after streak flew into the sky. Volley after volley of black arrows rocketed up, some screeching and swerving, most flying true, dozens upon dozens of the projectiles. They flew in a cloud, a screaming flock, blasting black smoke as they arced wide of the city, just as the others, over the walls and dropping against the wind.

When they hit, the sound was rolling thunder. Out of sight around the city's curve, those on the rampart could only fall silent as the first cracks and pops on the wind were joined by a constant rumble, crashing waves of explosive impacts.

Finally, they faded, the last of the black arrows whiffling drunken into the gorge, the smash of their percussion spent. The city stood in silence, choked by the floating drifts of black smoke and stone dust, shocked mute.

Then came the creaking, grinding sound, of shifting, shattered stone. Chel needed no view of the bridge to tell what made it. With initial glacial slowness, the first lumps of ancient stone flaked and fell, followed ever faster by their neighbours, until the tumble and thump of chunks of broken stone echoed around the gorge. Chel pressed his hands to his ears, unable to bear the noise, unwilling to hear the shrieks of anyone caught on the bridge as it fell. Numbness consumed him, an odd distance from the world, the constant sounds of terror and destruction pushed into the background beneath his heartbeat.

His heart was beating very fast.

Shouts reached them, cries and bells from across the city. Messengers pelted from darkened hallways, superfluous.

'The bridge is fallen,' Matil said, her eyes glazed.

'Exalted. Exalted!' Tarfel was focused on the scene below. 'The engine is moving.'

The hidden team dragged the great wagon forward, lumbering over the broken ground of the plateau, across the front of the city. Around it. Robed figures scuttled in its wake, its escort sliding around with it.

'They're going for the other bridge!'

'Where are your own engines?' Chel demanded, his voice scratchy and shrill. 'Your skein bows, your mangonels?'

'The Stop,' she said, gaze still somewhere over the plateau. 'The city has not faced a hostile army in decades.'

'Well, it does now.'

Tarfel was staring down at the trundling engine, calculating its path. 'How long will the city last if the second plains bridge is sundered?'

Matil did not answer, but the seneschal was at her elbow. 'We have water from the wells and aqueducts, but our food stores are . . . minimal. We have not . . . prepared.'

'Nobody could have foreseen this!' Ghiz snapped, elbowing into their conversation. Tarfel's mouth twitched, but he said nothing. 'Exalted, we must sally! That engine will cut us from the plains!'

The engine halted, a thin ribbon of smoke already rising into the wind above. It rocked on its giant wheels, shuffling, then settled. A moment later, the first black arrow screeched into the sky, fizzing off over the gorge. It climbed and stalled, dropping soundless into the chasm.

Chel watched it drop from view, his eyes darting straight back to the engine. It was only a hundred strides from the bridge's end. 'Lord Ghiz is right. I don't know how long it will take them to reload their engine and find their range, but that time is shrinking.'

Ghiz stared at him, eyes narrow, angered by his impertinence but unwilling to snap at support. He smoothed his moustache with tense fingers. 'Exalted?'

Matil's jaw was clenched, the muscles bulging beneath her ears. 'Sally. Sally now.' Ghiz was away, rattling in his gleaming armour, a flurry of lieutenants in his wake, frantic signals rung out by horns from the ramparts. In the courtyard below them, horses whinnied and stamped as their riders mustered, and the second gate groaned open.

'Ghiz!' Matil called down from the rampart, as another black arrow hissed overhead. 'Destroy that thing! Burn it to the ground!'

He saluted as he mounted, then spurred his mount away

at the head of the column, through the archway and toward the outer gate.

'He's going out himself?' Chel found himself surprised.

'Lord Ghiz likes to lead by example,' Mira the seneschal replied, her expression neutral.

Matil summoned the wall's commander, issuing unrepeated orders with firm intensity. The engine had shifted again, dragged onwards and around by the team behind its great iron shield, while its operators scuttled around its hidden rear, preparing another great volley. The smoke over it was thickening.

The outer gate opened, and the engine's activity froze.

Chel heard the hoofbeats clearly, the slow clap of iron shoes on bridge stone, thickening and merging as the column rode out. At first they were at a walk, a jingling procession of heavy lancers, mounts, and men gleaming in the morning sun. Some carried flaming torches, despite the day's bright warmth. Ghiz rode at their head, a long pennant bearing the Serican Butterfly and his family crest behind him. At a signal, the column broke into a trot as one, the beat of their hooves an amplified staccato.

'Why don't they charge?' Chel demanded. The smoke was rising thick over the engine now, and after their initial shock its operators had resumed their activities. 'Why are they moving so slowly?'

Tarfel's eyes took in the whole of the plateau. 'They're waiting to see what confronts them, I imagine, Vedren.'

Bells rang out over the plateau, thick and dolorous, mournful as the grave. Someone had picked an apposite signal for the church's armies. At the outer wings of their ranks, two infantry formations began to move. They marched forward, weapons aloft, whatever dirge they sung lost beneath wind and cavalry. Around the engine, confessors emerged, ringing it with a bristling band of spears.

Ghiz dropped an arm and the lancers charged. They roared forward, their sound at once a deafening cacophony. They rode with speed and precision that defied the heavy mail that cloaked both riders and beasts, moving as a sinuous wave, rumbling off the bridge and onto the plateau in a rising cloud of blinding dust. Panicked, the engine operators fired, and a half-loaded volley streaked away into the crystal sky. Dozens of black arrows screamed through the air, fizzing and spiralling over the gorge. Some found their mark, dark news from the lookout towers around the city relayed swiftly to its Keeper.

The confessors around the engine dug in behind their spears, a wall of gleaming steel between the riders and the dark engine. At either flank, the church infantry had picked up speed. Chel recognized a pennant, crudely affixed beneath their standard crook. The Company of Stars, Fest's mercenary company, absorbed and redeployed as a mere cog of the church's machinery. He wondered if Fest was among them.

The lancers bore down on the engine, then at the last moment they veered, pulling wide instead of crashing into them. They rode past the engine and its startled defenders, circling beyond, riding toward the plateau's edge as they curved. The confessors swung with them, turning to face, entirely oblivious to the crossbowmen who had reached the bridge's end, armed with the first batch of augmented weapons delivered from Kosh's workshop.

The first volley of bolts cut into the engine's defenders like a rain of teeth, dropping screaming confessors as they punched into unarmoured backs. The men scuttled for the safety of the engine as the second volley slammed against its iron shield, but on its far side they met only the oncoming lancers, wheeled and charging again from the flank. The remaining men were crushed against the engine's side, their spears abandoned, their formation shattered.

'Yes!' Chel whispered. 'Now destroy it!'

The lancers disengaged and rallied, reforming in a square behind the engine. Some of their number took a moment longer to rejoin the formation, returning from the back of the engine with spears and sabres bloodied. Its operators had ceased to operate.

The church infantry was closing, the near flank advancing with spears low, the far side making for the crossbowmen by the bridge. Chel waited for them to fall back to the safety of the walls, but instead they made a break for the engine, dashing with weapons over their shoulders to where the lancers waited. The former Company of Stars pursued them, breaking into a run, closing the distance.

Matil spoke angry Serican to those in earshot, then turned to Tarfel and Chel. 'What are they doing? Why is that infernal machine not already aflame?'

The crossbowmen reached the engine, forming into a ragged line to face their pursuers. The lancers moved again, splitting down the middle. Half wheeled inwards, turning back onto the pursuing mercenaries, while the remainder went wide, circling slowly back toward the plateau's edge, moving to flank the confessors. Both units ceased their advance, consolidating their formation, levelling their spears. They began to move again, step by step, like the imperial hedgehogs of old. The lancers slowed, circling, prowling like cats.

The engine rocked, then lurched forward a few strides.

It slowed, then lurched again, beginning a glacial turn toward the bridge.

'Gods,' Matil whispered. 'He means to take it. The fool!'

Bells pealed once more over the plateau, and the mercenaries and confessors redoubled their advance, ignoring the cavalry, closing on the engine. The crossbowmen huddled back against it, firing half-volleys at both units, thinning but not slowing the dense ranks. The lancers wheeled again, their threat ignored, and began to pick up speed for another charge.

Chel saw it, but it was Tarfel who spoke. 'Exalted, you must order their retreat,' he said, one hand on Matil's arm in defiance of propriety. 'Get them back immediately.'

She ignored his grip. 'If they fall back now, the bowmen and their weapons will be lost, and the men exhausted for nothing. If this is all they commit, the horse will rout them. Fool he may be, but Ghiz has played a bold hand.'

Chel was beside his prince, voice urgent. 'The other engine, at the back of the plateau. It is moving. They are bringing it to bear.'

Her voice was guarded. 'On what?'

'On the first engine.'

Their collective gaze fell back on the great dark mass of wood, iron, and alchemy, its hidden team lurching slowly back toward the bridge under unfamiliar command, while crossbowmen pressed against its great iron shield, firing blindly at the approaching pincers of confessor and mercenary spearmen. Behind those columns, beneath rising plumes of bleached dust came the lancers, two halves of a column converging on the loping squares.

'Their own men are too close, they can't possibly take the risk—'

Tarfel's voice was unlike anything Chel had heard from him. 'Exalted, you don't know my brother at all.'

Matil met his gaze, held it for a moment, then spun away, calling in urgent Serican. Horns blared from the city walls, signal flags snapped high on their runners.

The confessors crashed against the crossbowmen as the lancers crashed against the confessors. In the midst of it all, the second engine fired. Chel saw the jerk, the twitch of the wheeled edifice, then something like a swarm rose into the air from behind it. It spread as it arced, wide and thin, dispersing like a dissipating flock, countless dark, round objects, almost too small to discern.

Tarfel recognized them. 'Oh, no,' he said. 'Oh, no.'

The spreading cluster passed its apex and began to drop toward the men and horses around the engine. 'What is it?' Matil said, watching the objects fall. 'What are they?'

The prince was ghost-pale, thick beads of sweat on the fuzz of his upper lip.

'Demon eggs.'

They fell like stones, pelting the combatants and their surroundings, clattering from helmets, pinging against the engine's great iron prow. Men cried and yelped when struck, and horses shied, and for a moment Chel was baffled, thinking that this fearsome weapon was little more than a giant sling. Then he saw the first jets of angry smoke from the fallen objects, heard that same alchemical hiss, and was at once afraid.

Small pops and flashes lit the melee, bursts of acrid smoke, cries and sprays of vivid blood. They grew in number and frequency, pattering like distant lightning in the dim centre of the combat as horses screamed and men wheeled in panic. Formations broke as confessors and house guards alike tried to flee the sudden fiery bursts that surrounded them.

'Vedren, the engine!'

The horn blasts from the wall urging retreat were lost in the sounds of chaos and panic, the near side of the plateau already drenched with thick and choking smoke. Only those closest to the engine saw the lick of flame along its underside, heard the popping and hissing that issued from within. By then it was far, far too late.

A massive explosion ripped the engine in half, a blast of two parts, a heartbeat of force. The iron shield twitched as the engine's body dissolved in a wall of flame, then it detonated, a miniature blinding white sun, summoned from nowhere, expanding over the plateau until Chel could see nothing but its fierce light through his eyelids. A booming crash squeezed them open again, in time to see the great black ploughshare wheeling through the air, one bounce on the bridge in its wake. It smashed down again, shearing against the bridge's hard stone, one half skittering over the arc and smashing through the rail, the other pinwheeling along the structure's length, a murderous whirl, shedding broken shards of black metal as it flew. At last, it crashed against the rail and fell back, jagged and inert, behind it a trail of cracked stone and dark iron daggers.

Hunched and blinking, Chel looked to where the men had been fighting around the engine. Already the wind was blowing the smoke clear, although a thick, black column from the wagon's blasted remains was replenished as fast as it could dissipate. Around the smouldering crater lay only burning wreckage, the earth blackened and torn, gouged and pock-marked by shrapnel and explosion. It took him a moment to pick the figures from the steaming scene, to establish them as figures at all: few were whole, fewer still were moving. He flinched away when he started to identify isolated limbs. Somewhere, improbably intact, a riderless horse trotted, aimless and confused, moving in widening circles from where her rider had vanished from existence.

On the rampart, the atmosphere was shocked and terrified. One of the torn spears of metal had ripped over the crenellations and embedded itself in the wall behind the frozen assemblage of worthies. It was still quivering. Moans and whimpers drifted over the wind from the first gate. Chel could already see other impacts along the battlements, see the archers and spearmen laid low along the structure, crying for assistance, or in some cases, very still.

'Shepherd's mercy,' breathed Tarfel. Chel realized his hands were shaking uncontrollably.

Matil was to one side, alone for a moment, stone-faced, still resplendent in her armour. As silk clad nobility scuttled from the rampart, she turned and barked commands, jolting transfixed guards into action.

Mira, her kind eyes now wider and more distant than before, lingered behind Chel and the prince, bound by duty but desperate to be elsewhere. When a guard captain appeared on the rampart a moment later to report to the Keeper, she continued to translate their words, devoid of alternative purpose.

'Survivors from the field?' Matil asked the new captain.

'Uncertain, Exalted. Many wounded. We have not yet tried to collect them.'

'And Lord Ghiz?'

'Uncertain, Exalted. He was close to the engine when it . . . When . . .'

Matil bared her teeth, not a smile, a downward expression of something animal but controlled.

'And the north-eastern bridge? It stands?'

'Critically damaged, Exalted. It was never a sturdy—'

'Can we repair it, and continue to evacuate the city?'

'Uncertain, Exalted.'

Matil took a long breath, knuckles white on her clenched fists. 'Captain Temel, you now have acting command of the house guards, and with it, defence of the city. I suggest you start seeking a greater degree of certainty if you wish to keep this rank.'

'Absolutely, Exalted.'

She rubbed at one eye with her knuckles, then rubbed at her jaw. 'Very well. Rally the cavalry reserves, find out who we have left after Ghiz's folly, and start moving people away from this end of the city. Send men to the workshops. We need engineers to ascertain the damage to the bridge. We cannot afford to be cut off from the plains for more than a few days. And at the workshops, if you see—'

Shouts had been ringing from the outer walls for a while, but now they reached the rampart. The seneschal ceased her translation and stepped to the wall, peering out over the plateau in alarm.

'They are coming again.'

Movement at the back of the plateau, ripples in the ranks through belching smoke. The red formations were moving.

'Fuck's going on, little man? Sounds like a fuck-up wrapped in a fiasco.'

Rennic was behind them, Lemon and Foss at his back, gazing out over the battlefield with practised eyes.

'Where have you been? How did you get up here?'

'The boys and I weren't considered noble enough to

warrant an invitation to the premium gatehouse.' Lemon nudged Foss. 'Had to let the big fella charm us in.'

Foss coughed, shook his head. 'Truth is, they're a little short on guards right now.'

More shouts from beyond, and a sense of something moving through the air, dropping toward them, a swooping flock. Something pinged off the stone beside them, hard and dark, bouncing away with an alchemical hiss.

'Fucken hells!'

Lemon swept downward, scooping up the object with one hand and hurling it out over the wall. It soared away into the pure sky, then exploded in a sickly flash and a savage burst of caustic smoke.

'You all see that, eh? I just—'

The other demon eggs detonated, and the first gatehouse erupted in fire. Great gouts of flame roared upwards from the battlements, from inside the courtyard, from along the walls. Chunks of stone blasted out over the gorge, great cracks tearing through the shaking structure. House guards and staff alike were thrown and shattered, slammed against rock or shredded by hurtling debris. Shouts and screams rang out amidst the bells and futile horns, cries of pain and panic, pleas and entreaties and calls for absent mothers. One cry went up after another.

'The gate is burning,' Mira the seneschal said, her voice small in the bedlam. 'The gate is burning. The gate is lost.'

Chel could see it, the changed light in the courtyard below, the bright flare of flame beneath the outer gatehouse. The first of the three barriers was breached.

'Come on.' Matil was somehow looming over them, stone dust in her hair and a single trickle of blood at one temple. 'We are falling back to the next gate.'

With a crumbling sigh, the outer gatehouse tipped, then collapsed in on itself, sending another great plume of dust into the wind. It dropped from solid blocks of desert stone to a steaming pile of rubble in seconds, taking all remaining souls on the battlements along with it, pulverized amidst the crush of tumbling rock. Over its ruin, the cracked span of the bridge was revealed, chipped and smoking from two dozen charred impacts. Beyond it, on the plateau, on came the lines of red-robed infantry, the stomping ranks, and at their centre, the second great engine, the launcher of demon eggs.

'Not packing the walls with kegs, then, eh?' came Lemon's bitter commentary. She mimicked Rennic's growl. '*What are they going to do, throw them across the gorge?* Looks like they found a sturdy fucken arm!'

One of the council worthies was at Matil's feet, grasping at her, pleading. The seneschal translated his words without inflection or pause.

'We must surrender him, they will level the city and sink us into the gorge. We must give them what they want.'

There, a nervous look toward Tarfel, quick and guilty. The prince seemed magnanimous – or dazed – enough to let it pass. Chel wondered how Matil could possibly refuse.

She ignored him, stepping away from his entreaties, one ear cocked. 'They are not firing again. Why are they not firing again?' Her eyes scanned the devastation before them, and fixed on the bridge. A chunk close to the wall had fallen away, torn as if bitten, not far from where the ruin of the engine's iron shield lay. Whole sections of the bridge's walls had been smashed away. Small cracks spidered over its surface beneath soot and dust, widening as they neared the fallen bite.

'The bridge,' Chel said as she nodded with him. 'They don't want to risk collapsing it themselves.'

Matil turned to Rennic, her eyes burning. 'Then you were right all along, Master Rennic. We must bring down the bridge of my ancestors.'

Lemon was nodding along. 'Aye, right,' she said. 'And how are we going to do that, then?'

# THIRTY-TWO

Dolorous bells rang out over the plateau, and the marching ranks began to pivot. Steadily they shifted and merged, until a giant red-robed wedge stood just beyond the bridge's far end. Chel could almost pick out individual faces, dead-eyed or seething with righteous ire, weapons gripped tight in calloused hands, unburdened by doubt or equivocation. They parted, forming an aisle to their formation's centre, making way, the glimmer of their armour mingled with the heavy swish of their robes. Behind the first ranks stood another wagon, far smaller than the engines, almost of a size Chel considered normal. It was thickly plated with the same dark metal that had shielded the first engine, low on reinforced axles, a chipped bell dangling from a swaying gibbet above its empty bench. The team that had pulled it into place were cut loose, sent cantering back toward the church lines.

Matil leaned forward. 'What are they doing now? What is that wagon?'

Chel saw the narrow dust-plume approaching from the

depths of the plateau and knew it immediately. He blinked, an echo of the past flashing past his eyes. A circular chamber at the top of a citadel tower, converted to a holding cage, its gate a rotating mechanical marvel; before them a giant in plated steel, impervious, invulnerable, a wolf's hide cloak flowing from his shoulders, its head proud from his helmet.

'It's Hurkel.'

The chariot thundered through the ranks, sending lead-footed confessors sprawling. The two steaming horses at its head were fully barded, little more than shimmering beasts of metal, great hooves crunching on loose stone. Hurkel stood tall, a monster of metal, wolf cloak streaming into the dust behind. He closed on the armoured wagon then eased the reins, rolling to a stop in its shadow. Chel heard the clank of Hurkel's harness over the wind's lull, and remembered the great metal legs, stiff and solid, braces for his shattered knees. He remembered with satisfaction, and trepidation.

They waited – the ranks of confessors at the bridge's end, the nervous defenders among the ruins of the walls. Blood pounded in Chel's ears as he waited for Hurkel to stomp into view. Behind the wagon, the chariot's horses stamped and steamed.

Very slowly, the armoured wagon began to move. It wobbled at first, shifting on its reinforced axles, then it was rolling, advancing at a grinding pace, but advancing none-theless. It began to move toward the bridge.

'Fuck me,' Chel said, 'he's pushing it? Alone?'

As one, the first ranks of confessors stepped forward, marching onto the bridge. They marched ahead of the wagon, shielding it with their bodies, their bodies with their shields, chanting as they came.

Matil snarled. 'They mean to finish this today. Barricades! Archers!'

Mira gave an imploring look. 'We should fall back to the inner gate—'

The Keeper's glare stilled her words, and she repeated her cry. 'Archers!'

Reserves of reserves scuttled into view, pressed against the rubble of the collapsed gatehouse in the courtyard, manning the walls that remained above and around it. Volleys of arrows and bolts swept the length of the bridge, ineffective at first, then scoring hits as the confessors advanced. Overhead, another clutch of demon eggs flew high over the gates. Cracks and blasts echoed from within the city where they fell. Screams carried over the wind, along with the sound of falling stone. Cursing, Matil wheeled on her beleaguered staff. 'Evacuate this side of the city!'

One of the seneschals quibbled, raising the challenges of such an order, as well as the problem of the wrecked bridges to the plains. The Keeper neither screamed nor shouted, but her words, left untranslated by a trembling Mira, sent the man fleeing from the rampart as if a black arrow had lodged in his nethers and was driving him to a skyward expiry.

The confessors on the bridge were over the apex, but dwindling, and some sported shafts jutting from bloody wounds, the colour of their robes masking the extent of the injury. The plated wagon rumbled into view, no longer obscured, but with no team to aim for, the archers could do little to slow its progress.

'What do you think it is?' Tarfel asked, gesturing toward the coffin-like wagon. 'It's all wrong for a ram. A close-range launcher of some kind?'

438

Rennic paced beside them, seemingly itching to join the fray. 'What kind of assault is this? Where are their own archers? Why are they marching ahead of the wagon, not hiding behind it?'

'Maybe this time they do intend to stack the walls with kegs,' Chel said. 'With the first gatehouse gone, there'd be no risk of destroying the bridge.'

'Saints' breath, of course,' the prince said. 'Exalted, flame arrows!' Matil turned, questioning. 'That wagon, it is likely loaded with the black powder. They mean to destroy the gates with it. We must detonate it before it reaches us.'

Matil stepped back from the rampart, lamenting the loss of the first batch of Kosh's crossbows and their armour-piercing abilities, muttering to herself on the whereabouts and moral character of the woman she'd put in charge of the workshops. Behind her on the bridge, the wagon rolled inexorably onward as the first of the fire arrows dropped like dying fireflies around it.

'It's not working,' Chel sighed, watching the flaming arrows bounce and flutter from the wagon's armoured carapace. 'They're not catching on it, the armour's too thick.'

'Maybe oil, once it's close enough?' Tarfel suggested.

'By then it'll be too fucking late for the gate,' Rennic grunted. 'We need to stop it on the bridge. We need to bring that metal monster down.'

Behind them, Matil had begun pacing the rampart. At once, she stopped. 'All the armour in the world can't save a man from a knife through his eye-slit,' she muttered, then turned away, barking orders. She called and gestured to a nearby flunky, cowering beneath a tower doorway. The man dashed over, carrying her helmet.

Tarfel looked at her in shock. 'Exalted, you're not . . . ?'

She smiled, low and pursed. 'I hope it will not come to that, but some things require the personal and public attention of a leader. Mother was never slow to bring that up. Here—' She fished around her neck, removing the Keeper's chain, then pressed it into Tarfel's hands.

'What? I can't—'

'There's none in the city who will see to your welfare better than you will. Anyone else would sell you to them before the breath left my body.' She turned to the tower that overlooked them, wherein lurked the remainder of the council. 'The moment I set foot on the bridge, Prince Tarfel has command of the city, until the moment I request its return. Do we understand?' She repeated the question in Serican, extracting promises and oaths from all in earshot.

'Well,' she said with a small grin, 'that's likely the best we'll manage from them. Let us wish each other luck, and pray for the best on all outcomes.'

Tarfel nodded, swallowing, desperate, and made the sign of the crook, much to Matil's amusement. Calling for her horse, she strode from the rampart.

A moment later, Kosh came huffing up from the opposite stairway, a bundle of oilskin in her arms. She was sweaty, distracted, singed, and pungent, moving like a startled bird over the rampart. She blinked in confusion at the scene before her, the collapsed gatehouse, the massing troops on the bridge, the absence of Serican Keeper.

Chel intercepted her. 'Kosh, what tears you away from your work?'

She blinked again, slow to recognize him, then offered the bundle. 'A messenger . . . several messengers. They said the new crossbows were lost, demanded more. I have only this.'

Chel opened the bundle. Within lay her original work, her demonstration piece. He nodded his thanks and turned for the rampart.

'Wait,' she said, one girlish hand outstretched. 'Where is the Keeper? Where is the Lady Matil?'

'In the courtyard below. You should know . . . she has called for her horse.'

'I see.' Their business was concluded, but Kosh made no move.

'You should get out of here, Kosh. This is not a safe place for anyone.'

'I would prefer to remain.'

'Really?' He changed tack. 'What of your work, of our project? Surely it needs your attention?'

She shook her head, her eyes scanning the seething rubble in the courtyard below. 'It is complete. I can do no more with it without you.'

'Without me?'

'Indeed.'

He looked down at the crossbow in his arms. 'Then I will be there as soon as I can.'

'Foss, Lemon. Time to get below. We've got our work cut out.' Rennic was at his shoulder, peering over at the weapon. 'Oh. That for me? Got any bolts for it?'

\*\*\*

Rennic hunched over the crossbow, perched against the thick stone of the rampart wall. 'Come on, you beetroot-faced fucker,' he murmured. 'Let's test the thickness of that tin suit.'

Chel saw Foss and Lemon reach the courtyard below,

fanning out across the rubble among the sparse defenders. Chel hoped it wouldn't come down to them.

Its confessor guard shot down or driven back, the powder-wagon was half-way over the bridge, pushed over the peak of its arc with a great shunt from the armoured giant in its shadow. It lurched forward, edging away from the steel-clad figure at its tailgate, and in that moment Rennic fired.

The bolt arced over the wreckage of the gatehouse, whistling over the bridge. It slammed into Hurkel's head, coming to a shivering halt, jutting from between the eyes of the snarling wolf's head. Hurkel rocked backward and dropped from view behind the slowing wagon.

Those on the walls held their breath. The wagon rolled to a heavy stop.

'Have that, you f—' Rennic began, then fell silent. The wolf's head had appeared over the wagon, the bolt still proud of its furry brow.

'He's still up. Little man, we're going to need more bolts!'

The wolf's head sailed through the air and thumped down onto the cracked stone of the bridge beside the wagon, the empty pelt cape flowing after it. With a grinding screech, the armoured wagon began to move again.

Tarfel had left the cover of the rear doorway, and was peering beside them. 'Can you shoot him again?'

Rennic gave a withering look. 'Now he's hugging his gut to that wagon? No, princeling, there must be three fists of black iron between us and his vitals, and even our alchemist has limits.'

Chel expected a correction from Kosh, but none came. The wagon rolled onward, its pace increasing, horse collars bouncing empty before it.

'You could shoot him once he's beneath us, but . . .'

'. . . It'll be a bit fucking late then, yes.'

'Then what in hells do we do? He'll be at the gate in moments! Where in God's name is Matil?'

The rider thundered out from beneath them, pounding over the debris in the courtyard, leaping the bulk of wreckage where the gatehouse had fallen. Tall in the saddle, armour gleaming, the rider carried only a shield and a long spear, pennant streaming from its end: a swan.

'Five hells,' whispered Chel, 'it's her.' He felt Kosh go still beside him, as if she were holding her entire body rigid.

The Keeper clattered onto the bridge, throwing sparks from hot shoes. The wagon rumbled on toward her, toward the wrecked gatehouse and the vulnerable structures beyond. Matil bore down on the trundling wagon, flying over the stone, closing the distance in mere heartbeats. Then, at the last, she swung wide, dropped the spear, and steered her horse straight into the wagon-side. Horse and rider slammed shield-first into the dark metal of the wagon's flank at a full charge, rocking it upwards. The two nearside wheels left the ground and for a moment, the wagon tipped on to two wheels, hanging in mid-air. The horse staggered back, dazed, lurching drunkenly to one side. Its rider came with it, loose in the saddle, flopping from impact.

'It's going to tip!' Tarfel cried in triumph.

The wagon wobbled, two wheels spinning useless in the air, then, to the collective dismay of the watchers on the walls, it groaned back downward toward the bridge. The wheels smashed down onto the stone, held for a heartbeat, then the axles collapsed. The wagon slewed as its support gave way, swinging around on shattered wheels until it came to rest, perpendicular to the path of the bridge, still thirty strides from the walls. There it lay in a rising dust cloud, axles split, wheels ruined, its iron belly pressed against the battered stone.

The wall erupted into cheers, chanting their Keeper's name, singing her praises, jeering the surviving confessors who lurked at the fringes of bow-range at the bridge's far end. In the lee of the wagon, Matil reeled on her befuddled horse, slowly coming around to the success of her actions. Blinking, she raised one battered gauntlet in salute to those on the walls.

The arm came from nowhere, from the shadow of the dark wagon, viper-quick and grasping. It snatched the Keeper's leg and yanked, dragging her from her horse and out of sight behind the wagon.

Kosh gasped, her entire body flinching. 'No!'

The horse danced away, still dazed, uncertain of what it was supposed to be doing. Slowly, it began to walk back toward the gates. The Nort grabbed Tarfel with both hands, almost screaming. 'Save her!'

He looked back in panicked impotence, then down at the chain still held tight in his sweaty grip. Understanding dawned. 'Captains—!'

'Look!' Kosh squealed beside him, in delight or dismay. 'Look!'

Matil rolled into the sunlight, face bloodied and coated in dust. She stumbled up to her feet, helmet loose on her head, dented shield still strapped to her arm. Hurkel's massive armoured shape loomed over her, its metal grinding with his every step.

'Come on, you meat-stack,' Rennic rumbled. 'Come out where I can see you and let's put this to bed.' Something pinged in his hand and he ducked back, cursing. 'Nine goat-fucking hells,' he cried, 'not now!'

Chel couldn't take his eyes off the scene below. 'What is it? What's happened?'

'Fucking string's snapped! Nort! Do something!'

Kosh blinked and shivered as her eyes refocused, brain adjusting to the task at hand. She looked around the ramparts. 'Wait there,' she said, and scuttled away, as if there were nothing else occurring beyond the wall.

One of the captains approached, face etched with worry. He rattled urgent words, which the seneschal translated. 'Do we sally, your highness? With the walls undefended, the red men on the bridge will advance.'

Tarfel nodded, whey-faced. 'Hold. For now. But be ready.' He swallowed. 'Be ready for my command.'

On the bridge, Matil drew her long, straight sword, keeping her shield pressed against her body. Chel suspected she had already broken her arm. He felt his shoulder throbbing in sympathy. Hurkel advanced, towering over the gold-armoured woman, a giant in black iron. She swung, slashed, stabbed, each blow of her sword meeting only impenetrable plate metal. The giant continued his stomping advance, good hand empty, the other a gleaming metal trident. Her blade boomed away once more from his shell, and then he lunged, wrapping the prongs of his fork-hand around the blade of Matil's sword and twisting. With a cry, she dropped the weapon, and as it clattered to the stone he lunged with the trident again. She dragged the shield in front of her body, but the prongs punched straight through and into the arm beneath.

Despite the wind, her scream echoed across the city.

Matil fell to her knees, free hand struggling against the

445

gruesome spikes that transfixed her arm and pressed into her body beneath. Hurkel bent over her, driving the fork-arm forward again and again, a slick grimace pulling at his uneven mouth with every thrust. Then, with his remaining hand, he picked up Matil's fallen sword.

He turned to face the city, yanking the stricken Keeper with him, and began to speak.

'The fuck is he saying?' Rennic muttered.

Chel shook his head. 'Can't hear over the wind.'

'Bombastic prick. Where is that fucking alchemist?'

Hurkel was still speaking, gesturing with the sword and occasionally refreshing the Keeper's screams with a fresh twist of his trident hand. Then he reached some kind of crescendo, and yanked her to her feet. Slowly, Hurkel made his way onto the smashed wagon, clambering stiff-legged until he stood upon its groaning roof, then dragged Matil out into empty air above the bridge, dangling by her ruined arm, still impaled upon his fork-hand.

Kosh came bustling back onto the rampart, a bundle in her arms. 'I have enough for a temporary repair, although the force of another shot may snap it again. Really, it needs to go back to the workshop for a proper replacement, but it was only ever a prototype, and in the newer models I've—' Her gaze slipped beyond the battlements to the bridge and her mouth formed a small O of horror.

Rennic filled her vision, crossbow extended. 'Just fucking fix it!'

Hurkel was speaking again, his words lost to the wind, while Matil hung limp and lifeless from his extended arm. Chel had to give horrified respect to the man's strength; the Keeper was a solid woman, no waif, and he had her entire body weight swaying from his replacement hand.

Hurkel roared something at the walls, presumably in triumph, then raised Matil's sword.

'Hurry up, Nort,' Rennic growled, one eye on the bridge.

'What is—'

'Just hurry the fuck up!'

Hurkel swung. The first blow smashed against the Keeper's stranded shield, tearing a chunk from its edge. Hurkel hacked away, bellowing all the while, hewing through wood and metal, splitting the mail beneath. Then bright blood sprayed, and with a sickening crunch the sword bit bone. Matil's screams pierced the wind as she sagged lower, muscles tearing, then Hurkel delivered the final blow. The Keeper dropped like a sack to the bloodied stone beneath, while Hurkel threw down the sword and tore the ruined shield from his metal prosthesis. Feet planted wide on the wagon roof, he raised the shield over his head while blood streamed from the severed arm still strapped within, and roared his challenge at the walls.

Wordlessly, Kosh pushed the crossbow back into Rennic's outstretched hands. 'Finally,' he tried to say, but his voice faltered, and he swallowed the word. The Nort began to edge away from the ramparts, her gaze like cracked glass, on the verge of shattering. Rennic slotted a bolt against the newly drawn string, and met the little Nort's fractured glance.

'I will put this between that fucker's eyes.'

He propped the crossbow back against the fortifications, drawing a bead on the rampaging giant above the wagon. Already the confessors were flooding forward onto the bridge, their own shields held high in triumph and as protection from archers. An arrow flashed from the wall, slamming against Hurkel's armoured hide. It splintered on impact, falling away as shards. Hurkel was laughing.

'Laugh it up, metal man,' Rennic muttered. 'Let's see you chuckle with a bolt in your teeth.'

'Wait!' Chel had one hand on his arm, meeting his glare with a gesture to the bridge. 'Look.'

On the bridge, Matil was moving. Mutilated and bleeding heavily, the Keeper had dragged herself upright against the back of the flattened wagon, and was leaning lop-sided against it. Her remaining arm flapped against its thick hatch, leaving streaks of rusty blood on the metal.

Rennic froze. 'Nort. Nort!'

Kosh stumbled forward, her mind a thousand miles away.

'I need fire. I need a flaming bolt. Like in the citadel, you understand? Just like that.' He grabbed her arm, shaking her, forcing her to acknowledge him. 'Can you do it?'

Hurkel ripped the dismembered arm clear of the shield and hurled it to the dust below, laughing. Another shot from the walls pinged from his armour, increasing his mirth. Behind him, the confessors advanced. They had begun to chant again.

Kosh focused. She grabbed the bolt and withdrew to the back of the rampart, rummaging in the bundle she'd brought. A moment later, she scurried back, handing Rennic the bolt, a thick wad of something dark slathered around its shaft.

'What's—'

She only shook her head, then extended her hand, ready to drop something onto the bolt. 'Ready?'

Rennic slotted the bolt, and took aim. 'Almost.'

On the bridge, Matil flailed at the metal hatch. The sounds of her one-armed attempts reached Hurkel at last. Frowning, he began to stomp toward the wagon's end, making it tremble with every step.

Kosh looked beyond Rennic, and her eyes widened. 'She's alive!'

Hurkel reached the wagon's edge and saw his victim beneath him, her hand on the hatch handle, and roared a murderous challenge. The confessors were a wall of red robes approaching the wagon, shields high against the tepid rain of arrows. Their chants were clear up on the walls now.

Matil opened the hatch. It swung wide, revealing a dark interior stacked with pitch-sealed kegs, and as Matil collapsed back to her knees, she grasped the closest, dragging it into the light.

'Now,' Rennic said.

Kosh didn't move.

'*Fucking now!*'

The Nort started, and emptied her hand. Something sparkled, and with a flash the bolt was aflame. Choking back a cough, Rennic sighted through streaming eyes, and fired.

Matil was already moving, crawling away like a three-legged cur, when the smoking bolt hissed from the walls. It streaked down, heavy and wobbling, and missed the exposed keg. Instead, it hit the inside of the wagon's hatch and ricocheted within, lost from sight. A curl of acrid smoke blew in its wake, joined a moment later by a thin plume from within the wagon.

Hurkel's eyes widened. He glanced at the smoke, at the wall, at the crawling form of the maimed Keeper, leaving a thick trail of blood in the dust. Then Pentarch Hurkel leapt from the wagon, landing in a clashing heap of iron and frantic rage, scrabbling back from the smoking wagon toward the confessors. Their advance faltered as those in

449

the vanguard saw their commander's retreat, and a moment later the smoke blew over the column, leaving men choking and turning to flee.

Kosh pointed down at the crawling Keeper, who had made it as far as the shattered iron shield from the first engine, hope kindling in her voice. 'Can we—'

Something flashed within the wagon, bright and fierce, and then it tore itself apart in a pounding roll of balled flame. Panels of iron blasted into the air, flying as if blasted from another infernal engine, smashing against the walls, the sides of the bridge, the fleeing confessors. Chunks of flaming metal soared into the morning sky, arcing out over the gorge before vanishing into the darkness, their plumes of filthy smoke borne onward by the indifferent wind. Confessors and city guards cried out in pain and terror as molten metal rained around them, a smoking chunk of black iron as big as Chel's fist cracking the stone of the ramparts beside him.

The rising wall of smoke began to clear, aided by the wind. As the inky fog lifted, it revealed Hurkel, lying prone on the bridge, his armour steaming like a hot cooking iron. It revealed swathes of confessors struck down by flying debris, their screams and cries carried away with the smoke. It revealed no trace of the wounded Keeper, nor the great chunk of iron shield beside which she'd crawled. And it revealed a great rent in the bridge of the ancestors, a blasted hole where the wagon and chariot had sat, which crumbled and spread as Chel watched it. In a rising puff of stone dust, the unsupported sections either side of the gap collapsed inwards, crumbling back to stumps from pillar to the ruin of the city wall. When the collapse at last waned, a gap of thirty strides stood between city and bridge, beneath it only the dark yawn of the gorge and the spindly aqueduct below.

Hurkel lay at the lip of the collapse, and to Chel's disappointment he began to move. He climbed to his feet, tearing at his armour, shrieking for assistance from the cowering confessors nearby. He snatched at the panels, trying to tear the steaming metal from his flesh, howling and cursing and stomping. At last, the confessors bore him from view, as the red tide fell back from the bridge one more time.

Shouts from the ruined courtyard below brought people running. With shock, Chel saw Lemon and Foss picking their way through the debris, and over Foss's shoulder lay the slumped and mutilated form of Matil. She was unmoving, deathly still, but their calls for help were answered by running guards and the few staff who remained at the gates. A messenger appeared a moment later, one stride ahead of the guard captain, delivering an update via Mira the seneschal to a dazed and startled Tarfel.

'She lives, but perhaps not for long, highness.'

He nodded too many times, his head shaking like a rattling cart. 'Bring her doctors, surgeons. Bring her everyone.'

'Of course, highness.'

They looked back at the shattered gatehouse, the smoking ruin of the bridge, the massed army beyond it, licking its wounds.

'And get everyone out of here. Off the walls, out of the gatehouses. Get them to the back of the city.'

The captain frowned, long moustache drooping. 'Abandon our posts? I do not understand.'

Tarfel pointed at the wrecked bridge. 'Fear of bringing

down the bridge was the only thing holding back their bombardment. Pretty soon, someone over there is going to remember that too.'

The man's eyes flickered, then with a swift bow he turned and began crying orders. Chel and the others joined the exodus, retreating back through the twisting stairs and narrow passages that interwove the walls, expecting at any moment to hear the whistle and blast of demon eggs.

As they reached the streets beyond, the first explosions tore at the walls.

# THIRTY-THREE

The remains of the council were in disarray, but this time Tarfel was in the thick of their quarrelling. With Mira the seneschal as his mouthpiece, the scattered remnants of Arowan's decision-makers found themselves cowed by the newly assertive prince. As he spoke, his fingers worried at the Keeper's heavy chain. Like Matil, he seemed loath to string it around his neck while its official owner still lived.

The Keeper herself lay in the chamber beyond, bandaged and inert, in the same bed her mother had vacated only the day before. Kosh stood in the doorway, staring but going no further, suddenly small and utterly alone. Somewhere beyond the thick walls of the tower, soft booms heralded another barrage of demon eggs from the plateau.

Tarfel stomped over to where Chel leaned against a pillar. He looked flushed and angry, but also a little pleased with himself. 'Constitutional crisis?' he said. 'It's a crisis all right, but the constitution is clear, Vedren, not that they'll hear it. Matil has granted me command of the city until she recovers and requests its return.'

Rennic was crouched on the pillar's far side, keeping a critical eye on Foss and Lemon's game of stones. 'Or she dies.'

Tarfel pursed his lips. 'Indeed. Then it would become a council matter once more.'

'How much do you trust the guards at her chamber?'

Tarfel offered a hard smile. 'The assignments are doubled and their shifts irregular.'

'Looks bad for the city, either way,' Rennic went on. 'Losing two Keepers in as many days, smacks of carelessness.'

Even Lemon thought that was a little tasteless. Unconcerned, Rennic pushed himself to his feet against the pillar. 'Well, Acting Keeper, what have you told them?'

The arguments were continuing in Tarfel's absence; Mira the seneschal was a harried presence in their midst and while the words were unknown to Chel, the tone was unmistakable.

'That I know my brother. That taking this city is part of his imperial dream, and the only way this army stops is if it is made to. The situation is more dire than any of those perfumed gadflies ever envisaged, but the collapse of the bridge at least buys us time.'

Rennic nodded, half a smile beneath the thick black beard. Either he agreed with the assessment, or he was amused by the prince calling the local nobility perfumed gadflies. 'The lookouts say they're building towers.'

'Yes. Or something like it. We may only have a few days before they try to broach the gap.'

'Assuming they don't try something else in the meantime. There are more engines down there.'

'Indeed.'

'You know, if they'd brought the bridge down when I suggested it, many more people would be standing here today. Our friend the Keeper included.'

'Oh, it's easy to snipe, isn't it? To criticize?' Tarfel's anger resurfaced. 'You've never had to rule! To balance lives like a merchant!'

'Hey, I've led—'

'You've never *ruled*. Not like this. Not like any of this.'

Rennic's sharp smile returned. 'Enjoying your turn at the reins of power?'

Tarfel ran his hands over his face, rubbed at his eyes. The flush had paled, leaving him hollow-eyed and pallid as ever. 'Do you think she'll survive?'

Rennic shrugged. 'I've known some survive worse. I've known many ride the ferry from far less.'

Foss shifted, his attention lifted from the game pieces on the marble before him. 'She's a tough lady, the Keeper. Lem and I found her under that sheet of metal – she crawled behind it before that wagon went up. Wouldn't have done that if she'd intended to expire on that bridge.' Beneath his eyeline, Lemon rearranged two of the smooth stones, a look of studious innocence on her face.

'Aye, Fossy,' Rennic said, 'but when's intention carried the day?'

Foss met his gaze. 'More times than its lack.'

Lemon blinked, eyes flicking from one to the other. 'Sometimes I don't have the first fucken idea what yous two are blathering on about.'

'Worry ye not, Lemon,' Rennic grinned. 'That feeling goes both ways.'

Foss cracked a smile. 'Evil days, my friends.'

'Evil days, Fossy.'

'Well, clearly things here are under control,' Tarfel said with a huffy smoothing of his collar. Above them, something popped, and one of the great windows of coloured glass shattered, bursting inwards in a rain of rainbow shards. The council fled, squealing, as razor-edged slivers smashed against the marble behind them. Chel and Tarfel ducked behind the pillar with the others.

'Now if only we could do something about that bombardment, before they level the bloody place!'

Chel's eyes fell on Kosh, unmoved in the chamber doorway.

'Soon,' he murmured. 'Soon.'

\* \* \*

They'd relocated from the rotunda, with its tall windows, exposed at the city's front, to new chambers within the thick walls of the Keeper's palace. Sacks of sand stood piled in the window arches on the southern side of the rooms, blocking out the sounds of renewed bombardments, reducing the flow of cool night air to a trickle. The atmosphere within was hot and stale, the light from smoking oil lamps flickering against the angled walls.

Lemon laid out their places on the low table, insisting on preserving the same seating arrangement that saw her beside Foss. She set a platter for Kosh, but the engineer had since returned to the workshops after her unhappy visit to Matil's chambers. Tarfel ate in the council chamber, and Loveless was an empty space.

'At least the food's still good, eh?' Lemon said as she ushered the servants back out of the door. 'Even in reduced quantities. Perks of being mates with the new Keeper.'

'Acting Keeper,' Chel said. 'Until Matil recovers.'

'Aye, right. Course.'

He had resolved not to drink too much, given what would likely follow in the morning. He almost managed it, too. As evening drew on, he found himself sitting lower and lower, his eyelids heavy, his brain a mass of churning fog.

'What,' Lemon said, trying to pour out more wine, '*what* do you think happens . . . ?'

'When?' Rennic had something wet in his beard.

'When we die.'

'When you die, Lemon, there will be parades somewhere.'

'No, no, I mean . . . Like, is there more? Is there a judgement? Another go around? A "thanks for playing"?'

Rennic puffed drooping strands of hair from his face. 'Getting philosophical for a rationalist, aren't you?'

'What do you think happens?'

'I think there's pain, and darkness, and then nothing. Fuck knows I've seen enough others die, and they've not mentioned much more than that.'

'Aye, but—'

'If it's convictions you're after, maybe you'd be better off addressing the Foss.'

'Fossy?'

Foss had spoken little during the evening, and drunk less. He seemed lost in thought, but looked straight up.

'Lots of wiser folks than me have theories and proclamations on that, friend.'

'But what do *you* think, Fossy?'

The big man sat back with a sigh, resting his hands on the back of his head. 'I don't know, my friend, I truly don't. I know what the church preaches, what the Articles claim,

457

in all their varied voices. But me? Whatever else the end means, I hope it brings peace.'

Lemon nodded, then raised her cup. 'Aye. Peace.'

Foss raised his in response.

'Peace.'

\* \* \*

'Wake up! Wake up, Andriz!'

Awake, and thirsty. Regretting many of the previous evening's decisions. Kosh was bent over him, thin fingers digging into the flesh of his arm.

'What? What? Is it even dawn?'

Her dark eyes were wide, almost glowing in the light of the lone candle in her other hand. On inspection, he doubted she'd slept that night. He wondered if she slept much at all now. He'd expected her to be grieved by Matil's maiming, but he hadn't expected the fury that burned behind her eyes. She seemed animated by it.

'Not yet. Come on, get up.'

'Why? What's happening?'

'All is ready.'

\* \* \*

The temples and churches were full of the injured and terrified, their moans and whimpers melding with the anxious sounds of the besieged city even in the dark of night. The pops and bursts of demon eggs over the city lent a savage tension to the atmosphere, where death could fall from the sky without warning at any moment. The citizens kept off the streets, staying ensconced within the lower buildings, praying that the scattering clusters of explosions would lack the concentration to bring the upper towers down upon them.

Kosh led the way to the workshops across the plaza, hunched against the wind, paying no heed to the threat of aerial explosives, her every step an expression of mute fury. The intensity of her rage had taken the others aback; she radiated anger like a cloud. Only Lemon seemed oblivious, or indifferent.

'What's all this cloak and denanigans about, then?'

'You don't have to come along, Lemon. You and the others could go back and get some sleep.' *It might be your last chance*, he didn't add.

'Aye, right, and miss whatever antics you and friend Nort are cooking up? I think not, wee bear.'

'It's not safe out here.'

'Betwixt you and me, bearly, it's not safe anywhere for a poor wee lass of Clyde, down on her uppers, up on her downers, and anything in-between.'

'Lemon, are you still drunk?'

'I think the better question, bearskin, is why aren't you?'

Chel put one hand to his thudding temple. 'Just lucky, I suppose.'

Kosh led them all through a doorway he didn't recognize, into a darkened corridor. Guards stood tall at their approach, clearly accustomed to seeing Kosh. After a moment's hesitation at seeing Chel and the others with her, they opened the inner door. Chel filed in after Kosh, and Lemon, Foss, and Rennic followed, some of their walks steadier than others.

'What in hells are all these?'

Kosh spoke at last, curt over one shoulder as she moved

toward a narrow, winding stairway at the back of the chamber. 'Looms.'

The loom operators looked up at their entrance, surprised, uneasy. Chel and his companions were unwelcome visitors.

'They're still working? Even now?'

'The siege won't last forever. When it lifts, this city's silk will be ever more prized. No matter who carries the victory.'

'That's brutal.'

'That's economics.'

Lemon stopped beside one of the looms, a large construction of wood and lacquer. She began tracing its mechanism with one finger, to the increasing distress of the woman operating the machine.

'How does this work, then? Is this hooked up to the water wheels below? Or is it the windmills? Aye, that's clever.'

'Leave that!' Kosh snapped. 'You should not even be in here – outsiders are forbidden. I was given special dispensation.'

'Your smuggy balls are showing, Norty.'

'As is your inebriation.'

'At least in the morning I'll be sober.'

'That is an unsupported assertion.'

Chel ground his teeth. 'Can we move on?'

The Nort flared her nostrils, then marched for the stairs. 'Follow me. And touch nothing.'

\* \* \*

The tower platform had changed since he last saw it, now loaded with a mass of reels and odd, boxy constructions, their shape blurred by the fluttering of the torches at the platform's edges. The wind fell away with an unexpected suddenness, blocked off by a tall wooden barrier, suspended by some of the criss-crossing ropes.

'You've been busy,' Chel said, taking it all in.

'I've been working.'

'It's ready? We can use it now?'

Kosh looked around. The night sky was scattered with great washes of sparkling stars, rivers of twinkling light in a blanket of black so deep it seemed almost violet. Around them, the wind snapped at the silken pennants on every tower-top, at the long silken banners that hung in the streets. They were between bombardments, and for a moment, high over the city, everything seemed peaceful.

'No.'

'No?'

'We must relocate to another platform for the launch. We need the right conditions, a strong and consistent wind, and greater height.'

'Then why are we up here now? To show off?'

'Someone must transport them to the launch location. And . . . there is another complication.'

Kosh moved forward, setting to work on erecting one of the constructions. A boxy structure of silk and thin wood took shape, something wide and multi-tiered.

Rennic had taken a few cautious steps onto the platform, eyes narrowed, prodding at one of the stacks with a wary boot. 'Fuck's all this, little man? You going into dressmaking up here?'

'You,' Kosh said, pointing past Rennic to Foss. 'Hold this.'

Foss peered from the doorway, where he'd remained.

'Not much of one for high places, you understand, friend.'

She scowled and demanded Rennic approach. He did, taking the boxes in his hands, allowing her snaps of care and criticism to wash over him. 'Now over your head.' He lifted, his eyes now little more than black lines in the gloom. The uppermost tier surpassed the wooded barrier at the platform's end, fluttering in the fierce wind from the plains.

Kosh beckoned Chel. 'Hold this.'

A thin pole, attached to a narrow cord.

'And sit back on this.'

Another pole, a little longer than the first, secured at either end with rope. Kosh looped the rope over him, cross-wise, then tied it at his back.

'When you said "complication",' Chel said, watching her activities with growing unease, 'what exactly did you—'

'You, savage,' Kosh gestured to Lemon, who flicked a gesture involving two of her fingers in response. 'Take hold of that pulley.'

'This one?'

'That is your pudendum.'

'Aye, right, so it is. This one, then?'

'Yes, that one.'

Lemon gripped a rope, which Chel's nervous eyes connected to the wind-shield.

'Seriously,' he said, one hand tugging at the rope that wrapped him, 'what's the complication?'

'Now, hold these strings. Do not release your grip on the handle.'

Chel did his best to grip both the small pole, and the fistful of thin cords she passed him. They looped up into the arms of the structure that Rennic held over his head, separating and running over its bones through tiny metal loops.

'Why exactly am I—'

'The complication is the strength of the wind in this place. It is far stronger, and more persistent, than my nation's standard approach would handle. This necessitates certain changes.'

'What kind of changes?'

'For one, a greater mass to stabilize the structure. In addition, a secondary control point, local to the device. This should allow for the desired precision of delivery. Savage, release the catch.'

'Wait, wait, wait, are you saying—'

The barrier dropped. The wind rushed over the platform, and the tiers of boxy silk leapt from Rennic's outstretched arms. With the fluttering of heavy wings, the object rose fast into the sky, extending to its full height. Around him, Chel heard the whisper of spooling cord. He felt the ropes in his hands go taut.

'Just what is—'

Chel took to the air. The ropes around him snapped tight, and with a lurch his feet were dragged from the platform and into the night sky. A terrible vertigo overcame him, suddenly disconnected from solid ground, the torchlit buildings swimming beneath his gaze, the drop to the darkened plaza below utterly fatal. He felt like he was falling even as he rose, his brain's certainty of impending death overwhelming all other thought. The wind tore at him, yanking the structure above him ever higher, dragging the ropes suspending him with it. It could only be a matter of time before he was blown up and into the clouds, carried aloft and away, lost to the heavens then dashed to the earth below on the wind's caprice. At long last he realized he was screaming, and paused to draw breath.

Something twanged beneath him, and with a jolt his upward progress ceased. The structure remained airborne, floating on the wind, while he dangled beneath, staring down at the moon-washed points of the towers and domes below.

'Stop looking down, idiot!'

The Nort sounded very close. With great effort of will, Chel tore his gaze around, toward the origin of the voice. He was hanging from the silken box, itself kept airborne by the fierce wind through its sails, a rigid tether anchoring it back to the platform behind and beneath him. Kosh stood not five lurching feet from him, hands on hips, a look of quiet satisfaction on her face. He was barely two diagonal strides above and away from the platform, despite his all-consuming sensation of flying free and uncontrolled.

'Concentrate on the handle! Can you direct the *kayt*?'

The *kite*. He pulled at the handle in his grip, teasing it to one side. Above him, the structure shifted, and he felt the whole thing begin to lurch sideways. He pulled in the other direction, overcompensated, and found himself fluttering hard the other way. After some trial and error, he managed to correct his movements, stabilising once more. With surprise, he realized he was enjoying himself.

'What are the strings for?'

'What?'

'The strings!' He yanked at a couple of the bundle of thin cords she'd passed him, those that travelled up into the kite's body. Nothing seemed to happen.

'What?'

He tugged at a couple more, then the rushing died in his ears, and he was falling. The kite dropped from the sky and he fell with it, until the tether wrenched at his body and arrested his fall. The kite fell past him, dropping toward the plaza below, then stopped fast, held by the same tether that rooted him to the platform. For a moment, he dangled in space, the kite spinning below him, the terrible impact of the fall working its way through his midriff. He gazed down at the plaza, this time without the overwhelming nausea. There were people down there, holding torches, and it looked to him like they were watching. He waved.

Then, with a creak, the tether began to tug him upward, reeled back up toward the platform, a pendent fish on a hook. Strong hands grabbed him and hauled him back aboard, and a moment later the kite followed, lifted by Foss and Rennic with something approaching reverence.

Chel sat back against the boards, solid beneath him at last, and felt only disappointment.

'What happened?'

'The wind dropped.'

'The wind dropped!?'

The Nort shrugged. She seemed more concerned with checking the kite for damage. 'It can happen.'

'What if it happens again?'

'That's why you have the tether. And you will be higher, from the other tower.'

'But . . .' He gestured beyond the walls, over the gorge, toward the army camped on the plateau. The camp fires were a thousand twinkling lights across the dark expanse. 'What if it happens out there?'

The Nort completed her inspection, stood, nodded to herself. She started walking back toward the door. 'Pray to your god that it does not.'

\*\*\*

Rennic was walking close to Kosh as they descended, crates of folded silk stacked in his arms. Her anger seemed like sunlight to him, her simmering fury returned now the testing of the kite was complete.

'Are you well, alchemist?'

'I am . . . incandescent.'

'That display up there, that . . . *kite*. It'll hurt them?'

'Used correctly? They will be *seared*.'

'You want vengeance, don't you?'

She stopped short, sending the others into an uncomfortable pile-up. She breathed deeply, lost in the middle distance of the gloomy tower.

'I want justice.'

Rennic laughed, a single puff of air from his nostrils. 'We all want justice, alchemist, it's only ever a question of whose.' He paused in thought. 'Hey, can you make something . . . Something that can break that armour of Hurkel's?'

Her eyebrows lowered, deep furrows crossing her brow. At length, she said, 'Not for certain. But I can do something that goes around it.'

\*\*\*

A crowd was waiting for them in the plaza, seemingly not discouraged by either the cold depths of night or the threat of imminent bombardment. At first, Chel took them for well-wishers, come to cheer on the brave stalwarts resisting the invaders through ingenious means. But in the dancing torchlight, there was something in their eyes, something of their travel-stained clothes, a detachment, a burning zealotry, that told him they wished them far from well. He recognized some of them, by appearance at least: refugees from the roadside, the wild-haired types who'd been building a shrine on the plateau, joined by others, some from the city, some from far beyond. Their arms snaked with whirling tattoos and designs, spreading like tree roots, and their stares were hostile.

One of them stepped forward, a long, blackened branch in his hands, halfway between walking stick and weapon. Exactly what Rennic had done when he had posed as a beggar. The man gestured with the stick, up at the tower overhead, and barked something in a dialect Chel didn't recognize. Another approached, a smaller woman, her arms rich with whorls. Everything blurred in the low light, but to Chel the lines looked much like the scars that had adorned the arms of the crazed box-preacher in Denirnas. The woman he'd saved from the Rose.

'What are you doing up there?' the woman asked, translating or moderating. Her accent was southern, her features battered and blocky.

A step ahead of Chel, Kosh waved an irritated hand. 'Get out of my way.'

'You're the alchemist,' another member of the assembly cried. 'You're the one doing it all.'

Kosh raised an eyebrow. 'Doing what?'

'Offending the Mother!'

Chel blinked. God's breath, not here. Not now.

'You're building machines, unnatural engines, as bad as those raining fire on us!'

Kosh's eyes narrowed. 'Yes,' she said, slowly. 'But these are to . . . defend you.'

'She admits it!'

The cries from the mob rose in pitch, and they began to shuffle forward, enclosing the doorway. 'The skies are her domain! You defile it with your perversions!'

Of course they're maniacs, Chel thought, edging back toward the door and nodding for Kosh to join him. Who else would be out at this hour, in a city where death could fall from the sky at any moment?

He bumped into Lemon coming the other way. 'Who's this bunch of numpties?'

'Defiler!' the chant went up. 'Defiler! Defiler!'

'Oh aye, dribblers, is it?'

Foss emerged from the doorway, momentarily filling it, standing up to his full height beyond. Rennic was behind him, his crates parked, a wicked knife already loose in his grip.

'Friends,' Foss said, his voice somehow carrying over the noise of the mob, 'I'm sure all we have here is a misunderstanding.'

'You're one of them! You are party to the desecration of the Mother's domain!'

'The Mother . . . of Storms, yes? Mistress of the Skies, Sender of Lightning, Spirit of Eternal Vengeance?'

Their momentum faltered. 'Yes,' the woman said. 'She commands the air and the heavens.'

'And when she is displeased?'

'She smites her enemies with thunderbolts, razing them in pillars of flame!'

'Of course, of course.' Foss was relaxed, friendly, disarming, nodding along with every claim. 'And you are her devotees? Her chosen people, her prophets?'

The woman's cheeks darkened a shade. 'We are the Children of the Storm. The prophets walk among us. We have overcome war, plague, and famine, all to spread the word of her glory, to tear down the false god of the hated church.'

'And your journeys are a testament to her power,' Foss said, sincerity welling from his gaze. 'But tell me, friends,' he continued, shifting a little, keeping the bulk of the group in his line of sight, 'do you see many storm-clouds massing overhead?'

Gazes went skyward. 'No,' one of them admitted.

'But surely, if whatever took place in this tower so offended the Mother, she would smite it with lightning? Burn it to the ground?'

'It is her will! We must act for her!'

Foss frowned. 'But she is mighty ruler of the skies, she can act without limitation – unless you are questioning her power . . . ?'

The man who had shouted looked suddenly very alone. Foss steamed on. 'Or is it possible that the Mother does want you safe, and that her enemies beyond this wall are the focus of her ire? Devotees of the false god, who even now rain fire onto the innocents of this ancient and holy city? It is possible,' he went on, taking slow, easy steps forward, as the crowd shuffled back before him, 'that the Mother has sent this wind that we might use it? That we might return that fire whence it came, and scour her enemies from the land?'

A few were nodding. Not everyone was convinced.

'Friends,' Foss said, looming over the front ranks, his hands out in entreaty, 'this is not a safe place to linger. The Mother needs all of us whole, but you especially, for the struggles ahead, when the armies of the false church are repelled, and her message must be carried to the peoples of the lands. Who among you has the strength to answer her call?'

Hands shot up, and cries of assent.

'Then go, now, back to shelter. Wait for your moment. The Mother will make all clear, I have no doubt.'

'Praise the Mother! Praise her!'

They were off, chanting, wailing, dispersing into the twilight. One or two remained, uncertain, uneasy at what had happened but unable to express why. Then they, too, shuffled away.

'Fucken hells, Fossy, you can turn it on, eh?'

Foss said nothing, mulling, as he went to reclaim his share of their kite-cargo. At length he said, 'When you hear enough prophets, eventually you start to see . . . patterns.'

'They all say the same thing?' Chel asked, shifting his own burden in tiring arms.

He shrugged, still gazing into the lamp. 'Their proclamations tend to have a lot in common, friend.'

'That stuff about the false god, the church—?'

'The church of Vassad, of Hurkel, is no longer the Shepherd's. It costs me no angst to decry the monstrosity of man that besieges us.'

Rennic twirled the knife around in his hand before stowing it in a sheath. 'Shame,' he said, retrieving his crates. 'Thought we'd end up cracking some heads. Fuckers looked like they needed a kicking, lest they find their balls and come back for another try.'

Foss shook his head with a smile. 'Behold the incarnation of churchly virtue.'

Rennic tried to spread his hands while keeping hold of his cargo. 'Hey, they started it.'

Chel grimaced, images of Preachers' Plaza in Denirnas swimming in his mind. *I have a feeling that was me.*

'Come!' Kosh snapped at them. 'Dawn is approaching, and we have many stairs to climb.'

# THIRTY-FOUR

The platform wasn't like the one they had tested on. It projected from the upper spire of the workshop's tallest tower, a thick balcony extended with buttressed planks, whipped by frigid wind beneath rushing clouds the colour of burning copper. Thin strips of pallid blue peeked between the trundling formations, while a simmering burnished band grew at the rugged north-eastern horizon. Chel squeezed between boxes on tired legs, never more conscious of the absence of any sort of railing on the projection from the tower-top, trying to keep up with the little Nort steaming ahead.

'This is . . . very, very high.'

The former chief artificer had been waiting for them, and was now hunched over the now-familiar boxy construction of silk and thin wood, working at cords like sinew. Beside her, sand-backed crates stood stacked, their lids loosened, and the artificer was attaching something small and dark from within to the kite's structure.

Rennic and Lemon lingered at the platform's edge, where

the wind-shield, here recognizable as the stalled sails of a windmill, deflected the worst of the wind's stinging caprice. His load passed on, Foss took a step, felt the platform creak beneath him, and retreated.

'If it's all the same, friends, maybe I'll watch from downstairs . . .'

Their surroundings remained gloomy, despite the expansion of the glow at the horizon. The camp on the plateau was cast in deep indigo, shaded by cloud and mountains. Lines of torches twinkled along rows of what Chel presumed to be tents. It was unnerving to be able to see it so clearly from the tower-top.

'How far can the kite travel?'

Kosh looked up. Her gaze passed right through him, stopping somewhere out over the plains. 'As long as the wind holds, the tethers will hit their reels at a thousand strides.'

'A thousand strides? You're sure?'

She shrugged, a muscle beneath one eye twitching irregularly. 'The weight of the tethers will affect the lift, of course, but they are light, and they are strong. An abundance of silk has many advantages.'

'Wait, tethers plural? Does the kite need more than one?'

She smiled, loose, deranged, and stepped to one side.

'Two kites? But . . .'

'The munitions we have prepared are small but dense, and each affixing will increase the mass of the endeavour. Our preparations have been rushed and are likely to have incurred a significant failure rate where ignition is concerned, meaning a greater number of munitions may be required for any given target. Beyond a certain threshold, however, it would be simply unsafe to load the vessel any further, given both risk of collapse and accidental detonation.'

'Aye, that's reassuring,' Lemon muttered.

'Thus, in order to cover sufficient ground given our timescales, two vessels became a necessity. Each can operate independently, dividing the plateau in half.'

Chel stared at the second kite. It looked identical to the first. 'If there's another kite, we're going to need another pilot, yes? Will you be joining me?'

'The risks are far too great,' Kosh said, unblinking. 'It would be an act of terrific stupidity to risk my abilities and expertise on such a thing.'

'Whereas I, of course,' Chel said, 'am inherently disposable.'

He frowned when she said nothing to contradict him. 'Then who's coming up with the disposable Andriz? Your friend there?' He gestured at the former chief artificer, who ignored him.

'Don't worry, wee bear, you were born lucky, remember? You'll be right as rain.'

'The second pilot needs to be both small enough and light enough to operate the mechanisms without upsetting the flight model, and possessed of enough strength to steer against the volatility of the wind. That rules out my companion, as it does the mercenary, and the large man retreating downstairs.'

Foss was indeed heading for the tower door. He paused, mid-step, a look of shamed apology on his face.

Lemon looked at Rennic. Rennic looked at Lemon. 'When she says "mercenary", does she mean—'

'Me,' Rennic said.

'But that—'

Chel split an enormous grin. 'Oh, my Lemon. You are going to love this.'

\*\*\*

'This is against nature's laws! The Clyde is an earthbound creature!'

'Be quiet, savage, you are wasting time. Once dawn breaks the camp will begin to disperse.'

'I'm gonna freeze in that fucken wind!'

'You should count yourself lucky, you'd be naked for reasons of weight control were it not for the risks of exposure.'

Both kites were aloft, held up by Rennic and a very uncomfortable Foss, while Chel and Lemon were strapped beneath. Kosh and the artificer gave them their final instructions.

'The payload is delivered via the string bundle – yank each to release a cluster. You will find lift – and therefore range – easier to come by, the more you drop, but ensure you retain enough munitions for the most distant targets.'

Chel stared into the indigo of the silent plateau, its lines of torches still winking in the predawn light. 'I don't want to hit anyone, just the engines and their ammunition. How will we see what we're aiming at? It's still darkness down there.'

'Look for where their torches and watchfires are not. They will not want to keep naked flames close to their black powder dumps.'

Kosh signalled the artificer, and she retired to the lever that released the wind-shield. Chel could already feel himself being lifted by the fierce wind that flowed over and past it.

'One more thing,' the Nort said as she checked the final coupling. 'Keep to your separate sides. If the tethers become tangled, you may pull each other out of the sky.' She leaned in close, immune to Lemon's screeched protestations beyond. 'I have to say, Andriz, I am envious of your position, to be able to soar like a bird over this ugly mass, to leave it all behind. But, of course, the risks to me are too great.' She patted his arm. 'I hope you are as lucky as they say.'

Chel didn't even see her signal. The wind-shield dropped, and the full force of the elements blasted over the platform. Before he could speak, the kite snapped tall and out of Rennic's hands, and then with a lurch Chel followed, his feet lifted from the ground, the handles stubborn and heaving in his hands. From the corner of his eye, he saw a flash of silk and orange and knew that Lemon was away, clear of the platform and screaming with him into the dawn. The tethers spooled behind them, worked by the engineers, kept taut like fishing line, their bulwark against a sudden disappearance into the brightening sky.

Hands on the handles, thick bunches of thin cords wrapped around them, Chel soared. The city fell away beneath his feet, the domes and towers strange and receding from his vantage overhead. Now he could see the terrible damage of the bombardments, the charred craters, the smashed stone, some areas still smouldering, sending belches of dark smoke up into the sky beside them.

Still the wind tore at them, urging them forward, only the tethers and their wrestling of the handles maintaining the serenity of their ascent. On either side of him, dangling from the upper structure, the dark clusters jingled and sang, rattling on the currents of their climb. They were smooth, oblong things, their noses pointed and flimsy, their tops ringed with spiralled silk. Each looked bigger than Chel's fist, and reeked of menace.

To his right, he saw Lemon rock and swirl in her kite, fighting to keep it level as the wind yanked them onward and upward. He leaned on his handle, pulling closer, although not so close as to risk tangling the tethers.

'You all right?' He had to scream to make himself heard over the wind.

'Aye, wee bear, just fucken peachy!'

'Can you control it?'

'If you can control your fucken self!'

The walls flashed below, then the gorge was beneath them, hundreds of strides over the smashed ruin of the bridge and the spindly aqueduct beneath. It seemed utterly black, a chasm of pure darkness. Then the wind tugged at them, and the misty lip of the plateau rolled beneath their dangling feet.

'Ready?'

'Fuck off!'

'Here we go!'

Chel leaned into the handles, and looked for where the fires weren't.

\* \* \*

Shapes flashed beneath, dim blurs, pale against the dark of the plateau. Chel tried to steer his kite along a line of torches that marked a road through the camp, fighting against the wind's own opinions, starting to lose the feeling in his fingers and ears. The clustered weapons dangling from the construction's wings above his head jingled constantly over the creak and rustle of the kite's structure, and he began to worry about them knocking together and immolating him in mid-air. Just out of his vision to the right, Lemon was a fluttering white oblong, rising and falling on the waves of air, and no doubt still screaming.

The first rays of dawn had lit the limpid eastern sky, and suddenly he could see, the fuzzy blurs of the plateau taking shape, rows of tents and larger structures, rolling wagons, milling fighters. The camp was already alive. All it would take was for one of them to look up and notice their drifting forms, hundreds of strides above, and things would take an unwelcome turn.

The bundled cords pulled at his numb fingers, anxious to be released. Already his arms ached, his back aflame despite the chill of the wind's embrace. Needless to say, his shoulder was throbbing, a surly and neglected pulse beneath the rest of his aggravations. The sheer joy of flying in the morning sky had paled as the physical efforts took their toll. A voice at the back of his mind started to whisper that he'd made a dreadful mistake.

'Fuck this,' he muttered, fixing his eyes on a largish structure, inherited by the church forces from the refugees who'd formerly occupied the plateau, well clear of any sources of flame. *If I'm going to freeze and fall to my death, I might as well make the place interesting before I go.*

He realized he had no idea how to aim. Calculations formed in his head, the speed he was travelling, his height and rate of climb, the speed of the wind, the likely arc of the falling munitions. He had absolutely no idea what to do with any of it. He yanked the kite straight, straining and sweating from the effort of fighting the wind, and lined up on the building. The sun was in no danger of cresting the mountains any time soon, but already the plateau was distinctly clearer. Guessing at how far a cluster might travel, he squinted, and pulled one of the cords.

His finger didn't move, frozen stiff. After a moment, he bent forward, gripped the cord with his teeth, and yanked. The kite lurched immediately sideways as one of the bundles loosed, falling away in the corner of his eye as the cord whipped through the little metal rings along the kite's structure. A moment later, it was gone and falling, a shrinking blob of dark metal. Chel dragged the kite back on track as the cluster fell away, fighting the kite's listing inclination now it was unevenly weighted. The bundle fell far straighter than he'd expected, each of the oblongs separating, spinning as they fell, nose-down and picking up speed. He could already tell they would drop short, their paths almost direct, far less than the arc he'd imagined. Half in correction, half to make the kite easier to steer, he counted to three then loosed a second bundle, this time from the other side of the kite.

The first cluster hit, one at a time, along a row of tents that preceded his target. The first did nothing, whumping into a canvas structure and disappearing from view, but the second ignited on impact, spraying fire outwards in a fierce orange halo. The ring of flame caught the others, and suddenly a fireball was ripping through the tents, blasting outward and upward in a crescendo of explosions. Chel felt the kite buck as the shockwave travelled upward through the air, followed by a wash of pleasantly warm air over his frigid skin. Shouts and cries spread through the camp, lit orange as the flames took hold.

Off to Chel's right, another flare billowed, this time in the midst of a row of wagons. Lemon had scored a direct hit. He could make out her kite, somewhere over the oily smoke and roaring flame, a small, pale box in the violet sky.

His second volley hit. The earth before the building ripped upward, then the door blasted inward and the roof exploded. For a moment, it looked like that was it, then a massive blast tore the structure apart, flattening the camp around it and sending a torrent of flame and smoke into the air. This time, the shockwave knocked Chel sideways, sending the kite swirling on the roiling air, making him battle to stay upright, let alone on course. Sweating and cursing, he fought back against the battering, fists tight around the remaining cords, mindful of their aggravated clattering above his head. Any moment, one would come free, knock another – or his head – and that would be it. Any moment.

The battering subsided, the kite levelled. Off to his right, another explosion ripped the dawn air, setting one of the mobile bell-towers aflame.

Chel found that he was laughing.

\* \* \*

Chel soared over the churning plateau, rising higher as he dropped one cluster after another. He'd taken to releasing them in pairs, one either side, and had refined his aim with practice. The weight of the tether dragged him and the kite backward and down, even as the wind howled them onward and upward. He'd long ago ceased to feel the cold, the ache in his arms and legs, the loss of sensation in his extremities. He was one with the kite, always ranging, always climbing, the figures milling in panic below now little more than smears against the paling earth. The mountain walls loomed large in his vision, but he was closing on his target: the area at the plateau's mouth, where workers toiled on their engines, where the church's pet alchemists must mix and load their murderous compounds. He had four cords left beneath his numb fingers, and he intended to make them count.

To his right, gouts of flame rolled over the distant earth, searing a clump of low buildings. Lemon was keeping up her own contributions. Bells rang out, dolorous, urgent, useless.

Something floated up into his vision, slowing, turning, tumbling away. An arrow, fired from somewhere beneath. His smile broadened.

'Nice fucken try, pal,' he said to himself, in an imitation of Lemon's accent. The confessors had spotted them, at least, but it would do them little good now. As long as the wind held and the tethers kept spooling, it was only a matter of time before those great engines burned.

\* \* \*

He was closing in on his target when Chel saw Lemon's kite buck in the air. It jerked as if struck, coming up short, sending the last of its munitions groundward as if in spasmic shock. Before the clusters had even hit, the kite began to veer, strung against its rigid tether, unable to climb, unable to progress over the plateau. With increasing speed, Lemon's kite began to swing inward, toward the plateau's centre. Toward Chel's own tethered path.

'Fuck,' he said, blind to the flurry of detonations below the advancing kite. 'Fuck, fuck, fuck.' Lemon had run out of tether and had lost all forward momentum. She might be able to hover where she was, but she needed to be reeled in immediately, or either the wind would drop or it would drive her into Chel's own umbilical and down them both.

The kite was veering closer. He imagined he could already hear her abusive screams. He looked down at his own tether, still firmly fixed, but the length of cord remaining on the spool, back on the platform, was a terrifying unknown. He was still a long way short of the line of engines, creeping closer but not fast enough. What if his own tether ran out, and he remained stranded, a sitting duck for the archers below as he floated downward.

Fifty strides to the engines. He had to reach them. Lemon was coming closer; was she steering toward him deliberately? Why weren't those on the platform reeling her back in?

Without prelude, the wind fell away. The rush in Chel's ears faded to nothing, and he felt suddenly weightless as his steady rise tailed off, the protesting whispers and creaks of the kite his only companions. The rush returned, not from the wind, but because he was dropping, picking up speed.

But still moving forward.

Forty yards to the engines, a hundred strides below. Chel's mind worked at triple speed, but he knew he was guessing. Hoping. In his periphery, Lemon's kite was dropping fast.

But it could work. Only one thing would blow it. As fast as he could move his frigid hands, he bunched the remaining cords together in one fist, then dug for his knife.

\* \* \*

Thirty strides and falling. Chel gripped tight to the swooping kite, the air now rushing against his chilled and battered face, hands locked by icy willpower. Untethered, the kite was almost beyond his control now, but there was no danger of stopping short. Chel was riding his momentum all the way to the plateau's end.

Twenty strides, and the figures beneath were growing fast. With them came the engines, their scale only now becoming clear. The machines were huge, their wheels as tall as a man, great black sheets of iron bolted to their extremities, their tender workings within. He had to reach those workings.

Ten strides, and he'd been seen. He could hear the shouts, the panicked cries, as his vision streamed and blurred in the teeth of the rushing air.

Five strides, and he forced the bundled cords from his grip. With a whispering swish the clusters were gone, and he yanked back hard on the kite's handle, trying to arrest his dive. The little bundles of oblongs fell away faster than he did, the kite's descent slowing momentarily as the huge engine beneath him began to fill the world. He was still moving forward, still dropping, but no longer plunging.

Something whiffled past his ear, and the side of his head felt suddenly hot. Above him, something tore a rent through the fabric of the kite's wing, and he felt it give to one side. He had dropped within crossbow range. Another missile followed the first, ripping through the upper tier, splintering wood. Chel felt one side of the handle go slack.

Behind and beneath him, the last of his clusters crunched against the massive body of the siege engine. He felt, rather than heard, the whoomph of ignition, then the cries that echoed around him took on a different pitch. He saw the growing light from behind him reflected by the barren flanks of the mountains in front, then it all happened at once. A blast of heat hit him at the same time as a head-splitting wall of sound and force, and the kite bucked and swirled, this time with enough force to throw him up and over. Tangled in his strapping, he could only watch as explosions ripped through the line of engines, each setting its flames upon the next, even as their panicking operators tried to haul them away before they went. As the blasts lit the plateau, they abandoned their task, fleeing for safety as flaming debris tore through the air. A chunk of something hit the kite, smashing through its upper tier, and Chel saw the desolate ground approaching with gathering speed.

The kite hit first, its impact softened by a combination of the wind's return and the sudden impromptu thermals generated by the blazing engines. Even smashed and ruined, Chel could still force enough lift from the whirling construction to give himself the chance to cut free. As it collapsed, smouldering, into the hillside, Chel bounced into the scrub, feeling every thump of its prickly embrace as he rolled, arms over his head and screaming.

It took him several minutes in the infernal, smog-choked aftermath to become certain that he was still alive. At least the feeling had begun to return to his fingers, albeit in an entirely unwelcome way. His entire body felt grated, knees and knuckles skinned, and sticky blood crept hot over one ear. His damaged shoulder lurked beneath it all, simmering, vengeful.

Chel looked out over the plateau. Through black and billowing smoke, he could just make out the city perched over the slit of the gorge in the shimmering haze of the fires of the burning engines, all the way across the other side of the plateau. Lemon's kite was vanished from the sky, her whereabouts unknown. The entire church army stood between him and safety.

'Well,' Chel said, wiping at the blood on his brow. 'Shit.'

\* \* \*

Shoulder pulsing and knees raw, Chel stumbled down the crumbling slope, toward the roaring flames of his wake. Engines were aflame, their huge blackened frames crackling, and still the occasional fiery pop signalled the detonation of something alchemical within. The heat was intense, even from a distance, but any of the church forces who'd survived the devastation had long since fled. Somewhere behind him the downed kite smouldered among the scrub, and Chel wanted to get as far away from it as he could before someone came looking.

Something moved, something huge, and Chel realized that one of the half-finished engines was rolling free. It moved slowly, as if pushed by an invisible hand, trundling forward even as it belched fire and roiling smoke into the morning sky. Chel followed it, moving in its wake, one battered arm held before his face to stave the burning embers blown clear. A plan was forming, half-baked: perhaps he could follow the burning engine all the way to the bridge as it cleared a path?

He heard shouts, horses, coming from one side. Limping as fast as he could, he scuttled around the far side of the giant, burning wagon, keeping its blazing bulk between him and the oncoming riders. He found himself beside one of its huge wheels, its outsize spokes revolving with almost comical slowness as the engine rumbled on. He looked up at the thick iron rims, scorched and peeling, rolling around higher than his own head, and had a sharp and sudden memory.

*A wagon, huge, black, forbidden, wheels the size of the moon, towering over him and stinking of death. Pale skin in the moonlight, a hand dangling free of the wagon's rail, flaccid, lifeless. Then away, dwindling into the shameful night, Chel's screams drowned by his mother's arms, holding him back, blocking his sight and sound. Denied one last sight of his father.*

He was screaming now, hoarse and cracked, collapsed in the dust of the plateau. The engine rolled on without him, coming to a gentle stop before its axles cracked and it fell in upon itself in a burst of flame. The chance for escape was gone, he was lost and alone on the burning plateau, an army between him and any hope of safety. Arms wrapped around his head, he screamed again into the dust, his frantic hands gripping his skull as if it were the only way to hold it on.

Hooves sounded beside his head, solid thumps through the insulation of his arms pressed over his ears. His breathing slowed. This was it.

A voice came from somewhere above, muffled through his charred sleeves.

'Aye, fuck, bear, there you are! Hurry up and get aboard, will you?'

# THIRTY-FIVE

Lemon sat on the driver's bench of one of the troop wagons, a lone horse in the traces, skittish under her command. Chel looked up, blinking away smoke and disbelief.

'How did you find me?'

'Aye, you're joking, eh? Look for the fuck-off explosions, there's your wee bear, every time. Now are you coming or what?'

'Where?'

'Seriously, wee bear? You're asking . . . Get the fuck aboard, will you?'

He hauled himself up beside her, the effort of lifting himself extraordinary and painful.

'How—'

'Later! Get in the back!' She geed the horse, who was only too glad to be moving away from the giant burning ricks that surrounded them. They rumbled away over the broken ground, picking up speed, pulling out from behind the columns of oily smoke. Tents and shanty structures flew past, some smouldering; frantic church troops were milling between them.

'There's a big old bit of metal there, do you see it?'

'Is this . . . Is this your kite?'

'Later, wee bear, later! Grab that metal sheet and bring it up here.'

He dragged it up from the wagon floor, sliding it out from under the folded kite. He had no idea how she'd managed to get that aboard. The piece of black iron was heavy in his arms, a former armoured panel for one of their engines, its exposed mounting a decent handle. Shoulder screaming in its socket, he levered it to the driver's bench.

'What's this for?'

'I think we're going to need it in a moment.'

'Why?'

'Because very soon they're going to realize that we're not on their side.'

Already the shouts were rising as they raced over the rough terrain, travelling faster than a wagon should, even in times of upheaval. Challenges went unanswered, and a moment later Chel saw crossbows ahead. Lemon steered the wagon for the roadway that led to the bridge, and Chel rolled the metal sheet around. A bolt thumped into the wagon's side, a second pinged from Chel's shield. He flinched, cursed, and the wagon kept rolling. His shoulder was screaming.

'How did you . . . pull this off, Lemon?'

'When I snagged the tether, I dropped what wee packages I had left there and then, not exactly the plan. Still, it went up like a fucken effigy, cleared the place out no bother. Then your lot went up over that way and the rest scattered. Found this wagon unattended, thought it might be prudent to see if you needed a lift.'

'And you brought the kite?'

488

'Aye. Now just keep that fucken shield up, bear, I am not dying here.'

'What if they shoot the horse?'

'They just lost a whole bunch of men and horses, won't want to shoot this one if they can help it.'

Another bolt pinged off the shield as Chel swivelled it to protect them both.

'You'd better be right, Lemon.'

'Aye, no kidding.'

They crested the rise of the plateau, still thundering at speed toward the bridge. Ranks and ranks of soldiers came into view, confessors, mercenaries, miscellaneous. Row upon row, ordered, marching, taking up position to the tolling of gloomy bells. The path to the bridge looked far from clear.

'We'll never make it.'

'Never say never, wee bear. We've got something they haven't.'

'And what's that?'

'Surprise!'

They rocketed past the troops, no longer fearing shots from in front. The ranks they saw were focused on what lay before them, not behind, either the broken bridge or some kind of roped construction behind it. Lemon steered for the bridge, then veered, dragging their foaming horse wide.

'What is it?' Chel called from over his shoulder, steadying himself on the rocking wagon. Every muscle in his body was aflame, the sheet of metal he gripped a final insult.

'Fucken bridge is blocked! There's something on it, something massive. We'd never get past.'

'The bridge is down anyway! How were we going to get

across it?' The wagon lurched again as Lemon corrected her course. They were heading for the gorge, but not the bridge. Somewhere off to one side. 'Wait, where are we going? Lemon? Lemon!'

'Told you, wee bear. Surprise!'

\* \* \*

The ranks of confessors were little more than blurs in the flying dust. Chel peered over the shield, over Lemon's hunched form, trying to make out their new destination. The flying bolts had fallen away, the church army's focus elsewhere.

'Lemon? Lemon! Where in hells are you . . . God's bollocks, what are you doing?'

'Aye,' Lemon called back over her shoulder, forcing the horse onward, ever faster toward the gorge, 'right, wee bear. I'll be needing you to drop that metal chunk about now, and grab the old kite, yes?'

'What?'

'Grab the fucken kite, bear, and tie us to it. Pronto!'

Chel looked past her, at the approaching gorge. At the little projecting stub of stone in their path: the old bridge, the fallen ruin. Fifty strides of its span were missing, long since dropped into the chasm beneath.

'You cannot be serious.'

'Do I look like I'm having a wee fucken joke, bear? Chop, chop now, any moment old Dobbin here is going to twig on our intentions.'

'I thought the Clyde was an earthbound creature?'

'Needs must, wee bear, needs must!'

The wagon bumped over the loose ground, re-joining

the ancient road that led to the stump of the old bridge. Great plumes of dust rose in their wake, carried away by the furious wind. Realizing Lemon was not only serious but committed, Chel dropped to his knees, scrabbling with the ropes and cords. He looped one over himself, finding the kite handles, then threw a second loop over his driver.

The stump was growing in their vision, wider and longer than Chel had realized from far away; it sloped up and out over the gorge, before it suddenly broke off, leaving nothing beneath.

'We tied?'

'Yes!'

'Then lift it high, because here we go!'

Chel could see nothing but the jutting spar of sand-coloured stone, and the blurred towering form of the city beyond it, impossibly distant. The wagon jumped and rocked as they mounted the stump, the panicked horse throwing sparks on the old stone. With a grunt, Chel braced his legs against the wagon-sides and hauled the kite upwards, lifting it into the oncoming rush. It reared in his grip, its upper tier ballooning taut, the wings lifting from his grasp. He felt the rope at his midriff snapping tight.

Lemon threw down the reins and scrambled to her feet, throwing her arms around Chel. 'Hold on, wee bear,' she said with a goggle-eyed grin. Chel worried that he saw madness in her gaze, but it seemed a little late to care.

The wagon crested the rise of the bridge and the horse saw the void ahead. It slammed down its hooves, scoring grooves in ancient stone, and tried to turn away. The wagon, propelled by vicious momentum, sailed on past, swinging then tipping as its wheels slid perpendicular to its motion. Straps snapped, and the wagon was free, skidding loose and slanting, travelling with impossible speed. Chel and Lemon swung and lurched with it, and then it fell away. The wagon pitched away beneath them into the void as the wind caught the kite full-on, and Lemon released the metal shield.

In a heartbeat, they were airborne again, sailing forward over the chasm toward the city, ropes cutting them like cheese-wire. The wind snarled and buffeted them, trying to drive them back, but their combined mass and momentum carried them onward even as the kite's lift faltered. Chel gripped at whatever he could hold, his every muscle aflame, his shoulder a stab of red-hot ire. Lemon only laughed, cackling around his waist into the howling wind, crowing her defiance to the skies.

He tried to shut his eyes, tried not to look, but terrible fascination dragged his gaze downward. The gorge was sailing by beneath them, a chasm of impossible depth, a thin white ribbon of water glimmering in its stygian depths. His stomach immediately tried to exit through his mouth, but his gritted teeth blocked its passage. The pillars of the great bridge rose up into the light like ancient bones, and strung between them, the spindly trench of the aqueduct, its frothing water sparkling in the sun. Something moved within those sparkles, crawling shapes like ants, but at this distance they could be—

'Heads up, wee bear!'

The wall was in front of them, the wall of the city, streaked and ancient. Chel was astonished.

'We're going to get over it! We're going to go right over it!'

The wind stumbled in the city's shadow, and they were dropping, little more than the speed of their fall keeping them travelling forward. Suddenly they were no longer sailing over the wall. They were heading straight for it.

'Shit,' said Chel, as ancient, weathered blocks filled his vision. 'Shit, shit, shit.'

The kite crested the wall. Chel and Lemon did not. Chel slammed into the stone, shoulder-first and gasping, his grip loosened and teeth rattled in his jaw, as Lemon thumped against his guts. Purple stars burst in his vision. They hung there, snagged on the baroque crenellations of the side wall, as the battered kite slid over the top and out of view.

'Aye, fuck,' Lemon moaned. 'Don't look down, eh?'

Chel looked down. The void waved back.

Lemon cackled again. 'Warned you! Now hold still, I'm going to climb you.'

\* \* \*

'You know what, wee bear, that could have been a lot worse.'

Chel limped down the steps from the deserted battlements behind her, clutching his everything. He could taste blood again, and his side was scraped raw as meat. His shoulder throbbed with particular malevolence.

'Maybe for you,' he said, spitting pink.

'Thought we'd only need to get over the gap in the main bridge, never thought we'd get over that one. Didn't see us getting up enough speed.'

'*What?* You mean—'

'All past now, wee bear, best not dwell, eh?' She nodded to a panicked citizen at the foot of the steps, who seemed astonished to see filthy and battered people descending.

'Don't you worry, we're with the prince. No, no! Not that one, the other one. The good one. And she's off. Ah, well.'

They reached the winding street, empty of traffic. Bells rang out across the city. Somewhere, up on the battlements, a ruined kite collapsed into a heap.

Chel attempted to roll the ache from his shoulder. It didn't work. 'I saw something, as we crossed the gorge. Looked like figures on the aqueduct. People.'

'The one that runs under the big bridge? The big broken bridge that they can't currently cross?' Lemon was beginning to gabble as adrenaline flushed through her. 'The unbroken aqueduct that runs straight into the bowels of the city where there's probably chuff-all defences, meaning a torrent of red bastards could come windmilling up our proverbial at any moment? That fucken aqueduct?'

Chel swallowed. 'Um, yeah. That fucken aqueduct.'

\*\*\*

They made for the gate, pounding through the ruined, winding streets, skirting debris and broken stone, trying to ignore the savage aches that riddled them. They spotted Rennic from the battered rampart above the third gate, Kosh beside him. They were fussing over something in the ruined courtyard below.

'Little man.' Rennic did well to keep the surprise from his voice. 'Good work out there, the bombardments have stopped. How the fuck did you get back into the city?'

Chel tried not to remember, suppressing a wince as he pressed one hand to his side. 'Unconventionally.'

Lemon was hopping from foot to foot behind him, still flooded with manic energy. 'Where's Fossy? What's the crack

494

here? Wee bear reckons he saw a tide of red bastards crawling in along the aqueduct.'

Rennic's eyes widened, their whites thoroughly bloodshot. 'Fuck. Are you sure, little man?'

Chel struggled to answer, parts of his body now refusing to answer instructions. 'Maybe not a tide as such . . .'

'Well, there's a quivering shit-pile of the bastards on the bridge right now, and very shortly they are going to be giving our front door a little tap.' He gestured to the battered second gate before them. It suddenly looked very flimsy.

'How? The bridge is—'

'We're not the only ones who can work great feats of engineering, little man,' he said with a nod to Kosh. She was still fussing over something, a contraption of wood and wire, large handles on one side. Chel had no idea what it was. 'They've built a tower and laid it on its back. They're going to roll it over the gap.'

That was what had blocked the bridge. Chel remembered the ranks and ranks of red-clad troops standing ready at the bridge mouth as he and Lemon had fled. 'They're coming above and below at the same time.'

Rennic's nod was grim. 'Surely looks that way. Lemon, Foss should be in the workshops, keeping an eye on things there. Our friendly mother-lovers may still be around. Find out where that aqueduct kicks out, and what we've got to defend ourselves with.'

'Righto, boss.' She skedaddled.

'What about me?' Chel felt himself shiver, despite the day's growing heat. 'Should we tell the prince what's going on?'

Rennic had turned back to Kosh's contraption. 'I'm sure our glorious leader has full command of the situation. You just missed him here, before he scurried off back behind some thick walls.'

'Oh? How was he?'

Rennic half-turned, speaking over his shoulder. 'Fucking dreadful. Still not wearing his chain. Living in constant fear of assassination by his own guards or being flung across the bridge by an angry populace.'

'Ah. Did he, uh, say anything?'

'Yeah.' He affected a girlish squeak, speaking as if his mouth were stuffed with plums. '"Don't let me down, chaps, if we don't see these buggers off, I doubt my death will be quick or pleasant."'

'It's like he's here with us now.'

Kosh stood back from her device. 'It is ready.'

Chel tried to peer past them. 'What is it?'

'A leveller.' Rennic nodded to himself, then turned to the guards huddled at the courtyard's edges. 'Right, you lot, bring in the rest. And if you want to keep your hands, best be careful as fuck.'

The guards set about ferrying jugs and pots to locations around the rubble-strewn courtyard. They kept their distance, but their curiosity about Kosh's machine was undeniable. Chel heard their whispers and concerned mutterings, and wondered himself. Over the wrecked outer wall, beyond the debris and the ruined bridge, the plateau was a sea of movement. Fires still burned across it, sending stinking black plumes into the morning sky. Somewhere, something large was moving.

'Can they understand me?' Rennic gestured at the meagre complement of guards manning the walls above. The guard captain nodded, and Rennic called up to them. 'Take shots as it comes, but be ready to fall back the moment they cross the span. Understand? Drop back to this courtyard, keep away from the gate.'

The woman's frown was deep beneath the sweat-grime, her once-gleaming armour pitted and scorched. 'We do not hold the gate?'

'They've learnt their lesson this time. That gate is doomed. But we'll be waiting for them here.' He patted the device in front of him, its apparatus peeking over the barricade. 'And we can always fall back to the last gate. They've got nowhere to go. Remember, on my signal, shields up.'

The captain nodded again. 'Shields up.'

'Rennic, what about the aqueduct? Can we send some guards—'

'Do you see any spare fucking house guards, little man? I need all these people and more. If this next bit goes to shit, I doubt *any* of our deaths will be quick and painless, yes? Now, alchemist. When I want it to do its thing, I pull this?'

'I will do it.'

Rennic blinked, then stared at Kosh through narrowed eyes. 'You sure? This isn't the place for you, remember? Too risky.'

'I want to be here.'

'And why's that?'

'To watch them suffer. For what they did.'

Rennic chuckled, black, bleak. Her nostrils widened in irritation. 'I mean it! Do not disparage me, mercenary! I have seen death before, plenty of it.'

'Ever pulled the lever yourself? Watched the light leave another's eyes?'

She didn't reply. Instead, she reached down and rummaged in her satchel, then withdrew a flattish object of wood and metal. It gleamed in her hands, and Chel saw it had straps and eyeholes. It looked freshly made. Memories of Denirnas Port flooded back, the little grill-man on the rooftop overlooking the bay, the masks strung on his wall. His stern-eyed daughter.

'Do you think,' Kosh said, moving to the rear of the device, the mask strung around her neck, 'that the big one will be among them?'

Rennic moved beside her, eyes on the gate. He put one hand on the device, feeling the bristling points. Chel ducked down behind them and their barricade. It seemed too late to do anything else now.

'I fucking hope so.'

'Good.'

Kosh pulled on her battle-mask.

\* \* \*

The archers on the gatehouse were firing. The thing on the bridge was in range. Chel tried to picture it, from Rennic's description, from the views he'd snatched on his cantering fly-past. Long and low, fat wheels torn from an alchemical engine, metal shielding likewise. A vehicle built with one purpose: to cross the broken span and hold the gap, impervious to fire and arrow alike. It would likely achieve its goal.

He peered forward at the odd device behind which Rennic and Kosh were braced, its levers and pulleys, odd torsions and wires. A leveller, Rennic had called it. He hoped they were right.

'Last chance, alchemist,' Rennic murmured. 'We'll be getting a polite knock at any moment.'

Kosh ignored him, her bone-fingers gripped tight on the device's levers.

'By the way, children, if this goes tits-up, we're not going to make it through the third gate. I want you to know that. What I said to the guards was a platitude.'

Kosh looked at him, her gaze cold and fierce as a winter storm through the eyes of the roaring mask. 'I am not a fool, mercenary. I know you were lying. Now be silent.'

He nodded, and watched the walls. Chel saw one of the archers drop, an arrow jutting. Short arrow, bright-fletched. He stared at the arrow, unblinking, then swallowed. He'd seen arrows like that once before, in a mountain gully, when they'd been ambushed by archers in tan and fur. Rennic had seen it too. He must have seen it. He was staring right at it.

Rennic looked back to the Nort.

'You really want to hurt them?'

The archers were falling back, abandoning the battlements, the gate with them. It was almost time. Kosh only grunted.

Rennic reached out and nudged the nose of the device downwards.

'Then aim low.'

Her jaw jutted behind the mask, but she said nothing. She was trembling, fine as a hummingbird's wings. Rennic's fist went up, a signal to the huddled guards: shields up.

'Hey,' he said, 'it's still not too—'

The gate exploded.

* * *

Fragments of wood billowed through a pulsing cloud of pulverized stone. A ripple seemed to travel through the gatehouse, then with a sudden finality it caved inwards, its pillars shot, the ramparts rumbling downwards into a steaming mass. The severed walls on either side of the churning mire stood proud, blasted but resolute, but within the fog of debris was only chaos. Chel peered past the others and over the barricade, over the device, looking into heaving murk. He could see the shapes that moved within, as the wind's current pushed the great plume of smoke and matter out over the plateau.

Rennic's cry went up. 'Here they come!'

The alchemist was unmoved, uncowed despite the explosion. Her masked eyes were fixed on the void where the gate had stood, the levers fast in her white-knuckled grip. Chel watched the shapes, saw a lumbering form picking its way over rubble, slow, ungainly. It had to be Hurkel.

He heard the creak of the mechanism in Kosh's grip, saw Rennic put a restraining hand on her shoulder.

'Not yet.'

She frowned but nodded.

The line of confessors was trudging into view, bobbing shapes riding the debris, others faint behind them. Tall, oblong, chanting something unfamiliar as they came. The lead troops were almost clear of the dust cloud and into the courtyard. He saw some of the surviving house guards poking out from their hiding places, one or two levelling their bows.

Rennic's voice was clear, calm. 'Not yet.'

The first of the attackers cleared the shattered gatehouse, not an armoured Pentarch at all, but a bullish figure in dust-streaked lamellar armour, holding a great metal shield most of his height, in front. Another followed, shield likewise high, with others at their flanks. A line of smaller, dusty figures loomed behind them.

'Oh, shit,' Rennic whispered. 'Mawn siege-breakers.'

The Nort flashed him a look of angry concern.

'Now?'

The Mawn were striding unopposed into the courtyard, spreading, shielding those who came behind. Chel could see their weapons now, see the light-armoured shapes scampering over the smoking ruins behind them. They were picking up speed, assured that their assault had blasted the defenders away, delighted at the lack of resistance.

Chel saw her from the corner of his eye, recognized the pattern of her gait as she descended into the courtyard. He saw her face beneath the helmet, sweeping the ruined defences, picking out the hidden defenders, realizing at last the trap that was set. He saw Grassi's hand go up, saw Rennic holding himself taut as a bowstring.

'Now.'

\*\*\*

The net burst from Kosh's device, a maelstrom of shrapnel strung with wire. It spread wide as it flew, enveloping the lead breakers, bearing them from their feet. It carved into flesh and splintered armour, savage cuts of wire driven on by jagged chunks of metal, blasted from the device by a spark and a roar of accelerant. The slicing wire tore beneath shields and wrapped shins, slashing the Mawn's legs from beneath them. At last it came to rest, the front wave of assault hobbled and downed, struggling beneath the merciless grip of the cleaving wire.

Rennic had already given the second signal. From around

501

the courtyard, the guards threw their clay vessels. Pottery shattered around the beleaguered Mawn, and their cries of pain rose to panic when the oil within splashed over them. The breakers struggled to free themselves against the cutting wire, scrambling to escape the sprays of warmed oil that doused them. Those at the back of the ranks, their progress blocked, tried to fight their way through to where they assumed their comrades were joined in battle. Screams and shouts filled the courtyard, and Rennic raised his fist to give the final signal.

She was staring right at him. Trapped beneath the scrabbling bulk of a stricken siege-breaker, the blood from the man's deep wounds running thick over her, she was looking straight at him. Her helmet was gone, her long hair spread thick around her. Grassi was staring into his eyes.

With great strength, she nodded.

Rennic gave the signal, and the courtyard billowed bright with flame. A filthy smell overpowered the wind, burning flesh, hair, and lacquer, screaming panic torn from throats by the hunger of the flames. Chel looked away, up at the sky, at the distant fractured wall. Then back, unable to keep his gaze away.

Rennic's hand rapped Kosh's shoulder, his eyes still fixed forward.

'Give me the crossbow.'

'What?'

'Give me the fucking crossbow.'

He lifted, drew, loaded, sighted, all with his eyes on her, wavering through the heat. She never looked away, never screamed or struggled, just held his gaze as her hair began to smoke and curl.

502

'Goodbye,' Rennic said to Grassi, and was sure she said the same.

He fired.

\* \* \*

The dust from the blasted gate was settling, somewhere out on the plateau, but the stinking fire in the courtyard roared ever higher. With a face like a tombstone, Rennic had ordered the guards to stop wasting their own arrows on the downed attackers. Instead, they circled the roiling pyre, jamming their spears wherever they detected movement, whether from mercy or vengeance Chel had no will to judge. He could bear the sight no longer, nor the smell with it, and retreated to the courtyard's edge, where the breeze kept the worst of the smoke off him.

'Rennic, the aqueduct . . .' Chel coughed, swallowed, wiped at his streaming eyes. 'Can we send people now?'

Rennic's eyes were fixed on the broken gateway beyond the fire, and the courtyard beyond it, waiting to see what would come at them next. Those Mawn who had escaped the conflagration had fled back toward the bridge, but any moment he clearly expected to see them return.

'Our friends of the cloth came and went half a dozen times yesterday, little man. You think this is their only throw today?' He spat into the rubble. It hissed. 'We might even see your pal Hurkel this time.' He turned to Kosh. 'How fast can you reload that thing?'

The Nort was staring at the pyre, the stench of burning meat swirling around her like a cape. The mask was slung around her neck. Rennic nudged her. 'Hey, how fast can you reload?'

Her eyes took too long to focus. 'It . . . it does . . . I . . .' She took a long breath and blinked hard enough for a trickle of tears to leave the corners of her eyes. 'It must be rebuilt. It was single-use.'

The lines deepened beneath Rennic's eyes. He looked around for the guard captain. 'Get your people back up on the walls. The gap in the bridge is plugged, and another wave of red fuckers is an inevitability. Be ready. Alchemist! We need the black powder, whatever you've got. We need to destroy that fucking gangplank on wheels.'

'There is no more. We have used all I could produce.'

'Then make more! Now!'

'I cannot rush the process! The steeping needs a day and a night! More is brewing in the tower.'

'When? When will it be ready?'

Already her gaze was returning to the snarling fire. 'Tomorrow, maybe. If all goes . . . well.'

'Fucking . . . what? Tomorrow?'

Chel pushed himself forward, stepping between the Nort and Rennic's growing fury. 'It's all right. We'll make do, right? Somehow.'

'Not if a thousand armoured confessors come stomping over that bridge in the intervening,' Rennic hissed in his ear.

The Nort was looking at her hands, blanched and shaking, still in place on the device's levers. Tears streaked the dust of her cheeks.

Chel lowered his voice, gave Rennic a warning look. 'Are you all right, Kosh?'

Grimacing, Rennic affected his best voice of concern. 'You did it, right? Made them suffer?'

504

Sobbing, she tore off the mask and ran from the court-yard. Rennic pushed a hand through his matted hair and took a long, foul-smelling breath. 'Norts.'

'Is she— Do you think I should—'

'She'll be fine, she got what she wanted. Archers! To the walls. Form new barricades. Get eyes on the bridge, and watch for movement. Flaming arrows on that engine if we can. They'll be coming again, and soon, and this time we've got nothing but our hands and our blood.' Chel had no idea how much they understood, or how seriously they took him, but the house guards were moving in the right direction, at least.

'Rennic, the aqueduct, the waterways. Can we—?'

He rounded on Chel so suddenly that the raw pain in his eyes burned through undisguised. 'What's your fucking headache here, little man? I cannot leave this gate! You find the problem, and you fix it on your own.' He let out a sharp breath from his nose, his voice dropping. 'On your own. Like everyone else.'

Chel said nothing, just a soft nod, then turned and pushed his aching body in the direction of the workshops.

\* \* \*

'Lemon? Foss?'

The loom chamber stood empty, its once clattering machines standing silent and dark. Chel felt alarm in his gut, hot and piercing. The looms were never unattended. The looms were never still.

'Wee bear? That you? Did you bring the cavalry?' Lemon emerged from behind the great silk engines, a half-axe in one hand. Her mania had left her, and her eyes looked red and puffy. She had a pretty impressive bruise forming on one cheek.

'Not . . . No. It's just me. Did you find Foss?'

She nodded, swallowed, gestured to the room's far corner. 'He wouldn't wait. Said someone needed to get down there, make sure . . . Took that little lass with him, the workshop woman. What do you mean, just you? Where's the rest? How'm I supposed to guide down an army if we're one army short of an army?'

'Things at the gate, there just . . . there aren't enough people. Wait— someone's coming!'

A small, ragged figure emerged blinking into the chamber from a hidden hatch in the corner Lemon had indicated. 'It's the chief artificer.'

'Aye, workshop woman, like I said.'

Chel and Lemon made for the corner, expecting the woman to be babbling with news. Instead she looked up at them expressionless, slack-jawed, her gaze a thousand miles away.

Chel saw the sprays of blood that criss-crossed her. 'Five hells, are you all right?'

She tilted her head slowly, bringing him into focus, and nodded.

'What happened? What's down the—'

Lemon grabbed the woman by her bloodied clothes. 'Where the fuck is my brother Foss?'

The woman's loose gaze swivelled her way. She gestured toward the hatch.

'Come.'

\* \* \*

The air in the caves was dank and heavy with the stink of ammonia. Chel edged through the darkness, trying to ignore the streaked scrapes of bat-shit along the passageway floor. The artificer led, stepping carefully, insistent that no torch could be permitted. From somewhere overhead came the thump of machinery, the clatter of the water-wheels and their racks of scoops, delving incessantly for water for the city above. The caves echoed with overlapping noise. The passageway itself was smooth, tunnelled, mined; much of the city's stone had been quarried from beneath it.

The artificer trotted on, her progress nervous but rapid, her thousand-yard stare no impediment to her progress, especially with Lemon nipping at her heels. Chel's eyes had to be adjusting to the darkness now; side passages glowed blue along their ceilings, luminescence pale and delicate. He stopped, turned. The ceilings were glowing. Thin ropes of light like lambent beads dangled in clumps from the cave roof, swaying gently in the breeze that travelled the passages, almost like they were breathing. They were beautiful.

He went to step forward, but the artificer had doubled back, one hand on his arm. 'Come.'

'What is that?'

'Worms. For looms. Come. This way.'

He gave them one last look, then followed her and Lemon down the passage, an odd, delicate feeling in his chest, a sense that he had seen something secret and wonderful.

\* \* \*

They almost didn't recognize him in the darkness. He looked like a formation of rock, standing motionless in the cool blue glow of the caves. He was slick from moisture, gleaming in the low light, but when he turned Chel realized that he was coated in blood.

'Fossy? You . . . all right, pal?'

Lemon approached him sidelong, one hand extended as if he were a jittery horse that might spook. Even Foss's hair was thick with blood, his braids hanging dark and heavy. For a moment, Chel thought he couldn't see them, couldn't recognize them, although his lips moved slowly in the half-light. His eyes were closed. Foss was praying.

He opened his eyes, and slow as breaking dawn a grin lit his face. 'Am I pleased to see you, my friends. Thought I was going to have to see this lot off myself.'

Lemon touched his arm. Her fingers came away stained. 'Any of this yours, old man?'

He shrugged, slow, tired. 'Maybe a little.'

'Aye, well, fun's over now, Foss-bot. Friend Lemon has arrived to sweep your glory away.' She looked down the tunnel, hearing at last the clatter and clink of gathering confessors. 'What's this lot you're speaking of?'

'Confessors. Came in through the water system.'

'How many?' She looked down, noting the slumped forms along the passageway floor. 'Left.'

'A lot. Guessing they're making their move, friend, and this is it.'

She nodded. 'Aye, right. Well, a bad move it is, no mistake.' She swung an arm around, stretched her back, reached for a short-axe. 'How about it, wee bear? You up for a scrap?'

Chel looked from one to the other. His shoulder burned like a forest fire, and he was covered in scrapes and bruises. He throbbed, and was quite sure he was exhausted.

'Do you reckon we can take them?' he said.

'Aye, easy.'

Chel looked to the artificer, who had stayed silent to one side. 'What do you think?'

She looked him up and down, to the blood-smeared Foss and the wild and dirty Lemon, and shook her head an emphatic no.

'Then I think we need a new plan, don't you?' He paused, trying to think, feeling the screaming ache of his muscles, listening to the slosh and tumble of water around the reeking caves. He turned to the artificer. 'There were quench tanks in the workshops. Does the city's water come straight up from here, or are there places it rests?'

The artificer blinked in the gloom. 'Reservoirs, yes. When wind weak, less water comes.'

'Can we get to any from here?'

Lemon was frowning. 'What are you thinking, wee bear . . .? That we . . . oho, I like where this is going!'

The artificer looked from one to the other, her face blank. 'Yes, large beneath the workshops.' She gestured upwards. 'Above our heads.'

'And does it have any sort of tap or drain?'

Now she understood. Her face went pale in the gloom, hands already raised and warding. 'No, no, very bad. Very bad!'

'All we need is enough to send them packing, flush them out, drench their gear. We just need to buy time before we can get reinforcements down here.'

The hunched little woman cast her gaze around, wild and panicked. 'Water in caves, very bad! Damage machinery, pumps, flood caves – kill worms!'

'Worms?' Lemon looked at Chel and Foss. 'What's she talking about?'

509

'The glow, friend.' Foss gestured to the cool light of the dangling bead-strings overhead. 'This is where all the silk comes from.'

'Ooh. Eerie.'

'Listen,' Chel turned back to the artificer, 'if we don't do something, those bastards are going to come at us, through us, and they're going to take the city. A bit of water damage seems a small price to pay to prevent that, right?' The woman stared at him, rigid, her head shaking back and forth. He felt anger flaring. 'Then you have a better idea, right? Anything?'

Still her head shook, and Chel pursed his lips. Too much of his body hurt for this. The sounds of armed men echoed down the passageway, growing suddenly louder.

'Lemon, reckon you can find this reservoir?'

The Clyde hefted her axe. 'Oh, aye, you try and stop me.'

\*\*\*

Despite the artificer's protestations, the clacking of the remaining water-pumps led them to their quarry. A miniature indoor lake, dark and placid, the termination of half a dozen of the pumps. Other water chains and pumps rose from its surface, carrying water up into the city wherever it was needed. Chel marvelled at the ingenuity, then set about finding some way to drain it.

Lemon found a series of grates cut into the stone, beneath them a narrow passage of sorts, a thin trickle of water running along its floor. She called for help, and between them Foss and Chel managed to lift one of the grates. Lemon dropped inside, then called a moment later. She'd found the sluice gates.

She traced the channels, looking for the water's outflow. She called for the others and showed them what she'd found: the passage emptied into the tunnel beneath, and from there the water meandered down into the lower caverns, passing, inevitably, through the wide expanse where the confessors gathered.

'A tweak of them gates, boys, and we turn this trickle into a rush. Flood them out, drive them back out at the viaduct. Drown the slow ones if we're lucky, send a good number out into the gorge.'

Chel paused. 'Drown them? I thought we could, you know . . . Just push them back . . .'

Lemon gave him an even look. 'Aye, wee bear, drown them. There's a cubic fuck-ton of water in this here wee lake, and the rate it exits is going to smash out the tunnels below like a fucken hammer. This will not be a bloodless act.'

Foss put one hand on Chel's good shoulder. It felt very, very heavy. 'This is grim arithmetic, my friend: we take the lives beneath of those who would take countless more above. We must make our choice, then make our peace.'

'I . . . I can't do it. It was hard enough trying to destroy their engines without killing anyone.'

'You need not, friend. But someone must.'

'Right. Right.' Chel offered a weak grin, then cocked an ear. 'Hells, it sounds like they're on the move.' Chanting echoed from the passages below.

Lemon nodded, suddenly urgent. 'Then let's get out of this tunnel and get those pricks wet.'

'I thought that wasn't your kind of thing, Lem.'

'Oh, shut up, Fossy.'

They made back to the grate as the sound of the chanting

grew, undercut by the clink and jingle of the confessors' armour. 'Twelve hells, it must be all of them,' Foss muttered. Lemon went up through the grate first, boosted by Foss below. Chel tried to climb by himself but was glad of the assistance, his shoulder growling at the exertion.

'Hoy, wee artificer, how'd you go about . . . Ah, pig-piss, she's legged it.'

Chel hauled himself up beside her. 'What?'

'She's gone. Probably off scooping worms into her drawers. Fossy, you'd best come up here.'

Foss hadn't moved. Dark blood was caked across his face and body. 'Someone needs to open the gates by hand.'

'Aye, right, there's going to be a rope or pulley or some kind of mechanism—'

Foss had one ear cocked, but even Chel could hear the growing thump of marching feet from below, the chanting loud enough to discern its refrain. 'Don't feel we've got the time for hunting around, my friend. These gates look old and . . . ill-used.' He began to stomp off down the tunnel toward the gates, water splashing around his boots.

'Fossy! Fossy!' She started to go after him, but he ordered her back.

'Stay up there, friend, I might need a hand up in a moment. Anyway,' he looked down at the gore that coated him, 'could use a little cleansing splash.'

Foss reached the gates, dark sheets of stone in the murk. Chel and Lemon peered down from the grate, watching anxiously as he waggled an experimental grip beneath the first. The confessors were almost below them now, their chanting clear and rowdy, confident in their ascension.

Foss crouched before one of the gates, jammed his

fingers against the water's oozing flow, and with a roar began to stand. For a moment, nothing budged, then with a screech of protesting stone the gate began to lift, the dribble thickening to a pour, then a steady rush. Already water was coursing along the passage floor, frothing beneath where Chel and Lemon perched and away into the darkness. Was that an interruption in the chanting that he heard?

Foss roared again, and drove the gate higher, thumping it against its stop. Water rushed between his legs, hard and black, driving him back from the sluice. He seemed happy to follow, the water pouring dark and cold beyond his knees, and he began to wade toward the grate. From below the chanting faltered, obscured by the rush of the flood, those beneath it shouting in surprise and alarm.

Chel saw it from the corner of his eye as Foss waded back to them, a twitch of the black stone gate, a spasm. The water gushed in fury from beneath it, pursuing the big man like vengeance. Then the gate rocked and squeaked, as jets of white foam sprayed from the wall around it. The side of the reservoir was collapsing.

Lemon saw it too. 'Fossy! Run!'

He was turning, slow, ponderous, sapped by the greedy river at his thighs. Foss watched the gate crack and tear free, great chunks of stone wall in its wake, the wall of white-capped water surging down the passageway toward him. Lemon's hand was outstretched, Chel's with it, crying for him to stumble on, to reach up and leap for safety.

Foss looked up, his eyes tired, arms hanging loose and wearied. A slow smile formed on his bloodied lips.

'Peace,' he mouthed, his eyes closing, then the torrent took him.

The waters raged for longer than Chel thought possible, as both he and Lemon thrust numbed arms into the foaming spray, again and again until they were soaked and weeping. When finally the deluge passed, the last of the gurgling waters fading into the darkness, the passage beneath lay stark, slick, and empty but for Lemon's hoarse and echoing screams.

# THIRTY-SIX

It wasn't the pain that woke him, but the sound: rhythmic, low and muffled. It was the pain that kept him awake. His skin felt rasped, his bones jarred and his shoulder pulsed, but inside he was scratchy and raw. He had no idea how long he'd slept, but angled daylight sneaked through the gaps in the sand-sacks that blocked the arched windows, scattering odd patterns on the tasselled rug. The sun was still high. It was the same day.

They'd found Foss in one of the lower tunnels, still breathing but unconscious, and it had taken six of the late-arriving guards to carry him up. Lemon had pumped what water she could from his lungs, but he had not woken. It was likely he never would.

The sound came again, an incessant, cracked-voice murmuring. Lemon was curled in the corner, Foss's corner, lying against his motionless form, her body wrapped around him. She was saying his name, over and over, whispering reassurances and promises of shared activities when he woke. From the croak of her voice, she'd been doing so for hours.

'You're awake.'

Rennic sat against a pillar, legs extended, staring at the dancing motes in the shafts of light. He looked dry-eyed but flattened, and had a nasty, charred smell to him.

'Yeah.' Chel paused, searching for something to say. The side of his head throbbed hot and angry. He had no idea what he'd done to it. 'About what happened, I—'

'No.' Rennic cut him off with a gesture, pushed himself upright. That was it.

Chel stood with him, clutching his battered body, rolling his shoulder in its socket in an attempt to quell its rebellion. 'What's going on? Outside?'

'A lull.' Rennic sniffed, made a face. Clearly, he wasn't at peace with the stink that clung to him. 'Their gambit in the waterways failed, and they're marshalling topside for their next assault. I doubt we have long.'

'Should we do a circle or somethi—'

'No!' It was Lemon who spoke, her voice shredded raw. She rubbed at her eyes with her sleeves, forcing herself up on her knees. She looked thin. 'Why the fuck would you do that, wee bear? Circle's for the dead.'

Chel looked from her to Rennic and back, his mouth half-open, his question unspoken.

'Fossy's the toughest lad I ever saw,' Lemon went on as she stood, half to herself. 'Once saw him swim Lake Tulum in winter, against the current, no bother. Docks boy, he is, grew up on the water. Aye, nothing to worry about, he'll be back up and about in no time.'

'He will soon be dead. Like all the others.'

Chel hadn't even seen the little alchemist, huddled in an alcove, buried in cushions. She looked no better than Lemon, drawn, red-rimmed, hoarse. She dropped from the alcove and waved a finger over Lemon's protestations. 'We are just meat, just sacks of rotting flesh, frail, mortal. Our lives ended on another's whim, without care or consultation.

'Your friend will die, and the rest of us will join him soon enough. I hope you feel proud of your existence, because it is all you will get. It is all any of us gets, and it . . . it . . . it is not enough! Life cannot be so cheap, that we as living, thinking beings are so easily snuffed out. A lifetime of memories, relationships, thoughts, hopes, fantasies – gone! In an instant!' She whirled on Rennic. 'Those people in the courtyard, they were trapped, defenceless. They were tricked and beaten. And you . . . you murdered them all! You burned them to ash!'

Now Rennic stood tall over the Nort, his nostrils flared, hands flexed rigid and trembling. 'You say too much, alchemist. My patience for plush-living, would-be warriors telling me the hows and whys of war is a desperately scarce resource. I invite you to shut your fucking mouth while it remains within your power to do so.' He put a finger under her nose. 'I asked you if you had the stomach, and you decided. You make your choice, then you make your peace.'

Chel twitched at the echo of Foss's words. The little Nort shook, from fear, rage or both it was impossible to tell, then stormed for the door. 'Your friend will never wake!' she called again as she threw it open. 'And our lives are ending!'

'Go on, get to fuck,' Lemon called after her, a sob squeezing at her throat. 'You useless fucking piss-baby!'

The door slammed, then opened again, slowly. A harried face appeared, one of the Acting Keeper's remaining staff.

'His highness the prince has asked for you.'

\* \* \*

Chel and Rennic followed the flunky along the deserted
hallways, leaving Lemon to her murmured ministrations.

The palace appeared silent, eerie, not even the distant
clatter of activity echoing from the bare stone.

'Words or deeds,' Rennic murmured as they walked.

'What?'

'Huh?' He blinked, went quiet. Then, after a moment,
he spoke. 'I was thinking of the first man I killed.'

Chel waited. 'And?'

'That was what my captain asked me, when she heard.
"Words or deeds".'

'For why you'd killed him.'

'Yeah.'

'Which was it?'

They climbed the wide stone steps slower than before,
Chel feeling the burn of each in his legs.

'Words.' He paused again, and Chel thought that was
it, but after a moment he continued. 'It was in an alehouse,
took exception to another drinker. I'd had a few myself,
and was . . . younger. Fresh riding with the company.'

'You killed a man in an alehouse?'

'No.' He smiled to himself, but not happily. 'Waited
outside for him, seething, struck with his back turned. He
was bigger than me, a lot bigger. Then.'

'And was your captain pleased?'

'No. Not by my answer, nor my actions. You know what
she said? She said that one day I wouldn't even remember
what he'd said, that it would all be meaningless.'

The flunky nodded to them. 'His highness is with the
guard captains. You will be seen next.'

'My gracious thanks,' Rennic replied with a snarl.

They waited in the hall, each leaning on an opposite wall.

'What did he say?' Chel said. 'Your first victim.'

Rennic was quiet for a long time.

'I don't remember.'

\* \* \*

The Butterfly Chamber stood shattered, its balcony blocked with sand-sacks, its upper windows smashed, its glossy marble floors littered with piles of debris. Its former insect occupants appeared long-gone, but a few of their bejewelled silk facsimiles remained, tattered and dangling loose by their strings, crass and garish. Tarfel stood by the blockaded arch to the balcony, looking haggard and stooped, hair hanging like string around his ears. The two seneschals who attended him withdrew at Chel and Rennic's approach.

'My friends,' he mustered an unconvincing smile.

'Tarf,' Chel nodded. Rennic merely grunted. In the far reaches of the room came the echoes of whispered, desperate words of those sharing what they knew could be their last conversations. 'You summoned us.'

'I'm not going to dress it up,' the prince said, walking toward the balcony. 'Things are bad. As you might say, this city is fucked.'

Rennic nodded, as if this matched his expectations.

'What happened in the caves below the city led to the collapse of one of the aqueducts, the destruction of countless pieces of water-retrieval machinery and the loss of water supply to over a third of the city, including the workshops. This is without assessing the loss of silkworms and habitat to the flood. The damage to the city's prospects is severe.'

Chel started to protest, but the prince held up a hand. 'But. *But.* Corvel lost a huge number of his troops when the aqueduct collapsed, not to mention those who drowned in the caves or were discharged into the gorge.' The prince nodded to himself, smiling, but Chel felt a certain sickness at the thought of his hand in their deaths. 'A swathe of their confessors are gone, as are most of their mercenaries and ancillaries. Your destruction of those Mawn at the gate was sublime, Master Rennic, and you have my thanks.'

The mention of Mawn jumped Chel's gaze to Rennic, his eyes searching, but the big man's stony expression made no admissions. 'Part of the job,' he said.

'Is it right that you lost someone in the defence of the caves?'

Chel stiffened at the prince's use of 'you'.

Rennic sniffed and looked away. 'No.'

'Ah, good, good. And as for you, Vedren, my dear, dear Vedren.' Tarfel put a hand on his bad shoulder, and Chel grimaced. The prince didn't notice. 'What you did with those . . . those flying engines, those silken birds, why, it was magnificent! You may have saved us all, and I will ensure that the people of this city hear of it. You'll be a hero!'

Chel smiled, despite himself. 'Part of the job,' he said. Rennic frowned.

Tarfel lowered his voice. 'I wanted to thank you, Vedren, for your words when we arrived. I . . . doubted myself, and you gave me the strength to go on. We wouldn't have made it here without you.'

Chel nodded, but his smile had frozen. Somewhere in his head, a voice was whispering, *this is your fault, all this death and chaos.*

Rennic intervened, impatient. 'What are the scouts saying?' he said.

'That they may sue for a peaceful withdrawal after all. Perhaps they come for another parley to demand departure payment, perhaps they simply vanish into the night. Their engines are laid waste, their supplies shredded. Most of their non-believers have deserted, or no doubt plan to. That leaves a sizeable force, but their situation is greatly diminished. Another few days, and the outriders despatched by Exalted Matil may yet cross their supply lines and cut them off from behind.'

'Have you heard from the outriders?' Rennic said, moving past the piled sacks of sand onto the shaded balcony overlooking the plateau. The others followed.

'Not since they left.'

'Then they may not be coming. And we may not have a few days.'

'Taking me prisoner can't be worth that much more to them, surely? They have lost so many, they must realize that taking the city grows beyond them, let alone holding it. Even if the army doesn't revolt, every day out there, away from the seat of his power, increases my brother's vulnerability. The south must be disintegrating by now, Ruumi's reavers, the hill tribes, the free cities – how long will the Names stand by before they demand he take action, or take up arms against him themselves?'

Rennic nodded to the gorge. 'They still hold the bridge, and their long-wagon spans the gap.'

'True. But the city's captains attend my orders, and have rallied – to an extent. It seems I've learnt a few things from my time with you lot after all.' The prince offered a thin smile, which Rennic ignored.

'They can always build more engines.'

Chel pushed forward. 'If they build more engines, we'll

torch them with kites, like before. If they come over the bridge, you'll trap them and burn them, like before. We can see them off, for as long as it takes. As long as we have the workshops, we can fight them back.'

'That, little man, presupposes an overabundance of the alchemist's black powder and its constituents. Sounds like your escapades in the caves may have cleared out the precursors. We've got nothing but what's steeping in the workshops as we speak.'

Chel's jaw was jutting. 'Then what should we be doing? If everything is so dire, and all our plans are fruitless? Hm?'

Rennic's eyes gleamed in the gloom. 'Sally in the night. Cross their bridge before they do, kill the sentries, take them in their beds. Set the camp aflame, and whatever witchfire remains, before they wake.'

Chel was staring back in horror. 'But they might be on the verge of surrender!'

'Something like that should make up their minds for them.'

'. . . And I don't believe we have the manpower to launch such an assault,' Tarfel said ruefully. 'Speaking of which, would you happen to know the location of our alchemical friend? I understand she was in Lady Matil's chambers earlier, and left in a state of some distress.'

'We saw her, yeah. She left. Don't know where she is now. Probably skulking in the workshops.'

'I see.'

'How is the Keeper?' Chel asked.

'She still has yet to wake, but she lives. There is hope.' The prince turned to the plateau, watching it glow red in the light of the waning sun. 'Vedren is correct: while the workshops stand, impaired as they are, we retain our strength. But the structures that underpin this city are desperately weakened. If Corvel had any idea, he'd exploit it to the hilt.'

Rennic moved next to him. 'And if the people of the city knew that handing you over would end this in a heartbeat, they'd throw you across the gorge.'

Tarfel didn't blink. 'Then they had best remain ignorant.'

Rennic's lips curled, something like a smile. Then his brow lowered.

'Movement at the head of the bridge. They're coming again.' He straightened. 'Looks like no surrender after all.'

# THIRTY-SEVEN

Rennic returned from a further conference with the remaining guards and their captain, tightening the straps on his armour as he traversed the rubble-strewn courtyard. Chel picked at his own mail shirt, still hanging together despite its rough treatment, heavy and hot in the day's thick heat.

'They're making preparations,' the big man said, then stopped and looked Chel up and down. Something burned behind his eyes, something dark and driven, but it wasn't aimed at Chel. 'You got the strength for this, little man? You want to head back, sit this one out with Lemon and Foss, I'd get it. You need the rest.'

Chel shook his head. 'I'm fine. Can't leave you unsupervised, anyway. You'd only fuck something up.' In truth, he was shattered, but as long as he kept moving he could push the exhaustion from his mind and his muscles. And Rennic's look worried him. He'd made little acknowledgment of Foss's mortal state, but after the violence of his reaction to Whisper's loss, after what had happened with Grassi, Chel could not shake the notion that the big man was about to do something suicidally reckless. Loveless's words echoed in his head. *Watch him for me.*

Rennic nodded, that snorted half-smile again. 'No doubt, little man.'

Chel followed him toward the low, blocky form of the third gate.

'What's the plan? Let them come at the gate, hold the walls?'

'Come at the gate? At this gate? Are you soft, little man? This is the last gate, the oldest, the weakest. This fucker hasn't been closed in centuries. A stiff breeze could level it. No, we're going out to face them.'

'Leave the walls? But—'

'Yes, yes.' Rennic bent and hefted a spear from a rack, testing its edge and flex, whistling it around his head and body in a sudden display of martial prowess. 'Hurkel will be leading them. No way they'd be coming otherwise. That arse-faced fuck has made this personal.'

'And that means we should ride to meet him?'

'He's arrogant, selfish, self-important – he'll want to be the one to break the last gate. Take him down, those red pricks will be dead in their tracks. Cut the head off the snake.'

'Why not just shoot him? Kosh's crossbow is fixed, right?'

He snorted, blew dust from the spear-tip. 'Little man, this is something that needs to be seen to be done.'

'And you think you can beat him, one-to-one? He's smashed everyone he's faced to mush, and he's plated like an engine. It's not like I can hit his knees again – tried that in Black Rock, and it damned near got us executed. It did for Dalim and Palo.'

'But this time we're not locked in a tower, and the terrain favours us. And old prune-face has a fatal weakness.'

'What?'

'You. He thirsts for you, little man. And that's going to come in handy.'

The day darkened, thick clouds the colour of a coal-face sliding overhead. Somewhere over the plains, thunder rumbled, echoing from the mountains. Rennic's manic smile widened.

'I'd say there's a storm coming, wouldn't you?'

He flexed the spear and made for the gate.

\*\*\*

He was at the front, of course, rolling on his chariot. His wolf head was lost or burned away, the skin beneath livid and scarred, and great black-scorched plates coated his form, but Brother Hurkel still moved with power and menace. He was coming for them, and behind him marched a legion of confessors. It baffled Chel that there could still seem so many of them, after the losses they'd suffered above and below ground. Corvel's army was no longer immense, but it still overwhelmed the meagre defenders who remained.

Rennic stood on the bridge, a few paces from the lip of the long-wagon's boards. Wreckage littered the bridge's ruined stump, chunks of stone and wooden fragments, even a couple of near-whole kegs, blasted clear of the conflagration that had sundered the structure beneath. Rennic hooked one of the kegs with a foot, then rolled it beneath his boot as he waited for Hurkel to arrive. Chel wondered if it still contained black powder, and if Rennic was in danger of blowing his leg off before their enemy even reached them.

Hurkel reined in his chariot before the long-wagon, crimson face lit with delight at the sight of Rennic and Chel, alone before the ruins of the collapsed gatehouse. Somewhere behind them, Chel hoped, were the last of the Serican forces, dug in behind the stones, ready to spring to their aid. He watched Hurkel dismount, his eyes like black marbles in his beetroot face, his chuckles lost to the breeze. Chel's grip tightened on his headless mace.

'Sand-crab! Faithless one! Have you come to treat? The Shepherd is ready to hear your confession.'

He lumbered up onto the bridging wagon, stomping over the reinforced timbers, a heavy club in his remaining hand. Behind him, the confessors formed up behind the wagon, their front rank tucked behind what shields they had salvaged. Hurkel stopped before the giant wheels that marked the wagon's extension, where its long platform projected across the span of shattered bridge. It seemed he was in no hurry to cross the void. He was still calling to them, arms wide and grinning.

Rennic stopped rolling the keg, flicked it on end. His eyes were black, his knuckles white around the spear's haft.

'Oh. Shut. *Up*, you metal meat-stick. You want the Andriz?' He nodded at Chel, who tried to look imperious. 'Come and get him, mangle-bollocks.'

Rennic took a step forward, and Chel went with him. Rennic paused, looked at him sidelong.

Chel pre-empted the admonition. 'You're not doing this alone. You can't take him by yourself.'

Rennic nodded. 'You're right. But remember—'

The fist caught him under the ribcage, driving upwards, bursting the air from his lungs. He reeled, wheezing, his diaphragm in spasm, as Rennic's arms guided him down and backward.

'Have a seat, little man. I'll call for you.'

Then Rennic surged away, spear leading, leaving Chel propped on the upended keg, arms wrapped around his midriff, gasping for air.

Rennic charged toward Hurkel, pounding onto the long-wagon's span. He was roaring. Hurkel mirrored his roar, giving a great bellow of ecstatic fury, then barrelled forward onto the wagon's platform. It bowed but did not budge against the stones.

They met with a thunder of steel, Rennic leaping fully from the boards to drive the spear at Hurkel's face. The armoured confessor twisted, shielding himself with one metal arm and threw out a shower of sparks as the spear-tip screeched over his metal covering. Then around came the club, whistling through the air as Rennic ducked.

The spear returned, jabbing, driving, smashing against Hurkel's steel shell. He was too big to duck, too ponderous to dodge, and Rennic landed hammer-blow after hammer-blow against the confessor's carapace, driving the bigger man back toward the bulk of the wagon. Great booms echoed over the gorge as each jab found its mark, drowning Hurkel's snarls and curses as he gave ground under the assault. Behind him, the line of confessors shifted, their glances twitchy; a few were taking forward steps toward the wagon's tail.

Rennic's attacks were slowing, his onslaught ebbing as Hurkel shuffled back toward his lines. For all its savage fury, all Rennic had to show for the dozen hits he'd landed were as many nicks and scratches on Hurkel's blackened plate. The metal beneath shone through the soot and tar-streaked surface and Rennic's spear-tip was already notched and blackened from the contact. Rennic ducked left then snaked right, throwing out the spear again, at last catching Hurkel's cheek above the metal wall. But the bigger man rode the hit, rolling around it and snagging the spear's haft with his pronged half-hand.

Hurkel twisted, and Rennic stumbled. Around swung the club again, and Rennic released the spear and threw himself sideways to avoid its crushing blow. The club smashed through the spear in Hurkel's fork-grip. Its shattered pieces dropped to the scarred wood beneath.

Rennic was back on his feet, a knife in his hand, but the mood on the ruined bridge had changed. Now Hurkel was ascendant, taking steady, heavy steps toward his adversary; Rennic matched his even pace in retreat, snatching swift glances to the sides where the gorge yawned beneath them.

Chel's breath had still not returned. He tried to gulp in air, but his lungs were unresponsive, intransigent. His head rocked and bobbed, his knees weak, watching Rennic forced back onto the long, creaking platform with the grinning Hurkel in pursuit. The confessors on the bridge had begun to chant. Hurkel matched his steps to the rhythm of their words.

Rennic tried an attack, a feint then a slash with the knife toward Hurkel's bloodied face. Too quick, the confessor's arm was up, then Rennic was falling backward as the club hissed past his arm. He turned back toward Chel, meeting his eyes, opening his mouth to speak. This was the signal. Chel tried to stand, to be ready, but he could not force the air down inside him.

The club hit Rennic square in the back, and with a cry, he flew. His body lurched across the platform, crashing into the boards at its edge, slumping and sliding and slipping from sight. For a moment, he was there, then his legs were over the side and he vanished.

Chel stared, open-mouthed, his winding forgotten. He felt cold all over, frozen in space.

Hurkel took a step toward where Rennic had disappeared, then stopped, and brayed a honking laugh over the gorge. Behind him, at the wagon's end, the confessors had paused their chant, but now it resumed with greater urgency. Hurkel swivelled his ponderous form toward Chel and began a slow stomp toward him. He was chuckling.

'Sand-crab! At last we shall attend to your soul. Prepare to make your peace, and receive the Shepherd's mercy!'

Chel forced himself to stand, sucking in thin breaths at last. The mace felt brittle in his hand. He wondered if the archers were still behind him in the rubble, whether one would be able to land a hit on Hurkel's unarmoured parts. It seemed a faint hope. How strange, he thought, after everything he'd experienced, to be killed by Hurkel in the end. Had the Norts not arrived when they had, Hurkel could have resolved this in Denirnas lowport and saved everyone a lot of bother.

The sky had gone black, and the wind had dropped. He felt the first delicate patter of rain.

His eyes prickled with tears.

*I was supposed to be lucky.*

Something moved in the blurred corner of his vision, something at the platform's edge. A dark-clad figure hauling itself back onto the timber, moving slowly, painfully. Bright hope bloomed in Chel's chest. He tried not to alert Hurkel, but already the confessors were shouting, their chanting fallen away.

The Pentarch turned as Rennic pulled himself clear, then up onto one knee. He was breathing with great difficulty. Part of Chel smirked at the irony.

'Didn't I kill you once already?' Hurkel bellowed, taking a step in Rennic's direction.

Wincing, Rennic ignored him. 'Little man,' he called, his voice strained. 'Keg.'

Chel looked down at the keg, his seat until a moment before.

'Throw me the fucking keg!'

He dropped his mace and grabbed the keg. With a grunt, he set it rolling, bouncing along the platform toward where Rennic knelt. Hurkel watched it roll, crimson face scrunched in deep suspicion. He quickened his stomping pace. Bobbling, the keg began to bounce wide, drifting off toward the edge. Lunging, Rennic grasped it as Hurkel closed.

'Let damnation claim you!' the confessor bellowed.

In one sharp movement, Rennic snatched up the keg and lifted it, both-handed, over his head.

'You first, fuck-stick.'

He hurled the keg at Hurkel's head. Instinctively, the confessor threw up his fork-arm, driving the points of his trident into the oncoming object. The battered wood of the keg split around his blow, flooding black powder down his metal-clad arm and coating him with choking dust. The shattered keg disgorged its contents over the confessor's body, piling around his steel-shod feet, clinging to the tarred and bloodied plates in clumps and runnels.

Hurkel staggered backward, coughing, shaking the impaled keg free, dropping his club to paw at his face with his remaining hand. He was a long way onto the platform, too far for any confessor from the bridge to reach him.

531

Rennic was standing now, poised at the fringe of Hurkel's powder-splash.

'Brother Hurkel.'

In one hand was another knife.

'Hurkel.'

In the other was his flint.

Chel's still-uneven breath caught. He wanted to swallow but could not. He wanted to shut his eyes but could not.

Hurkel cleared dust from his eye and looked at Rennic, looked at the blackened boards beneath him, the powder that coated his scorched plate.

Chel waited for the moment, transfixed. He didn't want to watch Hurkel die. He didn't want to see him live.

'Do you yield, Brother Hurkel?'

Chel blinked. Rennic met his gaze for the merest instant, his shoulders twitching in a micro-shrug.

'Yield, and leave this bridge. Take your red friends back to your pretend emperor. Tell him you lost.'

Hurkel's reply was a wordless howl, and he surged forward.

Rennic's hand moved very fast.

*Snap. Snap. Whoosh.*

The air around Hurkel went first, as the spark ignited the finest particles. Immediately the armoured confessor was surrounded by a blazing halo of light, then the powder on his plating caught, followed by his tuft of hair. Still he charged, as the flames spread down his body and lit the boards of the platform beneath him, surrounding him in an ocean of fire. Rennic was already stumbling backward, faltering for the platform's end where Chel stood motionless. Hurkel pursued, a black metal demon at the heart of a pillar of flame.

*I dreamt this*, Chel thought, as Rennic scrambled toward him and the screaming, burning beast came after him. *Or something like it.*

Rennic was shouting. Rennic was shouting at Chel.

'—back before he sets you off too!'

The platform was burning, the flames hissing steam as the rain thickened. Hurkel was burning, his heavy steps unsteady, lurching and lunging toward the bridge's broken end. His face was lost within the flames, just a blistered, screaming husk at the heart of the firestorm. He seemed to be heading for Chel.

'Little man!' Rennic was calling, patting out one smouldering sleeve as he made for the rubble. 'Little man!'

There seemed nothing human left in Hurkel's searing armour, but still it moved, staggering onwards as if by demonic will, step after halting step. In its wake it left a blazing trail, and already the platform was sagging as its timbers blackened and burned. The handful of confessors who'd started forward in Hurkel's pursuit fell swiftly back.

'I should . . .' Chel said, staring into the sizzling mass where Hurkel's face had been. The pain had to be indescribable.

Hurkel lurched, reaching the platform's end, only paces from where Chel stood. Already Chel could feel the incredible heat that boiled off the armoured form, seeing the plates blister and bubble within the tower of flame.

*Make your choice, then make your peace.*

The mace was back in his hand. 'I should . . . show him mercy.' He tensed to swing.

Hurkel swayed, stepped, and dropped from the edge. A puddle of flame marked his exit, along with a billow of choking black smoke. The world seemed suddenly darker. The rain was getting thicker.

Rennic called again, and Chel turned toward the city. He was thinking of Heali, the avuncular guardsman in the winter palace of Denirnas Port. The man who'd betrayed him, tried to stab him on the battlements, who'd fallen in flames to his doom below. The first man Chel had seen die.

'Told you . . .' Rennic wheezed, doubled over, 'I'd call . . . for you.'

In the distance, thunder grumbled, then the lightning hit.

Chel saw the flash, then his eyes had only the after-image of the thunderbolt, a pulsing line of purple-black from churning cloud to darkened city, sending a cascade of sparks into the lightless sky. For a heartbeat silence reigned, then the thunder rolled over them, a terrifying crack as if the earth had torn. The rain began to hammer down, a gathering rush of water borne on the wind's fury. In moments Chel was drenched.

Then he saw the bright burr of flames, carving outwards through the driving rain from the site of the lightning's discharge. The workshop tower was aflame.

Rennic was still bent double, trying to draw air into his battered ribcage. He waved an encouraging hand toward the gate.

'This has been a shitty day,' Chel said, pushing his aching legs back toward the city.

# THIRTY-EIGHT

Chel stood in the slackening drizzle, evening mist mixing with the steam from the smouldering ruin of the outer workshop. The building stood stricken, its tower burned to a smoking nub, the long assembly rooms shorn of wall and roof, their contents blackened and wrecked. He felt much the same, hollowed and collapsed, numb. His mind simply rejected the news, the sight before him.

Tarfel was beside him, standing in the steaming plaza, receiving reports with an expression of stone. He looks the part, Chel thought idly. He didn't blink when they told him the workshops were lost. Or perhaps he's simply past caring now.

Again, Chel looked around for Rennic, and again he saw no sign. He'd lost the big man in the race back into the city, and their paths had not crossed since. He wanted to sit down. He thought if he did, he would never stand again.

'. . . seems the new chief engineer, your northern alchemist, was inside when the lightning hit.' A captain was reporting to Tarfel, his accent near-flawless. 'She attempted to douse the flames, but the tanks were empty, the water drained from below. When she sought help . . .' He consulted his notes. 'A group calling themselves the Children of the Storm pursued her inside, and it seems their interventions exacerbated the damage. Had it not been for the actions of the Clydish mercenary, the engineer would doubtless have died in the fire.'

Tarfel nodded. 'Any other survivors?'

'Just the chief engineer. There are . . . bodies . . . inside, citizens and refugees, one of our seneschals, an attendant of Exalted Matil. We have the survivors of the group.'

'Take the chief engineer into protective custody.'

'Custody, highness?'

'*Protective* custody. Keep her somewhere safe, let nobody near her. She is too important to leave at risk.'

'And the others, highness?'

*Kill them all.* Chel felt as much as thought it, unbidden to the forefront of his mind. His mouth tweaked in a mirthless smile. So much for righteousness.

The prince paused, reflective. 'They have caused irreparable harm, but they remain citizens and potential citizens. Good people can have bad ideas. Hold them, and we will try them in more peaceful times.'

The captain saluted and marched away. Tarfel caught Chel's look and flashed the briefest of smiles. 'More peaceful times, Vedren, eh? Once the last stone of this city is levelled and its citizens ash, then we'll come back to our dear prisoners.' He walked to his next report, leaving Chel uneasy.

He walked to where Lemon lay, tightly bandaged, on a low pallet. They'd cleaned most of the blood off her, and beneath it she looked deathly pale.

'All right, wee bear?' she croaked. 'You're looking mighty

roughty-toughty. Get your arse handed to you on the bridge, eh?' When she grinned, blood shone from her teeth.

He offered the best smile he could manage. 'Looking good yourself. Is it true they pulled three bolts out of you?'

'Aye, right, three my freckled arse.' She blew at a loose strand of hair, freed from a braid and drifting across her blood-dappled face. 'Must have been at least seven. Easy-fucken-peasy.' She laughed, then winced, her arms so tightly strapped to her sides she could barely move. 'Ouchie. Ach, I told her those things were dangerous. I told her.'

'You saved her life.'

'Ah, what can I say? We do the strangest things for the ones we loathe.'

'Highness!' Another scout from somewhere. They were younger and younger.

'Yes?' came Tarfel's voice.

'Black flag at the bridge.'

Lemon offered Chel a sickly grin. 'Sounds like you'd better pop along, wee bear.'

'You'll be all right?'

'Me? My porters will be here any moment. Fossy and I are going to have a nice little lie-down upstairs. Go on, off you sod. Your day's not over yet.'

\* \* \*

Vashenda had aged in the few days since he'd seen her last. Chel wondered if she was thinking the same of him. This time she came alone but for a single hulking guard. He'd brought no one. He'd had no one to bring, and felt so numbed to danger by now that the thought of being betrayed and murdered seemed fanciful, not terrifying. They met at the centre of the bridge, Chel walking the surviving boards of the damaged long-wagon with a casual ease that masked his exhaustion. This time, he had no trouble staring past the blackened wood into the darkness below. He and Lemon had flown over the gorge, then soared back. Walking over it seemed . . . pedestrian.

'Sand-flower.'

'Where's your boss?'

She didn't rise to it. 'Sand-flower, you must bring the prince. His majesty has demanded it, and . . .' She leaned a touch closer, her gaze flicking to the armoured form at her shoulder. '. . . He is desperate.'

'Desperate?'

'I can say no more. But with the Pentarch removed, I can guarantee his safety at any parley.'

'What does Prince Tarfel have to gain by exposing himself to such risk? Your forces are spent. Your engines are wrecked. Your supplies are dwindling. You'll be in full retreat by noon.'

'Sand-flower, you don't understand.' She rubbed her palms against her hollowed eyes. 'He will never give up. We lost hundreds of men, drowned, in the caverns of the city, and his only words were that they had failed him, they had failed the kingdom. The . . . empire. The south has fallen to anarchy – reavers have swallowed the south-west, the territories are aflame . . . Even the rebel cities of the south are riding out, pushing their insurrections into the wider kingdom. He does not care. He has emptied our coffers in pursuit of the black powder. He has summoned the armies. All of them. Every oath-holder and pennant in the kingdom, every brotherhood. They must come to this place, to the ruin of the lands, because he has decreed it.'

'Sounds like your problem, not ours.'

'Either way, this is another war without end. He will throw his forces against the city, dash them on its rock until it sinks into the gorge, all to claim his brother. Or the lordlings of the wetlands will find their mettle and declare on him, and mire our nation in another war of succession. Your prince, should he survive beyond the morrow, will be just one more loose end in need of the blade.'

'So, we surrender? On your word?'

'Sand-flower, on my eternal soul as a servant of the Shepherd, I do not lie. You must bring the prince to his brother.'

'The word of a prelate of the Rose. Consider me *utterly* reassured.'

\* \* \*

'Did a chunk of stone land on your head? You cannot be giving this serious consideration.'

Rennic looked both wild and hollow, windblown and wide-eyed. He paced the rampart around Tarfel and Chel with an unnatural energy. Chel doubted he'd slept in the time since he'd seen him last; he'd simply reappeared on the ramparts, no mention of his whereabouts since the events on the bridge. He did not look rested in the misty evening light. Neither of them had mentioned their stricken friends, but the words not spoken yawned between them as wide as the gorge beyond the walls.

The ache of exhaustion hung heavy on Chel's bones, the pulse of his shoulder vying with a thousand other hurts, and beneath it all the savage, sinking yawn of worry for his friends. Vashenda's words played over and over in his mind, their echo of Tarfel's qualms when they arrived. What have we accomplished, after all? he thought. Set half the kingdom on a path to ruin, handed its people to bloodthirsty Horvaun, let tribal raiders thicken their arms, brought Arowan to its knees and Korowan to ash and dust. So many dead and maimed, all to keep Tarfel from his brother's clutches, and now . . . and now . . . ?

I was trying to do the right thing. I was trying to do my duty. I wanted to stop the wars.

But all I did was make new ones.

Tarfel stared from the rampart, over two shattered gatehouses and the broken bridge, to the distant flutter of the black flag in the banks of mist that sat thick in the gorge and rolled over the plateau, burnished crimson in the sun's dying light. It almost looked like a tide of blood.

'The city is doomed,' he said. 'The water system is wrecked, our links to the plains unusable. The workshops are destroyed, and with them our best hope at overcoming their greater numbers. We've lost what black powder we had, and our alchemist seems unable or unwilling to make more. Sister Vashenda is right, more troops will come, and bring more witchfire, more black powder with them. Without the alchemist's kites, without her weapons, they will level what remains. Assuming we don't run out of food or water beforehand.'

'And what difference will getting yourself killed make to any of that?' Rennic stopped before the prince, his finger extended, nostrils wide. 'They will murder you and put your head on a pole, and all this will have been for nothing. Nothing.'

He swivelled, his arm sweeping over the mist-shrouded plateau. 'These fuckers are lost and they know it. There might be more of them than us, but their engines are gone, their supplies too, and without that meat-puppet Hurkel they're just scared boys and grudging levies, a long fucking way from home. They will break, and soon.' He placed his hands on the parapet, his grip hard and trembling. 'And when they do, we will fall upon them like the wolf on the fold.'

Chel stirred. 'Massacre them in retreat?'

Rennic didn't even look at him. 'Don't worry, little man, you and your sad little stick won't be needed.'

Tarfel looked unmoved. 'If I declare, they will spare the city. It will have a chance to rebuild, to repair the bridge to the plains, for those trapped to evacuate.'

'Horseshit! It's a ruse, and you'd have to be a fucking fool to fall for it.'

Tarfel turned his head slightly. 'You address a prince and the Acting Keeper of this city, Master Rennic. Please mind your words where others can overhear.'

Rennic's eyebrows raised in furious incredulity, but he said nothing. The guards on the rampart, stationed at a discreet distance, shifted innocently.

Tarfel ran his hands through his matted, greasy hair and sighed. 'What a burden is command! How I wish Exalted Matil were back with us – she could take it from my hands and decide my fate.'

'You want to be a ruler?' Rennic snarled. 'Rulers decide. They wouldn't be called decisions if they made themselves.' He sniffed, looked away. 'Your *highness*.'

'Vedren? What do you think?'

Chel looked up from his dark ruminations. 'Hm?'

'Can they be trusted, Vedren? Your actions, and advice, have brought me this far after all. Can I trust this offer?'

His red, hollow eyes betrayed the true question: *Should I take this offer?*

Chel's throat felt very dry. He felt Rennic's furious gaze upon him, his burning expectation. It was clear what his answer was expected to be.

He swallowed.

'Yes.'

Rennic wheeled on him. 'Little man, you fucking—'

'The rest of the kingdom will be long wrecked before they retreat, and Arowan sunk into the gorge with it. This is the reverse of our intentions. The right thing now . . . the right thing is to give up the fight. Let our pride go.'

Tarfel nodded, breathing deep, then straightened the clasp of his cloak. With trembling hands, he unfastened the Keeper's chain from his belt and held it out to Chel.

'You're not serious!' Rennic was up from the wall, his hands up, in placation or threat. 'There's still a way to win here, to come out—'

'Vedren, you've been a sterling friend.' Tarfel extended the chain to Chel. He took it with numb fingers. 'Mind things for me until Matil comes round, eh? Perhaps I'll see you soon.'

He started walking toward the steps, holding himself very straight. Chel stared at the heavy, ornate chain in his hands, then threw off his lethargy. He lurched to the nearest guard, told him to hold the chain, and stumbled after Tarfel.

Rennic got there first. He blocked the stairway with his body, towering over the slender prince, a quivering wall of furious muscle. 'I will not let you go. I will not let you give yourself to them, after all we've suffered to keep you alive!'

'Get out of the way, Master Rennic. It's precisely because of that that I must go.'

'My friends are wrecked, you worthless shit! Maimed, fled or dead. Your death would make their loss for nothing!'

Tarfel stood very still, staring up at the brooding hawk-nosed face. He swallowed, then said, 'Then there's something you should know. Whisper's death: it was absolutely my fault. I meant what I said at the crossroads. Were it not for my self-involvement, my stupidity, she'd still be alive today.'

Rennic stopped moving, and something broke in his eyes. A ferocious punch sent the prince flying backward, thumping hard against the stone.

'You gutless fucker,' Rennic said, his voice low and eyes dark. 'Nobody kills you but me!'

'Rennic!' Chel was there at last, ponderous, weak. 'Rennic!' He threw himself in front of the big man, trying to drive him back as he loomed over the prince. The guards were moving, sluggish from shock. Chel wrestled against him, lacking the strength to do any more than slow his advance. Images of the fight in the mud of the crossroads flashed before his eyes, his mouth full of dirt, Rennic's foot on his neck. A repeat seemed on the cards.

A knee drove into his battered midriff, then rough hands heaved him out of the way. A knife flashed from Rennic's belt, but the guards were on him, a pair of them leaping and driving him to the stone beside Chel. A third kicked the knife from his hand, a sword-blade to his throat.

'Don't kill him.' Tarfel was on his feet, a long strip of blood running from nose to chin. 'He doesn't know any better.' Tarfel turned back to the stairs.

Chel pushed himself to his knees, fighting fresh waves of pain. 'Tarfel! Wait. I'm still your sworn. I can't let you go alone.'

The prince stopped. 'You're right, Vedren,' he said, turning his head. 'Hereby in the sight of God and these witnesses, I release you from your oath. Your service is ended.'

'What? Just . . . like *that*? After everything?'

'You've done more than enough, Vedren. Now as your prince, I command you: don't follow me.'

Then he was gone, footsteps echoing from the stairway.

Chel struggled up, as Rennic threw off the retreating guards. As Chel moved toward the stairs, Rennic growled. 'The fuck do you think you're going?'

'I can't let him just—'

'Lost your ears? You're released. No obligations. A free bird. You don't have to keep him alive any more. Time to choose, boy. A real choice, the choice of who you are, who you want to be. One of us, or one of them? Free man or lickspittle? Life on the road or at the foot of a prince's bed?'

'Why can't—'

Rennic shook his head. 'Know this, little man. You go off after him, the next time we meet it won't be as friends. Understand?'

A messenger pelted onto the rampart, then pulled up in confusion. 'Message for his highness. Where is Prince Tarfel?'

Chel kept his gaze on Rennic. 'Stepped away. I'm his first sworn. What's the message?'

'Two messages. Bridge to plains is repaired.'

'And the second?'

'Her Radiance, Exalted Matil is awake.'

Chel stared into Rennic's eyes, seeing only blackness. Whatever fury lurked within was cold and dark, and his voice was a caustic snarl. 'Don't you—'

Chel held the gaze. 'I'll make my own choices, Gar Rennic,' he said, in echo of Loveless's words. He turned to the messenger. 'I'll see that the prince gets the news.'

Butterflies in his gut, he made for the stairs.

\* \* \*

Chel pelted over the broken stone of the ancient bridge, swathed in drifting banks of mist that boiled up from the churning gorge. The world seemed close and muffled, the deepening twilight doing little to penetrate the rolling shroud that lay over the plateau. The only sounds were the slap of his feet on the slabs and the rasp of his breathing. It was easy to believe he was the only soul left alive in the world.

He saw the prince at the bridge's end, a vague silhouette beneath the lingering standard of the black flag. His muscles burning with acid, he sprinted after him, gasping to catch him before he reached the army's lines. A moment later the prince was gone, lost in grey. Chel gritted his teeth and pushed on.

He was two steps onto the plateau when something hit him across the chest and knocked him from his feet. Rough hands seized him and dragged him up, at the end of reddish shapes in his blurred vision.

'Fuck's this? Straggler?' said a voice.

'Bring him along,' came Vashenda's cold reply. 'Try not to bruise him.'

\* \* \*

The grand pavilion had several chambers, and they'd reached the threshold of the innermost. Tables stood piled with charts and candlesticks, odd marks of luxury – a fur-covered chair, a pile of silken cushions – dotted within the austerity. The pavilion was lined with a clutch of scarred and brooding types, lordlings and captains, looking lean and cold. No one was clean. A single brazier burned at the chamber's centre, its dark smoke wafting through a gap at the peak of the canvas roof.

Chel twisted against the grip of the men who held him, but it was more for the look of the thing. In truth, he was glad that someone was keeping him upright. The strength was gone from his limbs, and he felt only numbness from south of his chest.

Vashenda stood before the canopy to the innermost chamber. Tarfel was with her, manacles at his wrists. His head was lowered, but he stood taller than Chel remembered, his shoulders back, no attempt to wipe the blood from his face.

'Your highness Prince Tarfel,' Vashenda said, 'I present His Majesty, Chosen-Emperor-in-Waiting, Lord of Land, Sea and Sky, Heir to New Taneru, Corvel the Magnificent.' She drew back the canopy.

On the gilded seat within sat a suit of glorious, gleaming armour, a full plate masterpiece of metalwork and artistry. Lions roared across its breastplate, its shoulders were spreading trees of gold. Its helmet was tall and peaked, banded with thick and glossy fur like a mane. It shone like a star in the brazier's light.

It was empty.

Corvel lay on a pallet at the rear of the chamber, pale and shining. He pushed himself to his elbows as Tarfel shuffled into the room, and Chel was shocked to see how shrivelled he was, wasted almost to the bone. His skin looked yellow, and it wasn't just the brazier-light. His once-golden hair lay matted and sweat-streaked, but when he smiled at his brother he looked a flash of his old, beaming self.

'Brother, you came,' he said.

Tarfel nodded. 'I did.'

'Come closer, let me see you.' Tarfel moved closer, with reluctance. Chel couldn't see his face, but he guessed the prince's horror was obvious.

'Brother, you look tired,' Corvel said with another drunken smile. 'Have you been eating enough?' He broke away to cough, hard and long, into a cupped hand. The fit lasted longer than Chel thought possible, and Corvel collapsed back onto the bed as it passed. Bright blood stained his palm.

'I'll take this one.' Vashenda was at Chel's elbow, steering him away from the surprised confessors who'd held him. Chel looked at her askance, but she stared straight ahead, moving him to an empty space by the bunched canopy.

'Told you he was desperate,' she murmured. 'I wish to God you'd come before.'

'What—'

'Shh. Keep looking ahead.' He realized she was slightly taller than him, or perhaps he was shrinking from exhaustion. 'White plague,' she said after a moment. They were apart from the others in the pavilion, and it seemed Vashenda wanted someone to talk to. 'Strangest thing. Some pox-riddled peasant at a triumphal, just ran at him. Managed to cough on him before he was hacked apart. That was all it took, Shepherd's mercy.' She shook her head and made the sign of the crook.

Chel felt a strange coldness in his gut. He'd only ever

heard of one person speak of using the plague-afflicted as a weapon. But Spider was dead. Spider had to be dead.

Lemon's words again: *did you see a body? Nobody's dead until you see a body.*

Corvel was speaking again, and Tarfel replying, their voices low. Chel was close enough to listen if he strained.

'. . . My works, brother. I may not be able to complete the restoration. You must continue it, as my successor.' Tarfel was shaking his head, in disagreement or disbelief. 'The Empire is too important, it is the only way we can bring peace to these divided lands. Only through empire can we unify the peoples as one. Unity. Purpose. Greatness. You understand. Only one of my blood could understand.'

He stopped to cough again, less aggressive this time.

'You wanted only peace?' Tarfel said, his tone acerbic, but Corvel either missed it or ignored it as he quelled his hacking. The emperor-in-waiting laid back against the pallet, lips flecked with blood, sweat glossy on his brow.

'Brother, where are you? My eyes are . . . weakened.' Tarfel took a reluctant step forward, taking his brother's unbloodied hand with a look of revulsion. He kept his head averted, no doubt mindful of the danger of contracting the plague himself. 'Ah, Tarfel, my sweet baby brother. They found it, you know. The proof, in the archives of citadel. Everything we always knew.' He coughed again, rattling in his sunken chest. Tarfel turned his head away until it passed.

Corvel's failing eyes opened wide and delirious. 'Brother, it is our birthright. We are descended from emperors!'

Tarfel withdrew his hand, dabbed at something spattering his chest with a careful sleeve. 'Brother, why did mother kill herself?'

Corvel frowned, his eyes still unfocused. 'Does it matter?

She had served her purpose long before. She had . . . borne us . . .'

Tarfel's reply was a vicious hiss. 'And you never thought to . . . *mention* her?'

He moved close, leaning over the pallet, his face approaching his brother's. Only Chel and Vashenda could see them now. Corvel's breathing was coming in rattling rasps.

'Your Imperial Majesty,' Tarfel said, 'you look spent. Perhaps we should pray.' Tarfel rested his cupped hands on his brother's chest, the manacle chains spooling over him. Corvel's breathing grew shallow and tight, and panic clouded his staring eyes. His mouth moved, tongue flicking over bloodied lips, but no words came out.

Chel glanced at Vashenda, then at the others in the pavilion. They seemed oblivious, wilfully or otherwise.

Tarfel leaned in close, his head bent over his brother's chest, his back to the main pavilion. Ostensibly he was praying, but Chel saw the movement of his lips, the shape of his words.

'Do not fear for your empire, brother. You will soon be dead, and in your place . . .' The prince paused, allowing the full weight of his chained hands to rest on his brother's struggling chest. Corvel's eyes went wide, fresh blood livid at his mouth, the thin cords of his shrunken neck proud and trembling.

Tarfel leaned a little further over his shaking brother, the chains pressing down on his shrivelled chest.

'. . . I will destroy your every deed. I will scrub you from the archives.

It will be as if you never.

Lived.'

Corvel breathed sharply, once, twice, gasping for air, sightless eyes wide and white, roving in their sockets, then fell still: an empty, lifeless sack of bones. Tarfel stepped back as if in shock, dragging the manacles from his brother's collapsed body, then cried, loud enough for the rest of the pavilion, 'Brother? Oh, Shepherd's mercy, my brother, my last and only brother, how could it be?'

Chel was staring at him, his mouth dry. Had he just witnessed Tarfel killing his own brother? Corvel was motionless, what little colour had lit his cheeks now departed, leaving behind a cooling waxen husk. Chel looked to Vashenda, but she ignored his glance. Instead, she stepped forward, entering the inner pavilion. She walked past Tarfel, slowly approaching Corvel's pale and wasted form. She made the sign of the crook and said a prayer.

'The king is dead.'

'No!' The cry came from the back of the pavilion. Pushing himself forward came Esen Basar, Chel's ducal nemesis. 'He killed him! Kill the whelp, kill him now!'

Nobody within the pavilion moved, guardian confessors included. Vashenda raised an eyebrow, and Tarfel suddenly looked as pale and nervous as ever.

'Very well, I'll do it myself.' The young duke pulled a dagger from his belt. 'Justice for the king-slayer!' He charged across the pavilion, Tarfel in his sights.

'Sand-flower,' Vashenda said with a meaningful nod.

Chel crashed into the duke as he approached the canopy, checking the man's run with his body, hands still tied behind him. Duke Esen reeled sideways, staggering, then turned in outrage. Chel head-butted him as hard as he could, driving his forehead into the man's nose. The manoeuvre felt oddly familiar, even down to the burst of pain across the front of his skull and the blazes of colour dancing across his vision.

The duke dropped like a stone, the dagger fallen from his hand. Chel stood over him, swaying and blinking, looking to see what the confessors and guardsmen would do next.

'Brothers,' Vashenda said, addressing the slow-moving confessors now plodding, thick-armed, toward him. 'Seize that man.' Chel swallowed. 'He tried to attack the royal person.'

She turned to those assembled in the pavilion as the confessors grabbed the dazed and bleeding Basar and hauled him upright.

'The king is dead. Long live the king.'

Still blinking away the bright spots in his vision, Chel looked to where Tarfel stood beside Corvel's body. A thin smile played on his narrowed lips, a look of satisfaction at a job well done. He did not meet Chel's eye.

'You know, sand-flower,' Vashenda said, sidling up to him. 'Our previous meetings have been, perhaps, unrepresentative. Let our understanding be reborn in the light of the Shepherd's mercy.' She offered a sly smile. 'Again.'

# PART IV

# THIRTY-NINE

The verdant hills hung heavy with dew beneath a sky like silvered steel. Dark smears of distant rain drifted at the rolling horizon, and the air smelled strongly of spring. Beneath a cacophony of birdsong, Chel stared down at the foaming grey waters of the Roni, swollen and fast with meltwater in the aftermath of the thaw. Now spanning the river's full width, atop three great pillars of glistening white stone, stood the restored Taneru bridge, its smooth arc travelling beneath three ornate, spiralling towers of the same, all the way to the steep drop of the far bank and the black outer walls of Roniaman beyond. On the distant ridge overlooking the city lurked the Imperial Palace, the vanguard of the restoration efforts. Already there was talk of returning the court to its marble halls.

The voice of Tarfel Merimonsun, called Tarfel the Young, King of Vistirlar, preceded his arrival, carrying over the busy camp. '. . . Once we're over the bridge, quick wave to the plebs on the free way, grand ceremony at the Dome then back up the free way to the citadel and we can crack on with the feasting. Let's hope the weather holds, eh? Be a shame for the great unwashed to get . . . washed out.'

The attendants giggled out of all proportion at the king's words. Chel didn't turn. The churning waters at the base of the steep bank had him mesmerized.

Creaking footsteps announced the king's presence at his side. 'Magnificent, isn't it, Vedren? Turns out some of my brother's endeavours were genuinely in service of restoration after all. I shall be thinking of him as we ride over it. Albeit not fondly.'

'Ride over what?'

'The bridge, Vedren, the bridge! Look at it! It's a masterwork. That carving, those towers, they must have worked from records, I don't know how. Let's hope this incarnation lasts a bit longer than the one before, eh?'

'Yeah.'

'Are you all right, old chap? You seem a touch down. Still thinking about the siege?'

'Mm-hm.'

'Well, nothing to dwell on there, God's truth. You did more than anyone to avert bloodshed, and certainly can't be blamed for what happened. Which reminds me, Her Radiance Exalted Matil has sent her felicitations on this august occasion, and her regrets that she cannot attend in person. She's up and about now, I understand, although she has rather a lot to deal with, as you can imagine. She sent a rather generous gift nonetheless, it's piled with the others on one of the carriages . . .'

Chel didn't turn to look. The king noticed. He leaned in close, his voice low, intimate. 'You mustn't brood, old boy. I know you feel like you lost some friends, but in truth, they weren't really our friends at all, were they?

They were mercenaries, paid to abduct us – well, me – and they would have cut our throats at a stroke if the winds of profit had blown otherwise. So come on, chin up. It's a big day.'

They'd had no chance to speak in the aftermath of Tarfel's sudden elevation; as head of the kingdom, he'd been whisked away, absorbed at once into the machinery of state, and Chel had barely seen him since. Tarfel's new minders, the royal staff, regarded Chel with a sort of wary respect, which could have been worse, but seemed to go out of their way to keep him at a distance from their new charge, to whom they had taken with unseemly enthusiasm. On reflection, that distance had suited Chel just fine.

The king put a heavy, gauntleted hand on his shoulder, and at last Chel turned.

'God's balls,' he murmured, 'that's . . .'

'My brother's armour, yes.' Tarfel flexed his arms and shimmered, even in the watery spring sun. His nose had healed a little off-centre, and it gave his face an unexpected, weathered look. Even his beard was coming in, a dark moustache and whiskers giving his face a novel definition.

'It fits you?'

'Needed some adjustment, of course. Turns out I've got a couple of inches on the old boy. Royal smith assures me I'll grow into the girth.'

'No doubt.'

Tarfel signalled to his staff, hovering at the edge of earshot, then turned back to the camp. 'Come on, Vedren, it's almost time. Don't make that face, it would have been a shame to let all Corvel's preparations go to waste. Need to put on a good show for the citizens. God knows they've had little enough cheer of late.'

Chel watched the troops assembling at the camp's edge, their armour less ornate and gleaming than the new king's, but no less intimidating. Someone had taken inspiration from the golden lancers of Arowan.

'Can you trust this bunch, Tarf?' Chel said as they walked back into the camp. 'I'm seeing a lot of a certain haircut growing out. At least half of them have to be—'

'Confessors, yes. Formerly. They've renounced the church, of course. I'm reviving the Order of Sentinels, you see, sworn in our first intake. Don't worry, my friend, you'll always be my first sworn, even released, but felt it was time to bolster the numbers, eh?'

'Is that wise?'

The king shrugged. 'An oath is an oath, Vedren, and they know the penalties. I suspect they'll keep each other honest. Otherwise . . .' He waved an airy hand toward the stakes that still lined the road that led toward the city, looming over the sparse, nervous traffic.

Chel pursed his lips. The sightless eyes of Esen Basar stared back from their distant, lofty vantage. Tarfel followed his gaze. 'I know you don't agree, old chap, but think of the message otherwise. I'm supposed to be unifying, remember? Can't go encouraging another half-dozen lordlings to try their hands. Still, we've got his lands to reapportion as favours, should encourage some bold displays of pre-emptive loyalty. Oh, don't worry, Vedren, I'm not going to try to make you a duke.'

Chel's smile didn't reach his eyes.

'Your Majesty. It is time.'

Vashenda had appeared, looking more formal, more elegant, more ostentatious than ever. She rode a glossy bay, and led a muscular grey stallion in one gloved fist. A mounting block followed, carried by a pair of earnest grooms.

Chel leaned close to the king. 'You've kept her around?'

'Who better to aid in dismantling a malignant monolith than one versed in its inner workings, eh? She's sharp. She'll be useful. Don't fret, Vedren. You don't have to watch my every step any more. I was born to do this.'

He stomped up the mounting block, took hold of the grey and hauled himself, armour and all, into the saddle. Vashenda passed him the reins, and a moment later, mounted King Tarfel was walking slowly toward the road, an armoured column forming up in anticipation.

Chel watched dumbfounded. 'You learnt to ride?'

'I thought it was time,' he called back. 'A king can't walk everywhere, or go bobbing along on a mule!'

Vashenda remained, looking down from her mount. 'Your animal will be along shortly, sand-flower,' she said with an icy smile.

'An ass, presumably? Or a sow?'

Genuine warmth touched the corners of her mouth. 'I don't want to ruin the surprise.' She geed the horse forward, then turned in the saddle. 'And don't worry, sand-flower, we've learnt our lessons. Any fucking beggar comes within a dozen strides, plague-ridden or otherwise, he'll be chunks in a heartbeat.'

Chel nodded, his own smile lukewarm.

'Most righteous.'

\* \* \*

Chel's fears were unfounded. His mount was a sturdy dun, barded in Tarfel's colours. He was urged to the column's centre as they set off along the road, to where Tarfel rode surrounded by his new sentinels. Vashenda rode at the column's head, carrying the royal standard, pennants fluttering slow in the damp air. The wagons and carriages, laden with favours, gifts, and tokens for the expectant crowds, brought up the rear.

'Come, Vedren,' Tarfel said, waving him closer. 'I want you riding beside me. You may no longer be my sworn, but I owe you my life many times over. This kingdom should thank you.'

Feeling his cheeks darken, Chel nudged his horse a token step closer. He tried to focus his mind on the positives. Corvel was dead, his dreams of empire stillborn. Tarfel had no appetite for war, Chel knew that better than anyone. And his intentions were good, his inclinations. He might just need some . . . *steering*, that was all. Through the choppy waters ahead. You don't desert a friend when he needs you most, that's what his father had once said. His father . . .

'Please, my dear Vedren, don't look so uneasy. Today is a celebration!'

Chel nodded, raising his gaze from the reins all the way to the silvery sky. 'I'm sorry, Tarf. You're right. I suppose, after everything, it's hard to shake the . . . the . . . foreboding.'

Tarfel met his eyes with a nod of surprising sincerity. 'I know what you mean, my friend.' From beneath his arm he retrieved a gleaming helmet, new, not the one Chel had seen in Corvel's tent. He lowered it onto his head, then flipped up the visor to reveal a complacent smile. 'But in all gravity, you must relax. Even if a hoodlum hacks his way through the sentinels, nothing's going to get through this.' He rapped the glorious breastplate, which gave a fitting thrum.

Chel nodded with a wan smile, but as they rode toward the bridge his thoughts roiled like the waters beneath their feet.

*Nothing's going to get through this—*
*Any fucking beggar—*
*The next time we meet, it won't be as friends—*

A kernel of thought had formed at the back of his mind and was growing, gathering speed, inexorable. An idea, or an image of one. There was something on the bridgeway ahead, a small celebratory decoration of sorts, coloured tassels waving in the wind. He looked up, sharply, up at the darkening sky and the approaching towers, white as washed bone, soaring from the elegant bridge. Strange things they were, with flared tops, odd balconies and projections.

*Was that—?*

'Now I know what you're thinking, Vedren, but we've stationed men—'

There, on the middle tower's exterior: a dark shape, nestled in the winding crevices of its structure. Moving. Climbing. Moments from the projecting balcony overlooking the bridge's span.

'Vedren, honestly, listen . . . Vedren. Vedren! Where are you going! Come back! Your king commands— *Vedren!*'

The dun's hooves threw sparks from the pale stone as he raced away.

\*\*\*

It took far too long to find the tower's entrance, a narrow doorway guarded by a couple of city watch. His screams to let him pass carried insufficient weight to move them, so he simply charged at them, bundling them out of the way with his good shoulder on dismounting. Then he was inside, pounding up the narrow stairway within, curling higher and deeper into the tower, only the slivers of pearly light from the stairwell's slot windows for company. The surprised guards gave chase, but slowly. They couldn't catch him. No one could catch him. Chel ran.

His breath echoed hoarse from the walls over the pounding of blood in his ears, each step sapping ever more of his frantic energy as he climbed above the bridge. He expected – *hoped* to hear a guard's challenge at any moment, the frenzied clamour of his progress should have been audible long before he hove into view.

But the tower remained silent above him, empty but for his commotion and the echoes of plodding pursuit from below, only the widening windows giving any sense of progression. A grey glimpse of the bridge below showed the column's advance, the first riders tramping grandly onto its re-laid white stone. Chel redoubled his pace, lungs burning, legs burning, the old stone of the steps flaking and crumbling beneath his boots.

It was almost a relief when he found the guard. The man lay face-down in a cramped hallway of ugly grey stone close to the tower's summit, his back to a wide window arch. His throat had been carved, and the floor was dark and viscous from his oozing blood. Panting and dizzy from the climb, Chel leaned down and touched the man's cheek. Cold, too cold for the recently deceased. From the volume of tacky fluid surrounding him, the man had likely been dead for hours.

The thumping echo of footsteps from the stairway behind

propelled him onwards. A door stood at the curving hall-way's end, closed but for a narrow grille. Dark and bloody footsteps led from the dead guard toward it and Chel followed them, merging them with his own. The door was locked, and stoutly so. Chel gripped at the grille and pulled, first gently, then with greater force, until he was rattling it in its hinges. It wouldn't budge.

'Yeah, I tried that too. It's a solid fucker, that one.'

Chel whipped his hands back from the grille and peered into the gloom of the chamber beyond. The voice did not match what he saw.

Two guards lay slumped in his cone of vision, their weapons loose at their feet, their necks slashed, as if taken by surprise and downed without a fight. The chamber bore signs of a struggle, however. In the pale light from its arched windows, Chel saw smashed furniture, an overturned table, broken crates and spilled food. Splashes of blood marked the walls, smeared in places with evident hand-prints. And at the centre of it all sat Spider. The silvery daylight shone from his polished dome, the glint of his many earrings creeping from the bloodied gloom. He sat with his legs splayed, his head bowed, his back to a splintered crate, in his gore-streaked hand a curved, black-bladed knife.

It took Chel a very long time to realize that he wasn't moving.

A figure drifted past the grille, white-haired and stooping, leaning heavily on a long staff. The figure shuffled toward the overturned table, righted it with a heavy foot, then leaned against it. Dark eyes stared from beneath the ash-coloured hair, below them an eagle's beak of a nose.

'Little man,' Rennic said, with a slight nod.

'Pig-fucker.'

'Only my friends can call me pig-fucker.'

The first drops of rain began to fall, plopping through the arch behind Chel, windblown, dark circles on its pale ledge.

'What happened here?'

'He didn't want to die. Took some convincing.' Rennic leaned back, unable to conceal his wince. Whatever he'd been through with Spider, he was far from unscathed.

'What was he doing here?'

'What do you think? He was going for a pair. A collector, that one. Obsessed with his own legend. I doubt that was the ending he had in mind.'

Chel rattled the door again. 'You going to open this? We can take a walk downstairs, tell the new king how you've saved his life. You can join the parade.'

Rennic was still staring at Spider's inert form.

'We always had the same ideas, me and him. Same view of things, same inclinations. We worked pretty well, had an understanding. Until now, at least.' He poked at Spider with the end of his staff, and the man slid sideways, flopping to the bloody stone. He was quite dead, eyes bulging from his sockets, livid purple tongue protruding from his open mouth. Rennic had strangled him.

'Of course,' the non-beggar went on, 'I was the thinker of the two of us. Look what he brought along to do the job.' He reached down and scooped up an ugly looking crossbow of dark wood from the floor, twanged the string. 'God knows what he thought he'd achieve with this. Wouldn't have made a dent in that steel tub.' He tossed the crossbow away. 'No, I was the thinker. That's why I brought this.'

Rennic reached down again, and Chel's innards lurched.

'Kosh's crossbow – what are you planning to do with that? Rennic? Rennic?'

Rennic ignored him. He pushed himself up from the table, leaving the staff propped, and began a slow walk toward the window arches at the edge of Chel's vision, the crossbow over one shoulder.

'He was my brother, you know that? Different mothers, of course, I'd never have tolerated the prick otherwise. But we both got our father's nose. Grew up together, joined up together. Suppose it's fitting it end like this.'

'End? Like what? Rennic!' The guards' footsteps were getting louder behind him, their panting filling the winding stair.

'Don't you ever get tired of asking questions all the time, sand-flower? It's exhausting. Here's one for you instead: I lied before, Rennic isn't my real name; you know what it means?'

'No, I don't. Rennic, open the door. The guards are coming. Rennic!'

'Nor do I,' he said, and knelt before the arches. He rested the crossbow on the window-ledge, then laid out six bolts alongside it. He began to load it.

'Rennic! Rennic stop!' Chel was ripping at the door again, slamming himself against it, hammering at the hinges. 'Rennic!'

The guards reached the stairway's end and found their comrade. Their shouts and cries were suddenly deafening in the tower's confines. Their eyes fell on Chel at the hall-way's end. Swords were drawn.

Chel saw their intent. 'Fuck,' he said. He kicked once more at the door to no avail, then his eyes fell on the window.

*Tried that too—*
The climbing figure.

Chel ran at the guards, who shrank back. Ignoring the acid burning in his legs, he jumped past them, up onto the window-ledge, pulling himself up to the shallow balcony beyond. The chill wind blew thickening rain against him in the sudden cold of the tower exterior, and somewhere thunder rumbled. He tried to fix his gaze on the horizon, keep his eyes well away from the swooning drop to the bridge and the gurgling waters beneath. He could hear the stomp and clop of the column below, its sounds blown up and around him, and the shouts of the surprised guards in the hallway interior.

There, a bloodied mark on the stone ahead: a footprint, and another beyond it. Before the guards could reach him, Chel turned and grabbed for the stone. Focusing only on one grip at a time, one bloodied mark ahead, he began to climb up and around the tower. The wind howled in his ears, blasting gusts of sharp rain over him, leaving the tower stone slick and darkened. He kept his eyes on the bloodied marks, the smears of Rennic's own climb, forcing his aching muscles to comply while his pulse hammered in his ears. The summit was in sight, a rail of thin stone at the top of his curling path. Greedily he snatched for it, hauling himself up, feet scrabbling, desperate at last to be back on something solid.

The rail gave, a crumbling chunk of stone left in his fist as he felt himself dropping. The empty air yawned beneath him, the sudden yank on his other arm jarring his shoulder, dragging it free, even as his feet scraped in vain for grip against the tower.

A hand snatched his forearm, arresting his slip, jolting

his straining shoulder. Another hand clapped over it, then dragged him up and over the crumbling rail. He collapsed to his knees on the rain-slick stone beyond as Rennic stood over him, thick streaks of black washing from his ash-clouded hair in the hastening rain.

'Thought I'd come up to greet you. Really half-arsed this restoration work, eh?'

From somewhere below came the sound of hammering. The guards were trying to get through the stout door. Chel concentrated on his breathing, trying to suppress the ugly throb from his shoulder, the rain-cut soaking of his clothes.

'Besides,' Rennic said, moving to the tower-top's far side, where a ladder led to the chamber below. 'It's a better shot from up here.'

He hefted the crossbow once more as Chel struggled to his feet, flicking rain water from his eyes. Over the lip of the rail, he saw the column spread along the length of the bridge. Tarfel had to be somewhere beneath them right now, riding proud through the rain in his glittering armour, oblivious to the danger that loomed overhead.

A peal of thunder rolled out from the hills, and a curtain of hammering rain washed over the bridge. Rennic raised his arm, sodden clothes hanging slack. 'You see? Even Almighty God doesn't want this bastard crowned!'

Chel took a determined step, hands open and wide, imploring, rain streaming down his face. He had to raise his voice over the rush of falling water. 'What are you doing, Rennic?'

'I'm finishing the job.'

'What job?'

'Torht's job, the Rau Rel's job, your job! What we started with Ruumi, what we almost accomplished in Arowan.

Destroying the church, lifting the curse from the land. Cleansing the corruption!'

'Corvel is dead, the Order of the Rose disbanded. It's over. We won.'

'Horseshit!' Rennic replied, setting down the crossbow and draping his soggy cloak over it. 'It's all still there. This is about more than just the man, remember? We have to pull it apart, or the next henchman down will simply pick up the reins.'

'It's not going to happen overnight, you need a little patience.'

'You said you cared about doing what's right! You abandoned us! After what he did!'

Rennic's snarl was instinctive, his hands clenching. Already they were circling, moving in a slow orbit, a bedraggled stand-off. Below them, the royal procession slogged onwards in the rain, hunched and leached of majesty.

'The right thing was letting go.'

'The wicked must be punished! He killed Whisper, he said it himself.'

'Is this what she'd have wanted?' Chel said, one eye on the shrouded crossbow. All he had to do was sling it over the side and Tarfel was safe. They were all safe. 'You throwing yourself away in petty vengeance? She knew the choice she made, denying her that is insulting her memory.'

He didn't even see Rennic move. An instant later, he was on his back in the slopping rain, feeling the echo of the cold stone at the back of his skull. The centre of his face felt very hot against the rain, the streaming sensation from his nose more than just precipitation.

Rennic stood over him, snorting, snarling, then turned his back, walking back to the crossbow. Blinking through water, Chel pushed himself up on an elbow, feeling the crest of the pain waves rolling out from his head. 'No matter what he said to you, it was just bad luck, and she gave herself that we could live. She decided. For once, break the cycle of vengeance.'

The big man paused, relaxing his grip on the soaking cloak. 'And the others, little man? Foss won't speak to me, he's taken up the cloth again, rejoined the fucking church that spat in his eye year after year. Lemon won't leave Arowan . . . They're broken, gone. There's nobody left.'

'Loveless is out there. You could—'

'She turned her back, made herself clear.'

'She left because she's pregnant!'

'She left because she chose to. Our paths have forked.'

'That's it? After everything?' Chel was back on his feet, wiping crimson rain from his battered face.

'It was her decision and she knew what it meant. She treads her path, I tread mine. To its end.' He swept back the cloak, snatching up the crossbow and setting it back on the rail.

'You'll do no good by dying.'

He didn't turn his head, but his eyes glowed sidelong. 'Then stop me.'

Chel launched himself across the stone, slamming into the bigger man's side, lunging for the crossbow. Rennic twisted, anticipating, the crossbow out of reach, a powerful elbow driven back against Chel's skull. He reeled, head ringing, scrabbling for grip against the splashing stone.

Rennic looked back over the rail, angling the crossbow again. 'Looks like they've stopped,' he said with his sharp smile. 'Perhaps to investigate the disappearance of the king-ling's lickspittle into this tow—'

Chel crashed into him again, this time driving him to the weathered stone. They tussled for the crossbow, Rennic's blows instinctive, his strength enough to wrestle Chel's hands away. He shoved him, clearing enough space to scrabble back and up against the wall. His breath was coming fast, and for the first time Chel saw weakness in his eyes. He had one hand at his side, the water running from it pink. The fight with Spider had taken its toll.

'Let me finish it!' he growled, his breath sharp little fogs. 'We were doing something *good*.'

Chel pushed himself half-upright. He was soaked through, coronation robes hanging slack and clingy against his skin. 'We were doing something necessary! And we did it. Things are different. They *will* be different. Tarfel isn't like the others! He's one of us, he's a friend. He can make a difference, do something good!'

'You think he's so different, little man? Ask him where the alchemist is.'

'What? Surely she's still in Arowan, with—'

'She's here. Ask to see her. All the silver in the south says you won't.'

'He's not—'

'You're telling me you're happy with this new dawn? The same confessors in golden armour?'

'All my doubt isn't worth throwing the kingdom into another anarchist convulsion. I won't let you do this.'

'Don't make me kill you, little man.'

'I won't let you kill me any more than I'll let you kill him.'

For a moment, something gleamed in Rennic's eyes. 'Are you going to kill me, then?'

Slowly, Chel drew himself to his feet. He drew the good

knife from its sheath. Rennic's eyes followed it, something dark and hungry within them.

'I don't understand you, little man. You've lost every fight you've thrown yourself into, but you keep coming back for more.'

For a moment, Chel's gaze travelled the horizon. 'It was never about beating people down. I fight because . . . some things deserve to be fought for.' With great deliberation, Chel tossed the knife away. 'But sometimes it's all right to stop fighting. Sometimes it's all right to walk away.'

Rennic looked to the blackened heavens, baring his teeth in exasperation, agony. 'We have to do what's right!'

'This isn't it.'

Rennic pushed himself up against the crumbling rail, and Chel saw the cracks from their impact behind him. 'How can you know? How can you always be so fucking certain?'

'My father—'

'Was a fool who threw his life away and doomed his family, and your quest for his post-mortem approval has damned us all!'

Chel felt a faint smile play upon his lips. 'Loveless said much the same.'

For a moment, the rage left him. 'Well, she knows whereof she speaks.' The brows lowered again. 'How can you claim any kind of—'

'You're right.' Chel stood drenched before him, hands empty, rain plastered to his skin. 'My father was a weak man, an accidental husband and parent, who wrecked his family's lives with his own pursuit of righteousness.'

Rennic was silent, and now the fury was gone from his eyes. Rain flowed in streams from his brows and nose, his hair clinging flat and dark around his face. When he spoke, his voice was almost swallowed by the wind. 'Then . . . how can you know?'

'I . . . I can't. I just have to have faith, in others, in myself. In Tarfel. He deserves a chance, the same chance you gave me, when you pulled me from a burning palace. That's why you saved me, right? Because I reminded you of your younger self?'

Rennic was so sodden it was hard to tell if there were tears in his eyes, but it was possible.

'Give Tarfel a chance to prove himself,' Chel said, taking a slow, squelching step forward. 'Give him the chance you gave me, the chance you never got. Tarfel could be a good king, a great king. He can do better, be better than any king we've seen in generations.'

'You're going to stand over him, are you? Bark orders in his ear?'

Chel paused. Rain was streaming down his face, he'd lost the feeling in his fingers and toes, but his eyes were back on the horizon, his mind cresting the clouds. When it came, his answer surprised him.

'No.'

'No?'

'He should make his own choices. But I'll be watching.'

The big man met his gaze. 'And if you're wrong?' he said in the quiet voice.

'Then it'll be my problem to solve once more.'

Rennic leaned back against the rail, a touch of humour back in his eyes. 'Oh, really?'

Chel took another step, this time with confidence. 'He goes the way of his brother . . . I'll kill him myself.'

A flash of a smile lit Rennic's battered face. 'Now that I want to live to s—'

The rail behind him cracked and split, and a chunk of tower-top fell away, Rennic along with it. Rennic plunged from view, Chel's lunging hands slapping from his body as he fell. Chel hit the cracked stone, arms outstretched, slick hands clasped on something. Plunging mass dragged him forward until he rocked against the rail that remained. His shoulder began to scream.

Rennic hung suspended from the broken tower, dangling free from Chel's agonized grip on his arm. Far below, the silver waters of the Roni rippled and churned in the downpour. Rennic swung in space, feet loose and sodden. He looked up at Chel through bloodshot eyes and grinned pink against the rain.

'*Really* half-arsed that restoration, didn't they?'

Chel could only grunt. The fibres of his muscles were tearing like so much old meat, and his shoulder grated in its socket. 'Climb. Swing. Something.' Rennic's weight was pulling him against the crumbling wall, and the cracks were spreading. Another chunk of ancient stone fell away beneath his shaking arms.

'You never give up, do you?' Rennic said. 'You daft bastard.'

'Hurry! Climb!' Another crack ripped along the wall by Chel's head, small stones pattering down the side of the tower, lost in the foaming waters below.

'Let me go, boy. I'll make my own way down. Nobody need know I was here.'

Chel's grip was iron, his arms and shoulders afire.

'No! Climb! Tell king, Spider dead—'

'I'm not going to be a king's pet.'

'Nor me! Service ended.'

'Then what are you doing here?'

'Fighting.'

The wall by Chel's shoulder began to disintegrate, cracks streaking like forks of lightning across it, flakes drifting free.

'Let me go, you dunce, your arm will go. I can make the window on the lower floor, dodge all those keen lads in livery.'

'No!' He was hoarse from screaming, his tears mingling with the flowing rain. 'Come back with me, stay—'

Rennic's voice was quiet in the heart of the storm.

'You were supposed to be lucky, little man.' He closed his eyes, letting the rain flow over him. 'Maybe you were.'

Rennic took a long, slow breath, as the rain ran down his face like tears.

'Be seeing you.'

Before Chel could shout a reply, Rennic put one hand over his, braced a leg against the smooth stone of the tower, and twisted. His spin wrenched Chel's arm from its socket, sending a white-hot burst of pain along his arm. He was momentarily blind, screaming at the sudden agony, good hand clutching at the trauma.

It took him several breaths to realize that his hands were empty. Rennic was gone. Bleary-eyed, Chel peered over the broken edge, but below lay nothing but the swirling ebony water of the Roni. And an open window, one floor down.

'Oh, you spiteful fucker.'

Drenched and broken, Chel laughed bitter tears in the rain.

# FORTY

'It's good that you brought this in. We wouldn't want it falling into the wrong hands.'

Tarfel looked odd with the thin crown around his head, but also somehow at home. Chel followed him, a step behind, dazed from both events and the leaf-thick concoction prescribed by the King's physicians. A gaggle of courtiers followed them at a respectful distance as they walked down the hall to the newly declared royal armoury.

One of the gleaming sentinels opened the door for them, and Tarfel carried the crossbow inside. The King's armour dominated the room on its stand, lit by tasteful lanterns, but the chamber glittered with trinkets. Chel thought he saw a suit of lamellar armour in the corner, but one item in particular caught his eye.

'Is this . . .' He reached out to touch it with his unstrapped hand.

'The glaive, yes. A coronation gift from our old friend Ruumi, now pronounced Blood-Queen of Liranetan. They must have dredged that bloody lake for it. She sent it along

with a message which was, I have to say, utterly inappro-
priate. I tell you, Vedren, it was filthy.'

'A proposal?'

'Oh, you could definitely call it that.' They walked back
to the hallway. 'Which reminds me, I need some help going
through possible marriage prospects, need to pin down an
alliance early. Especially as people are starting to ask
awkward questions about what I'm going to do about the
Horvaun war bands pillaging the south-west. I can only
have so many inquisitive people removed.' Tarfel read the
change in his expression. 'I jest, of course, Vedren. But the
situation is delicate, you understand.'

'Of course, Tarf.'

The king's look was keen. 'I need a new general, Vedren,
as you're well aware, and I understand if the position holds
no appeal, but how about becoming a special envoy? The
south is a quagmire of flaming razor-eels, and I could use
someone with a delicate touch who isn't tarnished by prior
associations. You'll need to re-swear, of course, but it will
come with a title. Not a dukedom, worry not, but something
with a consequential stipend at least.'

'A most gracious offer, Tarf. May I think about it?'

'Of course, of course. Actually, Vedren, on that note, it
might be best if you were to call me "your majesty", while
we're in public. Look of the thing, you understand. Respect
for the throne and all that.'

'I understand. Your majesty.'

'I knew you would. While you ponder, perhaps you'd
care to step this way? There's someone to see you.'

'Of course, your majesty.'

Tarfel set off down the hallway. As Chel went to follow,
he took one look back into the armoury as the stone-faced

sentinel began to pull the door closed. He thought he saw a flicker of movement within, perhaps only the shadow of the door in the lamplight. But as the door pulled shut, he could have sworn that the glaive was gone.

\* \* \*

It was strange to be walking the galleries of the citadel without fear of immediate arrest and imprisonment. Somehow, the place had lost its air of menace, despite scant transformation. Old scars lurked beneath the surface, though. Some stains would not wash out.

The stables were below, pungent and familiar. He wondered if he searched the packed earth floor, he might find the gouges left by Rennic's wild crossbow shots so many months before.

'Vedren.' The king paused, his young face pensive, then he spoke again. 'Vedren, do you think he's still out there? Do you think I . . . have anything to worry about?'

Chel took a long breath, flexed his shoulder against the strapping. It still hurt. A lot.

'No. Nothing at all.'

Rennic's words echoed in his head.

*Ask him where the alchemist is. Ask to see her.*

'Actually, majesty, I was hoping to stop by and see Kosh before I left, say goodbye to her. She's here somewhere, isn't she?'

Tarfel's smile froze at the very corners. 'I'm afraid that's not going to be possible, old boy.' Chel caught the flicker of his gaze toward the black tower that loomed overhead. 'Matters of state and all that, she's far too vital to risk, even to a friend.'

Chel worked hard not to turn and look up at the tower. *All the silver in the south says you won't.*

'I see. Of course,' he said. 'Your majesty.'

'Ah,' the king said brightly, Chel's words forgotten, 'and here we are.'

\* \* \*

'Brother Bear, you look like cold shit. Explain yourself.'

Sabina stood before him, resplendent in court finery and revelling in his speechlessness. She seemed to dance on her toes.

'Sab! You're . . . you're . . .'

'God's bollocks, Bear, how many more headwounds have you suffered since I saw you last? You're thicker than second-hand pigswill.'

'. . . here.'

The king cleared his throat. 'I'll, ah, leave you to it. I look forward to our further discussions.' He edged away, and staff descended on him like carrion birds before he made it three paces.

'I am,' Sabina declared, twisting a braid in one hand. 'Things continue to be "all well" and "deathly dull" at home, so I thought I would take up our new monarch's invitation. I'm just sorry I missed the coronation, it sounds like you had quite the day of it. Bloody north road was a swamp.'

'But . . . why?'

'Why, Bear? Your liege understands that he needs good people around him to unfuck this shitstorm, as you might put it. And you know me, I make friends, keep my eyes open. Plus, you know, not much call for raising the red

pennant of insurrection round our way.' She coughed.
'Any more.'

Chel looked from his sister to the hectored king and
back. His head was still swimming from the physicians'
murky brew.

'Home?' he said.

Her demeanour changed, the teasing levity replaced with
deep-eyed earnestness. 'They're safe and well, Bear, and
they'd love to see you. I understand you're off the chain
now, but if you're planning a visit, you need to understand
something: Mum is happy with the way things are. Only
return if you can be, too.' She slapped his arm. 'And if you
were really to turn your back on all this royal magnificence,
there might yet be a role for you back at the manor. Amiran's
not getting any younger after all and he might be glad to
have someone who could perform some of his duties around
the place.'

The mention of the word 'duties' set Chel's eyelid
twitching. Sab either didn't notice or didn't care. 'But stuff
all that, Bear, there's so much fun to be had at court. Did
you hear about the delegation from one of the free cities?
They're Andriz, like us! It sounds like your fame has
preceded you – I hear they were asking after you! We'll
need an official liaison to handle the formalities, of course,
it's the first time they've visited the capital in a generation.
Perhaps we should let your face heal a little first, we can't
have you scaring off the younger members of their expedition. Don't worry, Bear, I'll teach you everything you need
to know about living the high life at court.'

He could feel it, pressing in on him. It had been building
for a while, slowly, quietly, accumulating in the background
like gentle mist, then with sudden solidity it wrapped him,

crushed him, weighed him ever downward: Expectation. Obligation. Duty.

'I think,' he said, fighting the slur of his words. 'I think I would like to go to the stables.'

\*\*\*

'Are you sure you're all right to ride one-handed?'

His head felt much cooler in the chill spring air.

'I've done worse. It'll settle down in a few days, it usually does.'

Sabina watched as the grooms hauled Chel aboard his horse and retreated. 'You're *really* going? Turning your back on all this, on me?'

'Keep the place tidy, will you?'

'I beg your pardon?'

Chel settled in the saddle, checked the saddlebags and tested his riding posture. Still not good. 'Like you said, someone needs to unfuck this shitstorm. And as you kept telling me, you both spied in the court and survived as a confessor in the citadel with no help from me, or from anyone else. I can't think of anyone better qualified.' He offered her a pained grin. 'I have faith in you, Sab.'

Her cheeks darkened, and she coughed to cover her discomfort. 'Flattered, truly, but where are you *going*?'

He looked up at the sky and smiled. 'I'm going to . . . broaden my horizons. For a little while at least.'

She reached up a hand, rested it against his knee. 'I meant it, you know. Father would have been proud of you. They'd all be proud.' A tear glistened in her eye. 'How could they not?'

He reached down and clasped her hand, then nodded

back to where the young king stood in conference at the courtyard's edge, courtiers swirling around him like thunderclouds.

'Watch him for me.'

\* \* \*

Chel steered the horse through the cheerful crowds to the outer city. The riders shadowing him fell away as he reached the great gate. The sun had broken through the clouds, and the spring-bright landscape beyond the walls seemed somehow open, hopeful.

An image formed in his mind, an image somewhere of an alehouse corner: Foss dozing against the wall, hands resting on his stomach; beside him, Lemon trying to make a point through a drunken haze, her finger jabbing at the table and missing; Loveless with a sleeping baby cradled in one arm, a skin of wine in the other, her eyes dark and her smile mischievous; and standing over them all like a stern but proud father, a hawk-faced man with fire in his eyes and a mocking smile.

Chel liked that image. He'd find them again. One day.

The open country unfolded before him. With the sun on his back, Chel rode.

# ACKNOWLEDGEMENTS

It's a long road to publication for any book, and that's before you throw global pandemics into the mix. 2020 certainly didn't go to plan for most of us, and I'd like to extend an extra helping of thanks and deepest affection to everyone involved in getting *The Righteous* into your hands. May better times be ahead, and soon.

If you've read the acknowledgements for *The Black Hawks*, and I thrice-damned hope you have, then the roll-call of gratitude is much the same – the books were drafted consecutively, and many who suffered for the first got the second thrown in as a bonus. All those mentioned before are as deserving of thanks as ever, especially Jon 'Global Head' Brierley who was robbed of his second 'e' in the original printing. Sorry, Jon.

To that end, thanks once again to my literary agent and life coach Harry Illingworth, who continues to provide an inspiring template for the modern Yorkshireman, and all at DHH Literary Agency. To my fantastic editors, Natasha 'Cleaver' Bardon and Jack 'Oblongs isn't a word' Renninson,

Vicky 'Proof-pusher' Leech and all the production, marketing, and legal staff at Harper*Voyager*: thank you for creating this book and getting it out in the world. Thanks also to the perspicacious Verity Shaw and Linda Joyce, sublime cover designer Micaela Alcaino and magnificent cover artist Gavin Reece.

I'd also like to express a debt of gratitude to those who did so much to boost *The Black Hawks* upon its release, and make me feel welcome as a debut author in the process: Anna Stephens, Peter McLean, Ed McDonald, Nate Crowley, Den Patrick, Mike Shackle, and Peter Newman, and of course the incomparable Francesca Haig – thank you all so much.

And to the enthusiastic and glorious community of book bloggers and reviewers, further thanks are due: Andy 'eBook-wyrm' Angel, Dave Graham, Nicole Sweeney, Stefan of Civilian Reader, Matt Craig of Reader Dad, Chris Meadows, Nils Shukla and Mike 'Everest' Evans and the Fantasy Hive crew, Hiu and the Fantasy Inn, David 'Virtual Con Master' Walters and Mada of FanFiAddict, Night at SoManyBooks6, and all the reviewers and bloggers who featured the book. Thank you all for spreading the good word – both I and the surly oafs of the Black Hawks are in your debt.

I'd also like to give a mention to the Super Relaxed Fantasy Club, now unable to meet for over a year but very much in our hearts (and video channels); to Phil, Magnus, Caro, and all the team, and all the regulars (and irregulars). See you again soon.

Thanks once more to my three advance readers and ideation devices, James G Smith, Adam Iley and Laz Roberts. One day, chaps, we will see each other again, but until then: cheers.

Eternal thanks and adoration to my spectacular wife, Sarah, who has borne the brunt of 'my little writing habit' more than anyone, and to my daughters, with whose own brunt we have become abundantly over-familiar in the last year. Thank you for sometimes being asleep, and leaving a few walls un-coloured.

Finally, thanks and love both profound and immeasurable to my parents, Lawrence and Aureole, to whom this book is dedicated, and without whom it's statistically unlikely I'd have been around to write it. Thank you, Mum and Dad, and I will aim for fewer 'fucks' next time. Promise.